THE CHRISTMAS INVITATION

Trisha Ashley

BANTAM PRESS

TRANSWORLD PUBLISHERS
61–63 Uxbridge Road, London W5 5SA
www.penguin.co.uk

Transworld is part of the Penguin Random House group of companies whose addresses can be found at global.penguinrandomhouse.com

First published in Great Britain in 2019 by Bantam Press
an imprint of Transworld Publishers

A CIP catalogue record for this book
is available from the British Library

ISBN
9781787632189 (hb)
9781787630598 (tpb)

Typeset in 12/15 pt Adobe Garamond
by Integra Software Services Pvt. Ltd, Pondicherry

Printed and bound in Great Britain by Clays Ltd, Elcograf S.p.A.

Penguin Random House is committed to a sustainable future for our business, our readers and our planet. This book is made from Forest Stewardship Council® certified paper.

1 3 5 7 9 10 8 6 4 2

For my son
Robin Griff Aneurin Ashley
With love

Prologue

Incised in Stone

5 January 2016

It was Twelfth Night and an icy wind prowled around the Red House, occasionally causing a soft susurration of snowflakes against the window, or howled menacingly down the chimney.

'You have no teeth to harm *me*,' murmured Clara Mayhem Doome. 'You can huff and you can puff, but you can't blow *my* house down.'

Lass, her husband's spaniel, who had been temporarily banished to Clara's study from the hall while the huge Christmas tree was denuded of its baubles and tinsel, politely thumped her undocked tail on the floor.

'Blast,' added Clara, realizing that her microphone was still on and her words had been added to the end of her current crime novel as a strange postscript to the grand finale.

She deleted it, then switched off both microphone and computer and lay back in her chair, feeling that fleeting moment of catharsis that all authors experience after writing the final words of their current book . . . before the urge to start a new one sneaked in to occupy the empty space.

Professor Clara Mayhem Doome was a large, vigorous woman in her late seventies, with a boldly curved nose, bright dark eyes and a mass of silver-streaked steel-grey curls. She was clad in scarlet corduroy trousers and a rainbow-striped Peruvian jumper, across which marched a procession of llamas. This, together with the big silver sun and moon earrings she wore, had been this year's Christmas presents from her husband.

The room was spacious, warm and well lit, the walls lined with bookshelves and illuminated cabinets that contained chunks of stone, clay, wood and other hard substances, incised with the strange shapes of ancient writing. Clara was a world-renowned epigrapher, whose passion for deciphering anything not written on paper had become her career. She liked a little more dimension to her work, and thought that palaeographers, like her friend – or frenemy – Pookie Longridge, had chosen the flat and boring option.

Clara's large U-shaped desk was in the centre of the room, facing the long windows on to the garden, and the computers, monitors and laptop it bore reflected the different facets of her nature.

To the left, with an old-fashioned ball-and-stick microphone before it, was the computer devoted to the writing of her annual crime novel, which was her main hobby. In the centre was a huge monitor on which she could examine in minute detail photographs of bits of pottery, clay tablets or other inscribed surfaces, and which she could also move about like a virtual jigsaw puzzle until they fitted together. She was uncannily expert at spotting a 'join', as they were called. The computer to which this was wired was entirely dedicated to her profession, including the writing of her more erudite books, papers and articles. Her most recent book, in which she set out a new timeline for the development of three interlinked early forms of writing, had not so much set the cat among the pigeons in her field, but rather detonated a small explosion, leaving feathers everywhere.

The laptop on the right-hand wing of the desk was used to email friends and family, surf the internet and store personal photographs. She preferred things to be in compartments and imagined her mind as a richly nectared honeycomb of interconnecting hexagonal cells.

It was still only eleven in the morning, yet she had already studied the photographs of a few broken fragments of baked clay inscribed with cuneiform, which a colleague in the States had emailed to her, then sent back her opinion, after which she'd dictated the final chapter of her novel.

There was still a good hour before she could decently eat lunch, though good smells were wafting from the direction of the kitchen.

Cheese and onion pies, she thought, and perhaps some of Den's special savoury scones for tea later.

The sound of Henry's mellow and resonant voice and the higher treble of her great-nephew, Teddy, moved off towards the front of the house, so they must have finished with the hall tree and were about to start on the smaller, artificial one in the bay window of the drawing room. Henry, who adored Christmas and collected vintage and antique glass baubles, hung some of them each year on this smaller tree, and removing them carefully and restoring them to their storage places in his study would take some time.

Later in the day, her nephew Lex would help take down the Christmas trees and store the boxes of decorations in one of the attics. This substantial Victorian Gothic house wasn't short of those.

It had been another lovely family Christmas. She and Henry might have no children of their own, but her nephew and niece, Lex and Zelda, more than made up for that. And now, with Zelda's little boy, Teddy, living with them, there was a child in the house again to make Christmas extra special.

The room was warm and bright, the clock ticked and time seemed to ripple around her. In moments like this Clara often found herself thinking more and more about the past and how it linked to her present life, a train of thought stirred up by the brief autobiographical introduction she had been asked to write for her last crime novel.

To her surprise she'd found that she actually had quite a lot to say about her life, not all of it suitable for publication. But it would be enjoyable to write her full and frank memoirs, if only for future generations of the family.

With Clara, to think was to act. Minutes later she had created a new document and was intoning the foreword to her autobiography into her microphone.

An Inscribed Life

The Memoirs of Clara Mayhem Doome
Foreword

Late last year I was asked by the publishers of my crime novels to write a brief autobiographical note, to be included at the front of my next offering, Dead Clay.

They wanted something more personal than the outline of my professional achievements that graces my more erudite works on epigraphy.

But to me, the interesting parts of my life have mainly been those written in stone . . . or sometimes baked clay. What insight, I wondered, would it bring to the readers of my novels, to know such trivia as where I was born, that I preferred toast to breakfast cereal and rarely watched the TV from one week to the next?

But my publishers insisted that indeed they would be fascinated by such details . . . and I have to admit that despite my initial reservations, the exercise stirred up all kinds of long-dormant memories.

My husband, the renowned poet Henry Doome, pointed out that he has been examining and chronicling aspects of his life (and, later, by association, mine) through the medium of his work since childhood, but that is hardly the same as setting down the facts.

Anyway, as you see, I have now fallen prey to the lure of autobiography and so decided to pen a memoir – though for the family, rather than general publication, I think . . . unless it undergoes a radical editorial pruning at a later date.

I will start where I was born, in the village that lies in the valley below the house where I now reside, though I reserve the right to wander to and fro among my memories as the fancy takes me. Of course, I will always return here, for as Henry says, we are both firmly rooted in the village of Starstone, even if those roots are now washing about under the still waters of the reservoir.

Let us ripple the surface and stir up the silt a little . . .

Clara Mayhem Doome
The Red House,
Starstone Edge,
January 2016

1

Going Viral

Meg
November 2016

I used to think pneumonia was something that only elderly people and those with compromised immune systems got . . . but not any more. Autumn put off its bronze leaves and turned to stark winter before River finally sprang me from hospital and drove me home to convalesce, though I don't think they'd have let me go, had they seen the state of his ancient Land Rover. As it was, they looked slightly askance at his long silver hair, plaited beard and the medieval-style quilted tabard, worn over black tunic and trousers, which was revealed when he removed his stained and disreputable waxed drover's coat.

Outside, exposed to the chill air of the car park, I felt like a shrivelling hothouse plant, but I assured myself that I'd toughen up again, like I had after my last hospital stay, six years ago, when a car crash had ended the new life inside me that had barely begun. The anguish and mental scars of that loss had taken longer to heal than the physical ones.

My bags, packed by my best friend, Fliss, were already in the back and, once River had carefully wrapped me in an itchy hand-woven travelling rug, we headed straight out of London.

It didn't matter where I was, home would always be River's Farm up in the Black Mountains of Wales.

When he had first moved there in search of solitude and a life of self-sufficiency (within reason; there were some little luxuries, like good coffee, that he had no intention of doing without), the place had had a Welsh name that summed up its beautiful remoteness. But with the success of his first publication, *A Manual for the Self-Sufficient Vegetarian*, it was soon forgotten, and fan mail addressed to 'River's Farm', or even just 'The Farm, Wales', found its way there without any difficulty, as did a stream of fans and acolytes.

Over the ensuing years it had evolved from a simple commune into something far more complex, though at heart it had remained true to its roots and had been a wonderful place to grow up.

I fell fast asleep despite the Land Rover's almost non-existent suspension, and was woken only by the rattle as we crossed a cattle grid and bumped up the long track to the Farm. In the thick, woolly gloom of a winter afternoon, the dark conifers of the Forestry Commission woodland pressed up close against the fence to one side, while above us lights shone steadily from the lower windows of the house and the craft workshops in the barns. Between the hedges and trees to our left, lights from the yurts in the lower field flickered like a scattering of glow-worms.

I wound the window down a fraction and inhaled the heady scent of pine from the forest, mixed with a little wood smoke.

Soon I would be enclosed in the womb-like warmth and safety of the commune as if I'd never left – and how I longed for that!

It was the place I came for healing, though in my heart I already knew that with returning health would come the desperate urge to escape again.

I was quite right, too. By the start of December my flight feathers had grown back and I was more than ready to leave the downy softness of the nest again, where Maj, one of the long-standing members of the commune, almost suffocated me with mother love and tried to fatten me up with an endless succession of my favourite foods.

Well, apart from the occasional lunch like that of the previous day, when Oshan (River's son and my sort-of brother – relationships at the Farm are complicated), had insisted on cooking. Unfortunately he had turned vegan while spurning recipe books in favour of 'intuitive cookery', whatever that was. The result had both looked and tasted like butterbeans in chilli sauce on chopped grass. It probably was.

Only a few members of the original commune still lived in the house, like Maj and her husband, Kenny, while most of the rest had either left or moved into the yurt encampment that had sprung up in the lower field. Everyone still wandered in and out at all times of the day and night, so there was a complete lack of privacy. Of course, you could go and stand in one of the fields furthest away from the farmhouse, but even then, you might find Jerry and Luke with the goats, or an inquisitive donkey nudging you in the back and braying loudly, to give your location away.

In winter, after pneumonia, that option probably wouldn't have been a good idea anyway, though having survived the journey from London in River's unheated vehicle, there was clearly hope of a complete recovery.

I did have a slip of a bedroom to myself, over the front porch of the farmhouse, which was never used for visitors, even in summer, when the place was full with temporary helpers and the bunk rooms in the attic were crammed to bursting.

It was a privilege Oshan shared, though as River's son, he had a right to it by heritage, while I was awarded a granddaughter's rights from love.

For all official purposes, Maj and Kenny were my parents, Oshan my brother and River my grandfather. It had saved a lot of trouble and explanations over the years.

I did *have* a birth mother and so did Oshan, though both were quick enough to deposit their offspring at the Farm and depart, leaving their little cuckoos in the nest.

On the first Sunday in December, River reluctantly agreed to return me to the shoebox-sized Greenwich flat I'd shared until recently with Fliss.

As the miles vanished behind us, I shook off the last of the sadness I felt at leaving the Farm and began to look forward to being back in my own quiet space again . . . even quieter now Fliss had moved out. I would miss her so much and I also had the added worry about paying the rent on the flat on my own.

River broke into my reverie by saying, for possibly the third time, 'You should have stayed till after the Winter Solstice, Meg, if not the Yule Feast. Some of the family are coming home for it and they'd love to see you.'

By 'family', he meant anyone who had ever stayed at the commune over the last forty-odd years since he set it up, no matter for how long or short a time. And people did tend to return like homing pigeons, especially the ones who had grown up there, like me. We might all have felt the need to escape, but the umbilical cord frequently twitched us back.

'I don't want to leave the flat empty for too long, and anyway, I have commissions to arrange, things to catch up on and a living to earn,' I pointed out.

'You could take it easy for a while longer, though, Meg. Surely no one will want their portrait painted over Christmas?'

'Probably not, but I do need to add a few finishing touches to my last commission.' Like signing it, for instance. I was pretty sure I'd forgotten to do that before I was carted off to hospital.

While I preferred to paint the entire portrait from life, my sitters couldn't always spare me enough sessions so I took lots of photographs on my iPad. Those, and the sharp memory of the posed sitter in my mind's eye, meant I could complete the background later, if necessary.

Fliss had just got married, which was why she'd moved out. The wedding was another thing I'd missed during my stay in hospital, though to be honest, I'd really dreaded putting on that puffy-sleeved teal-blue bridesmaid's dress with matching capelet edged with fake swansdown and freezing my ass off for the day.

The things we do for love.

'So you really must come back for the Solstice ceremony on the twenty-first, even if you can't stay for the Yule Feast,' River was still urging, in his gentle, cultured and fluting voice, which went so well with his appearance: think of a small, slender, elfin Gandalf, silvery of beard and ponytail, bright eyes the pale azure of a summer sky. 'I can come back and fetch you.'

I was touched because it was a long drive, especially in that vehicle, and he was no longer young . . . though exactly how old I had no idea. He'd always seemed much the same to me: ageless and possibly immortal.

'I'll try,' I promised. 'And if I do, I'll be able to drive myself by then. I feel so much better.'

'Good, though Maj thought you really needed a few more days of nourishing home cooking. You're still too thin.'

It was true that my normally curvy figure was now fashionably skinny, but there was a limit to how much weight you could regain in one month, even on a hearty vegetarian diet, with liberal amounts of goat's milk cheese, yoghurt and extremely free-range eggs – when the very free-range hens obliged.

'There'll be visitors to the yurt camp too, because Posy and Simon are running a drumming and meditation retreat,' he said.

Well, that sounded irresistible, though the drumming would be just a faint rhythm on the breeze from the farmhouse.

He turned his head slightly and gave me his charming pixie smile, full of affection. 'We're your family and the Farm is your home: you'll always have a place there, and in our hearts.'

He was given to these slightly embarrassing expressions of affection but, none the less, I was touched and tears pricked the backs of my eyes. The aftermath of the illness was to make me more emotional and, in my darker moments, remember what I had lost and what might have been.

Still, if I could have chosen to have any grandfather in the world, I'd have picked River.

But luckily, I didn't have to, because *he* had chosen *me.*

2

The Vital Spark

River magically found a parking spot right outside my flat, something he often did . . . in the same way he frequently discovered the right change for a parking meter lying at his feet.

The basement flat felt dark, cold and empty when we arrived, though I knew Fliss had left the heating on low and popped in from time to time to make sure everything was OK. But the boiler was ancient and the pilot light often steered itself into extinction.

I switched on the electric fire while River vanished into the tiny galley kitchen, carrying Maj's parting gift: a basket of home-baked goodies.

Just as the long-unused bars of the electric fire began to glow dully and give off a smell of hot dust, the pipes emitted a sudden bronchial rattle and River came back into the room wearing the pleased expression of someone who had carried out an esoteric and difficult rite.

'I offered up the vital spark and it was accepted,' he announced. 'Our ancestors would call that magic.'

He should have looked slightly ridiculous, with his long silver hair tied back in a ponytail, the plaited beard and the black tunic, which had a hem embroidered with silver symbols, probably runes. He wore it over loose black cord trousers, tucked into baggy piratical boots, but somehow he got away with his style.

'Great,' I said, wishing that the vital spark of my life – painting – could also be rekindled so easily. At the moment it all felt a bit damply ashy and there was no sign of a phoenix, rising or otherwise. 'I'll make us a hot drink and then let's blow the budget and order a takeaway.'

After a month of having herbal brews pressed on me and eating meals that, however well prepared, often featured grated raw vegetables, nut roast and lentil loaf, I desperately wanted gallons of coffee and craved a Singapore-style fried rice with shrimp.

River always went for the Monk's Delight vegetarian option, then stole some of my shrimp. We were alike in that although lifelong abstainers from meat and poultry, we were not averse to the occasional bit of fish or seafood when away from the Farm.

'Good idea,' he agreed, and then added, 'There's a light twinkling on your phone. Perhaps there are messages with news of new portrait commissions?'

I glanced across at where the cradle of my cordless phone was indeed blinking a red eye. 'I hope so. A commission for the New Year would be good. In *January*,' I clarified, for in River's mind the New Year began the day after the Winter Solstice on 21 December. Sometimes I felt I was living with my feet in two entirely different worlds.

I suspected that at least half the phone messages would be from my ex-boyfriend, Rollo, deeply aggrieved by my lack of response to his latest catalogue of slights, affronts and occasional successes. He would have forgotten I'd had pneumonia about ten minutes after I'd told him, since over the six years since I'd ended our relationship he'd slowly become so self-obsessed I confidently expected him to implode one day with a loud pop.

'I'll go through all the messages in a bit and find out, but I'll need to increase my prices for any future commissions if I want to keep this flat on without Fliss, and even then, it would be a struggle.'

'You should move out of London now,' River suggested, contemplating the air around my head with his clear blue eyes, as if evaluating something only he could see. 'It's not good for your aura to be here.'

'I'm about as far out as I can get without actually leaving central London; I'm clinging to the edge of Greenwich by the skin of my teeth,' I pointed out. 'It's handy, especially having the little lean-to at the back as my studio. But then, I do seem to be increasingly travelling to my sitters' homes, so I suppose there's no real reason for me to stay here any more.'

Without Fliss, it wouldn't be the same anyway, for we'd been the last singletons in our circle of friends. It had been a bit of a shock when she had suddenly fallen in love and married in haste . . . though she definitely wouldn't repent at leisure, because Calum was such a nice man that he almost deserved her.

The tiny sitting room was already warming up and I removed my coat and went through to the kitchen to put the kettle on and fetch the takeaway menu. River would want to consider all the options before plumping for the dish he always had. It was a ritual. He liked rituals.

While I was spooning coffee into the cafetiere I could hear voices from the sitting room and assumed he'd turned the TV on, another novelty, since they didn't have one at the Farm (though they did have a laptop in the craft centre office now, and I suspected both he and Oshan occasionally watched programmes and films on that). But then, to my surprise, River called, in his beautifully posh voice, 'Meg, there's a visitor for you!'

I couldn't think who would be visiting me at this hour on a Sunday evening, other than the landlord, who seemed to operate only within vampire hours, but it wasn't him. The room seemed to be filled by a large, elderly lady who was wearing a voluminous heather-purple tweed cape. She had a mop of iron-grey curls streaked with silver, a bold Roman nose and dark, deeply intelligent eyes that appeared to sum me up at a glance: tall, too thin, pale as a wraith – in fact, colourless except for my hair, which one of the commune had rendered a verdant and interesting shade of deep green, using a natural vegetable dye. River had said I looked like a water sprite, but Maj had thought pink would have given my pale skin more of a rosy glow and, in retrospect, I thought she was probably right.

My visitor smiled, revealing a lot of strong teeth, and announced, like a particularly pessimistic oracle, '*Maim-doom!*'

The folds of the tweed cape billowed as she extricated a square, slightly gnarled hand adorned by a huge and ancient-looking carved carnelian seal ring and shook mine vigorously.

'You must be Meg Harkness.'

Something about that deep, upper-class and resonant voice, together with the smile, struck me as familiar . . . and then it clicked.

'You're Professor Clara Mayhem Doome!' I exclaimed. 'I watched that TV series you did, *Writings in the Sand*.'

'We pronounce our name Maim-Doom, and that programme title was ridiculous! They would call it that, even though the subject matter was the clay tablets we found *in* the sand.'

River had been looking on with interest. 'Ah, the famous epigrapher,' he said delightedly. 'I have your book of essays, *The Pre-Dawn of Written History*.'

He never ceased to amaze me. Put him in a room with an expert in any field, no matter how obscure, and he'd always have something to say.

'Oh?' My visitor raised her dark, straight eyebrows. 'You need the new, revised edition, because I've had to change course regarding one or two matters, after recently piecing together several fragments of an Assyrian clay tablet. You'd be surprised at the reluctance of museums and collectors to loan me their exhibits, even if I promise to work on them at the British Museum. But my days of constantly jetting round the globe are long gone and one can only do so much via computer graphics.'

'How fascinating! I must get the revised book,' said River.

'I wish you would buy it and then maybe my royalties would go into two figures!' She gave a deep chuckle.

I was fairly sure she hadn't paid this visit to discuss ancient inscriptions with River, happy though he would be to oblige. I could only think of one other reason . . .

'Do sit down,' I suggested, 'and tell us why you're here.'

'Oh, yes. Sorry to drop in on you unannounced like this,' she said, sinking into the unexpectedly smothering embrace of the sagging velvet sofa and then fighting her way upright into a sitting position. 'I got your email address and phone number from the Royal Society of Portrait Painters some time ago, but had no reply to my enquiries. The Royal Society just said you'd get into contact with me in due course and then babbled on about standard contracts and all that guff. So, being in London, I thought I might as well drop by and see if you were here. Obviously, it's about a portrait commission. Pookie Longridge gave me your address.'

'Would that be . . . Professor Priscilla Longridge?' I ventured.

'That's her.' She nodded and her springy dark grey and silver curls bounced vigorously, as did her earrings, which were in the form of tiny, brightly painted wooden parakeets in gilded cages. They swung mesmerizingly on their minute perches and I found it hard to drag my eyes away.

'I knew when I saw her portrait – lizard personified, my dear! – that you were the artist for *me*.'

'But I got the feeling that she didn't like her portrait,' I confessed, surprised.

'Of course she didn't, because it was a speaking likeness. You missed out only the forked tongue,' she said. 'But of course, it's such a brilliant portrait that everyone raves about it, so she can't say so! And it's the kind of portrait *I* want – a speaking likeness, warts and all.'

'I know a good charm for warts,' River offered.

'I haven't actually got any – I was speaking figuratively – though thank you for the offer,' Clara told him. 'Anyway, Meg – I hope I may call you Meg, since we're about to spend quite a lot of time in each other's company – here I am. In fact, I've popped round twice in the last week and found the place shuttered up, so my visit tonight was the final throw of the dice, because I'm going home tomorrow. Luck usually favours me, though,' she added complacently, 'and I thought if you *had* returned from whatever commission you were undertaking and were now free, I could quite easily take you back with me.'

She made this astounding proposition as if she was offering me a high treat and expected me instantly to fall in with her plans. Her personality was quite forceful, so I suspected most people probably did.

'I'm afraid that's quite impossible,' I said firmly. 'I've been away from home for the last two months and I got back less than an hour ago. I didn't answer your messages or emails because I left my iPad and phone here. They'll be as dead as a dodo by now.'

'A novel disinterest in modern communication technology from someone of your age,' she commented, then changed tack. 'You don't look a bit like your photograph on the Society's website. For a start, your hair was dark brown, except for a white fringe, like a frothy cappuccino. And your face is thinner . . . though you do look faintly familiar. We haven't met before, have we?'

'No, I'm certain we haven't. And I like to ring the changes with my hair colour,' I told her, then summoned a professional smile. 'I really *am* Meg Harkness, though! I've just recovered from pneumonia. After I got out of hospital River here took me home to convalesce.'

'River?' she queried, looking at him. 'Any particular waterway?'

He bestowed on her one of his more enigmatic smiles. 'No, just River,' he said, then told her he'd read another of her books, one about early Orkney runic stone markings, and there was a point he'd like to discuss with her . . .

'Not now, River,' I said hastily, but her eye had been caught by the runes printed in silver round the hem of his tunic.

'Turn around,' she ordered, and he obligingly twirled.

'Do you know what that says?' she asked.

'Yes: do you?' he replied tranquilly.

'Hmmph!' she grunted. 'So, I suppose you must be Meg's grandfather? You're not a bit alike.'

This was true, since I was several inches taller, for a start. Nor did I have his elegantly patrician features or sky-blue eyes.

'I'm Meg's grandfather in spirit and in loving regard,' River explained. 'There is no blood tie, but the commune is her family and my son, Oshan, is as her brother.'

That sounded a bit odd, but before she could demand any explanation, I broke in quickly, 'Anyway, I've been convalescing and although I mean to start taking commissions in the New Year, I have a few loose ends to tie up first.'

'In a way, then, the pneumonia was a stroke of luck for me, because it means you're not engaged on any other portraits at the moment,' Clara said, single-mindedly cutting to the chase. 'You're free to take my commission right away!'

'No, I—' I began to protest, but she carried on as if I hadn't spoken.

'You'll find the moorland air up there very bracing, you know. It'll do you a power of good. Rest and good food, fresh air . . . for, after all, one can't paint all day, I suppose.'

'Up where?' I asked, without in the least meaning to.

'Our house is in a small hamlet high on the Lancashire moors – big, roomy, warm, *very* comfortable,' she said, tempting me with its attractions. 'Even a studio, as one of the Gillyflowers fancied himself as an artist.'

'Gillyflowers . . . ?'

I felt myself struggling like a fly trapped in amber now. It had been a long day and I was starting to wonder if I'd fallen asleep and would wake up shortly in the jolting old Land Rover, the itchy rug tucked around me.

'It would take too long to explain now. You'll see for yourself.' Clara beamed at me, as one who has sorted everything out to her satisfaction.

River came to my rescue. 'Meg's had a month of rest, fresh air and good food at the Farm. She's only just got back.'

'That's all to the good, then, because she needn't repack,' Clara said. Nothing seemed to deflect her: she was a human juggernaut. She turned her attention back to me.

'I expect you'll want to get your painting gear together tonight, though. I'll pick you up in the morning. I have a hired car and driver, with plenty of room for everything.'

I stared blankly at her. 'But it's absolutely *impossible* that I should go to Lancashire with you tomorrow! I mean, I'm happy to discuss a commission with you and pencil it in for the New Year, but—'

She still wasn't listening. 'I want you to paint my portrait and my husband, Henry's, too, as a joint Christmas present to ourselves . . . and possibly posterity.'

She smiled happily and very engagingly. 'It will be such fun. I can't imagine why I've never thought of it before!'

3

Doomed

Apparently feeling that she'd sorted matters out to her own satisfaction, Clara levered herself out of the sofa's clutches and shook out her cape.

'That's that, then, and you can stay with us as long as you need to, Meg. I suppose it depends how quickly you work.'

'Actually, very quickly, once I've made the preliminary sketches: often only one or two sittings for the face. Then I use photographs on my iPad to put the finishing touches to portraits in my studio,' I replied automatically, while gathering my resources to persuade her that what she was asking me was quite impossible right now. 'But at the moment I can't—'

'I'm sure you'd much prefer to work entirely from life and since there's a studio at the Red House, there's no reason why not.'

I remembered earlier wishing the vital spark to paint would return and I reflected you should always be careful what you wish for, because now, despite my resistance, I'd begun to *really* want to paint Clara. Also, I'd realized that Henry Doome was the famous but reclusive poet, who, judging from his photographs, would also make an arresting subject . . . only not right now, when I'd just got home and was at such a low ebb.

I summoned up the dregs of my willpower and said resolutely, 'Professor Mayhem Doome, I'd be delighted to accept the commission and I'm sure we can come to some arrangement for early next year, but you must see that it's quite impossible before that.'

She gazed at me in surprise. 'I fail to see any difficulties. In fact, everything seems to have fallen into place most serendipitously.'

'Not really, because it's less than three weeks before Meg comes home again for the Winter Solstice ceremony and the Yule feasting. She's only here now because she had a lot of business to sort out,' River said. 'Nor should she be travelling up and down the country in the middle of winter so soon after her illness,' he added, entirely discounting the endurance test I'd already been subjected to in the old Land Rover.

Clara was looking speculatively from me to River. 'Did you say the Winter Solstice? Do you then celebrate the shortest day of the year and Yule at your farm, rather than Christmas?'

'We do indeed, and have a special ceremony in a sacred spot nearby, followed by a week of feasting and celebration. Meg *always* comes home for that.'

Well, I'd always at least made it for the ceremony, though the feasting could last even longer than a week, with much consumption of River's home-made mead, which always made the holiday memorable . . . or rather, unmemorable, since it was strong enough to fell hard-drinking men like ninepins.

'What a coincidence! We also have a ceremony every year at Starstone Edge, on the night of the Winter Solstice,' she said. 'Meg could go to that instead.'

'*Starstone?*' said River eagerly. 'I've heard rumours of the Starstone ceremony, and that it's based on a very old ritual!' Then he added wistfully, 'I'd like to see that myself.'

'Then there's no reason why you shouldn't. You can stay with us; there's plenty of room,' she offered. 'You'll be able to see how Meg's portraits are coming along, too.'

I opened my mouth to remind her that I hadn't agreed to start on the commission before the following January, but only a croak came out.

She'd certainly pressed the right buttons with River, however, because he was looking very tempted. 'That's extremely kind of you, but I'm never away from the Farm for the important ceremonies of the year, especially this one.'

I didn't see why he should deny himself this treat, whether I was there or not. 'But you said yourself last year that the climb up the mountain to ignite the bonfire was getting a bit much and you were going to hand over the ceremonial staff to Oshan,' I pointed out. 'He's perfectly capable of managing it on his own. You could still get home after this Starstone ceremony in time for the feasting.'

'I suppose I could . . .' he agreed, mulling it over. 'It's extremely kind of you to invite me, Professor Mayhem Doome.'

'Call me Clara, both of you. The rest of it makes me sound like a firm of dodgy solicitors. And I'm so glad you feel able to come.'

'If Meg's finished the portraits by then, she can return to the Farm with me after the Solstice,' River suggested.

I stared speechlessly at them both, for there seemed to have been a sudden seismic shift and it appeared now to be taken for granted that I was going to Starstone as Clara decreed.

'I'm sure she'll need a little longer than that to paint both of us,' Clara said. 'In fact, I hope she'll stay on and celebrate

Christmas with us, and then she can complete both portraits afterwards, at her leisure.'

'But I've never celebrated Christmas,' I objected, last ditch, because although I was perfectly capable of turning the suggestion down, the growing desire to paint Clara was sapping my will to resist any further. 'If I do begin the portraits before Christmas, then I'll go to the Farm after the Solstice and complete them in the studio.'

'Nonsense! Everyone should experience a proper family Christmas at least once in their lives,' she said. 'There'll be a house full, I expect, and Henry loves the traditions, so we'll have the tree, the stockings, the giant plum pudding . . . the even more gigantic cake, the—'

'I'm afraid I'm vegetarian, so I'd be a nuisance,' I interrupted hastily, though there was a certain fascination about the prospect offered. A proper family Christmas . . . what would that be like?

'No problem at all,' Clara said airily. 'So are we all at the Red House, in a manner of speaking. It's because of Henry: he's vegetarian most of the time, though he eats a small amount of fish and seafood too.'

'Pescetarian?' suggested River helpfully. 'But so are Meg and I – what a coincidence!'

'Perfect!' Clara beamed at us and gave a deep sigh of satisfaction. 'There we are then, that's all settled. Now, what time shall I collect you tomorrow, Meg?'

'I'm afraid that would be impossible, because I really *do* have things to arrange first,' I told her. 'Besides, I'd prefer to drive up in my own van.'

'You have a van?'

'A small camper van. I keep it on my friends' smallholding near St Albans and they drop it off here when I need it.'

That wasn't very often, and Freddie and Joe had the use of it the rest of the time, so the arrangement worked well. It wasn't as if it was a romantic old vintage Dormobile or anything like that, but a more modern small vehicle, narrow but tall, and containing only the modicum of living facilities. I could get all my painting gear in it and also safely transport tacky canvases, so I'd found it useful to camp in it when it was inconvenient to stay with my sitters. In fact, I often much preferred to do that, though in this case, it wouldn't be an option up on the Lancashire moors in the middle of winter.

Clara, having attained her main objective, conceded the point. 'In that case, you can follow me up to Starstone Edge as soon as you're ready.' She turned that force-field smile on me again. 'If you do decide to stay on over Christmas, Henry would be so delighted to introduce you to all the festive manifestations of the season.'

That all sounded a bit Jacob Marley.

'Most of the Christmas traditions are actually a late Victorian embroidering of old pagan rites,' River said.

'That's true, which makes them very suited to the Red House, which is Victorian Gothic of the most overblown kind. I let Henry have full rein over the celebrations: it's the highlight of his year, especially the tree. He always chooses one so tall, we have to decorate half of it from the stairs or using a stepladder.'

At the farm, we also had a pine tree, a small one, which was hung upside down in the hall and decorated with corn dollies, nuts, sprigs of holly, mistletoe and other symbolic odds and ends.

Christmas at the Red House sounded so interestingly different from anything I'd known, and it was tempting. But then,

I'd only just escaped from one house full of people, so did I want to be pitchforked into a party of strangers?

I needn't decide now, I reasoned. I'd go there and begin the portraits, and then, if it was all too much, escape with River back to the Farm after the Solstice.

Clara, mission accomplished, removed herself and the force-field of her personality back to the club she was staying at, leaving only a large dent in the sofa cushion to show she'd ever been there.

I think she'd used up most of the oxygen in the room, because I barely had the energy to eat the takeaway when it arrived.

When I woke late next morning, River had already set off for home. He'd left a pebble on the coverlet of the bed in the spare room, inscribed in pencil with the message, 'See you on the 21st!'

When I turned it over, I saw he'd added, 'May the Goddess bless you!'

But I think she already had, even though it might well turn out to be a blessing of the mixed kind.

Clara

I was born over seventy years ago in the Lancashire village of Starstone. My father, Cecil Mayhem (always pronounced 'Maim'), was the vicar there, a quiet, scholarly man with a keen interest in ancient languages and archaeology.

I grew up to all intents and purposes an only child, for my sister, Bridget, was an exceedingly last-minute arrival, long after we had moved to a parish in Devon. I was precocious and clever, and Father augmented the teaching of the small local school with lessons in such subjects as Latin and Ancient Greek, while Mother, the daughter of a diplomat, made sure I was fluent in French, German and Italian.

These lessons were shared by my great friend Henry Doome, second son of the family who lived in the local manor house, Underhill. Although almost a year younger than me, he was my equal in everything and even as children you could see the direction our careers would one day take. Henry was keenly interested in poetry and the interplay of words, while my early fascination with epigraphy was sparked by an ancient stone incised with runic markings that stood in the graveyard of the small village church. Henry and I spent ages taking rubbings from it and trying to decipher them.

Henry's brother, George, was his complete opposite, being vain, rather stupid and games mad. The only thing they shared was the fair, blue-eyed Doome colouring and the straight Grecian nose that appeared in so many of the family portraits.

George was sent off to prep school at eight and was destined to follow the family tradition of going into the army for a few years, a rite of passage presumably intended to instil a sense of discipline and turn the eldest son into an officer and gentleman. Of course, in his case that was a forlorn hope, for though he became an officer, he was never a gentleman, nor did he ever develop any discipline or self-control that I ever noticed.

Starstone was an ancient upland village, set in a beautiful valley, surrounded by hills that often bloomed over with the saffron and purple hues of gorse and heather.

As well as the church, we had a village hall, the pub, a general shop and a tiny school: everything you might need, right on the doorstep.

The pub, the Pike with Two Heads, also let rooms and was frequented both by anglers, keen to try their luck in the river that ran through the middle of the village, and by artists attracted by the rugged scenery and the striking inverted V of the Starstone (or rather stones, for there were two leaning together) atop the hill behind the Doomes' manor house, from which the village got its name.

The hamlet of Starstone Edge was clustered along the top road that ran around one side of the valley until it came to a stop at the upper end, by the rear entrance to the Underhill estate. Beyond that, it was just a gated farm track that wandered off over the moors in the general direction of Yorkshire.

But if you followed the road the other way, down the valley and through the clustered cottages and villas of the hamlet, you arrived at the large Victorian Gothic pile that was the Red House, home of the Gillyflowers. The name of the house derived from the red bricks that divided up the local sober grey stone into layers, like some strange cake.

There were no more dwellings beyond it, just the turning that would take you up over the moors to the village of Thorstane in the next valley, unless you headed down the scary hairpin bends of the Grimlike Pass to the small market town of Great Mumming, which to us at that time seemed an exciting metropolis.

This, for the first eight years of our lives, was our world.

4

Poetic Licence

I spent the next two days in a whirlwind of activity, including answering all my mail and messages, once I'd charged up my iPad and phone.

I'd been quite right about at least half the messages being from Rollo and, sighing, I deleted them unread.

He was four years my senior. When I first met and fell in love with him at a student party in my second year, he had a golden, mercurial quality, combined with a lot of charm. He could be very sweet then, too . . . but I suppose the spoilt child was always lurking within the man.

Rollo was a poet and one of the proprietors and contributors to a precious little quarterly magazine called *Strimp!* (Don't ask me why it's called that; I have no idea.)

By now he was also a part-time lecturer in creative writing, which gave him access to an endless supply of female students, though since he'd turned forty, all that mercurial charm had started to transmogrify into elderly Peter Pan, so perhaps it was drying up.

He was a performance poet, and came alive on the stage in a way that made his poetry sound a lot better than I suspected it really was.

As to his looks, imagine an ageing but still handsome cross between Dylan Thomas and Lord Byron, all red-gold hair, sulky mouth and brooding gaze, and you've got him.

My mind wandered back to that brief time six years before, when marriage and a family had finally seemed within my grasp, only to be snatched away again. I'd wanted a clean break between us after that. It was Rollo who insisted we remain friends, which would, he'd said, show that I didn't entirely blame him for the accident.

I firmly wrenched my thoughts back to the present, but there was no escaping Rollo, for he rang me on the Monday morning to demand histrionically why I was ignoring him.

'I've been ignoring everyone,' I told him patiently. 'I've had pneumonia, remember? Fliss told you and you sent flowers.'

'But that was ages ago!'

'I was very ill and you don't get over pneumonia in five minutes. I've been at the Farm convalescing since I got out of hospital and I've only just come home. How are things with you?'

I wedged the phone between cheek and shoulder and let him ramble on while I made myself coffee and ate a couple of slightly limp gingernut biscuits. I caught the odd phrase like '. . . she didn't really appreciate my work and then, when she saw me with one of the students, she . . .'

'Did she?' I murmured with absent disinterest. Since he flitted from female to female like a hummingbird visits flowers, I could join the dots without listening properly. I'd been the only woman he'd ever had a relationship with that lasted longer than a fortnight, even if it had turned out that I'd never had exclusive rights . . . but even now, so long after our break-up, he didn't seem able to function without constantly unburdening his soul and using me as a sounding board. That was *not* what friendship was about and, along with his increasing and unattractive self-absorption, it was a habit I'd like to break.

'But at least they appreciate my work in the States, and a new collection of my poetry is being published there next spring,' he finished on a triumphant up-note. He'd always been more popular in the USA than here.

'Well, that's wonderful, Rollo. I'm so glad. But I'm afraid I'll have to go now, because I'm off north on Wednesday to paint a portrait commission and I've got a lot to do.'

'But you've only just got back, you said so,' he said aggrievedly.

I thought of something, other than himself, that would interest him. 'My sitter is the wife of Henry Doome, the poet.'

I wished I'd kept this information to myself because he instantly became over-excited.

'*Henry Doome?*' he gasped, awed. 'They say he's turned down the Poet Laureateship twice! Of course he's a bit old hat,' he added, on a less exalted note, 'but still a Big Name.'

'Well, I'm supposed to be painting him, too.'

'He's said to be a total recluse these days and hardly ever gives an interview . . . but what a coup it would be for *Strimp!* if he'd talk to me and perhaps let us publish one of his poems. Meg, you'll have to prepare the ground before I contact him – or wait, maybe it would be better if I just happened to be in the area and dropped in to see you . . . and then you can introduce me and I'll take it from there.'

'Absolutely *not.* Are you mad?' I said, aghast. 'If you want to interview him, then you set it up yourself and don't try to involve me. I've never even met the man and I'm not going to try to persuade him into doing anything he doesn't want to.'

'But, Meg, it would be—'

'No,' I said flatly. 'I'll have to go now, Rollo, and I'm going to be very busy, so don't call me. I'll catch up with you when I get back.' *Or not, if I can help it*, I added mentally. Then I put the phone down while he was still being persuasive.

It didn't work on me any more: the magic charm had broken, like my heart, several years earlier.

I managed a quick chat on the phone with most of my closest friends, though none was free to meet up before I left, for they were all busy procreating, or child rearing, except Fliss, and I expected she'd be following suit as soon as physically possible.

She was the only one who did manage to meet up with me for coffee. When I told her all about my commission and Clara and everything, she said I'd probably vanish into the Bleak North, never to be seen again, and I must ring and email her with updates because it sounded fascinating.

'It's a pity you're going right away, though, because I wanted to introduce you to Calum's cousin, Rob. He's just your type.'

'I don't think I've got a type,' I told her. 'Or my type is extinct. I've decided I'm going to move to a little cottage in the country and devote myself to my Art.'

'Yeah, right,' she said, unconvinced, but since both my only serious (though on and off) relationship and my single attempt at motherhood had come to nothing, I thought I was finally embracing my destiny.

That reminded me of Rollo and I told her I'd come back to a load of messages from him and then he'd rung me.

'I can't imagine why you let him keep pestering you,' she said. 'I mean, you've no feelings for him any more, have you?'

'No, especially since he seems to be turning into some kind of self-obsessed monster. But getting rid of him is easier said than done, short of changing my phone number and email addie and moving house without telling him.'

'That would be a bit drastic,' she said. 'You'll just have to be brutally frank with him.'

'Yes, I've come to the same conclusion,' I admitted. 'I'll do it when I get back home after this commission.'

I blew the dust off my big folding studio easel and painting gear and packed them up ready to go. I'd exchanged cards with Clara, so I could ask her what size of portraits she envisaged, which was, as I might have guessed, large. Luckily I keep a stock of stretched and primed canvases in various sizes. I put in a few smaller ones too, because I had a one-woman show in a tiny gallery coming up in February and I was stockpiling work for that. I might have a little spare time and spot an interesting subject.

There was a wardrobe unit in the van, which took my easel, canvases and paints, so I generally just stowed a few clothes in two small drawers under the bunk. This time, though, I packed a suitcase and large holdall.

I didn't usually need an extensive wardrobe because I tended to live and work in jeans, T-shirts and hand-knitted jumpers. At the Farm, changing for dinner meant removing any garment that smelled of goat and replacing it with one that didn't. This time I wasn't sure what I would need, or even how long I would be staying. Still, since I didn't actually have that many clothes, and few that were really smart, I just packed everything.

Early on the Wednesday morning I finally headed North, Joe and Freddie having returned my camper van to me the evening before. Or rather, Joe returned it and Freddie followed him in their old 2CV to drive him home again.

Though they'd cleaned the van, it still smelled pleasantly of coriander and the other exotic herbs they grew in their ecologically heated greenhouses, along with several kinds of chilli peppers, which they sold to local pubs, restaurants, shops and cafés.

Freddie, at my request, had also brought me a large hamper of the jams and chutneys he made, for it had occurred to me that if I *was* to end up staying for Christmas, then some form of gift offering would be a good idea. And if I'd had enough by the Winter Solstice and decamped with River, it might sweeten my departure somewhat.

I wasn't sure how Freddie's new line, Fiery Fiesta Chilli Chutney, would go down, but no one could dislike the lemon, orange and lime curds he bottled so prettily, the jars wearing gingham mobcaps in the same colour as the contents and tied with matching grosgrain ribbon.

The good thing about travelling in my own cosy snail-shell home was that I could stop wherever I liked and make a hot drink and something to eat, without having to run the shopping gauntlet of the service stations in search of something vegetarian *and* edible, which in most of them would be akin to finding the Holy Grail on offer in the local supermarket.

I didn't do sat nav, but I'd checked the route via Google, which had also offered me views of a reservoir in the valley below Starstone Edge, where I would be staying. The photos had obviously been taken in high summer, with white-sailed little boats on a still surface that reflected a blue sky and a few snow-white puffball clouds. The amenities of the hamlet (the larger village in the valley having been flooded by the creation of the reservoir) included a seasonal sailing club, a handful of holiday cottages and a B&B. The delights of the area around Starstone Edge were described as good walking and birdwatching country, with sailing and fishing in the reservoir. I'd stayed in remote moorland areas before and strongly suspected that the whole place would shut down from early autumn to late spring.

The recommended route was via the village of Thorstane in the next valley, and then over the moors, the only alternative being a narrow zigzag pass, which I can't say I liked the look of, especially in the middle of winter.

I got lost twice after leaving the motorway, but eventually found myself winding my way upwards along ever narrower country roads until eventually I saw the sign for Thorstane. It was a large village with an ugly Victorian church, a couple of shops and, right on the furthest edge where the road began to climb steeply again, a large pub.

I stopped to take a look at it: it was evidently an old building, though now extended, and with a motel wing in what had probably once been stables and barns. It sported a sign: the Pike with Two Heads.

That struck me as being an odd choice of name for a pub on a remote bit of moorland, with not a river to be seen . . .

But there was no time to linger, because the afternoon dusk was already seeping in, as was the cold, the camper van heater not being terribly efficient. I started the engine again and set off, labouring upwards and then, with relief, over the crest and down into the next valley.

Far below a sheet of water gleamed dully, like polished pewter, and a line of toy buildings straggled along the road that edged this side of it. There were a lot of conifers crowding up to the water's edge and spreading up the hills on the far side.

In the other direction, the road snaked down the valley in a series of zigzags towards the dam. Slowly trundling up this route, and looking the size of a toy car, was a white pick-up truck. It vanished as I ran the camper carefully down the single-track lane, reversing at one point into a passing place when I met a tractor.

Finally, I reached the junction with the valley road and turned right . . . and there in front of me was the imposing and impossibly overblown shape of a Victorian Gothic mansion: turreted, pepper pot-towered, gingerbread decorated, gabled and many-chimneyed. It was built of some grey stone, divided by lines of red brick, some of it in herringbone pattern.

I'd come to a stop in order to gaze at the monstrosity in amazement. It was as if the architect had tried to include every element of Victorian Gothic in one house. This must be my destination. There couldn't be two of them.

The last of the light died and the façade turned dark, except for the many casemented or cusped and arched windows.

It was growing colder by the minute, so I set off again and turned up the drive, parking on a sweep of gravel behind what looked like the white pick-up I'd seen heading up the pass.

I got out reluctantly, thinking that, what with the rapidly vanishing light and the chill wind whistling round my legs, it didn't seem the most inviting venue I could think of for a cosy Christmas party.

A tall, wide-shouldered man, his dark curling hair whipped into a frenzy by the breeze, was lifting down a small boy from the passenger side of the pick-up. The child ran off up the steps to the house, a blue rucksack trailing from one hand. The door swung open and he vanished inside.

I was still shrugging into my old down-filled anorak when the man turned and took a step towards me . . . then stopped dead, staring.

I froze, and it wasn't because I'd caught the full blast of the icy wind whistling down off the moors, or the glacial expression of horrified disbelief in his dark moss agate-green eyes . . . eyes that could also look as velvet-soft as catkins.

But they weren't soft now.

Memories of the Lex Mariner I'd once known shuffled quickly through my mind: striding through the art college, his tumbled black curls, his long dark coat flapping, his winged brows and narrow face with its thin, curved nose that gave him the look of a young hawk, the sound of his deep voice raised in some artistic discussion . . . and another memory, long suppressed: the feel of his arms around me.

Then it all morphed into the man standing in front of me, an older version, with lines of pain and endurance etched on his face like a map of the past.

I felt myself flush hotly and then the blood drained away into my boots: old wounds might heal on the surface, yet underneath, remain raw. I never thought I'd see him again – and I hadn't wanted to.

The feeling appeared to be mutual, for without a word he swung on his heel, climbed back into his cab, executed a tight three-point turn and roared off, spattering me and my van in gravel.

Stoned – and I'd never even been guilty as charged.

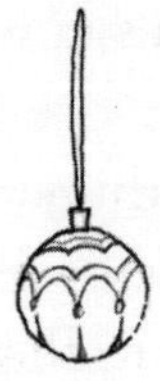

5

All Enveloping

A voice finally broke into my stunned reverie, in which, among other chaotic thoughts, a strong desire to get into the van and head straight back to London was forming.

'Miss 'Arkness?' it said.

I turned and found that a small, entirely bald man with a friendly, simian face was bobbing about next to me. He was attired in an over-large brown linen overall.

'Where's 'is 'ighness gorn off to in such an 'urry?'

The roar of the pick-up's engine receded like a lion down the valley and then was gone. Without waiting for an answer, the man continued, 'I'm Den, cook and dogsbody round 'ere. Yer to go in – drawing room's on the left. They're all waiting for yer. I'll bring yer cases, if you show me what you want, won't I?'

'Oh, right,' I said, finally getting my vocal cords to work and leading the way to the back of the van. 'Just that holdall and the suitcase. I'll leave the painting gear and everything else for later.'

'Right you are,' he said, swinging my luggage down. He sniffed, his flattened nose wrinkling slightly. 'If you don't mind me saying so, there's a strange smell in this 'ere van. Not *bad* – just . . . funny.'

'It's mostly coriander, I think. Friends sometimes use the van to deliver herbs from their market garden.'

'That would account fer it, then,' he said. 'And if you give me yer keys, I'll move the van round the side in a bit, where it's more sheltered, ain't it?'

I had no idea, nor could I quite place his accent. There seemed to be elements of Cockney, but overlaid with later strata that were less easy to pigeonhole.

I shut the door again. 'That man who just left . . .' I began, cautiously.

'Lex Mariner, Clara's nephew.' Den picked up my luggage as if it was as insubstantial as a cloud, which it wasn't, due to my having shoved several books in there, plus my wellies. 'She was expecting 'im to come in fer tea, be introduced to you, like, but 'e must 'ave 'ad something urgent to do. Maybe Teddy knows.'

I assumed that to be the small boy – could he be Lex's son? I took my tapestry shoulder bag and followed Den up the steps and through a vestibule with a half-glazed door into a vast hall, from which a grand staircase curved upwards into darkness. The eagle sitting on the barley sugar-twist newel post at the bottom looked as if it was about to swoop forward and carry me off in its huge talons.

Den nodded to a door on the left. 'In there. Unfreeze yer marrow while I dump yer bags and fetch in fresh tea – unless Tottie's already on the case.'

As he bent to pick my luggage up again, the collar of the brown overall rode down and I could see a tattoo on the back of his neck. It was a luridly coloured arrow pointing upwards, underneath it the words, 'This way up.'

'Interesting tattoo,' I commented.

'Ta. Got it done in Brixton. Passes the time, don't it?'

'I suppose it does,' I agreed, slightly startled. Could he mean Brixton as in prison? Did they spend the long hours tattooing things on each other . . . with sharp instruments? Surely not!

He plodded off upwards, refusing my offer to take one of the bags, and I turned my steps towards the drawing-room door. The hall was cavernous and dark, so that you could only just discern the outline of a vast coat-stand, wooden chairs with pointed canopies, a long table pushed against one wall and a grandfather clock ticking heavily away, like the heartbeat of the house. The floor was tiled in a beautiful pattern of oak leaves in ochre red and sage green, and the air was fragranced with lavender polish and pot-pourri, plus a slight overlay of damp dog.

But on opening the door, I blinked as I found myself in a very large room that dazzled the eye with light. It was painted a bright shade of golden yellow, to start with, hung with many gilded mirrors, and illuminated by a huge and glittering chandelier. The furnishings were an eclectic mix of twenties-style squishy velvet sofas and chairs, hideous camel saddle stools and Egyptian leather poufs. Ancient Eastern carpets hung on every spare bit of wall and a full-sized statue of the god Anubis was standing right next to me. He was wearing a gilded loin cloth and a very beachcomber straw hat with a frayed brim, adorned with a faded ribbon.

There were several people grouped around a roaring fire, like a slightly offbeat illustration for *Homes and Gardens*, and they had all turned to look at me.

Clara was sitting on one sofa before a large coffee table on which was a tray of tea things and a depleted plate of sandwiches. A thin, desiccated-looking middle-aged woman, with fair curling hair, sat on an upright brocade chair nearby, teacup in hand, while opposite on a mustard velvet chesterfield sofa was the small boy I'd seen earlier, leaning affectionately against a silver-haired and handsome elderly man, whom I immediately recognized as the great poet himself Henry Doome.

Rollo would have been dead jealous.

'There you are, Meg,' Clara said, with the beaming forcefield smile that I remembered only too well. 'Great timing, because Tottie's just gone to put the kettle on for fresh tea, and the cheese scones should be ready by now. I expect you're starving?'

'I . . . yes, I *am* hungry,' I discovered, surprised. You'd think the shock of seeing Lex Mariner again would have put me off food for life.

I was also freezing, so when she patted the sofa next to her I was happy to obey.

'Come and sit here to thaw out and I'll introduce you to everyone. And here's Tottie now,' she added as the door opened and a tall, weather-beaten woman of flatly angular physique, with cropped pepper-and-salt hair, and dressed in corduroy trousers and a checked shirt, pushed a tea trolley into the room with a rattle.

This sofa seemed to be an upmarket version of the one in my flat, for it enveloped me in such billowy softness that I wasn't sure I'd ever escape its clutches.

'Meg, this is Tottie Gillyflower, one of the household,' Clara said as Tottie removed the dirty cups and empty teapot and replaced them with a fresh supply in an entirely different pattern of china, before adding more sandwiches and a large plate of scones. The smell made me salivate.

'Ha!' said Tottie, by way of greeting, then shoved the trolley away into the middle of the room and planted herself opposite on the other sofa, next to the small boy.

'That's Henry, my husband, of course,' Clara continued.

'How do you do, my dear?' said Henry in a voice I recognized from broadcasts. We may have never had a TV at the Farm while I was growing up, but we had the radio. 'I can't get up because Lass is asleep.'

What I'd thought was a hairy black, grey and white rug spread across his knees was actually a spaniel. In fact, it now awoke with a snort and, opening its eyes, spotted me. A tail flapped a little, narrowly missing the scones.

'Teddy's in the middle,' Clara said. 'He's my niece's little boy, but he makes his home with us because Zelda is an actor and it's so difficult otherwise when she's on tour round the provinces, which she mostly seems to be.'

'It's a pity they didn't keep her character on in *Coronation Street.* That was really handy, since they film it so close by,' Tottie said.

'It was just a bit part, unfortunately,' Henry explained to me. 'You can't really make a big impression with only two lines to say.'

'That depends on how good the actor is,' Clara said.

'Mummy and Daddy are strange,' the little boy put in, fixing me with a pair of dark eyes.

'Estranged,' corrected Clara. 'Though the ways of modern coupling and uncoupling certainly *are* strange. Sybil, we haven't introduced you yet,' she added to the desiccated woman sitting in the brocade chair.

'Meg, this is Sybil Whitcliffe, Henry's niece. Her son, Mark, has inherited the family pile, Underhill, and is ripping the place apart so he can turn it into some kind of bijou wedding reception venue and country house hotel, so she's escaped over here to have her tea in peace.'

'So pleased . . .' murmured Sybil faintly. She reminded me of one of those plants that seem dead until you put them in water, when they spring back to verdant life. I thought she looked about fifty and would be pretty if you soaked her for long enough.

The door opened and Den, still wearing the brown linen overall, wandered in, took a cheese scone, which he ate in two large bites, then wandered out again.

Lass scrambled down and followed him through the door before it shut.

'It's her dinnertime, more or less,' Henry explained.

'We had fishfingers for lunch at school today,' Teddy said, looking up from a book he'd opened on his lap. 'But fish don't have fingers, do they? I asked Miss Dawn and she said, "Let's not get into one of your long discussions till after lunch, Teddy. Just eat it."'

'None that I've ever seen,' I agreed, beginning to feel as if I'd strayed into some Mad Hatter's tea party. 'I think they just make them out of minced up bits of white fish and call them that.'

'Good, because I don't want to eat real fingers,' said Teddy. He subjected me to a close scrutiny. 'Are you going to paint Aunt Clara?'

'She is, and Henry too, I hope, but Meg's recovering from an illness, so she needs lots of rest, fresh air and good food,' Clara told him.

'Your hair is very green,' Teddy observed, with one of those sudden changes of subject children are prone to. 'I can paint, too, so I might paint you with green hair.'

'That would be wonderful, Teddy. I'd love you to paint my portrait.'

'It's a very pretty shade of green,' Henry said kindly.

He should have seen it after Roz had first dyed it, when it was more dark emerald than waterweed.

He looked at me thoughtfully. 'And your eyes are a very unusual shade, my dear, somewhere between light green and turquoise . . .' He frowned. 'I seem to recall someone else with eyes of just such a shade . . .'

'You know, I thought the very same thing when I first met Meg,' Clara agreed. 'I can't remember where, though. It'll come back to me.'

I got my unusually pale hair and the colour of my eyes from Mum (though my father was also fair, even if more of a dishwater blond), but I thought it unlikely that her path had ever crossed with the Doomes. Still, coincidences *do* happen.

'You haven't been to India in the last few years, have you?' I asked hopefully.

'No, not for . . . oh, perhaps fifteen years. Time flies,' said Clara, accepting the change of subject without apparent surprise.

My sudden flare of hope died: Mum had vanished there some years ago and though that hadn't been unusual, she'd always previously resurfaced after a while. This time, however, she simply seemed to have been swallowed up and there had been no contact.

'My mother has the same colouring as me and she went missing in India a few years ago,' I explained. 'We haven't heard from her since, so I just wondered if your paths might have crossed.'

'No, afraid not,' Clara said.

'River went over there a couple of years ago to visit friends and went to see the owner of the bar where she'd been working.

The man still had a holdall she'd left there with her passport and other things, but she'd never gone back for them.'

'A complete mystery, then,' said Tottie, looking at me curiously.

'Meg was brought up in a commune in the Black Mountains and River is her adoptive grandfather,' Clara explained. 'Delightful chap. He's going to come and stay for a couple of nights for the Winter Solstice.'

And I, I thought, would now *definitely* be escaping with him afterwards if Lex Mariner was going to be around the place!

I didn't say that, though. My first impulse on seeing him had been to jump back in the van and make off, but I couldn't do that. I'd accepted the commission and I'd paint Clara's portrait. Then, if I hadn't completed Henry's, I'd decamp back to the Farm with River, promising to return later, though I wouldn't. I'd have to add any finishing touches back at the studio.

'Have another scone,' Clara suggested, and I realized I'd wolfed down the one she'd already put on my plate. 'It's a good couple of hours till dinner will be ready, so they won't spoil your appetite.'

'I do seem surprisingly hungry,' I admitted. 'It might be the cold air outside. The temperature appeared to drop rapidly as soon as I left Thorstane and headed up over the moors.'

'Yes, we have our own little weather system here in Starstone Edge. We're surprisingly high up, so in winter it's like living in a snowdome that a giant hand shakes from time to time,' Henry said, poetically. He had an attractively light and melodious voice.

'Grimlike Pass is only really driveable in good weather, so in winter we mostly rely on the road to Thorstane, and even that is often impassable because of snow or ice,' put in Sybil.

'We're much higher than Thorstane, but the local farmers usually clear the road over the moors in a few days,' Clara said nonchalantly. 'And the electricity lines and phone rarely cut out, though we have oil for the range and heating, and lots of logs, candles and lanterns, so we're fine if they do.'

'Den and I would much rather not cook Christmas dinner on a temperamental old range by the light of a candle,' Tottie said tartly, and I wondered how she – and indeed Den – fitted into the household. It was all a bit baffling and I felt too tired to get a grasp on all the relationships. Anyway, I expected they'd become clear in a day or two.

'I'd better get back,' Sybil said, putting down her plate and getting up. I saw then that she was in riding breeches and a heavy polo-neck jumper. 'I left Juniper in the stable and it'll be too dark to see where we're going if I don't set off now.'

'I'll come and see you off,' said Tottie, and followed her out of the room.

'We don't keep horses any more, but Tottie often borrows Sybil's spare hack and they ride out together,' Henry said. 'Our stables are always ready, if needed.'

'*I* can ride,' said Teddy. 'Sybil borrowed a Shetland pony from a friend last summer and taught me.'

'If Mark has anything to do with it, the stables at Underhill will be turned into spare guest or staff accommodation soon, and poor Sybil will have to pay for grazing her horses in the top pasture,' Clara said.

'Since George left her a good annuity, there's no reason why she shouldn't pay for her horses' upkeep, is there?' Henry said reasonably.

'Sybil never seems to *have* any money, though,' said Clara.

'Perhaps she's just the penny-pinching type, or has a secret vice,' he suggested.

'I can't think of any vice, other than spending too much on spring bulbs, that she could possibly have,' said Clara with a grin.

'Nor I,' he agreed.

Clara turned to me and explained, 'Mark was working abroad in hotel management when Henry's older brother, George, died a couple of years ago. Sybil kept the estate going until he finally decided to leave his job and come back.'

'He got all the plans in place to turn Underhill into a business first, though,' Henry pointed out. 'He realized he'd have to make Underhill earn its keep if he wanted to hang on to it. And if that's as a wedding venue, he'll have to make the money in the short season from spring to early autumn, so there's no time to lose!'

Henry rose to his feet. 'I think I'll go back to my study for a bit till dinner, my dear.' He stooped to kiss his wife, then smiled kindly at me.

'I expect you'll want to get the lie of the land and then settle in, Meg. I'm very glad you've come. Clara is so excited about the portraits and we'll have great fun over Christmas. I was hoping to settle with Lex about fetching the tree,' he added. 'But he must have had something urgent to do at the pottery and had to dash back. I expect he'll ring.'

As long as he didn't reappear in person, that was fine by me.

'This must be all very confusing for you, Meg,' said Clara. 'My nephew, Lex, has brought Teddy back from school today. It's in Great Mumming, where Terrapotter is.'

'Terracotta?' I said tentatively. I'd been a bit at sea during most of the conversation, but I'd come back to life at the mention of Lex's name.

'No, Terrapotter – it's the name of his business.'

'And . . . does he live there, too?' I asked carefully.

'Yes, in the cottage next to the pottery, the Old Forge.'

That was a mercy. Maybe he wouldn't come up to the Red House while he knew I was here.

'Teddy can go and change out of his uniform while I'm giving you the shorter guided tour of the house and then you can unpack and rest,' Clara said, rising without difficulty from the enveloping sofa. I floundered for a moment, trying to escape its clutches, then followed her.

I swear that sofa was trying to eat me up whole. I'd rather not be a set of dry bones found down the back of it one day, like a new take on the Mistletoe Bride.

6
Verdant

Clara led the way through the hall with about twice as much bounce as I'd ever possessed, even before my illness.

'Now, this door to my left is Henry's study, but we'll leave him in peace for the moment,' she said. 'He likes the view from the side window over the fields and down to the reservoir. When the weather is clear, he can see Underhill, the family home, at the top of the valley too, and the Starstone. All his favourite points of reference framed in one.'

She suddenly darted down a side passage, lit only by one dim bulb in an opaque glass shade painted with a Dutch scene of windmills and women in clogs and shawls.

When I caught up with her, she'd opened the door to a surprisingly large studio that must have been added to the house about a century ago. The floor was covered in ancient mottled brown lino, and a large studio easel of antique design stood importantly in the middle of it beside a battered table still bearing an artist's paintbox, its lid closed, and a large kidney-shaped wooden palette bearing the dull ghost traces of the paint that had last been scraped from it. Nearby lay a flat palette knife, two brushes and a rag, as if put out ready for the day's work.

It was a painterly version of the *Mary Celeste.*

The room was long and at one end was a model's dais, with a large, carved chair on it, facing the easel. The only other furnishings were a couple of smaller tables, a pair of battered easy chairs and some mainly empty bookshelves. A small, silent wooden clock eyed me balefully from the top of one of them.

Though the studio had obviously long been disused, it still held that faint scent of turpentine and linseed oil that was perfume to my nostrils. You can keep your modern acrylic paints, as far as I'm concerned: they smell vile and the colours are *dead.*

Faded green blinds were pulled down across all the windows, but above me I could see an expanse of dusky blue through the large skylight.

'Tottie's father had the studio built when he inherited the Red House,' Clara said, to my surprise. 'Of course, he was getting on a bit when Tottie was born, so he died a long time ago.'

'Tottie's father?' I echoed.

'Yes, Tottie's the last of the Gillyflowers and we bought the house from her over thirty years ago, on the understanding she continued to make her home here.'

'I hadn't realized that,' I said, then added, 'Wasn't it difficult for her to stay on in what had been her own home, once she'd sold it to you?'

I mean, call me nosy, but it was interesting.

'Oh, no, she said it was a relief that she didn't have the upkeep of a huge old house to worry about any more and could devote herself to the garden and her bees instead. Of course, we already all knew each other, so that helped, and we soon settled down together. I expect it's much the same in a commune, isn't it? You find your own interests and place in the group and . . . homogenize, as it were.'

'Yes, that's true,' I said, thinking about it.

'Tottie's father had spent a lot of time in France and Italy, learning to paint at various *ateliers*, but he was something of a dilettante. The family fortune came from their brewery, but he sold Gillyflower's Ales to a larger company and then lived on his capital. A bit like Henry's brother, George, who sold out of the army the minute he married an heiress, and had no sense with money . . . though Tottie's father doesn't seem to have drunk to excess, womanized or gambled, which is something.'

'I . . . suppose it is!' I was taken aback by this frankness and her words also cast an unedifying light on the late George Doome. The brothers were obviously totally unalike.

Clara turned to more practical matters. 'We had the studio rewired along with the rest of the house when we bought it and it's been updated again since, so there's lots of lighting. We had these wall lights installed.'

She demonstrated and the long wall opposite suddenly sprang into a patchwork of paintings of all sizes, stretching from floor to ceiling and with barely an inch between them.

I went across to have a closer look. 'Were all these painted by Tottie's father?'

'Yes, they're all Adrian Gillyflower's work. There are still one or two dotted around the house and several in Tottie's bedroom, but she moved most of them in here when she was attempting to run the place as a bed and breakfast. What do you think of them?'

I could see they were mostly portraits, or still lives of fruit and flowers, and his style appeared to have been totally uninfluenced by any artistic trends later than the eighteenth century.

'Competent but uninspired,' I said at last, cautiously.

'Yes, that's what I thought, too. You can learn technique in any art form, but not everyone can breathe life into it. But Tottie thinks Papa was an undiscovered genius, so we won't disillusion her.'

'No, of course not, I wouldn't dream of it.'

'So, will this studio suit you? Of course, you can set up camp in here, but paint me and Henry elsewhere in the house if you want to. See how you feel about it tomorrow, when you've settled in and got your bearings.'

We went out and she indicated another door that led to her own study overlooking the rear garden, the small library, which was apparently Tottie's domain but which she mainly used to store the materials for various kinds of craftwork, and the passage that led to the formal dining room, a garden hall with a cloakroom and the door to the conservatory off it, the kitchen and utility rooms. A faint clashing of pan lids and voices could be heard from that direction.

'That's Den and Tottie making a start on dinner,' she said. 'We'll leave them to it. Den can be quite an inspired cook, but Tottie has no imagination. She wasn't brought up to cook and clean, which was part of the reason her B&B business never took off. Dumping a loaf, butter and pot of jam in front of your guests when they come down for breakfast and telling them to help themselves to the stewed coffee on the hotplate, because she was off out to see to her bees, or do some gardening, was never going to go down well.'

'I suppose not,' I said, though if I'd been one of the guests I'd have quite liked that.

'It was home-made jam, though: she *has* learned to make preserves and pickles, and also wine and mead.'

'Oh? River makes a kind of medicinal mead from the honey bees at the Farm.'

'Then they'll have something in common to talk about when he visits,' Clara said. 'Tottie's officially our housekeeper-cum-gardener, but she's cast herself as occasional cook's assistant to Den. Den's such a blessing! Henry picked him up in Greece years ago, before we married. He'd just got out of the local gaol – some slight disagreement in a bar – and he's proved quite invaluable ever since. He can turn his hand to anything.'

'Really?' I said, thinking that Clara and Henry seemed to attach people to them. *I* was already starting to get the feeling that they wouldn't turn a hair if I never left at all either, just embedded myself in the studio and appeared for meals.

Not that that was likely to happen, with Lex Mariner in the offing . . .

'So, Tottie and Den aren't . . . ?' I paused, searching for the right phrase and Clara looked at me, puzzled. Then her face cleared.

'Oh, no, they're not in a relationship, just good friends,' she said.

I'd thought they seemed an extremely unlikely couple, but you just never knew with these things!

'That tattoo on Den's neck is . . . interesting. He told me he'd got it in Brixton. The prison?'

'Probably. He did have a chequered career before he met Henry, but just petty larceny and he could never resist an expensive car if he found one for the taking. He can drive Henry's vintage Jaguar whenever he likes now, though, so he doesn't do that any more.'

She turned and headed briskly for the main staircase. 'Come on, I'll show you your bedroom and the nearest bathroom, then leave you to unpack before dinner.'

She grasped the fierce wooden eagle on the newel post familiarly round the neck as she began to climb up to where, at the top, a passage led off on either side.

'Teddy's room, mine and Henry's, and Lex's are to the right,' she said. 'You're down here to the left, near Tottie.'

'I thought you said Lex didn't live with you?' I blurted out, startled.

'Oh, no, but some years ago he did live with us for a time, before he set up his business in Great Mumming. He often stays at the weekends, *and* over Christmas, too, of course.'

That did it! I'd be very sure to leave with River after the Winter Solstice and only hoped Lex kept clear till then. It was only a fortnight, so surely he could manage that? He must want to see me as little as I wanted to see him.

My room was right at the end of the passage and Clara threw open the door and switched on the light.

'It has a lovely view of the reservoir when it's light enough to see anything,' she said. 'There's a bathroom directly opposite across the passage and you do have a washbasin, which is as en-suite as we've got so far.'

'That's absolutely fine,' I assured her, because it was verging on luxury compared to a lot of places I'd stayed in, and while I was growing up, River had been more concerned with the ecological disposal of waste water from bathrooms rather than convenience.

Anyway, I found the room delightful, with little trace of the Gothic darkness that must have once prevailed, other than an imposing mahogany bed with a sort of half-circle of ornate woodwork jutting out above the head, from which hung heavy, looped-back faded red brocade curtains. It looked entirely suitable for a 'lying in state' and I would have to resist the urge to sleep on my back with my arms folded across my chest and my toes turned up.

The prevailing colour of the décor was a deep, old rose pink . . . and I really wished I'd had my hair done that colour, rather than green.

'It's lovely,' I enthused. And it was warm, too, which also was not the case in several country piles I'd previously stayed at while working on commissions.

'That little door over there leads to some stairs that take you up to one of the turrets – the pepper pot one. It's like a tiny sitting room of your own.'

It sounded very Rapunzel, though I didn't have enough hair for the role.

'There are lots more rooms in the attic that were once used for servants, but we only utilize it for storage.'

'What about Den?' I asked curiously.

'He lived in at first, but then we made him a flat over the garage. He likes his privacy and also, he can cook up the kind of food he enjoys there: bangers and mash, that sort of thing. I suspect he slips Tottie the odd bacon sandwich, too, but we don't ask.'

'It's a bit like that at the Farm, over fish,' I told her. 'River and I both eat it when away from home, but we don't mention it there.'

'You still call the Farm home,' she observed with interest. 'I suppose it's where your roots are, just as Henry's and mine lead directly to Starstone, even if they're now washing about underwater.'

I looked at her questioningly and she added, 'I was born and lived in Starstone until I was eight and the reservoir was built. My father was the vicar there. Henry and I knew each other as children, then met up again at Oxford.'

And now they lived at the Red House, looking down at where their home once was . . . and presumably *still* was, under the waters of the reservoir.

'Come down to the drawing room as soon as you're ready, Meg,' she told me. 'We dine at seven during the week, because of getting the child to bed at a reasonable hour.'

My bags were sitting in the middle of the faded carpet. When I was finally alone I resolutely decided *not* to reopen the can of worms that was Lex right then, but save it for later, when the first shock of finding him here and part of the family had worn off.

I unpacked everything into the large wardrobe and a chest of drawers almost as tall as I was, then washed in the bathroom opposite, which was old-fashioned, but had an electric shower installed over the claw-footed bath. The radiators were all warm and so was the water. Clara and Henry obviously liked to be cosy and had the resources to heat such a big house.

Back in my room, I debated what to wear for dinner. I suspected anything would be acceptable, which was just as well, since I'd left the Diors and Balenciagas at home, and as for the pleated silk Fortuny dress, it was at the cleaners . . .

I wear jeans and Converse sneakers most of the time, and my smart clothes are an eclectic mix of styles from the hippy to the vaguely trendy, though the latter is usually by accident. Tonight I put on a sea-green velvet tunic and darker green leggings, malachite earrings and scuffed Chinese velvet Mary Janes with a button strap. I was a symphony of verdant green from hair to toes.

I wondered if there was a Green Lady in mythology as well as a Green Man. I must ask River.

Clara and Henry were, it seemed, both thoughtful and friendly hosts, and I left my room with a calm sense of anticipation of the evening ahead.

7

In the Soup

Before I went downstairs, I couldn't resist looking at the sitting room in the pepper pot tower. A narrow spiral stair took me up into a tiny circular space with one slit window to the front, should I feel like some archery practice. It was simply furnished with a comfortable old tapestry armchair, footstool and small table.

It was so cute that I lingered longer than I should have, so that by the time I finally made it to the drawing room, I found everyone already gathered, imbibing sherry or whisky and soda, both of which I refused. Teddy generously offered to share his orange juice with me.

'No, that's OK, Teddy,' I said, and instead accepted a minute conical cocktail glass of golden mead from Tottie, which she had made herself.

I sipped it cautiously, but it was even better than the herb-infused kind that River makes to a very old Welsh recipe, though I wouldn't tell him that for the world: he's very proud of it.

Teddy had exchanged his school uniform for a rainbow-striped jumper, dark tracksuit trousers and Mickey Mouse slippers with sticking-out ears.

He saw me looking at them and said, 'I don't really like Mickey Mouse, but my dad sent them from America and I've only just grown into them because he got the size wrong. Clara said I should wear them till my feet have grown again and then I can choose my own.'

'I like them,' I said. 'If someone sent me Mickey Mouse slippers, I'd wear them.'

'He doesn't know how big I am because he never visits,' explained Teddy.

'But it's nice of your father to send you gifts. And he *has* been to visit you, but you were so small, you've forgotten,' said Clara.

Teddy looked unconvinced.

'Teddy's father is Radnor Vane, an American actor, though I think he's moved into directing now,' Henry said.

'When he came over here a few years ago he met Zelda, my niece,' Clara chimed in.

'Zelda shares a small flat with three other actresses in London, so it wasn't really suitable to bring a baby up in, especially since she's so often on tour. So Teddy lives with us and Zelda comes when she can,' said Henry.

'Mummy'll be here for Christmas,' Teddy said. 'She thought she was going to be Snow White in a pantomime, but she didn't get the part.'

'Well, lucky for us,' Clara said cheerfully.

Henry was still wearing the washed-out corduroy trousers, blue shirt and Fair Isle jumper he'd had on earlier, but his white hair was now sleeked back from his handsome, pared-down, interestingly bony face . . . one that would be very good to paint.

Clara and Tottie *had* changed for dinner, the former into a long red and black kaftan that looked as if it had been made from two bedspreads sewn up the sides. Tottie had on black velvet trousers, somewhat shiny and rubbed on the seat and the knees, and a lavender silk blouse, which did nothing for her complexion. Over this she sported a frilly flowered pinafore, which she now seemed to notice for the first time, for she took it off and stuffed it behind a cushion.

Immediately outside the door, someone suddenly beat merry hell out of a gong, apparently a signal for everyone to drain their glasses, put them down and rise to their feet. *Four* feet, in Lass's case. I hadn't noticed her lurking under the coffee table till she wriggled out.

'Dinner!' announced Henry happily. 'Come along, Meg. I'm ravenous and I expect you are too, after your long, cold drive.'

Den was standing outside in the hall with a dimpled and shiny copper gong in one hand and the stick in the other. I'm sure the air was still vibrating; the gong certainly was.

''Urry yerselves up or the soup'll have gorn cold,' he said. 'I'll fetch the bread, won't I?'

He vanished towards the kitchen and we trooped into the dining room. Henry and Clara disposed themselves at either end of the long table, which showed bulbous carved legs beneath a somewhat incongruous flowered oilcloth covering. Teddy, raised higher by a fat cushion, sat next to Tottie, while I was opposite, next to Henry. You could still have got several more people around that table.

As if she'd read my mind, Tottie said, 'This is as small as the table goes, but you can make it much bigger by putting in extra leaves.'

There was a soup tureen and a stack of bowls in front of Clara. She took off the lid and began to ladle soup into the bowls and pass them round.

'Has the soup got hard bits of bread in it?' Teddy asked suspiciously.

'No, it's not the kind you put croutons in, darling,' Clara said.

'And even if it was, you could just sink them till they go soggy,' Tottie pointed out. '*I* always do.'

Den came in with a silver filigree basket filled with bread rolls and went up and down with a pair of green Bakelite tongs, placing one on everyone's side plate. I took my napkin out of its carved wooden ring and found it was a square of kitchen towel.

'Run out of paper serviettes again, 'aven't we?' Den explained, depositing a warm roll on my plate, so that the scent of fresh bread tantalized my nostrils.

'Napkins,' Clara corrected.

'Napkins yerself,' Den said amiably. 'Napkins is fer babies.'

'If it was serviettes, napkin rings wouldn't be called that,' Clara observed.

It was obviously a long-running difference of opinion, because Den sang a throaty snatch of 'You say pot-a-toes and I say poe-tar-toes . . .'

'You haven't set a place for yourself,' Henry remarked. 'Aren't you joining us tonight, Den?'

'Nah, I've 'ad beans on toast, 'aven't I?' he said. He'd changed the brown cotton overall for a large blue and white striped cook's apron, which enveloped his slight figure from neck to ankle, like a strange Eastern robe.

'I might take a drop of soup and a bit of pud back with me fer me supper.'

'Fair enough,' said Henry.

'Going back to my place as soon as I've stacked the dishwasher,' Den added. 'Got something on the telly to watch, 'aven't I?'

'There's a TV in the morning room, but Den has the only decent-sized one on the premises,' Clara told me. 'He's addicted to football, darts and the soaps.'

'He can get the telly because of the masts growing on the highest hills,' Teddy explained to me. 'They grow there so they can make invisible waves bounce.'

'Satellites can bounce them too, and the masts didn't *grow* there, people put them there for communication purposes,' Tottie said instructively.

'Like the Starstone?' Teddy asked.

'I suppose so, in a way, though whether people wanted to communicate with each other, or with something beyond their knowledge, is a moot point,' said Henry, interested, then explained to me: 'The legend about the stone on the hill says that if on the Winter Solstice you can see the brightest star, Sirius, through the inverted V of the stones – there are actually two stones, leaning together – good fortune will bless the valley. Of course, you'd have been seeing it from Starstone village, so you can't view it from that angle any more.'

'Unless you're a fish,' said Teddy helpfully.

'Very true, Teddy,' said Henry. Then he continued, 'The stone is directly on an ancient ley line – do you know about ley lines, my dear?'

'Yes, River's very keen on them.'

I'd read the classic book on them too, *The Old Straight Track.*

'Then you know a ley line connects a lot of ancient sites, monuments, or geographical features in a straight line – too many for coincidence. The Starstone originally lined up with a carved monolith in the graveyard in the drowned village – it's now in the grounds of Underhill – then the church at Great Mumming, which has ancient foundations, and then on to the white horse carved out of the hill above Little Mumming too, though there's much debate about the age of that. It could be relatively recent.'

'I've always found ley lines fascinating,' I said. 'There's something magical about all these invisible threads crisscrossing and connecting the landscape.'

There was a pause while we all drank delicious soup and Teddy was admonished by Tottie for spreading butter as thick as mortar across his bread roll.

'Den says butter's good for you, and he lets me sprinkle sugar on top too when I eat it in the kitchen,' he said hopefully.

'I'll pretend I didn't hear that tooth-rotting revelation,' said Clara.

Henry polished the bottom of his soup bowl with the last of his bread and then resumed his lecture on the history of the Starstone.

'The ceremony that takes place on the night of the Winter Solstice has very ancient roots.'

'It's not much of a ceremony, darling,' Clara said. 'Just five men from old local families, going up to the stone, circling round it and . . . well, saying a few words.'

'Rhyming doggerel – and now it's four men and one woman, since I took over as the last of the Gillyflowers,' said Tottie.

'True, the Gillyflowers started to take part when an older local family died out,' agreed Henry.

'There's a bit of a bonfire on the ledge below the stones, where the onlookers gather,' said Clara.

'Yes, and don't forget the sixth performer, Old Winter,' said Tottie. 'He's waiting in a cleft in the rocks at the back of the ledge, Meg, and when the others go up to the Stone he suddenly appears and walks round the fire, until they come down again. Then the Green Man, who I suppose represents the New Year, or the spring, or something, banishes him.'

'It's all about renewal, rebirth, fertility and that kind of thing,' Clara said. 'The whole village used to turn out for it, but very few of the original inhabitants are left and so it's mostly just those taking part and their families. Everyone goes to Underhill afterwards for the Gathering and has hot toddy and treacle cake.'

'Sybil's kept that up since George died, but will Mark follow the custom?' Tottie asked. 'And he should be the Green Man instead of Henry, now he's home.'

'Good point, Tottie,' Henry said. 'I must speak to him about it, because although I haven't minded filling in for him it would be good to just watch the proceedings this year.'

'I *did* ask him and he said he wasn't interested in all that old rubbish,' said Clara.

'George wasn't really, either,' said Henry, 'but he was superstitious, so he did it anyway. And Mark might come round to the idea. I'll talk to the boy.'

'He certainly should, because going up there in the dark and the freezing cold dressed in robes and a lot of green frondy stuff isn't going to do you a lot of good at your age, Henry,' said Clara.

'If I have to do it, then I'll wear my thermals underneath.'

'I'll be all right, because other than the bird mask I traditionally have a cloak, so I can wear a lot of warm clothes under it,' said Tottie. She began to count off the members of the group on her fingers. 'There's me; Henry, filling in for Mark; Bilbo; Fred from the Pike with Two Heads; and Len Snowball, who is the gardener-cum-groom at Underhill . . . and then, since the last member of another old family has moved away, Lex had to be Old Winter last time.'

I was just pondering whether I'd heard the name Bilbo correctly when she mentioned Lex again. If he was taking part in the ceremony there would be no avoiding him. In fact, all conversational roads at the Red House seemed to lead to Lex, so I really needed now to confess that I knew him – or *had* known him.

But the conversation had flowed on and Tottie was saying, 'Mark's told Sybil that if she wants Len to give her a hand with the horses, she'll have to pay him herself. But I expect, if it comes to it, we can manage the horses between us,' she added comfortably. 'We do most of the work, anyway.'

The soup had long since been removed and we'd eaten the main course, a very delicious vegetable stew with savoury dumplings. I was beginning to feel my waistband tightening and now Den brought in the pudding and a big jug of rich yellow custard.

'You get off to your flat now, Den,' Clara told him, 'or you'll miss the start of your soap. We'll clear up and stack the dishwasher.'

'But Tottie's coffee's disgusting,' he pointed out.

'Mine isn't, though,' said Clara. 'Off you go!'

'Cheek!' said Tottie as he vanished, already untying the strings of his long, striped apron.

By now I was starting to feel extremely sleepy. My illness, the long drive, and the shock of seeing Lex Mariner again – all were combining to make my head swim and the voices come and go in a dreamlike way.

'Dear child, you're all in,' Clara said as we got up. 'You should go straight to bed and get a good night's sleep.'

I was too tired to resist and the thought of bed sounded so wonderful that, declining her offer of cocoa, I did just that.

And I did no brooding over the past that night, but instead slept like the dead in my catafalque of a bed . . . much like Lex's extremely late wife, Lisa.

Clara

We were a self-sufficient community in the valley, who helped each other in hard times and made our own amusements, mostly connected to the church year and the seasons.

Being so high up, Starstone could often be quite cut off from autumn to spring – and how we revelled in our freedom when the schoolteacher was unable to get over from Thorstane!

There was a pond on the Underhill estate where we and the other village children could skate when it froze hard, and an abundance of slopes to toboggan down.

Large, glassy icicles hung from every eave and window ledge, for central heating was uncommon back then. We would break an icicle off and hold it in our hands until it began to melt and our knitted mittens would be soggy and smell of damp wool . . .

Back in the vicarage kitchen, thawing out by the fire, we'd roast chestnuts on a small, perforated metal shovel until the sweet softness burst from the pierced shells.

Simple pleasures . . .

Christmas then was not so much about mass consumerism and eating and drinking to excess, but a magical time that started with the Winter Solstice ceremony in late December, was followed by the Christmas church services, Nativity and carol singing, then ended with Twelfth Night.

The origins of the Starstone on the hill and the annual Winter Solstice ceremony held there were hidden in the mists of time, but the whole village would attend. I remember the excitement of the bonfire on the plateau below the summit, the strange figures performing their torchlight ritual around the Stone and then my being carried home, half-asleep, through the dark night.

If the weather allowed, we would be taken to Great Mumming just before Christmas and the shop windows would be wonderfully exciting: the piles of jewel-bright apples and satsumas in the greengrocer's, the display of ribbon-bound boxes of chocolates in the sweet shop . . . not to mention the delights of the toy shop!

Henry's mother was a frail, gentle woman who died young, but she adored Christmas, and the tree at Underhill was always the biggest and most lavishly adorned in the village. I expect that's where Henry's love of the Christmas traditions and his interest in antique and vintage glass baubles really began.

We had a tree at the vicarage too, and it was a high treat to decorate it with the collection of Victorian glass spheres, bells, trumpets, birds and icicles that lay nestled in tissue paper for the rest of the year. I have them now – or rather, they are in Henry's extensive collection of old glass baubles.

8

Old Shades

Next morning, after some confused nightmares in which I was attempting to flee from a nebulous but terrifying monster, my escape hampered by deep snowdrifts in which I floundered helplessly, I slowly surfaced to the sound of howling wolves . . .

I was certain there weren't any wolves living in the UK any more, so after a dazed moment or two, I realized this howling was actually the wind wuthering shrilly down the chimney. It rattled the diamond-paned casement windows too, but since they were behind panels of secondary glazing, no draught stirred the drawn-back folds of the velvet curtains.

I seemed to recall that wolves played a part in my nightmare, too, so my subconscious must have registered the wind getting up in the night, and, since I was buried under a deep down duvet, *that* probably accounted for the snowdrifts. The ancient purple satin-covered eiderdown that had been on top of it, as an extra though entirely unnecessary layer of insulation, had either slithered off, or been thrown off by my struggles, for it was in a heap next to the bed.

I lay back against the plump pillows and thought about my arrival yesterday afternoon, and Lex Mariner.

I'd never expected to see him again *or* wanted to. He should have stayed firmly buried in my past, not returned well over a decade later, bringing back a memory I'd done my best to bury.

Now I felt again the hurt and anger of that time so long ago, and while it was true that I didn't have an *entirely* clear conscience about my behaviour on that night we spent together, the episode had been distorted and blown out of all proportion by Lex *and* his friend Al.

In fact, if Al hadn't sought me out in my studio space at college after Lex's wife, Lisa, died, to tell me exactly what he thought of me, I wouldn't have known the roles of both scapegoat and Delilah had been thrust upon me.

I think what had hurt most was that Lex must have told Al everything that had happened . . . or what he remembered, anyway.

Now, seeing Lex so unexpectedly had brought it all back, as raw as if it had happened yesterday, instead of – I did some rapid mental arithmetic – fourteen years ago.

What were the odds of my running into him here, in the wilds of Lancashire? Infinitesimal, I would have thought. And he'd looked at me as if his worst nightmare had come back to haunt *him*, too, though perhaps that was partly because seeing me had suddenly brought back the pain of losing Lisa.

He'd returned to college only once after her death, to collect some of his work, and when we'd come face to face in the corridor he'd turned on his heel and strode away before I could express my sadness at his loss – for Lisa had been a glowing, beautiful person, both inside and out. At the time I'd been puzzled and hurt, but later, when Al cornered me and in one furious, unstoppable outburst told me what he thought of me, I'd simply wanted never to see or even to think about either of them again.

How young we'd been! I was just twenty-two and Lex and Lisa only a year or two older. But I was not the person Lex had thought me then, and I'd changed even more over the ensuing years. For a start, I now understood the tragedy of loss so much better . . .

Whatever emotion my sudden appearance yesterday had conjured up in Lex, it had been powerful enough to make him turn round and leave without a word, like a ghastly reprise of our last meeting.

And if I'd had an ounce of sense, that's what *I'd* have done too: got back in the van and driven off, then sent some kind of apology to Clara later. Now, having missed my opportunity to make a fast escape, I was stuck here until after the Solstice on the 21st. Two weeks suddenly seemed like a very long time.

If Clara and Henry could give me enough sittings, I was very sure I could finish the major part of both portraits by then, for once the initial drawing on to the canvas was completed, I used a bold, almost impressionistic technique with a palette knife to apply the paint. When the spirit was with me, I'd usually finish the face within two sittings and the rest in four or five . . . or at my leisure, back at my studio.

I hadn't actually *agreed* that I would stay for Christmas, so I could say that I'd realized how much I'd miss the Yule Feast at the Farm with all my surrogate family, which I would, however alluring the thought of a traditional family Christmas had been before I found out about Lex.

Mind you, I already suspected that a lot of traditions at the Red House would turn out to be of the inhabitants' own devising, though probably just as much fun.

The image of Lex's face at the moment he had turned and clocked just who had arrived at the Red House yesterday slid unbidden and unwanted back into my mind. It was hard to define. Shock? Anger? Even a touch of contempt?

Still, now he knew I was here, he'd probably avoid the place until I'd gone, and if he did appear, I'd make myself scarce.

I sighed. There was no point in lying there fruitlessly going over and over it all. The sooner I set up my painting gear and got going, the better!

I showered, washing another layer of green out of my hair in the process, and dressed in jeans, T-shirt and a long, loose stripy knitted tunic with handy pockets. All were indelibly marked by oil paint, permanent souvenirs of portraits past – happier memories.

I twisted up my hair into a high knot – it was just long enough and kept it out of the way when I was working – and then I was ready.

Before I went downstairs I looked out of the window where, past the tops of a lot of majestically waving fir trees, I could see right down into the drowned valley. The dull, unpolished pewter surface of the water sullenly mirrored the surrounding hills and the dark pine trees that crowded up close to the shore, as if daring each other to take a dip in the icy water. They reminded me of the Forestry Commission woodland next to the Farm, which a few years previously had suddenly sprouted walking trails and a chalet café with a visitor centre.

I felt quite guilty as I went downstairs, because it was so late. The house was quiet, except for the grandfather clock ticking heavily in the hall.

Clara had told me breakfast and lunch were help-yourself affairs in the kitchen, so I went down the dark passage and opened the door at the end on to light, cosiness and the mouth-watering fragrance of warm bread.

'There you are, darling,' said Clara, a slab of bread and jam poised halfway to her lips. 'And very workmanlike you look, too.'

'I'm sorry I'm so late,' I said.

'Not at all, you were tired and needed your rest,' she assured me. 'Den and Tottie have taken Teddy to school and then they're going to do a little shopping. Tottie always gets the siege mentality at this time of year, afraid we'll get snowed or iced in, so she stuffs the larder and freezer until they bulge at the seams.'

'Do you often get snowed in?' I asked anxiously, for if they did, that might make my getaway difficult. Come to that, River might not be able to get here.

'Fairly often, but the road to Thorstane is generally cleared after a few days. Once we were snowed in for a week at Easter, though, and Tottie has never forgotten it!'

'I don't think I would have done, either,' I said, thinking that my tall, narrow camper van was certainly not built for difficult driving conditions.

'They'll be back shortly, I'm sure, and then Den can give you a hand bringing in your painting gear.'

'Oh, that's all right. Nothing's heavy and I'm used to carting it about.'

'Well, have something to eat, first. The coffee is hot on the stove and the bread is fresh from the oven. We have one of those bread-making machines, and Henry and Den have lots of fun experimenting with different types of dough. If men have to have a hobby, then producing something delicious is a good one. This loaf was so tasty it seemed a shame to toast it.'

'Yes, I'll just have it as it is too,' I agreed, and spread mine with butter and some of Tottie's own honey.

I suddenly remembered Clara saying that Tottie was an enthusiastic bottler, jammer and pickler, and I thought my hamper of curds and chutney upstairs would seem to be a bit redundant. I bet they hadn't already got any chilli chutney capable of blowing their socks off, though.

'Henry likes to work early, but now he's in the morning room, doing his t'ai chi,' she said. 'Lass is watching him. She thinks it must be some kind of game, but she doesn't know how to join in.'

I took a bite of bread and honey and chewed thoughtfully. This was not like any household I'd ever stayed in before whilst painting a commission, though it wasn't any odder than being brought up in a commune full of eccentrics. In fact, I already felt quite at home . . . or I would have done but for the Lex-sized fly in the ointment.

Clara soon retired to her study, in order, she said, to dictate the next chapter of her current crime novel, which she estimated would take approximately one hour, after which she'd show me the rest of the downstairs rooms and we could discuss when the first sitting would be and where I wanted to paint her.

She also added that she had work to do later, so I wasn't sure what she called the novel writing! Perhaps it was a hobby?

I took my second cup of coffee through to the studio and found there was quite a good light in there, especially considering it was December. Through the skylight I could see an expanse of icy blue, with ragged clouds scurrying across it, but the wind had stopped howling and instead just emitted the occasional disgruntled and perfunctory moan.

It still looked bitterly cold out there, though, so I put on my down anorak before going to search for the van, which I discovered parked round the back of the house in a gravelled sweep sheltered by the double garage and stable block and a stand of slightly battered conifers.

I ferried in my painting gear using the back door to the garden hall, resisting the lure of the conservatory that led off it, with its mass of greenery crowding up to press long, palm-shaped fingers against the steamy glass.

I expect that was Tottie's pigeon too, like the garden, and I'd be interested to see what she was growing in it.

I wasn't sure yet where I'd set up my easel, but meanwhile the ancient studio one was there, ready, and after carefully relocating the original owner's painting gear to one of the empty bookshelves, I set out my own.

There was something soothing to the soul about laying out the materials of my trade: the soft black pencils and putty rubber, a huge wooden box of oil paints, a palette and the mahl stick – a cane with loads of masking tape wrapped round the end to form a ball, which I used to keep my arm and hand off the wet surface of the canvas while I worked.

When I brought in the two large canvases intended for Henry and Clara's portraits, the breeze tried to carry me away, using them as sails.

The last load included a couple of good lights on tripods, the sort photographers use, which I'd found invaluable in the past. I tried moving the chair on the dais about and angling the lamps at it, but I still wasn't sure if I would paint Clara there, or Henry, or in their respective studies, which presumably would be full of items of meaning to them and imprinted with their equally strong, but very different personalities.

In daylight, the studio was rather nice, the walls painted a soft dove grey and furnished with a couple of battered but comfortable easy chairs, as well as the velvet-seated carved one on the dais. The dais itself was partly draped in a rug of faded splendour, which was surely too valuable to be thrown so carelessly about in an artist's studio.

The lino floor had a smell of its own, pleasing but indescribable, and evoked a recollection of making linocuts at art college during the foundation year, when we tried our hands at all kinds of art forms, from etching to pottery, before deciding what we wanted to specialize in.

In my case, I'd already decided: I wanted to study Fine Art, particularly portraits.

There was a knock on the door and Den appeared with a mug of coffee and two wrapped Italian biscotti, which he set down on one of the smaller painting tables.

'There you are, and the missus says she's nearly finished murdering some pore innocent and yer to go along to 'er study in ten minutes.'

That sounded a bit headmistressy, but although I did have something on my conscience, it was going to stay there.

9
Treasured Possessions

Clara's study was large and light, despite being lined with crammed bookshelves and several tall, glass-fronted cabinets containing what looked like bits of pottery, clay tablets, stone and wood.

There was a big U-shaped desk in the centre of the room, with various computers and screens on it.

Clara was seated before a small monitor, talking into one of those old-fashioned ball-on-a-stick microphones.

'*The blood ran richly red over the incised letters of the broken tablet and congealed slowly through the night, so that by morning the message appeared to have been filled with dark crimson sealing wax,*' she intoned deeply into the microphone and then stopped, clicked it off and turned with a smile that exposed her large and healthy teeth.

'There we are: one chapter a day and it all comes together in no time. This one is called *Written in Blood*.'

From the bit I'd heard, that seemed very appropriate.

'I'm afraid I haven't read any of your crime novels yet,' I confessed.

'Why should you? I only started writing them for fun and I certainly don't expect everyone to want to read them. But if you do fancy trying one, they're all over there on the shelf, so help yourself.'

She gestured to a long row of books nearby, which alternated between large hardbacks and shorter paperbacks, like a strange fossil spine . . . a spine of spines, in fact.

'*Stone Dead* was my first. Bit dated, but then, so am I.'

'I think I'd like to start with that one,' I said, finding the paperback and feeling strangely guilty about the hole it left on the shelf, though it was hardly akin to removing the keystone of the universe and watching the sky fall in.

Going by the array of computer monitors and equipment on the U-shaped desk, I wouldn't have said Clara was old-fashioned in *any* way.

'Can you get the internet OK here?' I enquired. 'I haven't tried yet.' In fact, I didn't think I'd turned on either my phone or iPad since my arrival, but then, I had had other things on my mind.

'Oh, yes, broadband. You have to be very unlucky these days to be beyond its reach. Just as well we have it, too, because I'm constantly emailing colleagues. And I've just got a new version of a very clever program to play with,' she added enthusiastically, propelling her sturdy wheeled office chair over to the middle monitor without rising from it and quickly bringing up a screen that showed several small fragments of incised clay tablets.

'Cuneiform, Hittite,' she explained. 'The pieces appear to be from the same clay tablet, but the images have been obtained from several different sources. Finds in the past were so often divided up and sold on to collectors and museums, not always with their provenance. But luckily I have a photographic memory for where I've spotted finds that might be part of the same inscription and with this program, you can bring them together to see if they really do fit.'

She demonstrated, moving the fragments about and turning them round. It was quite fascinating, like a jigsaw puzzle without the box, so you weren't sure that all the pieces belonged together, or quite how it would turn out.

'Of course, it's not as good as actually playing with a tray of pieces,' she said regretfully. 'You just don't have that same feel for what should go where, even if they are too broken to fit neatly any more.'

'I didn't even know you could do that on a computer,' I said. 'But then, I just can't seem to get interested much in the internet, or phones, or anything else my friends seem to find so riveting. Perhaps being brought up in the commune, with only a landline phone and the radio had something to do with it. I can't even get that interested in the TV most of the time, unless it's documentaries. I prefer to read my fiction and see the pictures in my head.'

'I understand what you mean. In my opinion, the internet is a good tool, but a poor master. And sadly, it does seem to have mastered and enslaved an entire generation – when they aren't binge-watching whole inane TV series.'

She had that spot-on, I thought.

'Don't you feel the need to tweet about the day-to-day minutiae of your life every five minutes?' she asked with a smile. 'My niece, Zelda, does that.'

'No, I'd rather just live my life rather than record it. And the same for photos. I want to look at things directly, not through a lens. I do take pictures of my sitters on my iPad, though, to help me with the portraits: to get the pose right each time, and to jog my memory for small details if I'm completing them in the studio.'

'You're a very unusual young woman,' she remarked, and I thought, but didn't say, that she was an extremely unusual old one. Not that *old* seemed the right term for someone so radiantly vital, and her mind certainly wasn't.

The light from the screen illuminated the interestingly strong bones of her face and I found myself looking at her now with the eye of a painter. She'd picked up a chunk of engraved stone that had been weighing down a heap of papers and was absently turning it over in her hands, the carnelian seal ring glowing dully as they moved. She was dressed today in a cherry-red jumper, black cord trousers and silver earrings in the form of ankhs. A long string of Egyptian turquoise paste beads hung round her neck, which contrasted wonderfully with the jumper.

Behind her was the bright patchwork of book spines on the shelves and, I now noticed, a tall wooden post carved with the brightly painted grimacing heads of various creatures. A bird squatted on top, reminding me of the fierce eagle on the stair post.

'Is that a totem pole?' I asked.

'A small-scale replica of one. I commissioned it when I visited Canada a few years ago and had it shipped over. The Customs people X-rayed it for drugs before they let me collect it, because they didn't believe that anyone would pay that much shipping for a carved post.'

'I love it,' I said. 'And I want to paint you just the way you are now . . . that is, if you wouldn't mind my invading your space?'

'Not at all – invade away,' she said amiably. 'When I'm working, I soon forget anyone's in the room anyway.'

I fished the iPad out of the depths of my tapestry shoulder bag, switched it on, then snapped her. She looked faintly startled.

'I want to get that exact pose again,' I explained.

'You can set your easel up right where you are now and leave it there as long as you need to,' she suggested.

'Great, but you'll have to tell me when I can start and how long you'll sit for each session.'

'You'll need good light, so I could give you an hour or two in the mornings, say from ten? Will that do? Not today, obviously – it's too late – and I want to show you round and let you settle in first.'

'That would be perfect, and perhaps when you're not using the room I could come in and work on the background a little, too.'

'There we are, then, all settled,' she said, turning off the computers and getting up. 'Come along – time for the sixpenny tour.'

By daylight the drawing room looked even bigger than it had the previous evening, and now the mustard velvet drapes were flung back from a square bay window recess, which had padded seats up each side, to reveal an impressive view.

'You can just see Underhill to the right. It's that squat, rambling house there, below the Starstone hill.'

'Oh, yes,' I said, peering out. 'The two stones on top of the hill do look like just one from this angle, don't they?'

'I suppose they do. I hadn't really noticed before,' she agreed. 'Luckily, Underhill was high enough to escape being drowned, though it lost most of the grounds at the front, which used to run right down to the edge of the village. That and Starstone Edge are all that are left.'

'I can see quite a few roofs,' I said.

'It's more of a hamlet than a village, though, and strung out along the road. Perhaps we'll have a little excursion up there later.'

'That would be lovely,' I said politely, though it looked a bit cold and bleak for hiking.

'Not that there's much to see at this time of year,' Clara continued. 'Most of the cottages are holiday homes now, only used in the summer, and it's a different place then. The Sailing Club opens up for the water sports enthusiasts, and the seasonal wooden café in the pinewoods by the water's edge for visitors: walkers, birdwatchers and the like.'

It was hard to imagine such a transformation, though I'd seen the pictures on the internet myself when I'd looked the place up.

It was a bit brighter out now and there were hurrying white and dove-grey clouds reflected on the water's surface, like a speeded-up film of the ever-changing sky.

Clara turned away and resumed her tour guide mode.

'Tottie's papa disliked Victorian Gothic, so he had most of the furniture put in the attics and replaced it with something that, if less in keeping, was more comfortable and functional. It's a strange mishmash, and of course Henry and I have added our mite to the mix. We seemed to have accumulated a lot of stuff over the years and much of it was in storage. We did have a flat in London at one time, but it was tiny.'

On the other side of the hall was a matching large room, which contained a TV with easy chairs drawn up around it, but otherwise had been given over to Teddy, for matting covered the rugs and his easel, paints, train set, farm, stuffed animals, bicycle with trainer wheels, sit-on tractor and myriad other toys occupied the space.

'Good heavens!' I said.

'Like an explosion in Hamleys toyshop, isn't it?' Clara said. 'Henry's a glutton for buying toys. You can't let Henry and Teddy near a shop unless you confiscate Henry's wallet first.'

'Fun, though,' I said. 'I don't think Teddy's going to run out of things to do on rainy days.'

'Oh, he's always busy. Henry and I are teaching him Italian and Greek, and he's already picked up the rudiments of hieroglyphs.'

As we passed through the hall, Henry opened his door and said, 'I thought I heard voices. Would you like to come in and see my little kingdom, Meg?'

'Henry chose this room because he's always liked writing in cramped spaces, like boot cupboards,' Clara said. 'This was the nearest he could get at the Red House.'

'Slight exaggeration, my dear, but it's true that I wrote some of my best poems in the hall of our flat in London. But here, you must admit, I have a real room, albeit not very large.'

It was very light and attractive, though, with most of the walls lined with light green painted bookshelves, well-filled. A desk with a laptop on it stood against one wall, next to a cushioned wicker basket in which Lass obliviously snored. Before the window was a battered pine kitchen table, on which reposed the kind of old-fashioned typewriter I'd only seen in pictures. It was black and gold, with ivory-coloured keys.

There was a sheet of paper sticking out of the top, with a thin column of words down the middle.

'I like to think straight on to the typewriter,' he said, following the direction of my gaze. 'I taught myself to touch type as a boy and old habits remain. I have to hear and feel the heavy clunk of the keys in order to create.'

'He does put his poems on his laptop afterwards, though,' Clara said. 'He's not a total technological heathen.'

'Far from it, as you well know, Clara! In fact,' he added turning to me, 'I'm constantly looking at auction sites on the internet, searching for ornaments and leaving bids.'

'Ornaments?' I said, surprised, because I couldn't really see him as a collector of porcelain animals or Cranberry glass.

'Baubles, bangles, bright shiny things, tra-la-la-la-la!' warbled Clara. 'But Henry doesn't collect jewellery; his passion runs instead to old glass Christmas tree decorations.'

'I've always loved them,' said Henry, drawing me over to what looked like one of those Victorian cabinets with drawers for the storing of ghastly things like birds' eggs, or butterflies and beetles impaled on pins. Above it was a glazed cabinet that lit up at the press of a switch, revealing sparkling rows of glass Christmas baubles in weird and wonderful shapes and colours. They all looked very old, fragile and strangely exciting.

'I keep most of them stored away and rotate the ones on display,' he said, opening the top drawer to reveal the usual divisions into little compartments, each filled not with an impaled insect, but a glass ornament in a nest of cotton wool. There were Santas, elves, pixies, fruit, flowers, clocks, angels, snowmen, musical instruments and birds with long tails of white spun glass, one of which looked remarkably like an ostrich.

'I'm constantly finding new shapes and designs,' Henry said. 'They started producing them in a German village called Lauscha in the nineteenth century and they were endlessly inventive. They still make them there.'

A larger drawer further down held bigger ornaments, and blown and silvered glass tree toppers – and one duller object that he lifted out and displayed proudly.

'This moulded papier mâché Father Christmas tree topper is over a hundred years old.'

I could well believe it, because it was a soupy brown colour, except for one or two clearly misguided attempts to tart him up a bit with glitter and cotton wool.

'He belonged to Tottie's family and originally his jacket was bright green. Red only became the dominant colour much later.'

'Henry's always bidding for ornaments online, when he can find them,' Clara said indulgently. 'I murder people as my hobby, but Henry collects shiny things like a magpie.'

'They don't all shine,' he said mildly. 'And we use some of them every Christmas to decorate one of the trees. They were made to be used and give pleasure, even if some of these are the sole survivors out of hundreds.'

'*Trees?*' I said, surprised. 'You have more than one?'

'Yes, we have a large real pine tree in the hall and a smaller artificial one in the drawing-room bay window.'

'We hang the antique decorations on the artificial one, because it's out of the way and the carpet is so thick underneath it that the ornaments bounce if they fall off anyway,' explained Clara.

'We often buy new ornaments for the big fir tree in the hall. There's an all-year-round Christmas shop in an old mill over near Little Mumming and Teddy loves going there to choose them,' said Henry. 'He adores Christmas as much as I do – and I hope you'll love your first Christmas here if you stay on with us, too, Meg.'

I opened my mouth to say that I was afraid I was definitely leaving the day after the Solstice, but Clara got in first.

'Meg's going to paint me sitting at my big desk, Henry.'

She turned to me. 'But what about Henry? In here, or the studio?'

'Oh, the studio,' I said without thinking. 'On the dais, with some good lighting . . .'

'I'll be happy to sit whenever and wherever you please, so long as I can read at the same time,' Henry said.

Lass suddenly awoke with a galvanic snort, looked vaguely at us and then hauled herself out of the basket and went to look pointedly at the door.

'It must be lunchtime,' Henry said. 'Lass is partial to a bit of bread dipped in soup.'

'Lass is partial to anything edible,' Clara said drily. 'It's a help-yourself meal again, Meg, usually at about one, but the pot of soup is always ready on the back of the stove by then, for when we feel like it.'

'Did Clara tell you that Den and I make the bread?' Henry asked. 'There's none of that mixing and kneading, you just pop the ingredients in the machine and turn it on.'

'Technology does have many advantages,' Clara said, leading the way out. 'Hmm, mulligatawny soup, I think – my favourite.'

10

Grimlike

There was no sign of Den or Tottie in the kitchen, other than a note explaining that they'd dropped off the shopping and gone out again.

'Probably a pub lunch, over at the Pike with Two Heads,' Clara said, after reading it aloud. 'Still, at least Den put the soup on the stove before they went off again.'

'We should take Meg over to the pub for lunch one day,' Henry suggested.

'Friday – they do a good fish pie then, though there's always a tasty vegetarian dish on the menu too, if you don't fancy that.'

'It sounds lovely,' I said.

Henry, now lavishly buttering a thick slice of wholemeal bread, said, 'I rang Lex up earlier because he dashed off yesterday before I could ask him about the tree and we're *already* a week into December!'

'Lex takes us to fetch the real Christmas tree in his pick-up every year, so we can bring it back with us. It's bound to be a whopper – it invariably is,' Clara explained to me. 'Henry always wants to put the tree up too early and then it sheds its needles long before the day!'

'Depends which kind you get,' Henry said. 'Some hold the needles longer than others and anyway, the scent lingers on, even if the tree is going bald. But in any case, I need Lex to bring down the artificial tree from the attic and the boxes of decorations.'

'*I* could take you to get the tree in my camper van,' I offered quickly, hoping to avert a possible meeting with Lex.

'Thank you, my dear, that's very kind of you, but you don't want a big tree in your lovely van.'

Clearly he hadn't seen the shabby interior, which already smelled of wet earth and exotic herbs, with a slight overlay of linseed oil and turpentine.

'Besides, it's become another annual Red House Christmas tradition, ever since Lex came home from his travels abroad and settled down to run the pottery. We all go to choose the tree, and this time you must come with us, Meg.'

I returned his kind smile with an effort. I thought perhaps this might be the moment to confess that I used to know Lex when we were at art college, but then, to my surprise, Henry pre-empted me.

'While I was talking to Lex on the phone, he said that he recognized you yesterday when he was driving off, Meg. Apparently you used to know each other slightly? Of course,' he added, 'Clara had told him she'd persuaded a portrait painter to come and spend a few weeks with us, but not who you were.'

'I . . . yes, *I* recognized *him*, too – I kept forgetting to mention it. He was at the same art college but he was a year ahead of me and studying ceramics, while I was doing Fine Art, so we moved in different circles.'

I didn't mention that the circles occasionally overlapped, once with catastrophic results . . .

'It's a small world,' said Clara. 'The older you get, the more evident that becomes.'

'Of course, he dropped out when I was about to start the first year of my MA and he the second of his and—' I stopped dead, realizing where this was taking me.

'Yes, poor boy, so tragic for him, but after Lisa's diagnosis I can see that he felt it was the only thing to do. I suppose you know they married and he devoted himself to looking after her until she died?' Clara asked me.

I nodded, dumbly as a tide of old guilt seeped in, making me feel less than a worm.

'Afterwards . . . well, he simply couldn't face going back to complete his postgraduate course,' she finished.

'We all knew about Lisa, of course, but . . . I'd no idea what happened to him afterwards.'

'He went abroad: just roamed around the world for a couple of years,' Henry said. 'I did much the same myself in my twenties and early thirties, though of course I kept getting drawn back to wherever Clara was, like a moth to a flame.'

They exchanged fond smiles. 'That was usually on some dig or other, for the first few years after I left Oxford,' Clara said. 'But we were like twins anyway: united even when apart.'

'Lex did any kind of casual jobs he could get while he was globetrotting,' Henry continued, 'but eventually he settled down in a Greek village, where they still made those giant terracotta pots in the traditional way – hand-thrown, you know.'

I didn't. I'd never really thought about it before.

'When he did finally come home for good, he stayed with us,' Clara said. 'Then he had the idea of setting up a business making his own version of the huge terracotta pots, for the garden.'

'And Terrapotter came into existence?' I finished for her.

'His old college friend, Alan, had been out to Greece to stay with him for a few weeks and learned the basics, and they decided to go into business together.'

My mouth opened and shut silently a couple of times like a dying fish, before I managed to utter, 'Alan Lamb, would that be?'

'That's right. I expect you knew him slightly, too, Meg?'

I nodded, speechlessly.

'Luckily, the Old Forge in Great Mumming came up for sale just then,' Henry said. 'It was a run-down cottage with a yard and a group of buildings behind it, including the smithy and what had been a brick kiln. Perfect, really. We staked him to buy it and then he and Alan became business partners. They're making a big success of it.'

'We'll have to take you over,' Clara suggested. 'Alan and his wife, Tara, live in a nearby cottage and have two delightful children, just a little younger than Teddy. Tara is Lex's late wife's sister. It's odd how things work out sometimes, isn't it?'

It certainly was. Horror piled on horror, so that my blood was now running cold. I'd be avoiding Terrapotter and Great Mumming as if the Black Death had broken out there and buboes were rife. In fact, I was now *desperate* to leave . . . which was warring with my equal desperation to paint Clara and Henry. I *had* to paint them but I was definitely leaving, never to return, at the very first opportunity afterwards.

Lunch over, Henry, as was apparently his habit whatever the weather, set out with Lass for a walk.

'I'm going to do a little work now,' Clara said, 'but if you want to pop in and draw a few sketches, or whatever preparatory work you do, I don't mind in the least. I probably won't even notice you're there.'

'That would be wonderful, thank you,' I said, because the sooner I got to work on the portraits, the easier it would be to escape at the same time as River.

'A little later we could drive up the Starstone Edge road, so you can get your bearings,' she suggested.

'Lovely,' I agreed, because at least it was in the opposite direction to Great Mumming and Lex.

But then she said, 'Just a quick spin as far as Underhill, though we won't visit Sybil, so we'll have plenty of time to pop down and collect Teddy from school and save Lex another trip up here. Luckily the weather is very mild for December, so we can use the scenic route down the Grimlike Pass.'

'Grimlike? That's a very odd name.'

'The story goes that whenever visitors asked about the road down the pass, the locals would tell them it was 'grim-like' and eventually the name stuck,' she said.

I could hardly wait.

Later that afternoon Den brought round an aged and battered white Range Rover and would have driven us, had Clara not insisted that she do so herself.

'I love to drive and, after all those digs in the Far East, no vehicle or road state is too much for me,' she declared, setting off with brio. 'At least here one isn't likely to round a hairpin bend and come face to face with a herd of camels.'

'No, I suppose not,' I murmured faintly, as we hurtled down the drive and then, with the briefest of pauses, shot out and turned right on to the narrow, but mercifully empty, road.

'Not much traffic about at this time of year, though it's different in summer, when all the holiday home people, the sailing and water sports enthusiasts, campers and the like infest the place,' she said cheerfully. 'The moment townies buy a four-wheel-drive vehicle, they assume all country roads are one way: the way *they're* heading.'

'The Red House is quite isolated really, isn't it?' I said, because it was about half a mile until the first cottages of Starstone Edge appeared.

'Isaiah Gillyflower built the Red House when Victorian Gothic was all the rage. He was a wealthy brewer who liked the imposing position of the plot, looking down on the village. I expect, like most of the second-homers, he only saw it in summer before he moved in. Lots of people buy the cottages here when the weather's lovely and then realize how awful it can be from autumn to early spring . . . and sometimes *late* spring. Then they either shut them up or sell them again.'

'It must be an entirely different place in summer.'

'Yes, a bit of sunshine and it's like Blackpool on a Bank Holiday.'

'I've never been to Blackpool,' I confessed.

'Really?' She turned her head to stare at me in astonishment, which seeing the speed she was driving at, I'd much rather she hadn't. 'You've never lived till you've eaten a stick of rock while walking along the Golden Mile, seen the Illuminations, or heard the mighty Wurlitzer in the Tower Ballroom. Henry and I used to take the nieces and nephews there sometimes when they were little and stayed with us during the school holidays. Their parents are my younger sister, Bridget, and her husband. They were in the diplomatic service, so often abroad. Now they've retired to New Zealand, where Lex's elder brother, Chris, lives.'

I devoutly wished that Lex had gone with them.

'You'll see the dam and the pumping house, or whatever you call it, when we go down the Pass,' she said. 'But in this direction the road is almost a dead end after Underhill. There's just a thin strip of track over the moors, which has endless cattle grids and gates to open, so no one much bothers with it except the farmers. If you keep going along it, though, you end up in Yorkshire. It's an old drovers' road.'

She slowed right down as the houses clustered closely together, presumably so she could gesticulate more easily with one arm.

'This is the centre of the metropolis of Starstone Edge, mercifully spared the Great Flood,' she announced, with a lordly wave that encompassed the terraced stone cottages huddled on either side, a couple of ramshackle wooden sheds, one with an ancient rusty petrol pump outside it, and a few semi-detached properties from the twenties and thirties.

A larger villa, painted an insouciant and incongruous lemon yellow and set back from the road, had a swinging wooden sign that had been shrouded in sacking.

'That's Bella Vista, run as a guesthouse during the season,' Clara said, with another wave that sent the Range Rover halfway across the road. 'Deirdre shuts it up in winter and goes to stay with her daughter in Australia,' she added. 'Then there's the Adcock family, who live in the end cottage of the next row and do a nice little line in looking after Deirdre's place, the holiday lets and the second homes, while their youngest son, Gil, runs the bar at the Sailing Club and keeps an eye on any boats stored there over winter.'

'They sound a very enterprising family,' I said.

'They are, to make a decent living here all the year round. The Sailing Club is a fancy name for something that's just a big hut, really, and most of the members only have little dinghies, or canoes and kayaks.'

I peered out of the scratched windscreen, having caught sight of a flat window at the end of the final, straggling terrace. 'Is that a shop?'

'Yes, that's Bilbo's – sort of a souvenir-cum-New Age affair, though he sells ice cream and drinks from a hatch in the side wall when there are tourists about. This time of year, he only opens if someone rings the bell and shows him the colour of their money.'

'Did you say *Bilbo*?' The sign over the shop had certainly read 'B. Baggins' and, in larger letters, 'Preciousss'. And now I came to think of it, they'd mentioned someone of that name as being part of the Solstice ceremony.

'That's right. The Bagginses are an old Starstone family, though he was Bob until he got totally Tolkiened. Such a lot of people seem to, don't they? And then the surname, of course – it must have been too much to resist.'

'I expect you're right.'

'Everyone calls him Bilbo now. He's not a bad chap. The family moved up here when the valley was drowned. It was a handy little general shop before Bilbo took over. He's got a wife and baby now . . . or I *suppose* she's a wife. I asked her once and she said they'd jumped the broomstick and were handfasted.'

'That's more or less the same thing,' I agreed.

'She's called Flower and the baby's Grace-Galadriel.'

'Quite a mouthful, for a baby.'

'It is, but I call her Gladdie.'

I wondered how that went down with the child's mother.

We were well past the last houses when a small lodge next to a pair of open gates appeared on our left. It looked habitable, if you were not claustrophobic. Maybe, I mused, Bilbo had a hobbit friend who lived there.

'That's the drive down to Underhill,' Clara said, making one of her grand gestures. I wished she wouldn't. 'It used to be the rear entrance until the reservoir took away most of the land in front of the house. The gardener, Len Snowball, lives in the lodge. He's a widower, a man of few words. His wife used to talk for both of them, so I expect he got out of the habit.'

The road ended at a wider turning place just beyond the lodge. Clara stopped to point out the farm gate that led to the road over the moors, which looked more like the shiny dark trail left by a giant snail.

'And the track that vanishes behind the gorse over there leads up to the Starstone. It zigzags about a bit, so it's not too steep a climb. You can even get a quad bike up it almost to the top.'

I peered upwards, but from this angle you could barely see the top of the joined stones.

Clara consulted a large wristwatch and started the engine again, turning round within inches of the ditch on one side. 'Better get going: I rang Lex to tell him we were collecting Teddy, so he didn't have to.'

The route down Grimlike Pass was hairy. I was glad we were on the left side of the road, hugging the cliff face, where rock scree had been steel-netted off to prevent landslides, for it was narrow with few passing places and the other side only bounded by a low stone wall. I noticed ominous light patches where it had been rebuilt, and below the ground fell sharply into a narrow valley beneath the dam.

'You can still see the old lower road,' Clara said, though I was happy to observe that she now kept both hands on the steering wheel. 'But no one uses it much, because you don't really want to drive up and picnic under a dam.'

'No, you certainly wouldn't!'

She whipped round the last few bends with panache and emerged at a T-junction with a slightly larger road.

'Left takes you to Thorstane and right, where we're heading now, to Teddy's school, and then, if you carry on, to Terrapotter and the urban delights of Great Mumming. It's the nearest place for shopping and metropolitan gaieties like cafés and wine bars.'

She turned in through a pair of stone gateposts too quickly for me to read the sign that was swinging in the stiff breeze and followed two more cars up a short drive to a large, ugly, foursquare late Victorian house.

'Here we are. And there's Teddy, just coming out with one of the Rigby sisters. There are three of them, all teachers and very good, but not really people persons, you know. Though they seem to communicate with the children all right, which is the main thing. Teddy is very bright, so we think he'll get into the grammar school later.'

Once Teddy had been installed in his child seat in the back, we set off home. I was more than relieved to find that Clara went the long way, by Thorstane, where we made a brief stop for liquorice allsorts.

'The Pike with Two Heads is an odd name, and especially for a pub up on the moors, isn't it?' I remarked, once we'd set off again and were passing it on the road that climbed up out of the village.

'There's a pike with two heads in the bar – I've seen it,' Teddy announced. 'It's dead and it's got stuffing in it.'

'It's a very old mutant pike from the river that ran through Starstone,' Clara explained. 'It was caught and used to hang on display in the village pub. Then when the reservoir came, the Golightlys bought this place – The Drover's Rest, I think it was named then – and renamed it. But they're very enterprising and have built a row of motel rooms at the back, as well as serving meals. They do quite well out of the locals in winter and the tourists in summer.'

'Mummy says Starstone Edge is at the arse end of nowhere,' confided Teddy.

'Well, it suits us, doesn't it?' Clara said to him, unfazed, as she changed down the gears for the climb.

We crested the hill, and below us in the gathering gloom shone the bright lights of the Red House and the long sparse string of firefly flickers from the village.

We swooped down into the darkness, between thorn hedges, and emerged on to the bottom road.

'Home is the hunter, home for his tea,' misquoted Clara, pulling up outside the front door of the Red House in a scrunch of gravel, under the great glass lantern that shone above the porch. 'We're home!'

11
A Moveable Feast

Afternoon tea was ready in the drawing room when we got back, so I thought it must be an everyday thing, not just laid on for my arrival, though this was a more low-key offering than the previous day, with sultana scones and a biscuit barrel full of digestives. I suspected all this food was not only going to put back the rest of the weight I'd lost while I was ill, but speedily insert me into a permanent fat-suit.

Tottie carried Henry's share and his cup of tea through to his study, since he was apparently still wrestling with an intransigent ode. Every so often you could faintly catch the staccato rattle of the typewriter keys.

Teddy had been sent to wash his hands and change out of his school uniform of black trousers and sweatshirt with 'Gobelins' across the front in swirling gold letters. I'd never seen a black school uniform before, but it suited Teddy, with his mop of dark curls and the aquiline nose so like his great-aunt's . . . *and* his uncle Lex's. In fact, Lex must have looked very much like Teddy at this age.

The strong features didn't really suit a small boy, but I knew he'd grow into them and turn into a handsome young man.

I don't usually want to paint children – their faces are generally so unformed – but Teddy would make a good subject.

It was just a pity I wouldn't have the time.

Teddy returned and, barely stopping to wash down a scone with diluted blackcurrant juice, fetched a painting book, planting himself firmly on one of the sofas next to me. (There were three sofas and this time I'd chosen the one that didn't try to eat me.)

'I bet you haven't seen one of these before, Meg,' he said. 'It's a magic painting book!'

'You're quite right. I don't think I've ever come across a *magic* one.'

He turned the pages, revealing old-fashioned pictures of ladies in crinolines, horses pulling ploughs and women in bonnets, feeding hens. The black outlines had been washily filled in with a limited palette of slightly mottled colours.

'I've done half of them already.' He turned a page to a fresh one, featuring a thatched cottage fronted by a border of flowers. 'You don't need any paint, you just use water and then the colours appear – like magic.'

'I'm not sure you can get those painting books any more,' said Tottie. 'I remember them from when I was a girl, but Sybil found a few unused ones in the old nursery at Underhill, when she was having a big clear-out after her father died, and she gave them to Teddy.'

'It looks like fun,' I said.

'It is,' agreed Teddy, 'but you have to stay inside the lines and not use too much water on your brush, or the colours run into each other. I'll show you.'

'Not on the sofa, darling,' said Clara. 'Put the book on the end of the coffee table.'

She pushed the tray containing the teapot up a bit to make room.

Den, who'd been silently sitting on one of the Egyptian leather poufs, consuming scones at a rate of knots, said he'd fetch a mug of water, if someone else would take charge of stopping Lass, who was lurking greedily beneath the table, from stealing the eatables. Soon Teddy was demonstrating the technique of producing colour from thin air. Or thin water.

He allowed me to paint one of the tall hollyhocks and it was strangely satisfying when it suddenly blossomed into a grainy yellow. It made me remember the time, many years ago, when the postmistress in the nearest village to the Farm had given me a small painting-by-numbers set of a swan on a river. I'd dutifully filled in each section with the numbered colours and then, stepping back, seen how surprisingly they blended together into a whole. I'd realized then that nothing in nature was one colour, but made up of many different shades, some of them quite unexpected. It had been exciting . . . and the oily smell of the little pots of paint a part of it.

Presently, Henry came in to have his teacup replenished and sat down next to Clara, who looked questioningly at him.

'Sometimes the words flow, other times they trickle, and occasionally you have to squeeze them out of the tube,' he said.

'Henry's writing a book of linked poems about Starstone and the Great Flood, pulling in several of the ancient stories of other great floods, including the biblical one,' Clara told me. 'It's sort of autobiographical. And I'm writing my actual memoirs, non-poetic and just for fun, really.'

'They both sound fascinating,' I said, though I wondered how Clara found the time to fit any more projects into her busy life.

I was already starting to become familiar with the very assorted inhabitants of the Red House and could well understand how they had compacted into the informal, workable, extended family unit it now was. It was much the way the core members of River's commune had settled down and taken their permanent places in the structure, while the summer helpers – transient yurt visitors and those who used the campsite – came and went like colourful flotsam on the tide.

I expect that was why I was so quickly feeling at home here, and had it not been for Lex's dark presence hovering just off-stage and due to take a more central role over Christmas, I might just have found myself sucked in and settled there indefinitely . . .

As if on cue, Clara said, 'Lex always starts his Christmas stay with us from the day of the Solstice, and it will be so nice for him to have an old friend here this year, Meg.'

'I'm hardly that,' I said quickly. 'And in any case, since the portraits should be well forward by then, even if not quite finished, I'll be able to leave at the same time as River. I've realized how much I'd miss the Yule celebrations at the Farm.'

Henry looked deeply disappointed. 'Oh, please don't run away before Christmas! It would be so much fun to introduce you to all the traditions.'

'Of course you'll stay,' Clara decreed. 'I know you're simply being polite, because you think you'd be intruding on a family party, but that isn't so at all.'

'No, indeed,' said Tottie. 'The more, the merrier!'

'*I* want you to stay, too,' Teddy said with flattering enthusiasm, looking up from the painting book.

'It's very kind of you, but I'm not just being polite,' I said. I knew I would have stayed in a flash, if it hadn't been for Lex.

'Well, there's plenty of time for you to change your mind later, if you want to,' said Henry kindly.

'True,' agreed Clara. 'And I'm certain that by the twenty-first, you'll be so happily settled here and painting away in your studio that you won't want to leave us.'

I decided there was no point in saying any more just then: Clara probably wouldn't believe I was really leaving until she saw me driving off!

'Does the pottery close right over Christmas?' I asked curiously.

'They do officially close down operations, though Alan and Tara keep an eye on things because they live nearby. Tara has her own little studio at the Old Forge, making jewellery. But of course, with two small children, Christmas is a busy time for them.'

The busier the better, I thought, because if I was going to be faced with Alan as well as Lex before I left, it would be the last straw.

'Do their children go to the same school as Teddy?'

'No, they're younger and at the local infant and junior school, which is where Teddy was until he entirely outran the teaching and we thought he'd be better at Gobelins.'

'Gobelins is a strange name for a school,' I commented.

'There aren't any goblins really,' said Teddy, looking up again, 'unless you count Miss Aurora's garden gnomes. It's just the name of the house.'

'I expect it was called after a previous owner,' said Henry. 'These things stick.'

'"Gnomelins" wouldn't have quite the same ring to it,' offered Tottie, and for some reason this struck Teddy as so exquisitely funny that he burst into irrepressible giggles and rolled about on the carpet. Tottie had to grab the water mug before it went flying.

Lass, unsure if she should join in with a game or protect Teddy, opted for the latter and tried to lie on him protectively.

Chaos ensued for the next few minutes.

After tea everyone scattered to their various pursuits and I went into the studio to brood over a sketch of Clara I'd made that afternoon, and which I'd pinned to the old easel. She'd settled down to work more or less in the exact pose I wanted, with the grimacing faces on the totem seeming to look over her shoulder and the light from the lamp shining on the honey-coloured piece of incised stone that she would absently pick up and turn in her hands, when she was pondering deeply.

I propped up the iPad displaying the picture of her I'd taken to set the pose, too.

Now I was officially back in the land of the living I was remembering to charge my various gadgets up occasionally, even if I didn't always turn them on. I dislike having my days punctuated by calls and messages and I certainly didn't want my phone going off while I was working.

But now I checked and to my irritation found several missed calls from Rollo and a series of voice messages:

Are you there?

Have you met Henry Doome yet?

Did you mention me?

Yes, yes and a resounding no, were the answers to those. In the next he said, *If he doesn't want to do an interview for* Strimp! *I've had a great idea.*

I bet he has, I thought, sighing as I scrolled down to the next.

He could write the foreword to my new poetry collection. He's old-school, but it would give it quite a cachet.

'Wouldn't it, just!' I muttered.

Ring me back, because I need to talk to you. I'm relying on you to pave the way before I contact him.

'In your dreams, buster!' I said aloud, then sent that back as a text message.

I checked my emails after that and found only two, one each from Oshan and River, sent from the laptop in the craft centre office at the Farm.

Oshan's said,

> Hey, sis! Pop says I get to wear the Cloak of Power and wield the Staff of Mightiness at the Solstice this year, now he's invited to stay with your current clients, though he's coming back afterwards for the feasting. He wasn't sure if you'd make it back with him or not, though.

I replied assuring him that I'd have completed the commission before the Solstice, and intended returning to the Farm in convoy with River.

River's email began, predictably, with,

> Blessings of the Goddess upon you, dearest child! I will be with you early on the 21st for I will be staying the previous night with my old friend Gregory Warlock, who has a museum of witchcraft in the village of Sticklepond, not far from Starstone Edge. I will bring my cloak and staff, in case required. Oshan is having to have much larger robes made for the ceremony.

He certainly would, for Oshan seemed to have inherited genes for height from his strapping Ukrainian mother, even if he got his deep blue eyes and fine features from River.

River's vaguely pagan ways had never quite added up to any kind of religion, so far as I could see, but by Goddess he always meant Gaia, the earth and all of nature. Gaia could apparently just shrug us all off the surface of the planet like annoying insects, if she felt like it, but I was so glad that to date she'd resisted the temptation.

I felt slightly soothed and comforted by the two emails: River and Oshan knew what kind of person I was and it definitely wasn't the monstrous one Lex had created in his mind and shared with Al.

But I still felt an urgent need now to talk about it to the one person who knew the whole truth: Fliss.

When I glanced at my watch, it seemed a good time to try. She taught art in a private school in the mornings and should be home again, though I had no idea if her brand-new spouse would be or not, since Calum had to travel abroad a lot for business.

She was alone, however, and we had a good catch-up, including all the details of her wedding that she hadn't had time to tell me during our brief meeting before I left.

'We did miss you, though,' she finished.

'And I was really sorry not to be there . . . but maybe not sorry about wearing that terrible bridesmaid's dress. It so wasn't me.'

'I don't know what happened in the wedding shop,' she confessed. 'There's a sort of Bridal Mania that sweeps over you and you just go with it.'

'Well, the knot's tied now,' I said.

'Yes, and we really need to get *you* knotted next.'

'I think I *am* well and truly knotted, just not in the way you mean,' I said gloomily.

'Is the family awful?' she asked sympathetically.

'No, it's not that. They've made me very welcome, even if Clara Mayhem Doome is a bit . . . overbearing. I like her, but I don't really know how to describe her, except that she assumes everyone will fall in with what she wants. And I suspect they all usually do. But her husband, Henry, is very kind . . . and paintable. I've really got my artistic mojo back.'

'But that's great, isn't it?'

'It is, and I'm really looking forward to starting Clara's portrait tomorrow. I've already done a drawing.'

'You're a quick worker, I know, but won't painting two portraits take you very close to Christmas?'

'Yes, and they've invited me to stay on, but you know I don't do Christmas. I always go home to the Farm instead, for the Solstice.'

'You could do something entirely different for once: aren't you tempted?'

'I might have been, because it does sound fun. But, Fliss, something dreadful has happened! It's made me wish I'd never come here at all and I'm leaving the moment I can possibly get away!'

'What on earth do you mean?'

'The first person I set eyes on when I arrived was Lex Mariner!'

'Oh, hell!' she exclaimed.

'Precisely,' I agreed drily.

Clara

As I look back at it, our childhood in Starstone seems a forgotten idyll – a village life that should have ended with the war, but instead was to be wiped out as if it had never been by the creation of a reservoir.

That last summer remains clear in my mind. On the surface we carried on doing what we had always done: messing about in the stream, riding Henry's pony, lessons in history and ancient and modern languages with Father and Mother . . . generally just being the precocious and happy brats we were.

Of course we were aware of the dark cloud hanging over the valley, even though we tried to ignore the changes taking place around us, as if by doing so we could prevent the destruction of our lovely village and community.

But people were already moving out and building work was well advanced on the wall of the dam at the lower end of the valley, where the hillsides pinched in. Maps had been pinned up in the village hall, showing the upper limit of the waters. It would spare the manor house and the hamlet of Starstone Edge, but soon everything else, so loved and familiar, would be fathoms deep and lost for ever.

*

At the end of that summer, our belongings were packed into a large van and we left for a new parish in Devon.

Henry was to go off to boarding school a week later and we said goodbye on the bridge, both numbed and unbelieving at the way our world was tumbling around our ears. When the moment came to leave, our hands had to be prised apart.

It would be nearly ten years until we saw each other again.

12

The Bare Bones

I was awake earlier next morning and I'd slept surprisingly well, considering. Perhaps being able to share with Fliss my shock at coming face to face with Lex had somehow helped, though the frequent references by Clara at dinner the previous night to 'Lex, the dear boy, is always so helpful with . . .' or '. . . and when Lex is staying here after the Solstice . . .' certainly hadn't.

While I ate my breakfast, Tottie told me Den had taken Teddy to school and then she discoursed enthusiastically about bees, gardening and horses, which seemed to be the only topics her weather-beaten face registered any passion about, though she did also seem deeply attached to Teddy.

Henry and Clara were apparently very early risers and had already breakfasted together and gone to work in their separate studies. I hoped I wouldn't disturb Clara too much when I set up my painting gear there shortly.

But after breakfast I found Den had returned and already moved my easel into position in Clara's study.

'I left the paints and stuff, though. Didn't know what yer wanted, did I?'

'Oh, thank you, Den,' I said gratefully. 'That's very kind of you.'

I popped my head cautiously round the study door and saw that a rattan mat had been laid over the ancient and beautiful carpet to protect it and the smaller painting table from the studio placed nearby.

Clara was already dictating dark crime into her microphone and took no notice of me, so I closed the door gently and went to the studio, where Den was contemplating the clutter on the big table.

'I dunno what else yer want.'

'Oh, that's all right, I can manage the rest, Den, and I'm sure you must have other things you want to get on with.' I'd noticed the large spanner sticking out of the pocket of his brown linen overall.

'Only a bit of a blockage in the downstairs cloakroom sink,' he said. 'Deal with that in a mo, when yer settled.'

He took the big wooden paintbox and a tiered plastic one full of things like pastels, Conté crayons, pencils, putty rubber . . . a small portable art shop, in fact, except that all the contents were battered and used.

I carried the canvas, the mahl stick and the jar of brushes and palette knives.

We tiptoed into the study with our burdens and then when Den left, closing the door silently behind him, Clara looked up absently, clicking off the microphone.

She blinked and said, 'There you are, Meg. Let me know when you want me to pose for you.' Then she clicked on the microphone again and resumed dictating, with no discernible pause for thought.

I'm sure she'd immediately forgotten I was there, but she'd already naturally fallen into the right pose, sometimes holding the stone paperweight and turning it over in her hands when she paused briefly between scenes.

I sketched her directly on to the canvas this time, in soft pencil, and then stood back and studied it.

Yes, I'd got it: the bones of the portrait were there, awaiting their fleshing out. I lightly erased the lines with the putty rubber until only the ghost of the drawing remained and then laid out my palette, before beginning to paint. I like to work using trowel-shaped palette knives at first, though later often dragging the paint together with a brush or even, sometimes, my fingers.

As always, as soon as I began, an electric energy seemed to take over my hand and make the sharp, sure movements that would create the flesh, the character and, I hoped, capture the inner essence of my sitter.

I was vaguely conscious of Clara's melodious deep voice dictating on while I worked.

'*The crumpled golden mask, slippery with blood, fell from the murderer's fingers and landed by some fluke askew over the terribly mutilated visage of Vernon Tate, spread-eagled like a sacrifice in the trench below . . . End of chapter eight,*' she finally intoned, then added, slightly plaintively, 'May I move, now, Meg? I've carried on and written two chapters today instead of one, but I'm feeling a bit stiff and it must be lunchtime.'

'I can hear Lass howling,' I said absently, stepping back so that the smears and squiggles of paint magically resolved themselves into Clara's face.

'That was my stomach.'

I looked up then as the import of what she'd said dawned on me. 'Oh, I'm so sorry! Yes, of course, do move! Just say whenever you need to stretch, or have had enough for the day.'

She got up, tall and sturdy, and stretched. Then she came round to have a peer at the picture.

'Hmm, interesting the way you've put a patchwork veil of colour over the bones of my face.'

'I like to start like that and then work over the wet surface more thickly afterwards. Sometimes I'm practically mixing the colours on the canvas.'

'Why are there random little blobs of paint dotted here and there over the rest of it?'

'Colour notes: I don't suppose you're going to be wearing the same clothes every day, for a start, so it will help me later.'

'Interesting!' she said. 'Well, I think we've both done a good morning's work, because not only have I written two chapters of the novel, but before that I added a little more to my memoirs. And after lunch, I'll be back to the day job. I've had an idea about that inscription I've been working on.'

I cleaned my palette knives and stuck them in the jar that I'd found in the studio, encrusted in ancient blobs of oil paint, like strangely coloured lichen.

The day had brightened and I carried the portrait through to the studio and set it on the old easel there, intending, once I'd had lunch, to spend the afternoon blocking out the background.

But it only seemed like I'd been back in the studio for five minutes before Clara winkled me out and insisted I go with her to Underhill.

'Sybil rang to invite us to tea. Tottie's already there because they've been for a hack on the moors. We can bring her back with us, which will save her the walk up, though it's much shorter over the paddocks. And Henry will collect Teddy from school and then they're going to call in on Lex at the pottery.'

'It's very kind of Sybil to invite me, but really, I'm here to work and—'

'To convalesce and have some fun, too,' she interrupted firmly. 'Come along. The fresh air will do you good and *I'm* curious to see what Mark is up to at Underhill. I haven't been there for ages.'

'Here we are,' announced Clara unnecessarily, driving through a stone arch and pulling up in the middle of a cobbled courtyard, scattering a gaggle of hens. They were the kind with frivolously feathery ruffles round their ankles, if hens *have* ankles.

The manor was a rambling, L-shaped low stone house of some charm, but no great architectural merit, having evidently been randomly extended and cobbled together over several generations. A large attached barn or coach house formed one side of the courtyard and I thought the original building might have started life as a farm.

'This was the back entrance to the house, of course, before they built the reservoir,' Clara said. 'Come along!'

I left the warmth of the car reluctantly, because heavy spatters of rain had been added to the icy wind and it felt as if someone was casting giant handfuls of water at us.

'It can't have been fun out riding in this,' I remarked, but Clara said Tottie and Sybil were tough as old boots and wouldn't let the weather stop them.

'Though Mark might, unless Sybil starts paying all the bills for the horses' keep and part of Len's wages for acting as groom,' she added sardonically.

'Did you say Sybil's son was turning Underhill into a wedding venue, or hotel, or something?'

If so, he could call it Bleak House; that would bring the punters in . . . not.

'Something like that. He's nearly finished converting the coach house over there into a wedding reception room, I think, but he's fallen out with the builders and he won't find any willing to come up here till at least the New Year – if they can even get up here then.'

That sounded ominous. The prospect of being snowed up in the Red House over Christmas with Lex Mariner was not an enticing one.

Clara led the way into the house through a large, metal-studded oak door and along a narrow passage, then, without any ceremony, threw open an inner door and shouted into the dark, cavernous interior beyond it, 'Coo-ee, we're here!'

Her deep, rich voice echoed around a very large hall, from which a splendid staircase ascended. There was about half a tree trunk in the vast open fireplace at the far end of the room, but since it was unlit, it was nearly as cold in there as it had been outside.

'There's always been a fire kept burning in here right through the winter, Mark,' Clara said, as a thin young man emerged from a nearby passage. He had very dark auburn hair and straight eyebrows twitched into what looked like a permanent frown, but he wasn't unattractive in a slightly foxy kind of way.

'I can't afford to keep huge fires going in all the rooms,' he said shortly.

'That's false economy in an old house like this, darling, because your central heating isn't up to much and you need to keep the whole place warm or it will soon get damp.'

He scowled at her, though her suggestion had sounded very sensible to me, then turned his brooding tawny eyes in my direction and stared.

It was dark in there, so what with my very pale skin and the green hair, I probably looked a bit spectral. He couldn't seem to take his eyes off me, anyway.

'This is Meg Harkness. I expect your mother told you I had a portrait painter staying with me over Christmas?'

'I . . . think she did mention it,' he said, his eyes still fixed on me. 'She's painting your portrait, Aunt Clara, isn't she? I'm Mark Whitcliffe,' he added to me, holding out his hand. 'The Doome – or doomed – heir.'

His wry smile was rather attractive and I found myself answering it.

'You wouldn't think he was a Doome really, because they're mostly fair and blue-eyed. He takes after his father,' said Clara. 'By the way, Mark, the hens are out.'

'Oh, great. I'll tell Gidney to round the little bastards up, before a fox gets them,' he said gloomily.

'Let's get out of this freezer and somewhere warm. Where's your mother?' Clara asked.

'In the morning room with Tottie. She's only just told me you were coming over, so Mrs Gidney's going to cut some more sandwiches.'

'Good, I'm ravenous. Come on, Meg, this way!'

As I followed her across the flagged floor, a door opened in a pool of warm light and two dachshunds raced towards us, yapping excitedly.

'Get down, Wisty,' said Clara, as the largest jumped up at her, while the other, who seemed to be barely in charge of her body, like a teenager still growing into it, sniffed interestedly at my feet and wriggled.

'This is Princess Wisteria of Underhill and that's the runt of her last litter, Pansy,' Clara told me. 'Sybil hasn't managed to offload her on to a buyer yet.'

'Oh, come in, both of you, do,' urged Sybil. 'It's so cold out there!'

The morning room was quite small and thankfully warmed by both a radiator and open fire of more modest proportions than the one in the hall.

Mark, who had followed us in and closed the door, had to reopen it, to let the two dogs back in.

Tottie was sitting near the fire with her long, booted legs stretched out.

'Hi, Tottie – good ride?' Clara asked.

'Yes, thanks, we had a lovely hack over the moors. We met old Jonas from Oxberry farm and he said there's a cold spell coming. He's always right.'

The weather seemed pretty cold to me already.

'I've told Mrs Gidney two extra for tea and it will be along in a minute,' Mark broke in abruptly and then added, rather resentfully, 'She's going to cut into the ham, which I thought we were saving for Christmas, Mum.'

'Oh, no – remember, we always have a Westphalian ham for Christmas, Mark, and it's on order.'

'Then cancel it! They cost a ridiculous amount and there'll be only the two of us.'

'Three, with Uncle Piers, and I think it's too late to cancel the order,' she said doubtfully. 'It's on its way.'

'Then cancel the turkey instead, because I'm sure you have some ridiculously huge bird on order, too. We can have ham instead. Or one of those blasted hens – they've got out again.'

Sybil began to look distressed and I said quickly, 'Please don't cut into the ham on my account. I don't eat meat.'

'And you know very well that I don't either, Mark,' Clara said. 'You go right back and tell her not to bother.'

He glowered and strode off again and we joined Tottie on a shabby tapestry sofa drawn up near the fire.

'I see what you mean about the penny-pinching,' Clara said to Sybil, who was making small distressed twitterings. She subsided into a chair and Wisty promptly lay on her feet. Pansy jumped up on to my lap and curled up.

'Push her off, dear,' said Sybil.

'It's all right, I like dogs,' I said. Even strange little sausage dogs with one flyaway ear, a kinky tail and a slight look of having been put together by someone with a sense of humour and their eyes shut.

'The boy's turning into a skinflint,' Tottie said.

'Oh, no, he's not that bad,' protested Sybil. 'It's just that the renovations are costing so much more than the estimates . . . and then, there's very little money to do it with, since most of what Daddy left was tied up in my annuity.'

'Henry said he'd left you enough to live on very comfortably,' Clara said.

'Yes, but not to pay *all* my expenses for the horses, as well as investing some of my income in the business, which was another of Mark's suggestions. His latest idea is that I earn my keep as some kind of receptionist-cum-hostess! He's considering turning the old housekeeper's room and bedroom near the kitchen into a sort of small flat for me.'

The prospect didn't appear to fill her with joy.

'Why? He can't want all the bedrooms for guests, surely?' asked Clara.

'He *says* he will.' I thought Sybil had forgotten I was there, but evidently she talked as frankly about personal matters in front of total strangers as the Doomes did, because she explained for my benefit: 'The plan is that the Gidneys will stay on as they are now. They live in a cottage in the grounds and Gidney looks after things generally while Mrs Gidney is housekeeper and cook. But Mark has two friends who will come to stay during the wedding season to cater exclusively for the receptions.'

'Which will be a short season, with the weather as it is up here – *and* if he gets the business off the ground,' Tottie said.

'He applied for all the permissions needed ages ago, before he came back permanently, and the barn is nearly completed,' Sybil said. 'The builders knocked through into the old scullery before they downed tools and left.'

'Mrs Gidney won't like sharing her kitchen, will she?' Clara said.

'She won't have to, because several of the small rooms behind it, which back on to the barn wall, have been knocked together into what will become one huge new catering-standard kitchen.'

'It all sounds very expensive,' Clara said, then added to Mark as he reappeared, 'What exactly *are* you planning for Underhill?'

Mark was carrying a large tray, laden with a teapot, crockery and a plate piled with sandwiches.

'If those dogs come anywhere near the food, they're going out in the hall,' he said, sitting down opposite and favouring me with another slightly smouldering, but seemingly approving, stare.

'Underhill needs to pay its way if it's to stay in the family,' he said to me, as if we were alone together. 'My grandfather didn't leave much money and what there was, was tied up.'

He gave his mother a look as if that had been all her fault.

'Your mother looked after George for several years with little thanks and no salary, so it was right that he should provide for her,' Clara said. 'She only had a bit of a widow's pension and what she made from breeding the dogs.'

'It needn't have been so much, though. In fact, you can't really need half of it, Mum, so I've no idea what you do with it all.'

'Oh, but it's not that much, Mark . . .' Sybil protested, looking flustered, so that I started to wonder if she might indeed have a secret vice, though it was hard to imagine what. 'Now I'm starting to pay for the horses' upkeep it's going to make quite a dent in my income: shoeing, feed and the vet's bills.'

'And it will have to stretch to paying some of Len's wages too, if he's going to continue as groom as well as my gardener,' Mark pointed out.

Sybil looked crushed and Mark turned to me again.

'I'm going to advertise the manor as a wedding reception venue – that will all be in the old barn and coach house, which I've thrown into one big room – and I hope to hold weddings too, eventually. Perhaps in the hall; the half-landing would make a great stage for the ceremony with the guests standing below.'

'I can imagine that,' I agreed. 'Or, at least, I could if it was brighter and warmer.'

'I only intend opening from spring to early autumn, because you can't trust the weather up here outside that. It means it'll have to be very upmarket and expensive, so I can make a lot of money in a short space of time.'

He'd obviously thought it out, but would people be willing to come all the way out here to the back of beyond for their receptions?

'I'll just shut the place up in winter, with the Gidneys to look after it, and go off to Italy,' he continued. 'I have a house there.'

Presumably his mother would also be shut up at Underhill for the winter with the Gidneys.

'I should be able to create six letting bedrooms with en-suite facilities, plus my apartment over the east wing and another suite of rooms for Art and Gerry.'

'Art and Gerry are Mark's friends,' explained Sybil. 'Art is a chef and Gerry . . . arranges things.'

'Gerry has a lot of artistic flair and he'll organize everything for the receptions – flowers, table settings, all of that,' said Mark. 'And Art will cater for the wedding dinners, or buffets, or whatever they choose, and cook for any of the bridal party staying here.'

'The boy has got it all planned out, you have to hand him that,' Tottie said, and the boy – who looked to be not much younger than my thirty-six years – scowled at her. It seemed to be his default expression. He should really have been born to an earlier generation because he was an Angry Young Man personified.

Sybil began to pour tea and Tottie passed plates. I was happy to see there were cheese and tomato sandwiches as well as egg and cress, and no sign of the ham.

Mark began to tell me all the details of his renovation ups and downs, which were amusing. His determination that he would finish in time to open in spring, no matter what, was quite admirable.

I did think he was being more than a bit mean towards his mother, but I could see he needed every last penny he could scrape together. And also, he must love Underhill to do it, though he seemed to love his Italian house even more, and waxed lyrical about the sun, the vines, the lemon tree in the garden and the beautiful views . . . which I must come and see on a visit one of these days.

After he made this suggestion I caught Clara's thoughtful eyes on us and blushed slightly.

Then she transferred her gaze to Sybil and said, 'I thought you'd found someone who was going to buy Pansy?'

Sybil sighed. 'I thought so too, and I did tell them I was reducing the price because she was not show standard, but then when they saw her they said she wasn't at all what they expected and went away again.'

'I think she's perfect – so sweet!' I said, stroking her silky head. She and her mother had been eyeing the food and sighing heavily from time to time, but making no attempt to scrounge. I suspected had Mark not been there, things would have been different.

'She's certainly taken to you, Meg,' Tottie said.

The feeling was definitely mutual, but did I need a little dog to complicate my life?

13

Grinched

Despite all his talk about frugality, Mark was doing full justice to the tea. The large number of sandwiches he ate seemed to have mellowed him a little, for he said fairly indulgently to the dogs, 'Funny little things!'

Seemingly encouraged by this thawing, Sybil said timidly, 'I had a letter from Uncle Piers this morning, Mark, saying how much he was looking forward to spending Christmas at Underhill with us again.'

'Does he know it's a building site? I mean, he hasn't been to stay with you since Mark got back, has he?' Tottie said. Then she explained to me, 'Piers Marten was a very old friend of Mark's grandfather and he used to spend a lot of time here.'

'He and George were as thick as thieves,' agreed Clara. '*And* as bad as each other. Luckily there was an extensive cellar at Underhill, so they could concentrate on drinking that dry during his visits.'

Sybil made a small protesting noise, but not with any great conviction.

Mark was looking angry again, which just meant adding another layer to his fall-back expression. 'Mum, I told you last time he suggested visiting that I'd had enough of him freeloading here . . . unless he has hidden talents in the plumbing, plastering or redecorating line?'

'He's the same age as Grandpa would have been – they trained at Sandhurst together – so he's not really up to that kind of thing, Mark, darling . . . and there's some sort of family rift, so he prefers to stay with us for Christmas and New Year.'

'"Stays" being the operative word, since he lingers on as long as he possibly can,' said Mark. 'It's a habit he'll have to break, because Underhill isn't a private house any more, but a business.'

'But it will still be *our* family home,' protested Sybil. 'And as to Piers,' she added anxiously, 'couldn't we—'

'*No,*' he snapped. 'For a start, I'll be working right through Christmas, painting and decorating and doing any other jobs I'm capable of, so I'm not hosting any kind of house party.'

'But surely you'll have a break over Christmas?' said Clara.

'Yes, darling, and you know we always have Clara, Henry, Tottie, Lex and Teddy here for dinner on Christmas Eve,' said Sybil. 'And then—'

'Not this year,' he broke in. 'It's all a big expensive fuss over nothing, so this time there'll be just the two of us. I'll take Christmas Day off and we'll have dinner as usual, and that will be it. I haven't got time to waste lolling about, overeating and making polite conversation.'

'You do remind me so much of Teddy's book about the Grinch who stole Christmas,' said Clara, and he gave her an impatient look.

'I shouldn't worry about Piers, Sybil,' Clara said. 'His ex-wife is a friend of a friend, and apparently the children take it in turns to invite Piers for Christmas, because they feel they ought to, family rift or no family rift, so he has got somewhere else to go.'

'I suppose you're right – and he did spend Christmas quite comfortably at his club, when Daddy was so ill – but it doesn't sound at all like our usual Christmas,' murmured poor Sybil. 'The opposite of what your grandfather would have wanted. He did enjoy Christmas so much.'

'Yes, it was about the only thing he and Henry had in common,' Clara agreed.

'If Grandfather hadn't lavished most of his capital on racehorses and high living, I might not be trying to turn Underhill into a business,' Mark pointed out.

Sybil sighed. 'I suppose you're right, darling. But one guest wouldn't make much difference, surely, so Piers—'

'No,' he said intransigently. 'That's my final word.'

'Sybil, why don't you come and stay with us for Christmas this year?' Clara suggested. 'If Mark ate his Christmas dinner with us, too, it would let the Gidneys have the whole day to themselves, *and* eradicate the need for an expensive turkey and all the trimmings. You can live off the ham while you're renovating, dear,' she added to Mark.

'Oh, *could* I?' said Sybil gratefully. 'That would be so wonderful, because it's such a building site upstairs and downstairs the dust has got everywhere, you have no idea.'

'I'll be surprised if your workmen return before the end of January,' Clara told Mark. 'You never know what the weather will do up here. A hard frost and the roads out could be lethal with ice.'

'I'll just carry on doing what I can,' he said impatiently. 'You go to the Red House if you want to, Mum, and you'd better write to Piers and tell him he can't come to Underhill because you're going away. That will settle *him*.'

'It's very kind of you, Clara,' Sybil said.

'Not at all,' Clara said. 'We'll love it.'

'Do come, it will be such fun!' urged Tottie.

'As long as you don't mind Wisty and Pansy?' asked Sybil.

'Oh, no, Lass loves playing with them,' Clara said. 'Mark, you will have Christmas dinner with us, won't you?'

'Thanks, that would be good,' he said ungraciously.

'It's going to be a full house. Henry will be so happy!' Clara said. 'Sybil, Lex, Tottie, me, Henry, Teddy, Zelda, Den and Meg . . .'

'But I'll probably have finished the portraits before then and left,' I pointed out.

'Oh, I'm sure you'll change your mind and stay on!' Clara said confidently. 'After all, you're supposed to be recuperating after an illness, so you need some time off, and then, you know, you might even fancy some other portrait subjects.'

That was acute of her: there were enough characterful faces in Starstone Edge to keep me busy for a year . . .

'Besides, Henry's dying to introduce you to all the delights of Christmas!' she added, then had to explain that to Sybil and Mark.

To my surprise Mark said he hoped I wouldn't rush off and then he invited me to come back soon so he could show me what he was doing to the house, which was kind of flattering until he added, 'I'd like your opinion on the paintings in the drawing room and the gallery upstairs. I need to sell something to fund the business until it starts to pay its way, and since Mum is totally against my parting with any of the ancestors, however hideous, it'll have to be the Stubbs.'

'School of,' corrected Clara.

'Daddy always said it really *was* a Stubbs,' Sybil insisted. 'And I'm sure it must be one of our ancestor's favourite horses. It's a very pretty grey Arab.'

'It *would* be a pretty grey Arab if there wasn't that slight suggestion that it had more than four legs,' Clara said.

'I'm sure I wouldn't be able to tell if it was genuine or not,' I told Mark hastily. 'I mean, I'd like to *see* it, but I'm sure you should get an expert opinion.'

'Mark's grandfather already did,' said Tottie. 'School of. He just wouldn't accept it.'

'It'll probably fetch enough anyway,' Mark said. 'One of the portraits Mother won't let me sell is a Lely and the insurance is horrendous. I wish I could sell that.'

'The insurance for a real Stubbs would have been even worse,' I pointed out.

'I suppose there is that,' he said.

'Why don't you get one of the big auction houses to take a look at them?' I suggested, but he persuaded me into agreeing to go over again in a few days and have a look.

When it was time to leave, I discovered I was holding Pansy in my arms, like a furry baby, and she did her best to go home with me.

'She *has* taken a fancy to you and, of course, I'd sell her really cheaply,' hinted Sybil hopefully.

'She's adorable!' I bent down to stroke her silky head. 'I'd love a dog, but I really can't afford it at the moment. And anyway, my current lifestyle, travelling so much, would make it difficult.'

Sybil looked disappointed, but seemed to accept that, though Pansy gave me a look of deep reproach when I left without her . . .

On the drive back, Clara warned me that Mark was a bit of a flirt, as she put it, but had never had a serious relationship that she knew about.

'Perhaps he has, in Italy,' I suggested.

'Possibly, but last time he was home he had a fling with Teddy's old nanny, Flora, who was visiting her aunt in the village, and I'm sure the poor girl thought it meant more than it did.'

I assured her that I wasn't interested him in that way, which I wasn't, especially if he was a love rat!

'He's very attractive in his own way, but not my type at all,' I said. 'I was engaged a few years ago, but I broke it off after . . . something happened that changed how I felt about him.'

Clara tactfully didn't ask me what that something was, which was just as well because I still found it very hard to talk about.

'So, no significant others, as they say, since then?'

'No, I decided the painting is enough for me – and a quiet life.'

'You'll certainly get a quiet life up here,' Clara said, turning into the drive to the Red House.

I went straight up to change and found there were short brown hairs stuck to my jeans, which made me smile. Pansy was such an imperfectly perfect dachshund . . . and perhaps, if I always stayed in my van, rather than in the sitters' homes, I *could* have a dog with me?

It wasn't really that practical, however, and anyway, I suspected that even if Pansy wasn't Kennel Club standard, Sybil would still want an impossibly large amount of money for her.

In our absence, Henry had picked up Teddy from school and they'd gone to visit Lex at Terrapotter.

Since the next day was Saturday, Teddy was allowed to stay up after dinner that evening. Henry was teaching him to play chess and Tottie, Clara and I played Scrabble. The lack of a TV in the room and people checking their phones every five minutes was just like being back at the Farm . . . restful. I hadn't even thought of my phone since my earlier call; in fact, it was probably still somewhere in the studio.

Teddy didn't want to go to bed at all, because he was excited about Uncle Lex coming over tomorrow to take the family on the annual Christmas tree hunt.

I intended lying low until they'd departed, so it was a blow when Henry said, 'Lex's staying here tomorrow night, so he can help put the tree up in the hall and fetch the decorations and the artificial tree down from the attic.'

'The boxes are kept in the top attic, which is up a ladder,' Clara said. 'A bit awkward. Perhaps you could help him get them down, Meg?'

My mouth did that silent goldfish opening and closing thing.

'We don't put up any fresh holly or other greenery till nearer Christmas Day, because it all looks so sad when it goes dead and crunchy, doesn't it?' said Tottie, before I could manage to speak.

'Uncle Henry, can I help you choose which of the old decorations go on the tree in here?' asked Teddy.

'Of course you can,' he said. 'I bid for some more recently in an auction and they should be arriving any minute. It was a big, mixed lot, though I could see in the online catalogue that there were one or two unusual ones, but the rest will be a surprise. A good one, I hope.'

'If it comes when I'm at school, you won't open it till I get home, will you?' Teddy asked anxiously.

'No, I'll save it so we can open it together,' Henry promised. 'Then you can help me catalogue it.'

At the back of my mind I was still dealing with the idea that Lex was not only coming tomorrow for the Christmas tree expedition – which I had no intention of joining – but staying overnight. I don't suppose he wanted to while I was there: it was just another of those annual festive traditions that meant so much to the family.

I found my voice finally and said brightly, 'Well, I'm sure you'll find a lovely tree tomorrow and while you're out, I'm going to work on the background to the portrait in your study, if you don't mind, Clara? Then perhaps you could give me another sitting on Sunday morning.'

'Oh, but you can't miss the Christmas tree hunt!' said Teddy. 'You have to come, Meg! We take a picnic and hot chocolate in flasks and everything.'

That sounded fun, except that the 'everything' included Lex.

'Teddy's right, you can't miss our little expedition, and you're entitled to the occasional day off,' urged Henry.

'I've only just got here,' I protested, and said I really would prefer to stay at the house and work, but as usual, Clara didn't want to take no for an answer and Teddy and Henry seemed genuinely upset at the idea that I would miss out on such a treat.

'We're not all going to fit in Lex's pick-up,' Tottie said, and for a moment I thought that was going to give me an escape route. But no.

'It doesn't matter, we always go in two cars anyway,' said Clara. 'Teddy and Henry can go with Lex and the rest of us in the Range Rover.'

'The Christmas tree plantation is near another reservoir called Rivington,' Tottie explained to me. 'There's a picnic area near the shore where we have lunch afterwards.'

'Then back we come with a huge tree, which will then shed its needles into the hall runner right up till Twelfth Night,' finished Clara.

'No, it won't, because we get a Norwegian spruce and they hold their needles best,' said Henry.

'Even a Norwegian spruce won't hold them till Twelfth Night, unless you superglue them on,' said Tottie.

When Teddy had finally gone up to bed, Henry showed me some more of his collection of vintage ornaments, and the bottom drawer of the cabinet, which contained Teddy's collection of antique papier mâché fish. These oddly shaped aquatic creatures were actually little boxes for sweets that you could fill and hang on the tree.

'I sometimes find one or two in mixed auction lots and he loves them, so now we keep an eye out for them.'

Henry was very knowledgeable and told me a lot of interesting things about their history and the difference between glass blown from a kiln-heated rod and lampwork, but really I just loved the sparkliness of the silvered glass baubles and the strange and often quirky shapes – snowmen, fruit, musical instruments, birds, pixies . . . you name it, they made it.

'The antique papier mâché Santa tree topper, which I showed you last time, always goes on the tree in the hall, to please Tottie. She's the one who misguidedly added that glitter and cotton wool when she was a little girl.'

'I actually like it like that,' I admitted.

'So do I, really, and even if it has ruined its value as an antique, it's increased its value as a family heirloom.'

He closed the drawer again on his treasures and we went back to the drawing room, but I didn't linger long because I suddenly felt very tired. I went up to bed, leaving Tottie and Clara discussing what to have for dinner next evening. The consensus seemed to be that it would be a pasta dish that Lex was particularly fond of . . .

The food, however delicious, would probably choke me if Lex was sitting at the same table.

I wondered if I could develop a sudden allergy to Christmas trees overnight. It seemed an idea with lots of promise, since It would not only get me out of the expedition tomorrow, but a tree in the house would give me a reason to leave as quickly as possible.

I just wasn't sure how convincingly I could put on an allergic reaction, and sustain it, under Clara's bright, clever eyes.

Clara

Father's new parish in Devon was warm and welcoming but I remained deeply unhappy at leaving Henry and everything I knew and loved behind me.

Then my mother's elder sister, Aunt Beryl, who was a wealthy widow with no children of her own, kindly suggested she paid the fees for me to be privately educated and my parents chose a small boarding school noted for the scholarship and intellectual achievements of the girls. Many had gone on to pursue degree courses at Oxford or Cambridge.

It was a stimulating environment and I also made several friends, all of whom went on to achieve considerable success in their chosen fields. But of course, I never forgot Henry. There always seemed to be some invisible connecting thread between us, as if we had been born twins . . .

Henry's father (his mother having died soon after we moved) was not the kind to write letters or send out annual Christmas cards, so all contact with the Doomes petered out, as these things do. Secretly, though, I intended that when I was old enough I would go and find Henry, but until that day I'd just have to bide my time.

*

In due course I was accepted, a year earlier than my peers, at Lady Margaret Hall, which was my mother's old college in Oxford.

Aunt Beryl had originally suggested that I be 'finished' abroad and then she could launch me on the London social scene . . . but I was quite determined on what I wanted to do with my life, and it wasn't an endless round of empty social events with a 'good' marriage inserted into the middle of it. When I told her this, and that my idea of fun was picking out an inscription on some ancient stone, she laughed and promised to support me through college instead.

She was to have more luck a few years later with my sister, Bridget. She proved more than happy to enter the social whirl of London, while I pursued my studies and embraced my chosen career.

I was never one to be deflected from my purpose.

14

Brief Encounter

We all met for breakfast early next morning and I tried my get-out-of-gaol-free card. 'I'm afraid I remembered last night that I'm allergic to pine trees,' I said casually, buttering toast.

'What makes you think that, dear?' said Tottie, who was combining the consumption of crumpets with the construction of a mound of sandwiches for the picnic. Den had just taken a tray of vegetarian sausage rolls out of the oven, which were also probably part of the moveable feast.

'The moment the Yule tree was brought into the Farm and hung from the rafters in the hall, I'd start to sneeze and my eyes would water,' I said. 'I really don't think it would be a good idea to come with you to choose the tree. I mean, a whole plantation of them . . .' I tried to sound regretful.

'I've never heard of anyone being allergic to *trees*,' Clara said, sounding very Lady Bracknell. 'I'm quite certain it must have been something else setting you off, Meg.'

'It does seem an unusual allergy, especially for anyone brought up in the country,' agreed Tottie.

'I think, my dear, that coming with us today would settle the matter one way or the other,' Henry suggested. 'Perhaps it was just dust disturbed from the rafters when the tree was hung up, or something like that?'

Had I really had a reaction, that would have been a possibility, seeing that no one ever dusted the huge beams of the farmhouse ceilings, or removed the cobwebs and their occupants ('our little friends', as River referred to them).

'Of course, if you start sneezing and your eyes stream the moment we get out of the car, then we'll know you were right,' Tottie said.

'Unlikely,' declared Clara. 'But if it happens, you can get back in the car and keep the windows closed.'

'She'd 'ave to eat 'er bleeding food in there too, seeing the picnic site's slap bang in the middle of the trees by the reservoir,' Den pointed out, waving the tongs he'd been using to transfer sausage rolls on to a cooling rack, to emphasize the point.

'I don't expect it'll come to that,' said Clara. 'Didn't you tell me you decorate the Yule tree with corn dollies, Meg? They'd probably be dusty by December; that'll be it.'

Since there seemed no getting out of the expedition, I said reluctantly, 'Perhaps you're right.'

Teddy, who'd been listening anxiously to this discussion, the spoon suspended above his half-eaten cereal, now said with flattering intensity, 'I *need* you to come, Meg. Do you want to drive there in the pick-up with me and Uncle Lex and Uncle Henry?'

'Bit of a squeeze,' suggested Den. 'Better in the car.'

I breathed a sigh of relief and Teddy seemed to accept this, for he said, swirling the contents of his bowl around, 'I like it when the chocolate comes off the cereal and goes into the milk,' then resumed eating.

'You make the most of it, because it's back to the wholegrain stuff after the weekend,' said Clara.

We left Den and Tottie assembling the picnic. Henry and Teddy got ready for a walk with Lass, since she'd be staying at home while we were out.

Clara said we had an hour to spare, so we retired to her study, where she briskly dictated another chapter of the crime novel, while I laid on paint with my little trowel of a palette knife. When I'm working, a sort of energy flows from my brain to my fingers; I can feel it, like an electric current. I'd missed that while I was ill, and I'd worried that it might never come back.

I immediately forgot about the expedition or anything else, so it was a shock when Henry put his head round the door and told us Lex had just pulled up and we'd better get ready to go, while they loaded the picnic hampers.

By the time I'd cleaned my palette knives and hands, and rushed upstairs to change my painty sweater for a warm tunic and my Converse pumps for short boots, everyone else was outside except Henry, who was heading for the door with a couple of tartan travelling rugs.

'There you are, my dear, and I've settled down Lass, so we're ready to go!' He handed me one of the rugs. 'You can wrap this around yourself in the car. You mustn't get chilled while you're still convalescent.'

'Come on, Meg, we're all waiting for you,' called Clara as I went down the steps, to the sound of Henry turning the big key in the lock behind me.

Lex, six-four of darkly brooding hawkish handsomeness, was leaning against the open driver's door of the pick-up and he gave me a sombre look.

'How lovely that you and Meg are old friends, Lex. But you can catch up later. We'd better get off now,' Clara said, and the expression in those dark green eyes turned sardonic.

Did he really think I'd told Clara that we'd been friends?

He said nothing, though, just swung an excited Teddy up into the cabin and got in the driver's seat. Henry nimbly climbed into the passenger side, next to Teddy.

Clara and Den were now arguing about who should drive the Range Rover, but Den won. (I didn't know how anyone ever got their own way with Clara; there must be a knack to it that I hadn't discovered yet.) She sat in the front next to him, still grumbling, while Tottie and I got in the back, an open wicker basket of Thermos flasks wedged between us.

The drive to Rivington was mostly along quiet country roads through farmland and I'd have enjoyed it if I hadn't known I'd have to get out at the other end and face Lex again. Or not. Perhaps he'd just stride off on those long legs of his and ignore me completely.

The Christmas tree plantation was up a rough track. Rows of trees in various sizes stretched away on either side.

'They cut the trees and net them up, ready for sale, nearer Christmas – another week or so – but early birds like us can choose one and they'll chop it down so we can take it back with us,' Tottie informed me as we all climbed out and stood in a chilly huddle by a barn.

We were now entirely surrounded by rows and rows of standing pine trees and the air was redolent with their heady, resinous scent. It reminded me of the Farm, with its dark forest edging up beside it.

'Here we are, completely submerged in a sea of pine trees,' said Henry, poetically, 'and you're not sneezing or anything, Meg.'

'My eyes are watering, though,' I said quickly.

'That's just this cold wind – we all have watering eyes,' Clara pointed out.

She examined me with her bright, dark gaze for other signs of imminent allergic attack and found none. 'It appears the reaction must have been to dust after all, which is lucky because you couldn't have avoided the tree once it was in the hall, could you?'

Only by leaving the Red House the moment the tree, along with Lex Mariner, entered it, I thought regretfully.

But you can't manufacture a full-blown allergic reaction without being a better actor than I am, so I abandoned that one.

Den was sensibly staying in the warm fug of the car, listening to the radio, until needed to help load the tree into the back of the pick-up.

As we all set off into the teeth of an icy wind – or in Teddy's case, ran off – I wished I was back in there with him.

Once among the ranks of trees it was more sheltered and I got interested in the different kinds and the way, as we moved from section to section, they ranged in size from cute tiny ones to huge monsters.

Among the latter were apparently some of the desired Norwegian variety and I stopped to see if I could spot the difference. Perhaps they were the ones with a rather beautiful blueish-green tint.

I looked up to ask Henry, only to discover that everyone else had moved on and vanished up the next row. There was no one in sight except Lex, who was standing watching me with his hands in his jeans pockets and a somewhat Grim Reaper expression on his face, though luckily there wasn't a scythe to hand.

Before I could stop myself, I said, 'Of all the rows of trees in all the world, you had to pick this one.'

Unfortunately, my mouth often tosses out a flip remark at entirely the wrong moment, especially variations on this line from *Casablanca*, and I could see this one hadn't gone down that well.

'I want a word with you,' he said flatly.

It was clearly show time, and if he was forcing the issue then maybe this was the moment when we could finally get things clear between us. I let go of the branch I'd been inspecting and straightened up to face him.

'Well?' I said shortly. 'I've already grasped that my arrival was a shock – and not a good one – but you can't have imagined *I'd* have agreed to come to the Red House if I'd known you lived up here.'

'You were the last person I expected to see when I brought Teddy back from school on Wednesday,' he said. His eyes darkened. 'It was like the past had come right back to haunt me.'

'Well, ditto,' I snapped.

'Then there was nothing to stop you turning round and leaving again, was there?'

'Don't imagine I didn't want to, because that was my first impulse,' I told him. 'But I'm a professional and I'd accepted the commission to paint Clara, and Henry, too.'

'She told me all about the portraits and she was really excited that you'd agreed to come, but she didn't mention your name.'

'No, well, she didn't happen to mention that you were her nephew either, until I got here and discovered it for myself. But when I found out you actually lived a few miles away, I thought it would be OK. I didn't realize you'd be around so much.' I shrugged, with a nonchalance I wasn't feeling. 'Now we have met it doesn't seem to matter so much, but I'm sorry if it's brought the past back. It's not a time I want to remember either.'

'What happened between us wasn't really *your* fault. I don't blame you for anything,' he said wearily.

'Big of you, considering I didn't do anything you could blame me *for*,' I said, though as always that small flicker of guilt stirred and I felt my face colour.

An unbidden memory of that fateful night came back at this inopportune moment and I could hear Al's voice, when I'd answered Lex's phone, demanding to know if he was there with me.

'Yes, but he's asleep and—' I'd begun.

'Then wake him up and tell him Lisa's taken a sudden turn for the worse. Her parents have been trying to get hold of him the last two hours. Give me your address and I'll be there in ten minutes.'

Numbly I'd obeyed and then said stupidly, 'But you're at work.' He'd had to leave the wine bar where we'd all met up quite early that evening, for his job at a hotel as night porter.

'Not any longer,' he'd said tersely and rang off.

Lex's voice dragged me back to the present, marooned in a sea of bristly green with a tall, dark, handsome and conflicted man, like the start to a low-budget movie.

'There's nothing to be gained by going over the past now, that's for sure,' he was saying. 'You're here and we'll have to deal with it, for Clara and Henry's sake.'

'You won't have to strain your civility for long because I'm clearing out the day after the Starstone Solstice ceremony.'

'Clara told me your grandfather was coming up for the ceremony, but *you* were staying on till the New Year.'

'Clara keeps telling *me* that, too, but I'm not. I have no idea how anyone ever gets through to her: she's like a human steamroller.'

'It's not just Clara who thinks you're staying, everyone else does, too. And if you're painting Henry's portrait as well as Clara's you can't do that by the twenty-first, can you?'

'Actually, I can, as long as they both give me a few sittings. I've already started Clara's portrait and it's coming together fast.'

I didn't mention how I now longed to paint the other inhabitants of the Red House, too – Den and Tottie, and even the slightly desiccated Sybil from Underhill – because that was a dream destined never to be fulfilled.

'Well, Clara said Henry is really looking forward to showing you a proper family Christmas with all the festive trappings, because apparently you've never experienced one.' He looked at me sceptically, one dark eyebrow raised.

It just showed how little he'd ever really known about me, though I suppose that cut both ways, for until I'd arrived here I hadn't known anything about his background either.

'We don't celebrate Christmas, as such, at home, so originally I did find the idea sort of interesting, but not any more.'

That was a straight lie, because I was becoming ever more fascinated by the whole thing.

'Running away? Could your conscience possibly be bothering you more than you admit?'

'Why should it?' I said coldly. 'I was only guilty of an act of kindness, after all.'

'That's one way of putting it,' he said drily.

I stared levelly at him. 'It's the *only* way of putting it, whatever your mad friend, Al, accused me of later.'

He looked taken aback. 'What do you mean? Did Al talk to you about that night? When was this?'

'Remember a couple of weeks after Lisa . . .' I petered out, because there was no tactful way of saying 'died'. I started again. 'Remember when you came back into college to collect some of your stuff and you cut me dead in the corridor? At the time, I thought you were either too grief-stricken to notice me, or embarrassed because you'd got drunk that night in the wine bar and told me a lot of very personal things.'

He pushed the dark curls out of his eyes and said, 'I did remember some of it . . . but I'd hoped I wouldn't run into you that day.'

'Al came and found me after you'd gone. I don't know what on earth you'd told him and why, but he laid into me as if I'd dragged you back to my flat and taken advantage of you in a weak moment.'

Then I remembered *my* weak moment again . . . or rather, *our* shared weak moment, and felt myself blush. Then the heat receded and iciness set in, because clearly he shared Al's version of what had happened. I could see it in his eyes.

'I've felt so much guilt since Lisa died, but I've been trying to put it behind me and move on, and then you come along and stir it all up again.'

'Well, I've said I'm sorry about that, but it was unintentional and soon I'll be gone. Feel free to carry on using me as a scapegoat for anything you did in the past, if it makes you feel better.'

He frowned down at me for a minute, as if trying to puzzle my attitude out.

'I don't understand you . . . but now you *are* here, you might as well stay until you've done the job. And I'm very fond of Clara and Henry, so I'll even put up with you over Christmas, if I have to.'

'Gee, thanks,' I said sarcastically. 'I'd so love to be the ghost at the feast.'

He shrugged. 'Please yourself. I usually stay at the Red House from the day of the Solstice – around the twenty-first – to the New Year, but if the weather isn't bad I can escape down to the pottery on some excuse occasionally. Al and Tara will be there for most of it. You do know Al is my business partner?'

'Yes, that really put the cherry on the cake. And Clara told me Tara is Lisa's younger sister, so there's whipped cream, too.'

He gave me another of his haunted, slightly smouldering looks. He'd have given Heathcliff a run for his money any day. 'We've all come to terms with Lisa's loss – Tara's parents, too. We've . . . settled into acceptance.'

That sounded comfortable. Pity I'd arrived on the scene and ripped the wound apart again.

'We all work together at Terrapotter. Tara's a silversmith and has a small studio there, but she helps out with the pottery and the paperwork, too.'

He looked down at me again. 'Please yourself whether you stay or go, as long as you don't disappoint Clara and Henry. I really don't care either way, now.'

I was starting to feel angry all over again. I hadn't done anything wrong and I didn't deserve this contempt. He might be eaten up with guilt about the past, but my imagined role in it had only been one small part.

Would he actually believe me if I forced him to listen to the truth about that night? I thought perhaps I'd better make the attempt, whether he did or not.

'Lex, it's time you heard what really happened . . .' I began resolutely, but I was too late: he'd already turned and was striding off.

'Uncle Lex! Uncle Lex!' Teddy was flying down the row of trees, pink-cheeked and excited. 'Did you and Meg get lost? Come on, we've found the perfect tree and it's *huge*!'

15

First Flower

I thought Clara gave us both a keen look when we joined the rest of the party, but no one else appeared to notice anything amiss and I kept as far away as possible from Lex as we retraced our steps through rows of increasingly Lilliputian fir trees to the large barn.

The chosen tree, which looked to me about the height of a house, had already been cut and wrapped in netting. It was soon loaded into the back of the pick-up, where it was secured with rope.

Then we drove down to the picnic area by the reservoir, where the contents of the hamper were set out on a large picnic table near the water's edge.

I found myself unable to eat much, however delicious it all was, though I was grateful for cup after cup of hot coffee or cocoa, from the giant Thermos flasks, because I was chilled not only to the bone, but to the heart.

Back at the Red House I could have made a quick escape into the studio, but I was so convinced that there was no way they'd get that huge tree into the hall, let alone standing upright, that I lingered to watch.

Den fetched a monumental green-painted metal stand and then the tree was somehow eased through the front door and vestibule into the hall, without taking out any of the stained glass. Then it was tilted up into the stairwell until vertical.

Finally it was clamped firmly into the metal base and manoeuvred into the perfect position in the curve of the staircase, the top several feet above my head.

There was some argument about which was its best side and it was turned a little to and fro until everyone was satisfied.

By then, quite some time had elapsed, and Tottie and Den, who had at some point vanished towards the kitchen regions, reappeared with the tea trolley.

'Picnic leftovers to finish off!' cried Tottie gaily, and, not having had any lunch, my stomach gave a sudden lurch and grumble of hunger. I can't say the thought of settling down in the drawing room *en famille* with Lex there was that appealing, though.

'I'll just take my tea through into the studio with me, if you don't mind,' I said, as Clara set out the cups and saucers, which today seemed to have been randomly selected from three different services.

She looked up. 'Oh, don't go, Meg. Why don't you just relax for a bit? You've already done some work today, and after tea I was hoping you'd give Lex a hand getting down the boxes of decorations and the other tree from the attic.'

'She doesn't need to. I can manage perfectly well on my own,' Lex said.

'I expect you could, but it's easier if there are two of you, because then you can pass down the boxes from the upper attic without climbing up and down that ladder,' said Henry.

'I can help too,' offered Teddy eagerly.

'Den would have lent a hand, but he's gone back to his flat for a bit,' Henry said.

'And I promised Sybil I'd pop down and help do the horses today, because Len's off,' said Tottie.

'Well, I want to do a little more work . . . and I expect Henry also means to vanish into his burrow for an hour or two,' said Clara. 'So if you *really* didn't mind, Meg . . . ?'

There was nothing for it but to agree. 'No, of course I don't mind. I'm glad to be of use. If there are two of us – and Teddy, of course,' I added hastily, seeing his mouth open indignantly – 'I don't expect it'll take long. I can stand at the bottom of the ladder while Lex passes everything down.'

Or perhaps dropped them on my head if the fancy took him, though boxes of baubles probably didn't weigh much so they'd only mildly concuss me. *Death by Bauble* sounded like a good crime novel title, though not the kind Clara wrote.

'Then I can carry them to the top of the attic stairs,' Teddy said.

'If you've finished eating, we might as well get on with it,' Lex said, abruptly getting up.

I hadn't – in fact, I'd only just finished a sausage roll and decided I could manage an egg and cress sandwich, too – but I drank my tea quickly and Teddy and I followed him, though I took the sandwich with me and ate it on the way upstairs.

I hadn't been up to the attic floor before, though I remembered Clara telling me they hadn't renovated it and it was mostly used for storage. The stairs were narrow and uncarpeted, and a door at the top opened on to a passage with small rooms opening off it that I guessed were once servants' bedrooms. There was another door at the furthest end of the corridor. Lex opened this and switched on the lights, illuminating a large, gloomy space filled with the shrouded shapes of large pieces of furniture, old trunks, boxes, broken chairs . . . the usual strangely assorted collection of items that seem naturally to accumulate in attics and lumber rooms.

Right at the back was the almost perpendicular ladder leading up to another level. It wasn't very high, but I wondered why on earth they'd decided to store the Christmas decorations up there, rather than more handily near the main door.

I didn't bother asking Lex, who had been silent all this time and now vanished upwards without a word. There was the sound of objects sliding across a wooden floor and then a long and ominous-looking canvas bag with handles was lowered down to me. I reached up to grasp it and found it surprisingly heavy.

'That's the tree for the drawing room,' said Teddy, and as soon as I'd set it down, he seized the handles and dragged it to the door, then along the passage to the top of the stairs.

'Plastic storage boxes next,' said Lex, and the first of them slid down the ladder into my waiting hands. They were quite light and had handles, which made it easier, and they bore handwritten labels saying things like 'Large baubles' or 'Lights'.

Teddy greeted each one like an old friend. 'This is the box with new glass ornaments. We get them from the Christmas shop in the old mill near Little Mumming and Henry says they're the collectibles of the future.'

'I expect they are,' I agreed, passing him a light box that was apparently full of tinsel and folding paper garlands.

The next was heavier. 'This one's full of the *huge* plastic baubles,' said Teddy, electing to drag rather than carry it. 'The plastic ones come in three different sizes and they're very bright and shiny. You need a lot of them for a tree the size of the one in the hall.'

The next box was cardboard, with a lid – large, rectangular and light.

'This is the big Father Christmas, who stands near the tree in the hall,' Teddy said.

'I thought Father Christmas lived in Lapland, not in a box in your attic!' I teased.

'He's not the real one,' Teddy explained seriously. 'He's got a pottery face and long red robes, but his body is just a big cone underneath, that's why he's so light.'

'Porcelain face,' corrected Lex's voice from above. 'I think that's everything.'

'No, the Angel Gabriel's missing,' said Teddy.

I heard Lex's feet on the boards above and dust spiralled down through the cracks, making me sneeze.

'You're allergic to attics, not Christmas trees!' said Teddy, and giggled.

'I think it's a dust allergy – your aunt Clara was quite right.'

'She always is,' said Lex, coming down the ladder with a box under one arm and making it look easy.

'One angel,' he said to Teddy, presenting it.

It took a few trips to ferry all the boxes down to the hall, where they were stacked up out of the way, except for the canvas bag, from which came the fake tree of obvious antiquity, though still a pleasing deep green colour. It had to be constructed from fat, fuzzy wire branches that slotted into a metal trunk. When put together and placed in the square bay window in the drawing room, it reminded me of a monkey puzzle tree. The bay was large, despite the padded seats up either side, so there was still room to move around the tree and to draw the old velvet curtains.

I did manage to escape after that, but only to my room to change and get ready for dinner. There was no time to think, which was probably just as well.

At dinner, I found myself at the opposite end of the table to Lex, which made the situation less awkward for me. The conversation was wide-ranging and interesting, too, so that I found myself sometimes forgetting he was there at all.

Den joined us for the dessert and then coffee in the drawing room, before he went off to his flat again to watch the telly.

'And probably to eat gross things like pork scratchings and salami,' said Clara.

'Well, he's at perfect liberty to eat and drink anything he likes in his own flat,' said Henry.

'He does,' said Tottie, handing me a mead chaser to go with the coffee, a strange combination of tastes. Not unpleasant, just weird.

Lex was sitting on one end of a sofa, stroking Lass's tummy, while she closed her eyes and sighed with ecstasy. His unguarded face looked tired, the shadows dark under his eyes, as if he hadn't slept for a couple of nights . . . maybe since I'd arrived on the scene. Only a few days had passed since then, but I felt as if I'd been here for months.

All the excitement had made Teddy tired. Eventually he just kept keeling over sideways with his eyes closed, so he was sent to bed.

He insisted that Uncle Lex do the honours of bath and bedtime reading, and after they'd gone upstairs the rest of us embarked on a game of Scrabble. Tottie and Henry were good, but Clara was the clear winner: never play word games with an epigrapher, because there's no way they're ever going to lose.

I didn't notice when Lex returned; he was just there when we'd finished the game, reading quietly by the fire.

And by then my eyes were closing just like Teddy's had and I said my goodnights and left them all to it.

But despite feeling so suddenly weary, once I was in bed, I couldn't sleep. I kept seeing images of a young Lex lying next to me, smiling drowsily down into my eyes . . . but unless I had False Memory Syndrome about what happened next, Al and Lex were both living in an alternative reality, inhabited by a totally different version of me.

I slid off eventually into an uneasy sleep, but my nightmare was not of that time, but a few years later. I relived the moment when Rollo's horrified face had turned to me after I'd told him I was pregnant . . . and then the car was veering off the road, a horrendous tortured screaming of metal added to my own, followed by a sudden eclipse into darkness.

I woke up just as I had in hospital afterwards, my face wet with tears and an aching emptiness where the baby had been.

After that, I didn't sleep at all.

From the look of Lex at breakfast, I don't think he'd slept any better than I had. He sat silently over his toast and coffee, though Teddy talked enough for all of us, mostly about decorating the trees later on.

Afterwards, Clara decreed that since she was behind with her memoirs, she would have a session on those, while the rest of us went out for a nice bracing walk, before an afternoon spent tree decorating.

'Though Den and Tottie said they were going to church,' she added.

'Soon as I've fetched the soup from the freezer and the banana bread's out of the oven,' Den agreed.

I didn't have him down as a churchgoer, and he wasn't, because Clara explained, 'Den's best friends with Fred Golightly at the pub, so they have a good catch-up while Tottie's at church.'

'Me and Fred's best mates, aren't we?' confirmed Den.

'You can paint me for an hour or so before lunch, Meg, while I dictate the next chapter of the crime novel,' suggested Clara.

'That's great,' I said. 'But I'll give the walk a miss and just work in the studio till then.'

'I think you should get some fresh air, Meg,' Henry said. 'Besides, Clara sometimes finds an empty house conducive to pushing through to the next stage of whatever she's working on.'

I could empathize with that: like most creative people, I loved feeling the warm, heavy folds of an empty house enclosing me in a world of my own.

'Yes, I've rather got bogged down in the years after we left Starstone for a parish in Devon, and before my arrival at university, which were pleasant enough, but so dull,' agreed Clara. 'I just need to tie up the loose ends and then move on to a more interesting stage of my life.'

'When we met again?' suggested Henry, and they exchanged one of those fond smiles that make couples who have been happily married for a lifetime resemble each other, however different their features are.

'I'm not going for a walk unless you and Uncle Lex come too,' Teddy said mutinously, and Lex gave me a sardonic look.

'Of course I'll come with you, then, Teddy,' I said, and went to get my boots and coat.

Henry, Lex, Teddy and I set out by the back door, where a wide gravelled path led through the middle of twin knot gardens and round the side of the vegetable plot, a polytunnel and some small fruit trees, until it finished at an opening in a hedge. Beyond that was a grassy area with a neat row of white hives, surrounded by lavender and rosemary bushes.

It was a peaceful spot, though I could hear the hens somewhere near the stable block.

We passed through a five-barred gate into a field and down a track that Henry told me led to the bottom paddock, where Sybil's horses were. It was a shortcut to Underhill, too.

It was bitterly cold and I'm sure I felt the occasional ghost touch of a snowflake. We didn't talk much, and Teddy ran about hiding behind walls and jumping out at us.

Two horses were in the lowest field, a bay and a bright chestnut, standing in an open-fronted shelter, pulling at hay nets. They glanced over their shoulders at us as we passed, but we were obviously not as interesting as the hay.

A stream ran through the paddock. Lass, who had been ambling along in a vacant but happy manner, suddenly came to life, galloped off and jumped into a muddy pool.

'You little stinker!' said Lex, when she finally responded to commands and emerged, shaking herself vigorously as we backed away.

'She's a chocolate spaniel now,' said Teddy, giggling.

'Yes, and *you* can help me turn her back to her usual colour when we get home,' Lex told him.

'Oh, I usually just shut her in the garden hall till she's dried off and then Den brushes most of the mud out of her coat,' said Henry. 'She does seem to have acquired a lot more of it than usual this time, though.'

'She has, and there's more than a slight hint of horse manure, too,' Lex suggested.

Lass showed signs of wanting to get back into this deliciously fragrant bath, but was firmly clipped to the lead and dragged away.

The land rose in front of us to the hilltop crowned with the Starstone. From this angle, I could see a sort of level space below it and a dark fissure in the rocks. We didn't head that way, but instead turned on to a downward path that came out at the road just before the gates to Underhill.

'We just follow the road home again now, through the village,' Henry told me. 'It's only about a mile.'

Lass, seemingly invigorated by her icy dip, towed him off briskly towards Starstone Edge, with Teddy skipping along beside him. Lex hadn't said a word directly to me all morning and now strode off after them, leaving me to bring up the rear.

When we reached the edge of the village, many of the cottages we passed looked shut up for the winter and there were few signs of life, other than spirals of blue-grey smoke from one or two chimneys and a dog barking in the distance, possibly from one of the farms, for sound carries strangely in valleys.

Someone was about, though: rounding a bend in the road we caught up with a small, thin woman pushing a baby buggy. The infant in it was almost invisible, having been inserted into a sort of hooded sheepskin footmuff affair. I could see only two closed eyes and a button nose.

The woman turned, revealing a face that was quite pretty in a rodenty sort of way – pointy nose and pouched cheeks. Her hair was much the colour of the mud Lass had rolled in, long and limp and appearing a little damp. But then, it had always looked like that . . .

'Moonflower!' I exclaimed. 'I'd no idea you lived here. I haven't seen you for years!'

She parted the lank fronds of hair and peered at me. 'Is that you, Meg? What are you doing up here?'

'Painting Clara's portrait,' Henry said. 'How nice that you know each other.'

'Moonflower lived in the commune at the Farm with her parents for a couple of years, before they moved on,' I explained.

'They always liked travelling about in the van, rather than being in one place all the time,' said Moonflower. 'We came here one day and camped down among the trees by the reservoir . . . and I met Bilbo and stayed. This is our baby, Grace-Galadriel.'

'She's . . . lovely,' I said, peering down at the infant. The button nose was a bit snotty from the cold.

Lex was standing silently watching us, but now said, 'Hi, Flower.'

Moonflower blushed and simpered, and I suppose you really couldn't blame her, because he looked like every dark and conflicted romantic hero rolled into one. I'd have fallen for him myself if I hadn't already been there, done that and burned the T-shirt.

'How's your mum?' she asked me.

'I don't know. She went to India to work in a friend's bar about eight years ago, but then took off to explore somewhere and never went back. We know she meant to, because she left most of her stuff behind, but she just vanished.'

'And you haven't heard a thing since?'

'No, it's a complete mystery. River went out there to see if he could find any trace of her, but nothing.'

'She must have died, then,' suggested Moonflower tactlessly. Empathy had never been her middle name.

That was my greatest fear too, though I still hoped for the best. 'River doesn't think so, but she might have had an accident, and then, since she left her passport and papers back at the bar where she was living, they wouldn't have known who she was. The trail was cold by the time River tried to find her, but he's sure she'll turn up again.'

'I remember now that you told us your mother had vanished. It's very sad, my dear,' said Henry kindly.

'It is, though actually I'd never seen much of her while I was growing up anyway, because she was such a free spirit,' I explained. 'She turned up at the Farm occasionally and was bright and fun . . . and then, after a while, off she'd go again.'

Lex, who clearly had no idea of my past, was looking at me curiously.

'Who brought you up, then?' he asked.

'The commune in Wales at River's Farm, where I was born. River's been a grandfather to me and two of the founder members of the commune, Maj and Kenny, were like parents. And then there's Oshan, River's son, who is my brother.' Seeing Lex was still staring at me, I added, 'It all worked very well and I had a very happy and secure childhood.'

'Oh, I loved it at the Farm, too!' Moonflower agreed. 'I cried for a week when we moved on.'

'I'd no idea about your background,' said Lex. 'That explains a lot!'

'Like what?' I demanded, but at that moment the baby woke up and made loud grizzling noises, while trying to fight her way out of the footmuff.

Flower said she'd better get home and feed her.

'Come and have coffee one day,' she said to me. 'Meet Bilbo.'

'Oh, thanks, Moonflower, that would be lovely.'

'Call me Flower; everyone else does. And we've some nice things in the shop, too, if you need any presents,' she added hopefully.

Presents? Well, I'd brought the hamper of jams and chutneys, either as a general house gift or a sweetener if I managed to get away after the Solstice, but I hadn't thought of individual Christmas presents.

But then, I'd no intention of still being at the Red House over Christmas, so I wouldn't need them, would I?

Back at the house, Lex and Teddy dealt with the muddy and very smelly spaniel and Henry vanished into his study with a vague smile.

I changed into something already spattered in oil paint and then Clara dictated a chapter of the crime novel while I worked on her portrait until lunch called. Or at least, it called Clara, because as usual I'd forgotten the time.

Lex was in the hall when we passed through it, taking the lids off the boxes of decorations. He looked up.

'There you are! I was just going to remind you about lunch, because we've had ours and we're going to start on the trees in a minute.'

'I forget the time. It's my fault we're late,' I said.

'It doesn't matter, because this portrait's going to be wonderful,' enthused Clara. 'There's magic in you, to draw out things about myself I didn't even know existed, Meg.'

'There always was,' Lex said. 'She won Young Portrait Artist of the Year soon after she started her Fine Art degree.'

I was surprised he remembered that, and I wondered if he was slowly starting to see the real me again – or the version he knew long ago – rather than the false one he'd built up in his mind over the ensuing years.

'Where are the others?' asked Clara, breaking into my thoughts.

'Teddy and Henry are in his study, choosing the decorations for the drawing-room tree. Sybil rode up leading the other horse and she and Tottie have gone for a hack, but she said she'd be back in plenty of time for tree-topping.'

I had no idea what he meant by the tree-topping, unless it was just that the entire household needed to be present when the final decoration went on the top?

'Right, then, we'll just have a quick bite to eat and then be back to help,' she said.

The soup was onion, topped with bread and toasted cheese and we ate it to some *basso profundo* snoring from Lass, who lay clean, crinkly and exhausted, in her basket by the stove.

Den was about to go back to his flat, and admonished us not to touch the Madeira cake cooling on the rack.

'You can have some fer tea, but 'alf of it's fer the trifle, ain't it?'

'Oh, good,' said Clara as the door closed behind him. 'He makes an excellent trifle with Tottie's bottled raspberries and a good layer of custard.'

Then, as I laid down my spoon, she rose and said energetically, 'Come on, let's help decorate the trees. It's *such* fun!'

16

Illuminations

I was now looking forward to the tree decorating, Lex or no Lex, and I think the Christmas magic was starting to slowly seep into my psyche.

The sound of Christmas carols was drifting sweetly out from the drawing room and Lex was up a very tall stepladder, winding fairy lights into the Norwegian pine, with Henry and Teddy assisting, or at any rate, offering advice.

'There you are, my dear,' said Henry. 'Lex's already put the lights on the little tree, and Teddy and I are about to get on with decorating it. Then we'll come and help you with this monster, won't we, Teddy?'

Teddy, who was pink-cheeked and excited, nodded. 'You mustn't come into the drawing room until it's finished, though, Meg!'

'All right, I won't. I love a surprise.'

'We're leaving the door open, but no peeking.'

'Cross my heart,' I assured him solemnly.

He and Henry vanished into the drawing room, while Lex, once he'd wound the fairy lights from top to bottom of the tree, began to help us sort out the baubles.

There were loads of the brightly coloured round plastic ones with faceted, mirrored sides, in every colour you could imagine. They came in three sizes and I began to hang the smallest at the top of the tree by going up the stairs and leaning over the rail, while Lex did the other side from the top of the rickety-looking wooden stepladder.

Clara started at the bottom with the largest of the baubles and met us in the middle with the medium ones.

There was a lot of going to and fro between the two rooms – for the scissors, or silk ribbon, or plastic hanging hooks – but I kept my promise and didn't even glance through the open door.

Den had returned at some point and sat on the wide bottom step of the stairs, unknotting a huge tangled rainbow of old tinsel. Slowly he extracted each strand and rolled it up into a coil: silver, gold, green, blue, red and brightest royal purple.

Teddy emerged from the drawing room and demanded all the silver and gold tinsel, but this must have been the final touch, for we were summoned in to admire their tree shortly afterwards.

It had grown dark, so the curtains were drawn, but the lights had been switched off so we could appreciate the full effect of the illuminated tree.

It looked so magical glowing out of the darkness that it took my breath away. The odd shapes of the old ornaments came alive and sparkled crazily. Bunches of purple grapes and green-capped pixies jostled with bears, spotted dogs and Santas. Small coloured spheres with deep, silvered conical indentations reflected the lights and there were icicles of clear twisted glass. Birds of all shapes perched among the branches with their long, white, spun-glass tails balancing their silvered bodies.

The metallic tinsel zigzagged down from top to bottom, like a mountain road sparkling in the rain, and on the very top of the tree was a small fairy with a skirt of crinkled pink crepe paper over a layer of white net.

When we'd praised it enough for Teddy's satisfaction we all returned to the hall to finish the big tree together, though now the first baubles had been placed, this one seemed more a race to see how many of the other ornaments we could fit on it.

'I've forgotten the chocolate decorations,' Clara said, suddenly. 'They're in one of my desk drawers.'

'The chocolate only goes on the big tree,' Henry explained to me. 'And well out of reach of Lass.'

Clara came back with the goodies: net bags of golden coins, little bundles of foil-wrapped chocolate parcels tied up with silver string and a big bag of assorted chocolate shapes – bells, candles, snowmen, Santas, reindeer and stars – with loops for hanging.

'Father Christmas puts one of those big bags of chocolate coins at the bottom of my stocking every year, with a tangerine,' said Teddy. 'I think he steals the tangerine when he comes in, because last year I counted all the ones in the fruit bowl before I went to bed, and in the morning there was one missing.'

Behind him, Henry winked at me.

'Perhaps he can't get enough of them in the sleigh, what with all those toys?' I suggested. We might not have ever celebrated Christmas at the Farm, but once out in the world there was no escaping the knowledge of things like Father Christmas's seasonal delivery service, with his red coat and sleigh . . . not to mention the relentless urging to spend ever more money on presents.

'I don't think so,' Teddy said, after giving this idea his serious attention. 'It's a magic sleigh.'

'That's true,' Lex said. 'But perhaps he keeps the ones in the sleigh for houses where there aren't any.'

This seemed to satisfy Teddy and we all joined in hanging up the chocolates above dog level, and some just above Teddy level too, so he wasn't tempted to overindulge and make himself sick.

We'd just finished when Tottie came back, her cheeks red from the cold. She was still wearing breeches and a heavy poloneck jumper, but she had removed her riding boots and was just in grey ribbed woollen socks.

'It's starting to freeze hard and one of the farm tractors is out with a gritter,' she told us.

'You're back in perfect time, Tottie,' said Clara. 'We've only this second put the chocolate decorations on the tree, so it's ready for the finishing touch.'

Henry vanished into his study and emerged carrying the antique papier mâché Santa that Tottie had so misguidedly tarted up with glitter and cotton wool in her youth.

Now she took it from him and climbed the stairs until she could reach over and ceremoniously place it over the topmost spike of the tree.

'Hurray! Let the Christmas revels begin,' called Henry, and everyone clapped. Tottie gave a mock bow and came back down.

'Right, let's turn on the fairy lights and off with the hall ones,' said Clara. Lex plunged everything into darkness except for the illuminated magic of the tall tree, which seemed to float in the air like some enchanted vision of fairyland.

'Oh, it's so beautiful!' I sighed. 'Both trees are, but in different ways.'

'When I was a little girl we had the old-fashioned candles in crimped metal holders that clipped to the ends of the branches, but we only lit them briefly and Daddy would stand by with a bucket of sand and the soda siphon, just in case,' said Tottie.

'We had those too,' said Clara. 'Mother was petrified the house would go up in flames.'

'I wouldn't even have electric lights on the tree when I lived here on my own,' said Tottie. 'The early ones were a bit dodgy.'

'Well, they're all quite safe now, especially since the house has been rewired,' said Clara. 'Those two-pin sockets and plugs belonged in a museum.'

'They were in my rooms over the garage before the place was done up,' said Den.

'Grooms and chauffeurs can't have expected much in the way of home comforts back in the twenties and thirties,' said Clara.

'Only cold water plumbing, too, poor bustards,' said Den.

'Is bast—' began Teddy, interestedly, but Tottie interrupted him hastily.

'Never you mind, Teddy. It's just another one of those Den words that you can't use until you're bigger than he is.'

'At the rate he's growing, that's not going to be long,' Lex pointed out.

'The house became so much brighter and warmer after you and Henry bought it,' Tottie said. 'And all those lovely bathrooms, too! Funny how you don't notice the lack of things like that in a house where you've lived your whole life.'

'I agree. The Farm is up in the Black Mountains and when I was a little girl it would often be quite chilly in winter,' I said. 'It was heated by only a range and a couple of wood-burning stoves back then, but it's all changed now, especially since River embraced solar power and had loads of panels put in.'

'I look forward to meeting your grandfather when he comes for the Solstice and hearing all about the Farm,' said Henry.

'Yes, *I'm* looking forward to his arrival, too,' said Lex enigmatically, with a look at me that I interpreted as meaning that he looked forward to it because it would mark the date of my imminent departure from the Red House and his life.

Teddy said he thought it was mean of River not to celebrate Christmas properly. 'Uncle Henry says you've never had a real one!'

'We celebrated the Solstice and then had a lovely Yule feast instead,' I told him. 'That was fun, too.'

'But Father Christmas didn't bring you presents, did he?'

'No, but we always exchange gifts on the first night of the feasting, usually things we've made ourselves.'

'I think *real* Christmas sounds much more fun,' he insisted.

Lex switched the ceiling lights on again and we blinked, back in the real world. The hall was richly redolent with the wonderful scent of pine.

A rattle heralded the arrival of Den with the inevitable tea trolley.

'Time fer a bite to eat, ain't it?' he said, wheeling the trolley into the drawing room ahead of us, then putting more wood on the fire.

I sank down on to one of the sofas in a state of exhaustion, what with all this decorating business, the long walk that morning, and all the emotional turmoil that had stopped me sleeping the previous night.

'Madeira cake,' Henry said. 'You have been busy, Den!'

'Nah, Madeira cake don't take no time at all.'

'I think you're a magician in the kitchen,' said Clara, and Den looked gratified.

Teddy began to tell Lex what was on the Christmas list he'd sent to Santa. It seemed both extensive and varied.

Then his mother, Zelda, rang and after a word with Clara, she put him on the phone. Zelda must have asked him what he wanted for Christmas, because he began reciting down from the top of the list all over again, but he was less than halfway down when Lex removed the phone from his grasp.

'Hi, Zelda,' he said. 'We've just finished decorating the trees, so Teddy's a bit over-excited.'

Teddy pulled a gremlin face at him, but having crammed another slice of cake into his mouth, he couldn't protest.

Lex listened for a few minutes and then said he'd relay that to everyone and see her soon.

'Is Mummy coming *now*?' asked Teddy, having eaten his cake. 'Will she bring me a pony?'

'No and no,' said Lex. 'She's shooting an advert next week and then has an audition, but she'll be here right after that.'

'As long as she really does come,' said Teddy, 'because when she's in a pantomime, she doesn't.'

'She'll be here, but I hope the roads stay clear for her,' said Clara. 'Fingers crossed.'

'Oh, I'm sure she'll make it, one way or another,' said Henry. 'She's very resourceful.'

I suspected she wouldn't have Teddy's pony under her arm, though.

'Her call reminds me, Meg,' Clara said suddenly. 'Your young man rang while you were all out walking this morning.'

'What?' I said, surprised. 'I haven't *got* a young man! *Or* an old one,' I added, as a horrible suspicion dawned.

'No, I remembered you telling me that, though it was definitely the impression he was trying to give me. His name was Rollo something.'

'Rollo Purvis,' I said resignedly. 'He's an extremely ex-boyfriend.'

I looked up and found Lex staring at me with his straight brows knitted in that strangely attractive, slightly hawkish way he had. 'Weren't you already going out with him years ago, when you were at college? He's that poet bloke who always turned up at student parties.'

'I was. Then we broke it off . . . and got together again later. But I finally finished with him over six years ago.'

'It doesn't sound like it,' he said.

'He's become a bit of a nuisance and likes to ring and unload his existential angst on me from time to time. Lots of people seem to like doing that,' I added pointedly and he gave me a black look.

'A poet? I thought the name sounded vaguely familiar,' said Henry.

'He is, and also runs a quarterly poetry magazine called *Strimp!*'

'Oh, yes,' he said, not with any great enthusiasm. 'I've placed him now.'

'Isn't he very good?' asked Tottie.

'Not if the examples of his work I saw in a copy of *Strimp!* someone sent me once are anything to go by, no.'

'That's what I thought, too,' I said, pleased to have my judgement confirmed. 'Some of it's quite clever, but somehow cold.' I turned to Clara to apologize. 'I'm sorry he disturbed you. I didn't give him your phone number and have no idea how he got it. I hope he didn't try to wangle an invite to visit?'

'I quickly gathered that that was the real purpose of the call when he started saying how much he'd love to pop in and see you soon, when he'd be in the area, and how wonderful it would be if Henry could spare him a few moments of his time and give him an interview for his magazine.'

'What cheek!' I exclaimed. 'I hope you told him to take a running jump.'

'I was fairly polite, considering he'd interrupted me while I was working, and also I wasn't sure if he might be a friend of yours, even if not your boyfriend. But of course, I told him there was no possibility of an interview with Henry.'

'He's quite likely to turn up anyway and try to charm his way in,' I warned her. 'Because he's not only pushy and thick-skinned, he has an over-inflated sense of his own importance.'

'I'm only surprised your relationship lasted so long, then,' said Lex, drily.

'He's changed a lot over the years – people do,' I said, meeting his eyes directly.

Lex gave me another of his knitted frowns: this one was so complex it was practically Fair Isle. 'Why didn't you just make a clean break, then?'

'I tried to, but he's so persistent, it was easier said than done.'

'Never mind, dear, you can retire to your little tower above your bedroom and unloose the slings and arrows of outrageous prose at him from there, if you want to,' suggested Clara. 'But if you ever decide you want to marry a poet, I'd hold out for a good one.'

'I think you're both as mad as each other,' Lex said, but an unwilling smile tugged at the corners of his lips.

Clara

I went off to Oxford, where both my parents had studied, though my poor mother had been considerably hampered by the restrictions that were then imposed on every aspect of a female student's life.

Even by the time of my arrival in 1959, there were still many rules and regulations we were supposed to obey, but largely ignored, or found ways around.

I settled gratefully into the studious atmosphere of Lady Margaret Hall, for many of my fellow-students were working towards an eventual career, often in teaching of some kind. My interests, however, lay in epigraphy, archaeology and ancient languages, and I had no desire to teach anyone anything.

Instead I intended to seize every opportunity that came my way to increase my knowledge, further my interests and gain experience in my chosen field.

No lingering elements of misogyny were going to deflect me: I set my course and any minor idiocies of that kind scattered before me like the lesser vessels they were.

Of course, it was fun to explore my new surroundings and meet the other students at Lady Margaret Hall, though one of them, a half-American girl called Nessa Cassidy, was to my dismay inclined to have what we used to term at school a 'pash' on me. Although she was by no means stupid – English literature being her forte, especially the Romantic Poets – she was also giggly, girly and with a head full of silly ideas about romantic love.

I firmly discouraged her and to my relief she quickly gathered a small circle of like-minded friends around her, though there was no shaking her off entirely . . .

Nessa was an orphan and, as she freely told everybody, an heiress, with American trustees who doled out the generous allowance with which she bought arty and expensive clothes and treated her circle to cream teas and the like. Since she was small in stature and already plumply curvaceous, I thought too much of this would soon render her quite spherical.

She was generally considered very pretty, having a short upper lip, a thick, creamy skin, fine white-gold hair and eyes of an unusual light greenish-blue.

I had forgotten most of these details until recently, when something brought them back to mind . . .

But more of that later, for I must tell you about something wonderful that happened in my second week at Oxford: I came face to face with Henry Doome in Cornmarket Street!

I'd have known him anywhere. He was a taller, wirier version of the boy I'd last seen in Starstone, with his handsome, bony face, straight Grecian nose and bright, cornflower-blue eyes. The wind was whipping his flaxen hair about and he looked as if he'd dressed in the first garments that came to hand that morning.

I don't expect I'd changed much either: the same tangle of dark curls and over-generous aquiline nose.

'Clara, there you are,' he said, as if he'd expected to meet me that morning. 'Still poring over the runes?'

'I've moved on to hieroglyphs and cuneiform, Henry,' I replied. 'Are you still scribbling the odd ode?'

We grinned at each other and then embraced warmly, though such public demonstrations of affection between undergraduates were discouraged.

And from that moment, the years that had parted us ceased to exist and our lives joined up again quite seamlessly.

We were in separate colleges, of course – they were not co-ed then – and our studies mainly pursued different courses, with some overlapping, like Ancient Greek. But we became as inseparable as was possible under the circumstances.

How wonderful it was to have a friend with whom I could talk on an equal intellectual footing and without constantly having to explain myself – just as it had been when we were children. But we were also soulmates, who could laugh together and share dreams of the future. I had no doubt that Henry would one day be a renowned poet, for his work was already then beginning to be published. For his part, he was absolutely certain that I would rise to be an eminent epigrapher.

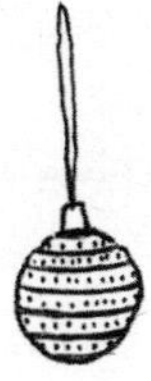

17

Eaten Up

Soon after tea, Lex announced that he would have to go back to the pottery, but Clara and Henry wanted him to stay for a proper Sunday dinner of nut loaf, with roast potatoes, onion gravy and all the trimmings.

'I hate you missing out on a good feed,' said Tottie, as if she'd just filled a nosebag with oats for him.

He certainly didn't look malnourished to me. His tall, broad-shouldered frame had filled out with what I suspected was solid muscle in the years since I'd last seen him. Probably due to pummelling the hell out of giant lumps of clay and carting huge pots about.

'We usually have dinner at about one on Sundays, instead of in the evening,' Clara explained to me. 'Then have Welsh rarebit or something simple later. But with the tree and everything, today's different.'

'I'm sorry I'll miss dinner too, Clara,' Lex said, 'but I promised Al I'd be back to help unload the kiln tonight. We've got a big order of urns heading off to a stately home tomorrow – a Christmas present from the owner to his wife.' He grinned suddenly and added, 'He asked me if we did gift-wrapping, but I think he was joking.'

'If he's not, I hope he has a couple of strong men to help him do it,' said Henry.

'He particularly wanted them to arrive tomorrow, because his wife's away and he can hide them in an outbuilding.'

'Let's hope they're what she really wanted for Christmas, then,' said Clara. 'I know it's what I want – another lovely giant pot for the garden.'

'Just as well, since that's what I always give you and Henry,' he said. When his face relaxed into amusement, he suddenly looked so much like the younger Lex I'd tumbled headlong in love with at first sight, so very long ago . . . First love, not the lasting kind.

Mind you, my second love didn't prove all that durable, either.

'I think I told you that Lex makes the most amazing huge antique-style pots and urns, didn't I?' Clara asked me. 'At least, their *shapes* are like antique ones, but when you look closely at the decoration and mouldings, you realize they're very contemporary.'

'The ones encrusted with barnacles or coral do look like antique ones, dredged up from the seabed,' said Henry. 'We must take you down to Terrapotter one day, Meg. I'm sure you'll be interested.'

I really was and would have loved to have visited Terrapotter . . . provided Lex and Al were not there, not to mention Lisa's younger sister, though she at least would have no idea who I was.

As if he'd read my mind, Lex said insincerely, 'Yes, why don't you come, Meg? Al and I would love to show you round.'

'That sounds so irresistible,' I said. *Not.*

I got up. 'Well, I'm going to take Clara's portrait into the studio and look at it for a bit, so I'll say goodbye now, Lex.'

Since I half-suspected he'd invented the reason for his early return to the studio in order to remove himself from my vicinity, I hoped perhaps our next and final meeting might be on the night of the Solstice, when I'd have the comforting presence of River to fortify me.

But I wasn't to escape another encounter before Lex left, because Teddy literally dragged him in to see Clara's portrait first.

'You don't mind, do you, Meg?' Teddy asked me anxiously, and I couldn't very well say 'Yes, I do!' because Lex was already inside the door, held fast by a small, relentless hand.

'Teddy insisted I—' began Lex, then broke off abruptly as his eyes fell on the painting, which I'd propped on the old easel. There was a long, still silence, like the aftermath of an avalanche.

The portrait had quickly sprung into shape and already Clara's face was leaping from the bones of the drawing, swirling into three dimensions with every slash and squiggle of paint. It seemed to be internally illuminated by the bright light of her intellect and character, rather than externally, from the screen of the computer.

'It's good, isn't it?' I said humbly, for a force outside myself makes that connection between my eyes and hands when I'm painting and I, Meg Harkness, am only the instrument it uses.

'It's not good at all – it's better than that,' he said at last. 'In fact, if you don't mess it up at the end with overpainting, it'll be bloody brilliant!'

He managed to drag his eyes away and looked at me in a new way . . . or rather, in a way familiar to me before he started imagining I'd turned into some kind of Mata Hari and tempted him with the apple of infidelity when he was having a weak moment.

It was the look not only of recognition, but of the respect that one artist of equal stature gives to another.

'I *always* know when to stop,' I said, and the expression in his agate-green eyes transitioned back to unfathomable again. Turning on his heel, he strode off without another word.

He's very good at that. If I tried it, I'd probably fall over my feet, or get my scarf trapped in the door, or something.

Teddy, wearing the expression of one whose protégée had proved her worth, called breezily, 'See you later, Meg!' and rushed off after his idol to say goodbye.

He left the door ajar and Lass wandered in, wrinkling her nose against the mingled aromas of linseed oil and turpentine, which she evidently didn't find as delicious as I did.

I remembered where there were a couple of biscuits, which had arrived with morning coffee the other day, and offered them to her.

She took them gently, one at a time, and ate them with appreciation. I expect she was hungry, for Den's voice suddenly called her.

'Lass? Din-dins!'

She paused only long enough to give my hand a hasty lick of gratitude and then left as precipitately as Lex had.

The kitchen door slammed a moment later and silence descended.

While I *knew* everyone was still in the house (apart from Lex), and busy as bees in their own little hive cells, I suddenly felt myself alone in it, shrunk to the size of a minute and oddly dressed porcelain doll in a gigantic Victorian doll's house.

I relived again that moment when Lex had looked at me as one artist does to another, recognizing an equal, for his work had been brilliant at college and he'd been set for success until he dropped out before the second year of his MA.

I was glad I'd shaken him into realizing I wasn't just some two-dimensional shadow-demon from the past, even if not shaken enough, perhaps, to make him open to the idea of listening to my version of events, otherwise known as The Truth.

But part of me was now sorry if my arrival had taken him back to a time of his life that was clearly still as painful to remember as ever, even if he'd got my small part in the tragedy completely wrong.

My reverie was finally broken by the door swinging wide open again with a creak, as if an invisible hand had pushed it, for there was no one there. Then the small wooden clock that sat on one of the bookshelves, and had been entirely silent until this point, suddenly began to tick loudly.

Weird.

I closed the door and was soon lost in the portrait again. It might be the best thing I'd *ever* painted . . .

I only emerged from the studio when I was summoned to dinner. The clock was still ticking, though the time was set for a parallel universe. Maybe it was the one Lex and Al lived in.

I wondered if I could face yet more food, but despite dinner being earlier because of Teddy having school tomorrow, my mouth watered when the fragrantly savoury nut loaf, roast potatoes, bright medley of home-grown winter vegetables and jug of onion gravy were carried in.

The starter had been melon balls, piled into old-fashioned shallow glass sundae dishes and topped with a swirl of raspberry sauce.

Teddy's enquiry, 'Aunt Clara, do melons have b—' had been firmly quashed by Tottie before he could properly get going.

We were all tired and the conversation desultory. Tottie's description of how she clamped her carrots in sand over the winter and put polythene tunnels over the winter cabbage nearly sent me to sleep.

Henry asked me if I'd enjoyed decorating the tree and I assured him, with complete honesty, that I had adored it.

He and Teddy seemed to have entered into a Christmas conspiracy to wring the last drop of relish from every festive aspect, from the Advent calendar that hung in the kitchen, with all the doors popped open to today's date, to release the chocolate Nativity figures within (though eating them seemed sort of sacrilegious), to the day they would put up fresh holly and ivy, and fake mistletoe.

'But *good* fake,' said Clara. 'The real berries are so poisonous, we're all afraid they'll fall down and that silly dog will eat them.'

'One year she ate a whole bowl of peanuts roasted in their shells, but luckily she threw them all up again in the garden hall,' Tottie said.

'Doubly lucky, because it's got a tiled floor so you can clean it easily,' pointed out Clara.

'Yer mean *I* could clean it easily,' said Den. He still had his blue and white striped pinny on, though he'd joined us for dinner. The rolled-up sleeves of his denim chambray shirt showed more tattoos on his wiry arms: one the dangling tail of what I thought must be a mermaid, because otherwise it would have to be a fish, and why would anyone have a fish tattooed on their arm?

'You know I'd have cleaned it up if you hadn't found it first,' protested Tottie.

'Any of us would; we're not squeamish,' agreed Clara. 'You soon get over that kind of thing when you've worked on digs in remote parts of the Far East, with no mod cons except hot and cold running fleas, don't you, Henry?'

'Very true, though at least here at dinner nobody offers you a plate with a delicious sheep's eyeball on it.'

''Ere's looking at you, kid,' drawled Den in a passable Bogart voice, and we all laughed, including Teddy, who can't have had any idea whose voice it was.

I helped clear the plates and carry in the dessert, starting to feel as if I'd lived there for months, rather than a matter of a few days.

'How is the autobiography coming along, my dear?' asked Henry, after chasing the last delicious bit of apple strudel round his plate and then laying down the spoon with a satisfied sigh. 'Did you catch up a little while we were out walking this morning?'

'Oh, yes, I managed to skim through the boring years at boarding school and the holidays in Devon, and I've just got to the bit where I've been accepted by Lady Margaret Hall a year early.'

'Only to find *I'd* been accepted by my college almost *two* years early, so we were starting there together,' said Henry.

'Well, we always were both smarter than most of our peers,' said Clara without false modesty. 'That's probably what drew us together when we were growing up in Starstone.'

'Clara and I just literally bumped into each other in our first week at Oxford and it was as though we'd never been apart,' Henry said reminiscently.

They beamed lovingly at each other and I envied their long and happy marriage, which wasn't something that seemed on the cards for me.

'You may have to jog my memory for the Oxford years, Henry. Most of it's a bit of a blur: classes and picnics, lectures, talks, tennis, cycling round the countryside . . . swimming in the river . . .'

'Wasn't Oxford still trying to segregate women from the men back then?' I asked.

'There were still a few archaic rules and regulations, but it was 1959 when I went up and they'd never quite managed to put women back in what they thought was their place after the war. We just quietly did what we wanted to do, without making a song and dance about it.'

I could certainly imagine Clara doing whatever she wanted to do!

She explained to me that she and Henry had been so bright as small children that her father, a great scholar, had given them extra lessons in Latin, Greek, Ancient History and Egyptology, while her mother, a gifted linguist, had taught them French, Italian and German.

'Of course, we didn't realize then that we were quite bright. We just thought the other children we knew – especially my brother, George – were a bit dim,' said Henry.

'George *was* dim,' said Clara. 'Big, bluff, self-centred, handsome and entirely stupid.'

'Not *entirely*, Clara!' Henry said mildly, then turned to me and explained: 'George followed family tradition and went to Sandhurst for army officer training. He sold out not long after he married.'

'He liked the idea of being an officer in uniform, but he really fancied himself as some kind of playboy,' said Clara critically. 'Whenever he could get leave he usually went up to London, but during our first term at Oxford he came to visit Henry.'

Something about that particular memory made her shake her head and sigh. 'It would have been better if he hadn't.'

Henry said, 'He was always trouble, because women fell for him like ninepins and he never treated them well.'

'Only the idiotic ones,' said Clara crisply. 'Hmm, it's amazing what you push to the back of your memory over the years, isn't it? The next part of my memoirs will certainly have to be edited out if I ever decide to publish it.'

She and Henry exchanged glances that I couldn't quite fathom, a shared moment from the past, I assumed.

'Shining a light into dark corners of your life is all part of writing a good memoir,' he told her.

'That's poetic, that is,' said Den.

Teddy seemed to be fighting sleep, his eyes closing and then jerking open again. Any minute now Tottie would notice and whisk him off to bed.

'You know, I always felt a little guilty that I inherited the part of my mother's money that was secured to her when she married,' said Henry. 'I know she did that because George, as the elder son, would have Underhill, and she thought it would make it all fair. But my investments all flourished and I ended up a lot better off than he did.'

'He'd have been fine if he'd lived within his means, but once you start spending your capital it's a slippery slope,' Clara said. 'And that dreadful old crony of his, Piers Marten, just encouraged him. They were always off to Monte Carlo or the Riviera, and even when they were home they spent most of their time at racecourses.'

'You're right, my dear,' Henry agreed.

'I had a rich and generous aunt,' Clara told me. 'She left all her money divided between myself and my sister, Bridget. That's how we managed to buy the Red House and come back to Starstone Edge.'

'And it's all worked out wonderfully well,' said Tottie. 'Happily ever after!' She rose. 'Come on, Teddy, before you fall asleep in your chair. Time to go to bed.'

His protests were half-hearted and he was borne away with the promise that Henry would come up and read to him when he was in bed.

Henry and Clara were still reminiscing about their Oxford student days when we went through to the drawing room and I became increasingly aware that there was some event, or mystery, in their shared past that they were not talking about, an elephant tiptoeing round the room.

Or maybe even round the house? Perhaps that was what had jarred open the studio door and set the old clock ticking?

I told Henry that I'd like to make a start on his portrait as soon as possible, or some initial sketches, at least.

'I'd like you to pose in the studio – if you don't mind – on the dais and with Lass sitting at your feet.'

'Or, more likely, *on* my feet. She does have a way of pinning one down.'

'My portrait seems to have taken shape so rapidly,' said Clara, when Henry had gone up to read another instalment of *The Water Babies* to Teddy, and Tottie had brought in fresh coffee. Den was right: she did make it very badly.

'Your face only needs one more session at most and then a little more work on the hands,' I agreed. 'It's just background and final touches after that.'

'Well, you did tell me you were a quick worker. I just hadn't realized it was *this* fast!'

'It's all a matter of style. If I was painting a traditional oil portrait, I'd be building it up slowly in layers over time, but my technique is more impressionistic. That's why I told you I could probably complete both portraits by the time of the Solstice.'

'I expect you could, but you might as well take your time over the finishing process and then I hope you'll relax and enjoy Christmas with us. There's no real need for you to rush off, is there?'

Little did she know!

Then she startled me by saying thoughtfully, 'I thought you and Lex were old friends, but you don't seem to have much to say to each other – though, of course, he *is* very quiet and intense.'

The last part was probably due to his being eaten up by guilt, but it was just as well she hadn't heard what we were talking about among the Norwegian pines!

'Since he was in the year above me in college, we didn't know each other very well,' I told her, which certainly seemed to have been true. 'I did sit for Lisa for a clay portrait head, though – she was good at those. And so kind and sweet and funny, as well as being beautiful.'

She'd seemed to have it all. What happened had been so cruel.

I'd sat for her in my first term, when I was still at the stage of infatuation where I blushed every time I saw Lex. I'm sure she noticed; it just didn't bother her, and why should it? He wasn't likely to look at anyone else when he had Lisa, and anyway, mine was a humble first love, adoring from afar. I'd got over it long before I met Rollo.

'Yes, Lisa was a lovely and very talented young woman,' agreed Clara. 'It was a complete tragedy for both of them, though since they were only in their early twenties when they married, I do sometimes wonder how things would have worked out in the long term.'

'I think my sudden arrival brought all the memories back again,' I said. 'I do feel a bit guilty about that.'

'But you couldn't help that, my dear. Don't forget, he sees Alan and Lisa's sister, Tara, almost every day, so it's not as if there isn't a constant reminder already.'

No, I thought, but I'd dredged up a different bit of memory and a muddy extra layer of guilt.

Since I couldn't keep my eyelids open any longer I went off early to bed, feeling that climbing the stairs was a bit like scaling the Matterhorn and wishing I could climb on the back of the big wooden eagle and be carried up there in a swish of wings.

18

Raking the Embers

I was still furious with Rollo, so on Monday morning I rang him up from the studio.

'It's me,' I said abruptly when he answered.

'*Darling!*' he began fulsomely in his most mellifluous voice.

'Don't you darling me after ringing here and trying to give Clara the idea that we're in a relationship, just so you could wangle your way in and interview Henry!' I snapped. '*And* you interrupted Clara when she was working.'

'But I had to do something, because *you* didn't seem to want to prepare the ground for me at all.'

'No, I bloody well didn't want to prepare the ground! And how the hell did you get the phone number for this house?'

'You can get any phone number these days,' he said ambiguously. 'You never replied to any of my messages, so there was nothing else for it. I mean, this interview with Henry Doome is *important*, Meg.'

'Only to you – and in your dreams! There's no way I'm letting you use me to get your foot through the door.'

'Oh, come on, Meg,' he wheedled. 'A real friend would already have smoothed the way, ready for when I turned up.'

'A real friend wouldn't have suggested it in the first place. You *use* people, Rollo, and I've had enough.'

The message didn't seem to get through, because he said, 'Did you tell this Clara that we *weren't* in a relationship?'

'Clara Mayhem Doome, Henry's wife. And yes, I did, but she'd guessed what you were after, anyway.'

'I expect I can still work that angle; she'll just think we've had a lovers' tiff,' he suggested.

I was about to put him right about that in no uncertain terms when he added, curiously, 'What's Henry Doome like? He's supposed to be a total recluse.'

Something came over me.

'He shuts himself in his study from morning till night and rarely speaks to anyone except family.'

'I thought you were going to paint his portrait?'

'I am, but I've had to take a vow of silence while I'm working, never turn my back on him and only wear the colour green.'

There was a pause. Then he said uncertainly, 'Are you making that up?'

'Of course not. He's a *little* eccentric. I mean, he won't talk to *anyone* unless they're wearing green, so it was a wonderful stroke of luck that I'd dyed my hair dark emerald before I came here.'

'Why green?'

'Oh, I was bored with it and wanted a change.'

'No, I meant why is *Henry Doome* so fixated on that colour?'

'I think it must be because of the Green Man,' I improvised quickly.

'Which green man?'

'You know, *the* Green Man, the ones from old folklore that you see on cathedral doorknockers with leaves sprouting out of their mouths. Symbolic of growth and rebirth and spring and stuff, I expect.'

Rollo abandoned the topic and said confidingly, 'The thing is, Meg, I mentioned to my American publisher that I might be able to get a brief foreword from Henry Doome for my new anthology and they're *very* keen on the idea.'

'More fool you, then, for counting your chickens before they're hatched.'

He ignored that. 'And if we could get Henry to give me a brief interview for the magazine as well, it would hugely boost our subscriptions.'

'What, into triple figures?'

'Ha, ha,' he laughed coldly. 'You've never really appreciated the importance of *Strimp!* in showcasing rising young poets, have you?'

'It mostly seems to showcase you and Nigel, and you're both the wrong side of forty.'

Risen and then sunk, like a pair of sad sponge cakes.

'I'm not forty!' he declared indignantly. 'We're the same age, Meg.'

'Rollo, you're a good four years older than me. Don't forget I met you in my second year of my Fine Art degree and you'd already finished your MA in creative writing by then.'

He didn't dignify this with a reply, but instead tried the honeyed voice again. 'Pleeease, Meggie, try and persuade Henry to see me.'

I held the phone away for a moment and stared at it as if it had verbally assaulted me. Then I put it back to my ear and snapped, 'No! And nobody *ever* calls me Meggie.'

'You're being very selfish and unreasonable about all this. I'm surprised at you and deeply hurt.'

'Me? *I'm* being selfish and unreasonable?'

'Look, darling, I'll be up in York in a few days, taking part in a big poetry-reading event, so I can easily drive over to see you after that, on my way back.'

'You can easily get stuffed, Rollo! And Starstone Edge is a remote moorland village, so no one's going to believe you were just passing by, unless you're wearing a drover's coat and driving a flock of sheep.'

'I'm sure they'd believe I'd detour just to see you, Meg. I'll take you out for lunch and then, when we go back, they're bound to invite me in and then I can—'

'I think you've missed your true métier and should be writing fairy stories instead of poetry, Rollo,' I interrupted. 'I'm here on a professional engagement, not to be your Trojan Horse.'

'Mare,' he said. Or maybe that was 'meh', as in an expression of disgust at my lack of cooperation.

'Well, Rollo, fascinating as it's been chasing our tails round in a small conversational circle, I'll have to go.'

'But, Meg, I really would like—'

'It's more than time you grasped that I don't care what you would really like any more, Rollo. That all ended six years ago, remember? I should have insisted on a clean break then.'

'I suppose you still blame me for the accident and losing the baby and now you've found the perfect way to pay me back,' he said, with a vicious spitefulness I hadn't thought him capable of.

'If you think that, then you never really knew me at all. I always blamed myself more than you. I shouldn't have told you the news while you were driving, though I didn't expect it to be such a shock you'd go right off the road. And I saw the horror on your face and realized later in hospital that you'd only *thought* you wanted to settle down and start a family, but when it came to the reality, you'd run a mile. Right back to Mummy, in fact.'

He began to bluster, but I cut him short. 'There's no point in going over it all again, or looking back – and there's certainly no place for you in my future. I'd already decided when I left London that we needed to make a clean break and I didn't want to see or hear from you again. So this it: the parting of the ways. Have a good Christmas with Mummy, Rollo. In fact, have a good life. Only don't bother telling me about it.'

I switched off the phone while it was still making bleating noises. I felt a sense of catharsis and of having cut something toxic out of my life, but my hands were trembling slightly. I'd known all his faults: vanity, selfishness, infidelity, yet I'd thought he'd been as fond of me as he could be of anyone. Now, though, I could see he was just like one of those wonderfully beautiful (if slightly overblown) parasitic orchids. I hoped I'd snipped his aerial roots and he'd wither off out of my life.

It was only then that I realized the door was wide open. It must have been off the latch and Lass had nudged her way in, because she was sitting looking pointedly at the drawer where the biscuits had come from.

'No luck, Lass – they're all gone,' I told her. She sighed heavily and followed me out of the room, but turned off towards the likelier pickings of the kitchen, rather than to Clara's study.

Clara was leaning back in her chair, long legs crossed and eyes shut in deep thought, tossing the stone paperweight from one hand to the other, but she opened her eyes when she heard me close the door.

'Was that you shouting a few moments ago, dear?'

'I suppose it must have been, though I hadn't realized I was doing it. I rang Rollo, to tell him exactly what I thought about his attempt to use me to get to Henry.'

'I expect you feel a lot better for it. There's nothing like clearing the air.'

'You're right, I do! And I hope he's finally got the message that I never want to hear from him again.'

'You sounded pretty definite from here,' she assured me, with a Cheshire Cat grin that exposed all her teeth.

I'd brought the canvas with me and now I set the portrait on my easel and she got up and came to look at it.

'It's taken so short a time – and yet, there it is, the distilled essence of Clara Mayhem Doome!'

'I'm glad you like it. I just want to do a little more work on your hands, if you wouldn't mind keeping them still, while holding the stone paperweight?'

I went to get my paints and when I returned she obligingly did so. While I worked, I found myself telling her a bit more about Rollo and how we'd met at a student party. 'He was very handsome . . . like a cross between Byron and Dylan Thomas.'

'Difficult to imagine,' Clara said. 'I can see Byron was handsome, and must have been magnetically attractive to a certain kind of woman, but I've always thought he was a complete tosser.'

I had to agree with her on that one.

'When I first knew him, Rollo could be quite sweet and very charming . . . and also unfaithful, as it turned out. I gave him a second chance, and then a third, after he'd had a health scare and it had made him want to settle down and start a family.'

I sighed. 'He even talked his mother round. He'd always been afraid of crossing her because she was very well off and paid for his flat and car, but she'd never liked me.'

'I find that hard to believe.' Clara sounded genuinely and flatteringly astonished.

'Oh, she wouldn't have found any girl good enough for her darling boy, but my strange upbringing and my mother having been adopted were major flaws. She seemed to think not knowing who your real grandparents were was a big deal when it came to having children. All those unknown genes waiting to pop up.'

'An odd way of looking at it,' Clara said, turning her bright gaze on me. 'So your mother was adopted?'

'Yes, as a newborn baby. But it didn't work out well and she ran off when she was a teenager – then ended up at River's Farm.'

'Interesting,' she murmured, and then fell silent while I added a few final touches to the background and fell back to take a searching look at the portrait.

'I think it's time to stop. It's finished.'

'Then let's call everyone in to see it!' she said, jumping up and clapping her hands. 'How exciting! And I can hardly wait to see what you'll do with Henry!'

I was looking forward to that, too, but before then I'd have to find an art shop: I'd come away from home in such a rush that I'd left behind my big spare tube of flake white. And my putty rubber, which should have had a slightly stretchy and squidgy consistency, had gone hard and crumbly.

Where Rollo was concerned, the new me was also hard, but definitely not crumbly.

Over lunch it transpired that there was a good art and craft shop in Great Mumming, and when Henry heard that I intended driving there that afternoon he offered to take me himself.

'I'll go to the wine merchants and get a couple of spare bottles of whisky and sherry.'

'If you're going into Great Mumming, then you can bring Teddy up from school afterwards,' Clara suggested.

'But I could easily go in the camper van myself, and I can pick up Teddy too, if you like?' I offered.

'It's no bother at all; the Jag needs a run out,' said Henry. 'I'll just take Lass for her walk and then we'll set off.'

Den, who had been standing at the work surface water-icing some kind of sponge cake while whistling quietly between his teeth, now turned and said he'd go with us and do the driving.

'Tottie's got a feeling we'll be snowed in fer Christmas, so she wants to cram the freezer and larder full to bursting, like a bleeding squirrel.'

'Who's a bleeding squirrel?' asked Tottie, coming in at that moment with a long string of onions in one slightly grime-encrusted hand.

'You are,' said Den. 'Gimme a list of what yer want from Great Mumming, and I'll see what I can do.'

Henry and Den bickered about who was to drive the car, but Den won and, having finished his icing, put a huge glass dome over his cake and took it out to the larder.

'Den does so love driving the Jag and I don't get it out of the garage so much in winter,' Henry whispered to me.

Tottie had hung the onions up from a hook on a metal rack high over the table, from which already depended a smaller string of garlic and bunches of dried herbs.

'That looked like one of Den's marmalade cakes with lemon icing,' she said, appreciatively. 'Did you lot leave me any soup?'

Clara vanished back into her study after lunch and Henry went off with Lass. Tottie offered to show me the conservatory and I fetched my iPad and sketchbook from the studio and met her there.

A warm, damp and deliciously earthy smell enveloped me as I followed Tottie along the paths that led through the rampant foliage, though after meandering to and fro for a while, I realized that they all met in the middle, under a sort of cupola, where there was a paved area with wicker basket chairs and a low table.

'Henry and Clara like to sit in here occasionally. They love the heat, though of course I keep the air moist, too, because most of my plants are from the tropics.'

She'd proudly displayed her exotic, carefully nurtured charges: pineapples, bananas, lichees, kumquats, lemons and small oranges, among other things, *and* a coconut palm in the biggest pot I'd ever seen. The only thing I felt it lacked was a couple of chattering monkeys and some gaudy parrots.

'Please don't show this to River when he visits, because it'll give him ideas!' I begged her. 'I don't think the solar power is enough to heat something this size as well as everything else.'

'It does cost a lot to heat, Henry says,' she admitted. 'I couldn't afford it when I was here on my own, but Clara and Henry wanted to restore the whole house to its former glory and we had lots of fun planning what we'd have in here.'

'I can imagine – like making your own little corner of Paradise! River would so love it. He does manage to grow peaches and nectarines under glass, and keeps trying grapevines, though Oshan thinks we're too high up for it to be worth it.'

'Oh, I don't know, he might manage it with the right vine. Come and look at mine.'

She set off down a small path I didn't think we'd taken before and stopped under a leafy canopy.

'Table grapes – we get loads of the black ones, but the green are less prolific in the fruiting. They can also sometimes be a little sharp and acidic.'

I felt an immediate affinity with the sharp and acidic green grapes: my sweetness had all been crushed out by recent events.

I'd taken lots of photos as we went round and now I asked Tottie if she wouldn't mind posing for one, and perhaps I could do a quick sketch?

'It'll only take ten minutes max,' I said persuasively, but she was looking flattered and agreed instantly. I pulled up a wicker chair and had her stand in front of one of the pineapples that grew in a raised bed, reaching up as if to pick an almost-ripe fruit, though from the angle I was at, the pineapple appeared to be resting on her head, with the curved, serrated spikes of the foliage forming a green crown around it.

When I showed her the iPad, she said she looked like Carmen Miranda and I should go for it, so I drew her like that . . . and perhaps, if I had time, I'd ask her if I could paint her too . . .

19

Snakes and Ladders

I googled Carmen Miranda when I was back in the studio and found lots of pictures and old film clips of an exotic-looking lady, sometimes wearing nothing much except a lot of fruit on her head. I was tempted to add a pair of cherry earrings and a banana or two to Tottie's ensemble. And it would be lovely if she was holding something like a basket . . . or a cornucopia overflowing with produce.

Rollo had left a couple of messages on my phone, which I deleted unread: I'd just keep deleting him out of my life until he gave up.

I'd missed a call from Oshan, though, so I rang him back.

'Pop's wondering what to bring his hosts as a thank you, for inviting him to stay for the Solstice,' he said.

Oshan was the only person who didn't call River by his name, but by the irreverent Pop, which he'd done since he was a small boy and a visiting American had asked him where his pop was. We'd both thought this was hilariously funny at the time.

I thought about what River might bring. 'Not anything fruit or vegetable, because Tottie – one of the household – is an ace gardener and she's got all that sewn up. In fact, she's just been showing me round the conservatory, which is huge and heated and full of things like bananas and pineapples!'

'I hope to God it doesn't give Pop ideas!' he said. 'The solar power isn't going to stretch to it.'

'That's exactly what I thought. We'll just have to hope for the best.'

'Back to the question of the gift: he wondered about some of his medicinal mead.'

'Tottie also keeps bees and makes mead too. Don't tell River, but I think hers is much more delicious, like golden nectar.'

'Maybe I'd better head him off the mead idea too, then.'

I ran my mind over the various things the craftworkers made in the barn, or sold in the shop.

'One of those big Cellophane bags of crisp gingerbread stars, pierced for hanging on the Christmas tree, that Maj sells in the café would go down well,' I suggested. 'They're big on Christmas here and there's the most enormous tree in the hall.'

'OK, and she's selling a sort of super Dundee-style cake this year, too, with tons of glazed fruit all over the top.'

'Perfect. They seem to eat a lot of cake.'

'I'll tell Pop and then he can sort it out with Maj,' said Oshan. 'I think there might be one or two Yule gifts coming up with Pop, too, just in case you decide not to come back for the Feast.'

'I'd made my mind up I was *definitely* coming back but now, suddenly, I'm not so sure,' I said slowly, speaking more to myself than him as I realized my feelings had undergone a change. 'It's starting to feel as if I'd be running away . . . And besides, not only am I painting *really* well here, but I think I've been struck by Christmas madness and I want to experience the whole thing.'

He didn't ask me what I'd be running away from: but that's Oshan. If I wanted to tell him, then I would.

'You can make up your mind when Pop gets there, can't you?' he suggested easily.

'True, and since Starstone Edge is often cut off by snow at this time of year, it may not be in my hands whether I leave or not. Or in River's, come to that, if he makes it in the first place!'

'Oh, I expect he will. I mean, we're used to bad weather up here, so he'll have the snow chains with him and a shovel and everything.'

'He might well need them, because he'll have to take a single-track road over the moors from the next valley to get here.'

'It sounds like you've strayed into *The Land That Time Forgot*,' Oshan said, amused. 'Are there any dinosaurs?'

'I have to admit, the valley does feel a bit like that.' I paused, then added, 'There's someone here who was at art college with me, though he was a year ahead so I didn't know him that well.'

'If you're snowed up together, you'll probably get to know him a lot better,' Oshan suggested.

'Or it might turn into one of those old cosy crime novels, where the characters are snowed up in an old house and there's a murder,' I said tartly. 'But there's someone else living in the village that we *both* know. Do you remember Moonflower?'

'What, that drippy girl with long brown hair who was here for a couple of years? Her parents lived in a converted horsebox?'

'Yes, that's her. She still looks much the same, but now she's married to a man who has a shop in the village and they have a baby. Round here they just call her Flower, though.'

'It really is a small world,' he commented, and then added, 'Here's Pop. I'll just tell him what you suggested as a present.'

I could hear a conversation in the background and then Oshan came back on. 'He says that sounds fine about the biscuits and the cake and he's gone to talk to Maj. He's bringing goat's cheese, too.'

To be honest, I've never been that keen on goat's milk, cheese or yoghurt, which always tastes to me profoundly of goat, though I do like the goats themselves.

'My robes for the Solstice ceremony are finished and Pop's bringing his with him to wear for the ceremony up there, even though he's only a spectator.'

'Good idea,' I approved. I didn't see why he should be done out of dressing up this year, when he enjoys it so much. Getting enrobed . . . which reminded me of being taken to a posh restaurant in London once, where the menu described the pudding as being 'enrobed in a rich chocolate ganache' and I was quite disappointed that it didn't arrive with an ermine train and a tiara, too.

Henry and Den bickered about which way to drive into town, before deciding to go down the pass and back the other way.

The vintage Jaguar was a gleaming dark red thing of polished beauty and descended the pass in a stately manner. Halfway down, an ancient Land Rover with three sheepdogs in the back squeezed past us with a roar. The driver even took one hand off the steering wheel to wave.

'Local farmer,' explained Henry. 'But even they don't go up and down here when it's really bad.'

'Told yer it would be OK today,' Den said, taking the last bend and emerging on to the wider, flatter road at the bottom.

We passed Gobelins and then were into the edge of the small market town where Den slowed, so I could take a look at the old smithy, now reborn as Terrapotter. There was a large green sign across one side of the long, low, ancient-looking brick building, though I didn't have time to register more than that there was a central arch in the building with windows over it. I suppose if it was an old smithy originally, they'd have had to have driven carts and carriages through into some kind of courtyard.

'We can stop on the way back, if we have time,' Henry suggested, though I sincerely hoped we wouldn't.

There was a small car park in the centre of the town near the slender engraved granite obelisk of a war memorial and a stone horse trough. The art shop was on the far side of the square, so we arranged to meet back at the car when we'd all done our shopping.

The art shop was surprisingly large, well-stocked, and had the good quality oil paints I preferred. Then I found a box of ready-cut mounts for pictures or photographs and thought I'd get several small ones. I could sketch the various inhabitants of the Red House – human or otherwise – and then they'd make nice presents to leave . . . or give, if I was still there. The jury was still out on that one, but the balance was teetering towards the Stay side.

Then I spotted a complete artist's box, the kind with pull-out winged trays, full of tubes of paint, oil pastels, pencils . . . everything a budding artist could possibly want. At a price, of course, but oh, how much Teddy would love it! I couldn't resist. They had rolls of gaily coloured Christmas wrapping paper at the till, too.

I'd spent a small fortune and I must have been in there ages, but I couldn't see any sign of the others having returned to the car, so I went into a nearby hairdresser that looked trendy and asked them about the hair colouring I fancied, a shade of pale ashy old-rose pink that I'd seen one or two women sporting lately. They actually had it in stock. It was a new line and, they assured me, entirely free of harmful chemicals, so though it probably wasn't as ecologically friendly as the green dye, at least it might last a little longer. They offered to remove the now pale snotty green tint from my hair and then dye it for me then and there, since they were not busy, but I told them I didn't have time.

And then, since it seemed to be render-yourself-penniless day, I wandered into the shop next door and tried on a long dress in squares of fine corduroy in muted jewel colours. It had a low-ish scoop neck that made the most of my fast-returning curves and it was cut like an old-fashioned riding dress: it fitted to below the waist, where there was a peplum frill, then fell, long and drapey, to my ankles. It was like a new take on the kind of old-hippy garments that Maj and some of the other Farm residents favoured. They'd probably mug me for it when they saw it.

The clothes on that rack were made locally in a nearby village, the shop assistant told me while folding the dress into tissue paper before inserting it into a bag with the name of the shop on it: East Island.

I was still pondering that one, when she added that the village was called Halfhidden and was the most haunted in Lancashire.

That sounded fun and I'd have been tempted to visit it, except that this was hardly the time of the year for sightseeing.

Heavily laden, happy but broke, I staggered out with my purchases and headed for the car before I found anything else to buy.

Den and Henry were loading shopping into the boot of the Jaguar.

'There you are, my dear – perfect timing,' Henry said. 'And I see you've had a successful shopping expedition!'

He and Den managed to wedge everything in, though a couple of bags had to go behind one of the seats. Not the one with the art box in, though, because I told them what that was and they hid it in the boot in case Teddy got curious on the way home and poked about among the bags.

'How kind of you!' Henry said. 'I think paints are on his Christmas list, too. He'll be so delighted.'

'We've just fetched the castle 'e wanted from the toyshop, 'aven't we?' Den said.

'I ordered it and Den's bought a family of plastic dragons to go with it.'

'Going to paint them up first,' Den said. 'Bit of silver on the scales.'

Henry pushed up his sleeve and consulted a battered old wristwatch. 'Oh good, we have time to call in at Terrapotter on the way to collect Teddy from school. Lex's bound to give us coffee and you'll be interested to see the pottery, I'm sure, Meg.'

I'd forgotten he'd mentioned that idea earlier, and I was so thrown that I almost said I was allergic to clay, but luckily remembered in time that this gambit hadn't worked with the Christmas trees.

'Isn't it getting a bit late?' I suggested instead. 'And I'm sure they must be way too busy for visitors right now.'

'We'll have about half an hour to spare and the school is only a minute or two away. Lex won't mind, because that stately home consignment has gone off and they've dispatched most of the stock ordered for Christmas ages ago. This is actually a quiet time for them.'

By now I'd squeezed myself into the back of the car between Teddy's child seat and the overflow packages and we were heading for the Thorstane road. I resigned myself to my fate.

Henry was still talking. 'Alan's wife, Tara, makes very interesting jewellery and sells it online, as well as through shops, so she tends to work till the last post goes. I mean the last posting of parcels before Christmas, of course, not the trumpet one.'

However, I was pretty sure *I* heard the trumpet version sounding as we turned through the archway that pierced the front of the mellow brick building and came to a halt in a stone-paved yard surrounded by a hotchpotch of outbuildings.

'Interesting old place, isn't it?' Henry said. 'The original smithy was that large building to the left. That's the pottery now, but there was an old brick kiln at the far end . . . and then some of the other buildings had people like stonemasons working in them at one time. It's had a varied life, but it was empty when we helped Lex to buy it.'

'A right dump, it was, and the cottage at the front falling down,' Den said.

'A slight exaggeration,' Henry said as we got out. He led the way through a small Judas door cut into the large one that filled the front of the old smithy. It was labelled 'Office', though when we got in, that seemed to mean an unoccupied cubbyhole to the left, with a desk and computer screen.

We were in a large room with the original cobbled floor and it was filled with the varied shapes of huge terracotta pots, mostly fastened to wooden pallets, ready for delivery. It reminded me of that terracotta army in China . . . but actually, once my eyes adjusted to the gloom, it was more like a strange version of Ali Baba's cave, except no one popped out of a pot.

A door to one side opened and Lex appeared, a mug in his hand. 'I thought I heard a car, Henry. Trust you to turn up when I've just made a pot of coffee!'

'I hope there's enough for three extra, because I've brought Meg to see the pottery, too,' Henry told him. I'd been hanging back till then, so I don't think Lex had spotted me.

One dark eyebrow went up. 'So I see – but you did say you'd bring her down here one day.' From his tone I inferred that he hadn't expected me to fall in with the plan, though.

'Well, there's plenty of coffee. This one's for Al – he's slip-casting in the back – but help yourselves while I take it through.'

We went into a small room with a stove, table, microwave and a big glass coffee pot on a hotplate.

Den said he'd be mother and pour, and then rootled around in an open tin of biscuits for one with chocolate, but I refused them when he offered them round. I thought they'd probably choke me. I wished I was somewhere – anywhere – else.

There was a small electric heater and I was just warming my hands when Lex returned and picked up his own mug. His dark green eyes regarded me over the rim thoughtfully. 'I suppose now you're here, I'd better give you the guided tour.'

'We haven't really got time,' I said quickly. 'We don't want to be late collecting Teddy.'

'Oh, there's plenty of time for a quick look,' he said, then to my surprise, added, 'I'd *like* to show you what we're doing.'

It occurred to me that there seemed to have been some kind of small but significant seismic change in Lex's attitude to me since I last saw him in the studio. Perhaps he really had been so shaken by Clara's portrait that he'd actually started seeing the real me again, the one he'd once known, rather than the alternative version he'd constructed over the years.

In fact, he now appeared quite *eager* to show me round, though Henry and Den elected to stay where they were, and after only a few minutes I'm certain Lex had entirely forgotten who I was, because his enthusiasm for what he was doing was so great.

He showed me the finished pots and described where he'd learned to make each individual shape. The only thing they had in common was that they were all terracotta and large, some of them *huge*.

'I learned most of my craft in Greece,' he said. 'It takes about twelve to fourteen years of practice before you're said to be an expert at throwing the biggest pots, so when I started up Terrapotter, I was really still officially a beginner.'

Many of the finished pots were decorated with impressed or raised designs, often very subtle: faces, sea creatures, swirls of seaweed, coral growths . . .

He'd taken something traditional and made it unique and his own, and I was deeply impressed.

'I do most of the designing and make the moulds for decoration,' he told me. 'Al helps me throw the pots. It's a two-man job for the biggest ones, because you throw them in two or three pieces and then put them together.'

'That sounds tricky,' I said as he led me through into another big area.

'It's the fun part!' He grinned, a hint of the old Lex back again. 'We have to buy the clay in. I mix three kinds together in a long process of washing and sieving out the grit and impurities, then put it through the pugmill a couple of times, before it's ready.'

There was a lot of machinery involved, though all quiet at the moment: I supposed production had stopped for Christmas. 'I can see you need such huge quantities that you couldn't wedge it by hand, like they do in college,' I agreed.

'The blend of clay had to be trial and error too, before I got one that was right – not too porous, so water doesn't freeze inside it and crack the pots in winter.'

I saw the big throwing wheels and then the racks of pots drying out in the chamber above the kiln, before they were fired.

The staircase up to that was fairly steep and I wondered how they got the pots up and down again, until I noticed a large old pulley-style hoist, like a sort of ancient dumb waiter.

'Heat rises, so when the kiln's firing its warm up here. There'll be one final firing before we stop for Christmas.'

'Can you leave all the clay and everything for a week or so?'

'Yes, if it's either in the tanks or wrapped in plastic to keep it damp,' he said. 'We're going to load the kiln later, which takes a while. Al designed a really clever system of hand-pressed interlocking smaller planters that fill in the lost space around the big pots,' he enthused. 'You can add them on in any direction, or stack them, and they're very popular in garden centres.'

Those did sound a clever idea, but I was sure Lex was the real original mind behind the business.

I liked the smell of damp sacking and clay. It took me back to art college where, apart from the scene with Al, I was mostly very happy.

'That's the kiln room through there,' Lex gestured. 'Tara has a small kiln of her own that fires very high, because she combines porcelain and silver in her jewellery. Her studio's next to the office.'

'Yes, Henry told me about her,' I said, and if she hadn't been Lisa's sister I'd have been interested to see what she made.

By this point I was perfectly certain that Lex had forgotten I was anything other than a fellow artist who would appreciate what he was doing. Now he told me how sometimes, if things were quiet, he did a few random ceramic sculptures just for fun and they sold well in a gallery up in Halfhidden.

'A painter runs it – he's really good – and he only stocks artwork that's first class. People come long distances to visit it and pay good prices.'

'It's strange you should mention Halfhidden because someone just told me about the village. It's haunted, isn't it?'

'They've certainly made a big thing of the haunted trail around it and built it into a tourist draw. There are teashops and this gallery, and an architectural salvage place, too – not to mention an ancient Roman bath in the woods and a pub nearby called the Screaming Skull!'

He grinned again and the years fell away. He'd always had that dark, attractive gypsy look about him, a touch of devil-may-care, and it hadn't completely been extinguished over time by the grief and guilt.

I found myself laughing. 'Now I really *will* have to go and look at this place, if the weather lets me before I go.'

That, unfortunately, seemed to recall him to the present and to who I was. His face sobered. 'Let's see what Al's doing. He's in here, but I warned him I'd be showing you round when I took his coffee in.'

'Let's *not*—' I began, but he'd opened the door by then and there was Al, glancing briefly up at me from the bench.

Then he went back to concentrating on carefully pouring slip into a cast, tapping it to release any air bubbles and setting it aside. Only then did he look at me directly and his expression wasn't any friendlier than it had been the last time I saw him.

He was tall – though not as tall as Lex – loose-limbed and with nondescript brown hair and hard grey eyes.

'Long time, no see, Al,' I said.

'When Lex told me you were staying up at the Red House I thought you'd at least keep clear of the pottery,' he said.

'Al, let's not go there,' Lex said wearily. 'Let it go: Meg's leaving in a few days, when she's finished the portraits, and it was Henry who insisted on stopping here today so she could have a quick look round.'

'The quicker the better,' Al said. Time did not seem to have taken the edge off his anger. I'd always suspected he was more than half in love with Lisa himself, which might have had something to do with it.

I was starting to feel angry all over again when a thin, red-haired girl came in, a dimmed and fuzzy version of Lisa, who must be Tara. It was evident from her expression as she looked at me that she knew about the past – or at least, the parallel reality version.

'So you're this Meg Harkness! Al's just told me all about you.'

'So you're Lisa's little sister,' I said, returning her inimical stare.

'Al, you really shouldn't have told—' began Lex angrily, but broke off as Henry suddenly appeared in the doorway behind Tara.

'Oh, there you all are! Meg, my dear, we'd better leave now, or we'll be late. You can come back again another time because I'm sure you're finding it all fascinating.'

'I'm as riveted as a nest of snakes by a mongoose,' I said, following him out, but I don't think he heard me.

Lex caught me up by the door and grabbed my arm, pulling me back. 'Meg, I hadn't realized Al had told Tara about that night. I'm sorry they—'

'Oh, get potted!' I snapped, and then, wrenching myself free, stepped through the Judas door into the darkening afternoon.

It's hard to brood – or even seethe – in the company of an over-excited eight-year-old, or among a lively group of people over tea, when they very naturally want to discuss their day.

When I finally slipped away, Teddy followed me into the studio, where he finished the picture he'd started of me with green hair. Luckily he'd painted the hair while it was still greener than its present ever-fainter tint. I, in turn, sketched him.

Dinner, and the ebb and flow of conversation over it, soothed the tensions away a little more, but anger was still bubbling somewhere beneath, like molten lava, and if I was ever alone again with Lex, Al and Tara, I was sure it would erupt dramatically and I'd put them all right in no uncertain terms.

Not that I thought they'd believe me, but the truth should out, I could see that now.

Tomorrow I'd start Henry's portrait. I knew I could complete enough of it to leave after the Solstice with River, but now, not only did I *not* want to, I'd become convinced that fleeing would seem like an admission of guilt and an act of cowardice.

Clara

The joy of our reunion in that first Michaelmas term was only slightly marred by an early visit from Henry's older brother, George, who was now an army officer and based somewhere within reach of Oxford.

Henry brought him to tea in my rooms, where we were permitted to entertain our male friends during the afternoons, because obviously nothing of an intimate nature could possibly take place until after the danger hour of seven in the evening.

George was now large, handsome, in a ruddy-faced, bold kind of way, and had the same cornflower-blue eyes and fair hair as Henry. He looked bored even while politely expressing pleasure at meeting me again.

Nessa must have caught sight of the arrival of this manly embodiment of her wildest romantic fantasies, for not five minutes later she intruded under some pretext. Of course, she and George immediately hit it off and began a heavily flirtatious conversation, so that there was no getting rid of her. Indeed, we became a foursome for the rest of his leave, and very tiresome it was, too.

I was glad to see the back of him, but Nessa was full of gushing enthusiasm, having cast George as the perfect, gentle knight of the legends and poems she so adored.

I warned her not to lose her heart to him because Henry had told me he'd had several affairs, despite having a fiancée of long standing.

Nessa assured me I was quite wrong about his character and that George had already told her about the engagement. 'It's just a family thing that he's trying to end without hurting this girl's feelings.'

This seemed unlikely, for Henry had also said that George's fiancée's main attraction was that she was an only child with wealthy, doting parents and he hoped that once they were married he could sell out of the army and embark on a life of idle pleasure, which seemed to be his only ambition.

I suspected that Nessa ignored my advice and was in contact with George, and perhaps had even met him since that first introduction . . . but if so, I hoped the attraction would quickly fizzle out.

'Though by now he probably knows she's an heiress, because she tells everyone. She even told you,' I said to Henry.

'Yes, but she's also told everyone that she won't gain control of her capital until she's thirty, so that's not going to tempt him to jilt his fiancée for her, is it?'

I hoped he was right. Nessa might end with a broken heart, but I'd warned her and could do no more.

My life had become so full of interest and pleasure that I soon forgot all about Nessa and George.

Henry and I had begun to plan for the Christmas vacation: he was to return home to the vicarage with me to reacquaint himself with my parents and then I would travel up to spend the

New Year at Underhill, the family home at Starstone Edge. It was the first time I would have returned there since I was eight, when the reservoir was built, and I viewed the prospect with mixed feelings. While I longed to go back to the place where I had been so happy, the village itself would be invisible beneath the water.

Henry's father was gregarious and I would be one of a house party that would include George's fiancée and her parents.

But before that, in November, something disquieting happened.

Nessa had obtained leave to go to London, ostensibly for the purpose of seeing her dentist, but really to stay with her godmother, Lady Leamington, and attend some grand Society party.

I was not much interested . . . until I glimpsed her, early on the morning of her departure, getting into a car with George.

I sincerely hoped that he was just driving her to London, but as Henry said later, there was nothing we could do about it anyway and perhaps she'd just wangled him an invite to this fabulous party too.

Nessa returned in an unusually quiet and subdued frame of mind and showed no inclination to confide in me, other than describing the grand party and the famous people she'd met. She didn't mention George directly at all, but instead threw out a few dark remarks about the animal instincts and earthiness of men, and how they had no romantic souls. This made me think George had perhaps made a heavy pass at her on the way to London and disillusion had set in.

Nessa turned to her studies with renewed interest and solaced herself with the company of her coterie. I'd already suspected that she preferred women to men and perhaps she now had some inkling of that herself . . .

She spent Christmas in London with Lady Leamington and on her return seemed to be forever dipping into a box of chocolates, or consuming cream cakes, so that she rapidly began to resemble the sugar plum rather than the fairy.

20

Resolution

Henry kindly gave me the first portrait sitting early next morning and I spent ages getting the light right, so that it shone on his bony, interesting face under the fine, silvery hair. It also had to shine on his book, for he was reading an old paperback Agatha Christie.

'Clara doesn't rate them – she says Agatha Christie's all plot and no character,' he said – 'but I can happily read them over and over again, even though I know what happens.'

'I'm reading Clara's first crime novel and really enjoying it,' I told him. 'She's a lot gorier than Agatha Christie.'

Lass, who had come in with Henry and, without any prompting, arranged herself over his feet like a black, grey and white rug, went straight to sleep.

'Perfect,' I said, stepping back. I took a photo on the iPad for reference, then decided to draw straight on to the canvas without any preparatory sketches, sweeping the soft black pencil over it until the bare bones of what I wanted to show filled the space. Then I stared at it for what must have been a long time, for Henry finally broke the silence.

'How is it coming along?' he asked. 'I didn't like to speak before, you looked so intensely absorbed.'

'The drawing's really come together quickly. If you don't mind, I'll just make a very quick pencil drawing of you in my sketchbook, too, then you can relax.'

This one wasn't anything to do with the portrait, but to go into one of the mounts I'd bought, as a present for Clara.

'I'm perfectly comfortable, if it won't take long, because I'd like to do a little more work before lunch.'

'Five minutes,' I assured him, flipping the sketchbook to a clean page and setting it on the easel, in place of the canvas, which I propped against the wall.

'I think your grandfather will be surprised at the speed at which you've worked, Meg. I'm looking forward to meeting him. He sounds such an interesting chap.'

'He is, and he's never stumped in any conversation, either, which I think is because he's so naturally curious about *everything*.'

'It must have been an unusual upbringing at the Farm. Clara told me about your mother having been adopted and not knowing who her birth parents were.'

'Yes, she was, though I can't say she ever seemed inquisitive about it. But she's always been someone who lives in the present, rather than looks back at the past,' I said. 'The adoption wasn't a success, so in the end she ran away and ended up at the Farm. And that's where I was born and stayed.'

'A surrogate family,' he suggested.

'The perfect one. I do *know* who my father is and I've met him – he lives in France now – but there was no real connection.'

I sighed, laying down my pencil.

'I do wish I knew what has happened to Mum. River feels strongly that she's still alive.'

'I'm sure you're right,' Henry said gently, then seeing I'd finished my sketch, bent to wake Lass. 'My feet are warm, but quite numb.'

When Henry had gone back to his study to work, the morning was well advanced and I thought I'd go and visit Flower.

The sky had that slightly ominous leaden tint and a fine, sleety rain was falling, but I decided to walk anyway. It was only about ten minutes away, hardly worth getting the van out for.

Flower, looking damper than even I probably did after my walk, let me in at Preciousss by the shop door. It sounded like a million small jingle bells, due to the long string of fabric elephants holding brass bells in their trunks that hung on the back of it. The shop was narrow, but stretched back a long way, an Aladdin's cave of wind chimes, dreamcatchers, bunches of scarves, swinging racks of clothes, pictures and posters, bookcases, shelves of dragons and other Tolkien tat, replicas of the Starstone, a basket of embroidered toe-post sandals (just the thing for winter in Starstone Edge), a case of silver and semi-precious stone jewellery, loops of thonged necklaces, trays of friendship bracelets, incense, joss sticks . . . It was a veritable New Age version of the treasure trove in Tutankhamen's tomb, but without the mummy.

The air was redolent with sandalwood, patchouli and possibly a hint of weed. Apart from the weed (River is very puritanical about these things), the smell was just like home.

'I've put all the lights on in here, because I was sure you'd want to look around before we go through to the kitchen and have some coffee. Grace-Galadriel's crashed out on the sofa in the snug with Bilbo.'

She was right: I did want to look around and it was all way too tempting. The counter, a tiny island in a sea of little baskets of smaller items, was soon piled high with my purchases and she even produced starry wrapping paper and rolls of Sellotape.

I'd already bought some Christmas wrap in Great Mumming, but I could wrap the one or two small gifts I'd bought for River in something more celestial.

I'd selected several things to take back for my family at the Farm, too, and Flower, cheered no end by all this spending, popped everything into two huge brown paper carrier bags. Then she thriftily turned off the shop lights and led the way into a small kitchen, which was heated by a very ancient stove and awash with felines, who all ignored me.

'How many cats are there?' I asked, picking my way through them to a wheel-back chair.

'Six,' Flower replied, filling a battered kettle and putting it on a hotplate. 'Tree, Leaf, Rainbow, Dandelion, Daisy and Sky.'

She pointed to each in turn as she named them, but only one, Tree, reacted. He gave her a dirty look, then stalked off under a chair. One of his front fangs stuck out over his lip, which gave him a somewhat malevolent expression, so I was glad it wasn't my chair he'd chosen to retreat under.

She made coffee and Bilbo came in for a chat, carrying the baby, who had now woken up and regarded me with huge, pale eyes.

She was almost a year old and I suspected was going to resemble both her parents, which was unfortunate.

Bilbo was a short, stocky man with a receding hairline, thin ponytail, a long nose that was bulbous at the tip and a lugubrious expression. However, he was very pleasant and chatty, wanting to hear all about the time when Flower was at the Farm and what we used to get up to. Flower had loved the donkeys. I expect that's why she cried for a week after they left.

After a bit he went back into the snug to play some kind of *Lord of the Rings* game on his computer.

Flower said, 'He does a lot of research on Tolkien, too – that's why we've got the computer – but we don't have mobile phones because they fry your brains.'

'I've heard that, too,' I said. 'I do have one, but I keep it switched off most of the time. And I have an iPad, but that's mostly for work.'

'It's all just *stuff*,' she said vaguely, offering me what was left of a tin of peanut butter biscuits. Bilbo had taken a big handful back to his lair with him.

She got on to the subject of Lex, whom she seemed to fancy, in a dim way. 'You'll see a lot of him over Christmas, because he always stays there from the Solstice ceremony to the New Year,' she said slightly enviously.

'I already know him a bit; he was in the year above me at art college.'

'Oh, then you know about his wife dying? It was terribly tragic and I think it's blighted his life because he's never married again. I mean, he has gone out with one or two women, just nothing serious.'

She sounded a bit disappointed by this. I think she'd much have preferred him to be totally blighted.

'The Doomes had a nanny for Teddy until he went to school and she really threw herself at Lex, but I could see he wasn't seriously interested in her, just being kind.'

'Really?' I prompted. I remembered Clara telling me about the nanny, but in connection with Mark, surely?

'Flora, she's called. She's an orphan and grew up with her aunt, Deirdre, who runs a guesthouse called Bella Vista further up the road.'

'Oh, yes, I remember passing that one. Clara says Deirdre's in Australia, so it's shut up for the winter.'

'Everything in Starstone Edge shuts up for the winter,' Flower said gloomily. 'Flora trained in childcare and then her first job was looking after Teddy, but she didn't live in; she stayed with her aunt.'

'That must have been very convenient all round,' I suggested.

'It was a bit awkward for Lex when he visited the old folk and she wouldn't leave him alone, but then, she's been out with every unattached man within ten miles and she always starts planning the wedding after the second date,' she said surprisingly cattily.

'That must put them off,' I commented, though now feeling slightly sorry for this unknown Flora.

'Clara found her a good nanny position in London but she's changed jobs several times since. In between she stays with her auntie, and last time she was home Mark was at Underhill too and she set her sights on him.'

Well, Clara had said he'd had a fling with the nanny. 'I suppose she already knew him?'

'Yes, it's a small place and he'd often visited because his mum moved back to Underhill after she was widowed, to look after old George Doome, her father.'

'Did Flora get anywhere with Mark?' I asked. Call me nosy, but this was all very interesting!

She considered this. 'They went out in his car a lot and Bilbo saw them in the pub a couple of times.'

I didn't think that constituted a serious relationship, but I filed the information away for future reference, though I suspected Mark's flattering interest in me had mostly been because he hoped I'd give him free advice about his paintings.

'It'll be great if you're still here for Christmas, Meg,' Flower said, changing the subject. 'Me and Bilbo put a Christmas tree in the snug and we're going to tell Grace-Galadriel that Father Christmas is a wise elf.'

'How lovely,' I said.

'The Doomes always have a big Boxing Day morning party at the Red House. Everyone's invited, so we go to that. Nibbles and drinks.'

'Sounds fun,' I said, then looked at my watch and got up. 'It's late – I'd better get back for lunch.'

'You could stay and have something to eat with us. It's lentil soup and I can easily open another tin.'

'That's kind of you, but I'd better go. I need to do some more work, anyway. I'm not here on holiday.'

I thought Den's home-made soup would taste a whole lot better than the canned too, not to mention the fresh, crusty loaf I'd seen Henry removing from the breadmaker earlier.

Grace-Galadriel had all this time been sitting stolidly and silently on a rag rug among a sea of cats, chewing at a rusk, but now slowly toppled over backwards. I feared for her head if it struck the stone floor beyond the rug's edge, but instead it landed heavily on a ginger cat. It squirmed out as Flower was scooping the baby up and walked away in an offended manner, only spoiled by its having the remains of the rusk sticking out of its mouth like a chewed cigar of Churchillian proportions.

I collected the brown paper carrier bags full of my purchases on the way out. The bags were the sort that go soggy and disintegrate in the rain, and outside it still looked distinctly and damply sleety. I'd have to walk fast or I'd be leaving a strange trail of random objects behind me.

'Drop in any time,' Flower urged me hospitably, waving the baby's arm goodbye. 'I'll probably be here. There's nowhere else much to go at this time of year.'

I didn't think there would be many places to go *any* time of year, but then, it must be beautiful in summer, so why would you want to?

I pulled up my anorak hood and stepped out briskly into the sleet, but had barely got going when a large black and glossy Ford Cherokee pulled up next to me and Mark was lowering the window and offering me a lift.

It didn't look like he'd counted the pennies when it came to buying himself a car!

I scrambled gratefully up into the passenger seat. 'Thanks so much, Mark! I know it's only a few minutes' walk, but these paper carriers are likely to fall apart long before I get there.'

'You've been buying up Flower's shop?'

'I suppose I have bought rather a lot,' I admitted. 'It's very New Age and not that different from the one in the craft centre at home, though they make a lot of the things themselves there. I was brought up in a commune on a farm,' I added in explanation.

'Yes, I've heard about that from Mum. And isn't your grandfather coming to stay soon, or did she get the wrong end of the stick from Tottie?'

'No, she's right, though River isn't my real grandfather, I just think of him like that. Clara was kind enough to invite him to stay for the Solstice ceremony, so he'll be arriving on the twentieth for a couple of nights.'

We were almost back at the Red House by then and I asked Mark to drop me at the end of the drive. 'I don't want to hold you up.'

'Actually, I'm only on my way to Great Mumming to get some more paint and sandpaper – and if you haven't had lunch yet, why don't you come with me? There's a pub that does great food.'

'That's a kind thought, but they're expecting me and I'm already running late. And actually, I went into Great Mumming yesterday, because I needed some art materials.'

He looked flatteringly disappointed. 'Then why not come up to Underhill tomorrow? I'd love to show you what I'm doing to the place. I'll pick you up after lunch.'

'That would be nice, if it fits in with Clara's plans, but I could drive up. I've got my camper van with me.'

'Oh, no problem,' he said. 'See you tomorrow!'

When I told Clara about the invitation she said she'd ring Sybil. 'When Mark brings you back, she can come along too and they can both stay for tea. The boy can't work all the time.'

'How old is "the boy"?'

She grinned. 'Oh, I suppose he must be thirty-one or so by now, but he seems a boy to me. What on earth have you been buying?' she added, looking at the bags.

'There was a surprisingly good stock of things in Bilbo and Flower's shop. I got a vegan cookbook for Oshan – he thinks he can cook, but he really can't – and there was a new book on ley lines for River and . . . well, I bought a few more odds and ends. Then in this bag there are two tunics, a purply-pink one and a powder blue, with pleating and little bells.'

And there was a pair of black harem trousers, though I certainly wasn't harem material.

'What with the new dress I got in Great Mumming, I've never bought myself so many new clothes all at once in my life,' I said. 'I don't know what's come over me.'

'They're all very pretty, so why not?" Clara said, admiring the tunics that I'd pulled out to show her. 'I love new clothes.'

'Now I've put weight back on, I fit much better into my old ones again.'

'You're just right, now,' she assured me.

'My mother's small and plump – or she was, last time I saw her,' I said. 'My father's the tall, stringy type, so I must fall somewhere in between.'

For the first time I noticed that there were distant hoovering noises above our heads and, now I came to think of it, there had been a van outside when Mark dropped me off.

'It's Tuesday, so Mary's Pop-ins are here,' she said.

'Mary's Pop-ins?'

'A local cleaning service from Thorstane. They send a team over every other Tuesday to give the house a good going-over, then in between, Olive Adcock gives us a couple of hours and changes the beds and that kind of thing. She's very obliging. Den likes to do the kitchen himself, though; he won't let anyone else clean it.'

She tilted her head, listening to the noises from above. 'They'll have finished upstairs in a few minutes and move down here, so I'm going out for a walk with Henry and you're welcome to join us. Tottie's going to Underhill to ride with Sybil.'

But I said I'd had enough walking in the sleet for one day.

I had a hasty lunch and a cup of coffee, then went into my studio to mount two sketches – Tottie and Henry – and by then the cleaners were finishing with the drawing room, so I retreated upstairs to my little turret, where I'd stashed the presents. I didn't think Teddy would go up there, but I'd already wrapped his art box anyway, just in case. One of today's purchases was also for him: a little bean-filled corduroy dragon. I couldn't resist it.

I decided to wrap everything and there was quite a heap of parcels when I'd finished, though I put the ones for the Farm back in the biggest bag.

Then I sat in the tapestry chair and read Clara's novel . . . and as the afternoon light faded, I reached the end.

I never saw *that* twist coming!

Downstairs, the house was shiny and clean and the scent of lavender polish competed with that of resinous pine. I could hear the tapping of typewriter keys behind Henry's door, but Clara's was wide open and she called me.

'Come in, Meg! Tottie's gone to collect Teddy and I'm dying to tell someone – look!'

She gestured at her screen, where several pieces of incised clay tablet had been roughly fitted together.

'Eureka!' she cried. 'And since I know that the same inscription is also engraved on to a stone temple slab, it would appear to be an edict sent throughout the land, rather than just a proclamation.'

I got the gist, even if not quite understanding what she was talking about. 'Wonderful,' I enthused, but she was already sitting back down at the keyboard. 'The pieces are from three different museums and two collectors,' she said. 'I must email them all and let them know . . .'

Seeing she'd forgotten I was there I tiptoed out again and closed the door quietly behind me.

After tea, which had taken on a celebratory air once Henry had winkled Clara out of her study, I went back into the studio and rang the Farm.

River answered and said he was all set to visit his friend Gregory Warlock in Sticklepond on Monday, before coming on to the Red House.

'I'm sure you remember me mentioning him. Besides having the museum of witchcraft in the village, he has written some works on ancient sacred sites, as well as novels.'

'Yes, I do remember,' I agreed.

'I'll have only a short journey onwards to the Red House from Sticklepond.'

I told him all about my visit to Flower and then he asked how the portraits were coming along.

'Clara's is completely finished and I've just started Henry's. I'm hoping they'll let me put them in my February exhibition.'

I hadn't asked them yet, but I was sure they would agree.

'I look forward to seeing them – and you too, my dear Meg,' he said, then gave me his usual Goddess-inspired benediction and rang off.

Before I could turn my phone off again, Fliss caught me and I told her about Rollo's behaviour and that I'd told him I never wanted to see or hear from him again.

'I told you you should dump him, right after the accident,' she said.

'I know and I wanted to, but he seemed to feel so guilty that I ended up agreeing we could stay friends, just to show I didn't blame him for what happened. And he did visit me several times while I was in hospital.'

'Only to inflict all those sad poems he'd written about how *he* felt on you.'

'Yes, there was that. And though he insisted he'd have supported me and the baby if I hadn't miscarried, that was easy enough to say then.'

Even now, I felt a pang of anguish fill my heart: the loss of the baby was something I'd learned to live with but would never be able to forget.

'Never mind, you've cut him out of your life now, that's the main thing,' Fliss said.

'I just hope he doesn't turn up after this event he's doing in York anyway, because I wouldn't put it past him.'

'After what you've just told me you said to him, he'd have to have the hide of a rhinoceros to do that,' she said, then asked what else had been happening.

I described the trip to Terrapotter and how Lex hadn't seemed so antagonistic this time, but Al and Tara had made up for him.

'Lex was cross with Al for telling Tara what happened in the past – or what he imagines happened. And he didn't know until I told him about Al having a go at me that time in college, after Lisa died.'

'Though, of course, Al wouldn't have done that in the first place if Lex hadn't talked to him about that evening, would he?' she pointed out.

'No, that's true, though I suppose Al could have put two and two together and made five all on his own, when he found Lex was with me.'

'I suppose it's made you even more determined to leave after the Solstice?'

'No, actually it hasn't,' I confessed. 'I'm painting really well here. Not only that, I've fallen in love with the idea of Christmas, too! And,' I added determinedly, 'I don't see why I shouldn't stay, whatever Lex thinks of me, because I've done nothing to be guilty about . . . or not much.'

'*Nothing*,' she assured me. 'And I think you're quite right: it'll be fun! The people you're staying with sound a bit mad . . . but interesting.'

'They are. Clara's just made a major breakthrough with a clay tablet inscription in cuneiform.'

'What's that, when it's at home?'

'An early type of writing: it looks a bit like a bird has walked across damp clay.'

'Like runes?'

'No, not at all like runes,' I said, from the depths of my new, if sketchy, knowledge of epigraphy.

'I've been invited to visit the owner of the local manor house tomorrow,' I said, changing the subject.

'Is he young, single and handsome?'

'All three – but about five years younger than me.'

'Oh, that's nothing,' she said airily.

'He also seems to be a bit of a love rat, so I wouldn't buy a wedding present quite yet, Fliss. I think he'd only marry someone who could plaster walls, or who knows how to use a cement mixer.'

I told her what Mark was doing to Underhill and she laughed and said she might be renovating a house herself soon, on a more modest scale, because the only way they could afford to buy a house would be to move out of London.

'There's no real reason for me to live in London now either. Being up here has made me realize how much I miss the countryside.'

'Just somewhere not quite so remote?' she suggested.

'No, or anywhere with Lex Mariner as a neighbour,' I agreed.

21

Still Life

Henry gave me another sitting next morning and I began to put paint on the canvas. The sound of my palette knife spreading paint on the surface and then, sometimes, scraping most of it off again, was for some time the only sound in the room.

Henry was a perfect sitter, seeming to relax into the pose, though I wasn't sure he was always reading, because sometimes the pages didn't turn for ages. Perhaps he was thinking about his long poem cycle instead, which sounded as if it was nearing completion.

I had thought that poets were all like Rollo and his slightly precious circle, or the sometimes earthier but more entertaining ones we heard at pub open mic sessions, but Henry was something else entirely.

He had the same thing that Lex and I recognized in each other, without false modesty, and that's brilliance at what we did. You can't be full of yourself about it, because you're merely the vehicle for this amazing gift that's been bestowed on you.

Mark fetched me after lunch in that huge black Cherokee thing. It had snowed on the tops last night and everything was looking sugar-coated and crispy white, like the enormous

Christmas cake under a glass dome in the larder at the Red House. Den had swirled 'Merry Christmas' in red icing across the top, then added a tiny reindeer, a huge robin and sprigs of plastic holly and mistletoe. I had a sudden mad vision of him up on the hillside with a giant icing nozzle, marking out a seasonal greeting . . .

Mark parked in the courtyard in front of the oak door and led the way in.

'Mum?' he called, opening the door on to the hall's dark chilliness, but there was no reply except for a faint echo. Or perhaps I just imagined that. Cosy, it wasn't.

'She must be out in the garden, or up with the horses or somewhere, but I expect she'll be back in a bit.'

If she wasn't, I thought, she'd probably get hypothermia, but they seemed a hardier breed up here and were presumably acclimatized to it.

'I'll show you those pictures first,' Mark said with his attractive smile – probably because he wanted my free advice, I thought cynically. With his longish dark auburn hair, straight nose, high cheekbones and pointed chin, he'd have looked like a Cavalier in a painting by Van Dyck if he'd been wearing a ruff.

'After that, I'll show you round and tell you what I'm planning for the place.'

I reluctantly parted with my coat, because it seemed rude to insist on keeping it on. Then we went upstairs to what he called the Long Gallery. It *was* quite long, the walls half-panelled in dark wood, with pictures ranged above them.

The Stubbs *wasn't*. In fact, I was pretty sure the Lely wasn't, either . . . but there *was* a small, but very dirty, Dutch still life in a dark corner, which I thought might be promising.

'I'd never have thought that was worth anything,' Mark said, when I pointed it out.

'I think it's good, but you can't really tell until it's cleaned – and I mean *professionally* cleaned and *not* wiped over with white spirit,' I added hastily, because I could see what he was thinking. 'If you tried to do it yourself, you'd remove almost all the value from it.'

'Oh . . . right,' he agreed reluctantly, so I think I got that one across in the nick of time.

'I've written down the number of the girl I know in a big London auction house. Why not invite her up after Christmas and see what she thinks? I suspect that little still life will make more than all the others put together . . . but if it was mine, I don't think I could bear to sell it.'

'But if it's valuable enough to pay for the rest of the renovations and keep us afloat until I've opened for business, then Mum will be pleased too. She doesn't want to part with any of the paintings really, but I don't think she's ever paid much attention to that one.'

'I expect your visitors will like to see the portraits of the ancestors. They'll be an added attraction.' Not quite the Lions of Longleat, perhaps, but something to look at. 'But I suppose the wedding receptions will be the chief moneymaker?' I said as I followed him back out of the gallery.

'Yes, and I'm determined we'll be open for those this spring. The letting bedrooms might have to wait a bit longer, though I'll need an en-suite room for the bride to use on the day.'

It didn't take him long to show me over the rest of the house, because although considerably bigger than the Red House, Underhill wasn't a vast stately home.

We had to negotiate an obstacle course of ladders, buckets and rolls of paper to reach the room intended as the bridal suite. A door had been knocked through into an adjacent bathroom and it had been refitted, but was otherwise bare. The bedroom wallpaper was half-stripped and the sections of plaster looked scabby and mottled.

'The rooms along this corridor have always been family bedrooms, but I'll have a new apartment in the east wing, and I'm creating a suite of rooms over the old kitchen for Art and Gerry. I thought Mum could have the old housekeeper's parlour downstairs, with the bedroom over.'

'Yes, I think she mentioned that,' I said, and I could see why Sybil might not be entirely enchanted with the idea after being the chatelaine of the house.

'Once the workmen downed tools, I realized I'd have to concentrate on finishing the bridal suite first.'

I hoped he'd have cleared the clutter of tools and materials from the landing before the first bride tripped – literally – down it, but I expect he would.

'Of course, I'd get on faster with the decorating if I had some help,' he hinted, but I didn't take him up on that one. I was here to do my own work, not be Mark's unpaid labourer.

We went back downstairs and into the old kitchen, where there was evidence of the Gidneys, but no sign of life. Mark said they would have gone to their own cottage in the grounds, since he and his mother would be out until dinner.

'This kitchen won't need to be changed, because there's going to be another catering-standard one through here . . .' He led me out past closed doors, which were probably larders and the like, and into a big room with newly plastered walls and ceiling. Here and there, bunches of wires and cables hung from holes.

'We created this from a couple of smaller rooms and you can see we've knocked a door through into the barn. The plumbing and electrics are done in here and a specialist firm will come and fit it out in early February.'

That wouldn't be cheap and I could see why he wanted to raise some money from the paintings.

He unlocked the new door that led into the coach house and went through. 'We've made this little anteroom, for when we're clearing the tables and as storage for the cutlery, china and table linen. Then there'll be swing doors into the actual reception area.'

He made a gesture as if pushing invisible doors apart as he passed through the space into darkness beyond and I stifled a giggle: he'd looked as if he was swimming off, breaststroke.

He turned the lights on in the barn, and I found it surprisingly big, with wonderful beams, whitewashed walls, and a series of high windows. There was one large area of glazing with a central door, where presumably coaches were once pushed inside, too.

I commented on the polished dark wood floor.

'I thought the original paving would look too cold, so I had this laid. It goes with the beams and brings the place together anyway, I think,' he said, and I agreed.

He turned on his heel, surveying the room. 'There'll be a long serving table at the far end, which can also be used for buffets, and then smaller tables that can be joined together in any configuration. The linen will be the very best damask, of course. Everything's going to be very, *very* upmarket.'

'I can imagine how it'll look,' I said, 'and once the kitchen has been fitted out and the furnishings are in, it won't take long to get ready to open for business, will it? You've already done such a lot in a short space of time.'

'I'll still need to get that bridal suite finished by then, though. And if I decide to perform wedding ceremonies here as well, then the Great Hall will have to have a makeover.'

We went back in there and it seemed even darker and chillier than ever, and not at all bridal unless you were a romantically inclined polar bear.

Mark had been talking to me as if he'd known me for ages and wanted to know me quite a lot better. But although I found him attractive and it was flattering that he was interested in me, I found I didn't fancy him in the least. Probably, from what I'd been told, just as well!

I realized he'd been talking for the last few minutes, and was gazing down intently into my eyes. Now he was saying. 'I'll spend the winters in my house in Italy. I'd love you to see it. It's—'

He was interrupted by the opening of a door and excited barking as the two little dachshunds rushed in.

Pansy made a beeline for me and jumped up and down against my legs, as if she was being bounced on a piece of elastic, until I picked her up. Then she licked my chin and wriggled ecstatically.

Sybil had followed them. 'Do come into the morning room, Meg. It's freezing in here!'

'You take Meg through, Mum, and I'll make some coffee,' he said. 'We'll have to set off quite soon, though.'

In the cosier small room, Sybil put another log on the smouldering embers of the fire and then, looking guilty, turned the thermostat on the radiator up a trifle.

While we waited for Mark to come back with the coffee, we talked about the pictures and the renovations.

'The bedroom corridor, especially, is such a mess at the moment that I'm very glad to be going to the Red House for Christmas, although I haven't heard anything back from Daddy's old friend, Piers Marten, after I wrote to tell him I'd be away this year. I hope he doesn't have to spend Christmas alone in his flat.'

'Best place for him,' said Mark callously, having come in bearing a tray. 'And you know very well he has family he can stay with. He'd just rather freeload here, guzzling good food and trying to drink the cellar dry.'

Sybil gave him a nervous and placatory smile and said, 'Perhaps my letter went astray. I'd better ring him to make sure he got it.'

'You do that,' agreed Mark. 'We don't want him turning up like a bad penny.'

I wondered just how bad this Piers Marten was. Mark certainly seemed to dislike him very much, though I think Sybil must have had a soft spot for him, to be so sad about putting him off.

We set off back to the Red House for tea and the dogs kept me warm in the back of the car by lying in a heap on my knees.

'Pansy's taken such a shine to you,' said Sybil, turning round to look at them. Her voice held a hint of speculation and if I hadn't known how much she'd intended charging the people who had backed out of buying Pansy, I'd have been sorely tempted myself, even if it would have made my life difficult when I had to travel about so much for work.

We arrived at the Red House just as Lex and Teddy had got out of the pick-up, so it was like *déjà vu*, but with an audience. At least Lex didn't look shocked this time when he saw me, just sombre, serious and slightly tight-lipped.

Perhaps it had been my parting shot – 'Get potted' – last time I saw him? It was possibly not my finest moment.

Clearly, though, it hadn't put him off staying for tea, because he followed us into the house. He'd greeted Mark in a friendly enough way too. I supposed they were relations, if only by marriage, and had seen quite a bit of each other over the years.

Teddy ran straight off upstairs to change out of his school uniform, while we found Henry, Clara and Tottie in the drawing room, cosily ensconced on the sofas in front of the fire.

Mark sat down next to me on one of the sofas and laid an arm across the back of it behind my head, in what struck me as a slightly proprietorial way . . . and now he was telling me again, in a low voice, how I'd *love* the warmth of an Italian winter.

'I expect I would, but I've no intention of going there any time soon,' I said firmly. Then I caught Lex, sitting in an oversized tub chair nearby, his long legs stretched out, looking so sardonically at me that I felt myself blushing . . . and even more hotly when I noticed that all conversation in the room had come to a halt and *every* eye was turned on us.

The blush was turning fiery when Pansy came to my rescue. She'd climbed on to my lap when I sat down and now jealously inserted herself in the small space between me and Mark and tried to rabbit-kick him away.

'Naughty Pansy,' I said, not meaning it in the least, and then Den provided another distraction by bringing tea in and decanting cups, saucers, teapot, a covered dish and a cake on to the coffee table.

Teddy followed him in carrying a small stack of tea plates and paper napkins. 'There are buttered potato cakes in the dish,' he told us. 'I like those, but they drip a lot.'

'An' this 'ere's a carrot cake, seeing Tottie grows enough bleedin' carrots to feed a stableful of 'orses,' said Den. 'I'm orf now to the flat fer a bit; leave the 'appy family to it.'

This seemed to have been said with no sarcastic intent and he went off, whistling 'Happy Days Are Here Again' between his teeth.

'He's such a character,' Sybil commented.

Her eyes wandered back in my direction again and I hoped she – and everyone else – hadn't got the wrong idea about me and Mark.

Henry asked me what I thought of Underhill and Mark's plans, and I told him I was impressed by how much he'd actually done already.

'It'll certainly be ready for the spring opening,' Mark said. 'But I'll need it all looking good before that, for the brochure and website . . . so I could do with a little help, especially with decorating.'

He'd already hinted as much to me, so I thought that one might have been directed at Lex, though *he* didn't take him up on it either.

'Meg thinks a teeny tiny still life of flowers and fruit, which I'd never really taken much notice of, might be worth more than most of the other pictures put together – isn't she clever?' Sybil announced.

'I'm not an expert,' I said hastily. 'I just think it might well be extremely valuable, so you won't have to sacrifice any of the family portraits.'

'I expect you're right and I don't think we'll really miss it at all,' she said. 'I can see we have to sell something, what with death duties and the renovations and—'

'Grandfather having tied up what was left of the money,' Mark finished, though since I'd found the still life, this didn't sound quite as barbed as before.

'We're so looking forward to having you here over Christmas, Sybil,' said Clara.

'And Mark for dinner on Christmas Day, though of course you're welcome to come over any time you like, dear boy,' invited Henry.

'That depends,' Mark said, looking at me with a meaningful smile. 'You said you weren't sure if you'd be leaving before Christmas or not, Meg.'

'Oh, I'm definitely staying now, if Clara and Henry will still have me,' I said breezily, with a look that cast the gauntlet at Lex's feet.

'Hurray!' cried Teddy. 'Meg's a favourite people.'

'Person,' corrected Tottie.

'Thank you, Teddy. I'm very honoured to be a favourite people.'

'I think you could become one of *my* favourite people too,' Mark said, and I realized he thought I'd changed my plans to leave because of him, which was a bit unfortunate.

Perhaps Lex thought so too, for he was giving us another of his sardonic looks, but Pansy didn't like the way Mark was leaning closer again, and decided to resume her pushing and kicking.

Mark put her on the floor. 'She can be a bit of a nuisance sometimes.'

'Oh, no, I just think she's funny,' I said, and then got up, took a teacup and a slice of the delicious-looking cake, and sat down next to Clara instead.

She smiled widely at me. 'I'm so glad you've made up your mind to stay, though I was sure you would. We're going to have a lovely family party, with lots of fun!'

Lex didn't look as if he remembered what fun was . . .

A faint cloud crossed Sybil's face. 'I must remember to phone Piers when I get back. He hasn't replied to my letter telling him I'm away this Christmas and I'm afraid he might not have got it.'

'I expect he has and he's just sulking,' Mark suggested. 'But you'd better make sure.'

'Don't worry about Piers, Syb,' Tottie said. 'If ever there was a man who could look out for himself, it's him. He's got family, so there's no reason why you should feel responsible for him.'

'No . . .' said Sybil, but she still looked troubled.

'Auntie Sybil, do you want to see my portrait of Meg with green hair?' asked Teddy.

'Of course, I'd love to,' she said promptly, and he went to fetch it.

'He's already very good for his age,' I said. 'He's got a real feeling for colour and form.'

'There's only the very faintest tinge of green in your hair now, Meg,' said Tottie. 'It must be naturally very light in colour?'

'Yes, so fair it's almost white,' I agreed. 'My mother's is the same.'

'Will you dye your hair green again, my dear?' enquired Henry. 'The dark emerald was quite wood nymph, in a way, and suited you.'

I wasn't too sure about that, but I thanked him anyway. 'No, I'm going to go for an entirely different colour next time.'

'Your hair was like white gold the first time I saw you – platinum blond, I think they call it,' Lex said, unexpectedly, then elaborated for the others: 'She materialized out of the shadows in a dark corridor in the art college – white hair, pale face, dark clothes. I thought she was a ghost and it was quite scary for a minute.'

'Well, *you* scared me, too, with that long black coat flapping out like the wings of some huge, dark bird swooping down on me,' I retorted, and our eyes met and held for a long moment. I think we were both seeing each other as we were on that day: young and with the world before us.

I shampooed my hair twice that evening and when I'd finished I was back to Silver Phantom mode again.

But not for long: soon I'd be a vision in rose.

Clara

As the new term wore on towards early spring, I settled ever more deeply into both my studies and my social life, which of course revolved around Henry.

I had neither the time nor inclination to pay a good deal of attention to Nessa, or I think I would have noticed what was amiss much earlier. However, the moment she came into my room one day, closed the door behind her and burst into a flood of tears, I immediately – and rightly – guessed she was pregnant.

She had been denying it to herself until now, but could do so no longer. I don't know why she chose me as her confidante, unless perhaps it was that the father of her child – George, of course – was Henry's brother.

Out came the whole sorry tale of that fateful London trip she had made in the autumn: George had indeed driven her down and they had planned to spend some hours together before she went to Lady Leamington's house. He'd borrowed a friend's flat, where they went first to drop her suitcase . . . or so she thought. She certainly hadn't expected him to behave the way he had.

'Like a wild animal!' she sobbed. 'And afterwards he said he didn't know why I was so upset, because he wanted to marry me!

And once the knot was tied and I had control of my money, we could go anywhere, and do anything, we wanted . . .'

'So then I expect you told him you couldn't touch the capital till you were thirty?' I suggested.

She shuddered again. 'He changed in a flash when he knew! I thought he loved me, but he didn't, it was just the money he loved.' She sat up straighter, a hint of backbone returning. 'But after the way he'd taken advantage of me, I wouldn't have married him if he was the last man in the world!'

Then she dissolved into tears again and wailed, 'I don't know what to do!'

'Does George know?'

She looked at me aghast. 'No! I never want to see or hear from him again!'

'Perhaps not, but under the circumstances—' I began, then stopped dead, as a complication presented itself to me. 'Nessa, I need to tell you something. Henry's gone home this weekend, because George is getting married. In fact, by now he will be.'

I kept our suspicions about the hastiness of the wedding to myself.

Nessa stared at me and then began laughing in a way that was working up to hysteria, until I dashed a glass of cold water in her face. Then she just huddled there, looking white and more than a little damp.

I'd been counting months. 'The baby must be due in the summer vacation, so if there was a way of keeping it secret till then . . .' I mused aloud. 'But I don't suppose there is.'

Nessa gathered herself. 'I can see now that the only person who can help me is Godmama. She'll know what I should do.'

She seemed very certain that Lady Leamington would be shocked, but worldly-wise enough to advise her, and on reflection I thought she was probably right.

She made me swear secrecy, which I did, apart from Henry: we were too close to keep things from each other and anyway, since it was to do with his family, he ought to know.

Henry was as shocked, angry and disgusted by George's behaviour as I was, but there was nothing to be done, for his brother and his new bride were by then on honeymoon and, besides, we were bound by my promise of secrecy.

At the end of the Hilary term Nessa went straight to London to confess all to Lady Leamington, who came up with a novel solution to the problem.

'She said I should be able to hide the pregnancy to the end of the Trinity term if I pad out my top half as my stomach gets bigger. People will simply think I've got very fat – and I have been putting weight on.'

'Will that really work? I asked sceptically.

'It did for one of her friends, so I don't see why not. That way, I can complete my first year and then I'll go into a private maternity clinic to have the baby.' She shuddered. 'It will be adopted immediately, of course.'

'You might feel differently when you see it,' I suggested.

'I don't want to see it, just get rid of it. And as soon as I've recovered, I'm going back to America to finish my degree there.'

I didn't say any more, because she seemed to have it all planned: cut and dried. There was a new, harder edge to Nessa, and she was still adamant that George should never know.

'I'll make a fresh start in America and all this will be like a bad dream,' she said, then added, fiercely, 'But I'm finished with men and motherhood!'

Really, for someone usually resembling sugar-dusted pink and white Turkish delight, she'd looked amazingly resolute when she said that!

22

The Image

I had another good painting session with Henry next morning, exciting and intense. The dabs and scrapes and blobs of paint placed themselves by some alchemy of the mind, and I knew that when I finally stepped back from the canvas they would all come together into a whole.

The sum was definitely more than the parts, for Henry's pared-down, handsome face began to take shape: the Grecian nose and high cheekbones, so like Mark's, his bony forehead and fine silver hair . . . the bright blue of his eyes in their nest of laughter and sun lines and those straight lips, with curved, humorous corners.

He'd brought his novel, but today his mind seemed firmly set on his work, the epic novel-length poem cycle about the drowning of the valley. While I painted, he told me a little about it.

'The strong sense of place still remained long after the village vanished under the water. In fact, it still does,' he said. 'My golden childhood with Clara wasn't washed away. It still exists and always drew me back over the ensuing years. Clara felt the same way.'

'I can understand that, because the moment I saw the valley, even *I* felt a connection with it. River would say that it was old magic and the ley lines drawing me in.'

Henry looked at me curiously. 'You felt that too? Interesting,' he murmured, then added, 'I wanted to show the effect of the drowning of the valley, not only on the human inhabitants, but from the viewpoint of the creatures displaced or drowned. The trees, the plants, the fish and insects – even the birds. The thrush that nested every year in an old watering can hung on the barn wall at the inn, the fox that used to hide in the vicarage greenhouse when the hunt came by, and the badgers in the copse over the humpbacked bridge, who led their own lives at dusk when we slept.'

His voice, low but wonderfully resonant, swept on. 'The silenced bells, removed to the big, ugly church at Thorstane, and the ancient inscribed pre-Christian stone that stood in the churchyard, which inspired Clara to take up epigraphy, now relocated to the Underhill estate. Much was moved, but you can't take the dead, or the weight of time that holds down a place, with you.'

He paused and seemed to come back from somewhere a long way away.

'It sounds wonderful and I can't wait to read it,' I said truthfully.

'It's nearly completed . . . and Clara, too, has almost finished her latest crime novel, though not her memoirs. I suspect,' he added, looking at me with a smile, 'that this one will end on revelations. Just as well she isn't intending it for publication.'

'Do you think Clara's memoirs could end up running to several volumes, like Dodie Smith's?'

'Probably only two. I think she's about to reach a moment of resolution, which would be a good place to end the first one.'

Some major discovery, perhaps, which would crown Clara's work in the world of epigraphy with added glory?

'If you could just stop speaking now for a few minutes while I paint your lips,' I suggested, 'then I think we'll be done for the day.'

And the face, at least, was almost at the stage where someone should take my palette knife away.

At lunch, Henry told me that Lex and Al were coming up at about two that afternoon to deliver the huge garden pot that was Lex's annual Christmas gift.

'Though of course Tottie decides where it should go and what should be planted in it, so really it's a gift for the three of us. This time we know it will be identical to the one in the middle of the right-hand knot garden in front of the terrace, so they match.'

'I'd noticed only one had a central pot,' I said, while silently blessing him for the warning, for the moment I'd had a cup of coffee, I took my novel (the second in Clara's series) and went upstairs to my turret room.

If there'd been a hatch, I'd have drawn it up behind me.

I heard Lex and Al arrive and peered out of my little slit window, just in time to see the pick-up, with an enormous terracotta shape roped in the back, vanish round the side of the house.

I didn't go downstairs till they'd driven off. Unfortunately, I didn't realize it was just Al leaving until I'd emerged from the garden door on to the terrace and saw Lex there with Tottie.

'I thought you'd gone!' I blurted.

'No, sorry to disappoint you.' His dark eyes were unreadable.

'I'm not disappointed, just surprised,' I said with dignity.

'I'm going to bring round the bags of compost for Tottie and help her plant up the tree in the new pot,' he said.

'What sort of tree will it be?'

'It's a box spiral like the other,' said Tottie. 'Henry wanted them to match, but he hates angles so we ended up with spirals.'

They went off round the side of the garage to where there was an old greenhouse and returned a few minutes later with Lex trundling a large wooden wheelbarrow piled with bags of compost.

Tottie followed, carrying a sizeable tree in a plastic pot. 'Take for ever to grow, box, so you might as well buy the biggest you can get for the effect,' she said.

The pot took two barrow loads of compost before it was full and firmly pressed down around the tree's roots.

Tottie wheeled the empty barrow away and Lex and I retired to the terrace to admire the effect.

Lex surprised me by suddenly apologizing for the way Al and Tara had behaved at the pottery.

'I haven't had the chance before, but Al shouldn't have spoken to you like that – and he certainly shouldn't have said anything to Tara about what had happened.'

I shrugged. 'I don't really care what they think, and when I leave after Christmas I'll never have to see either of them again.'

'I don't know about that. You looked very *friendly* with Mark yesterday,' he said pointedly.

'Don't be silly. I barely know the man and he's years younger than I am,' I said crisply. 'What he wants is free advice and unpaid labour, if he can get it.'

Lex grinned quite unexpectedly, with devastating effect. 'Oh, I wouldn't underestimate your charms,' he said.

I was just staring at him in astonishment, wondering if he was being sarcastic, when Tottie rejoined us, brushing earth from her hands.

'Looks good, doesn't it?' she asked, gazing critically down at the knot garden.

'Lovely,' I said. The intricacy of the twin knot gardens placed on either side of the long gravelled path did indeed look picture-book pretty.

'Al seemed a bit tight-lipped today, and he refused to stay for tea,' Clara said when we went in. 'You haven't fallen out, have you, Lex?'

'A slight difference of opinion, but he'll get over it,' he said shortly.

'Henry should be back with Teddy any minute.'

'Is it that late?' I exclaimed. We must have been out in the garden for ages. No wonder I felt frozen!

Teddy was excited to see Lex there again – but then, with every day that brought us closer to Christmas, he was excited, full stop.

'It's the last day of the school term tomorrow,' he told me. 'Father Christmas is coming and then we're having the school play. You're coming to that, Uncle Lex, aren't you? Meg is, and everyone else.'

It was the first I'd heard of my being expected to go, though of course, I knew all about the Nativity play, which Miss Aurora had apparently rewritten in more feminist terms.

'I'm sure they must limit the audience numbers,' I said quickly.

'Actually, there's lots of space, because the assembly room was originally the old ballroom at the side of the house. It has a wonderful parquet floor,' Henry said, as if that might be a major incentive.

'The chairs are the hideously uncomfortable plastic stacking kind, but the plays are always short, and then the refreshments are good. But don't let Teddy pester you into going if you don't want to, either of you,' said Clara.

'Of course Meg and Uncle Lex want to come!' Teddy said, looking deeply hurt, so we immediately had to assure him we did.

'We're taking Meg to the Pike with Two Heads for lunch tomorrow, Lex,' Henry informed him, which was *also* news to me, though I remembered that they'd said it would be nice to do that one Friday. 'Why don't you come, if you don't have too much to wrap up before the Solstice?'

'I think you're mean, going when I'm at school,' Teddy protested.

'But you'll be seeing Santa instead, and we can all go again another time,' said Clara.

Lex said he *would* join us at the pub. 'I have to eat, after all, and if I'm going to the Nativity play, there won't be time to do any work that afternoon, will there?'

Lass's nose was slowly inching towards the plate of Gentleman's Relish sandwiches and I pushed it further away. She gave me a look of deep reproach.

'It's nearly your dinnertime,' I told her.

'What's Den doing?' Henry asked.

'Making more mince pies, as if the freezer wasn't already crammed with them,' replied Clara, 'but he's made Eccles cakes, too.'

'Yum,' said Henry. 'You can't have too many mince pies.'

When we came in, Tottie had vanished to scrub the earth off her hands, but now she reappeared, though still attired in slightly grimy corduroy trousers and grey ribbed socks.

'I'm starving,' she said, loading a plate with sandwiches.

Clara poured her tea. 'We're all going to the pub for lunch tomorrow, Tottie.'

'Super!' she said, and I could see the young raw-boned and jolly version of her, who must have played tennis at Underhill and probably hockey at school, and now her enthusiasms had turned to horses, bees and gardening.

Den drove Lex home later, and Teddy and Henry went off into his study to unpack a box of baubles. The mixed auction lot of Christmas decorations had finally arrived.

Clara had retired to her own room to work, but Tottie remained sitting by the fire, reading a gardening magazine, and I curled up in a comfortable armchair with Clara's second novel. But by the time Teddy had run in half a dozen times to exhibit some fresh treasure from the box, we both gave up and went and watched the fun too.

Next morning, I painted Henry's long-fingered, sensitive hands and began on Lass, who always lay unbidden across his feet on the dais, in just the right pose.

Clara came in after a while to have a look.

'So different from my portrait . . . and yet, so distinctly your work,' she said, examining it. 'Henry's a typical Doome – straight nose, high cheekbones and fair hair.'

'Well, it *was* fair; it's white now,' he said.

'George was the bigger, cruder, glossier version of Henry,' Clara told me. 'Brassy gold hair, slightly popping blue eyes, tall, rugged, dim.'

'Sums him up pretty well,' agreed Henry. 'He felt sorry for me for being such a runt.'

'Ha!' said Clara.

Henry got up to join her and they scrutinized the portrait together, then turned as one and looked intently at me.

'Is there something wrong?' I asked anxiously.

'Not in the least. We're just amazed at your brilliance, my dear,' Henry assured me.

'I'm certain I could finish it tomorrow, if you could give me one last sitting, Henry?'

'I'm not sure there'll be time tomorrow. It might have to be Sunday morning.'

'Why, what's happening tomorrow?' I asked.

'We always take Teddy to the old Friendship Mill near Great Mumming to see Father Christmas and to choose our box of Christmas crackers. It's what they've always made there. The cracker making is only in part of the mill now, though, and the rest is a little museum and some interesting shops, including the Christmas one I told you about.'

'Oh, yes, I remember.'

'They have a very good wholefood café, so we always have lunch. Clara, Lex and I take him, but this year he wants you to come too, Meg,' Henry said.

'He's taken a real shine to you,' said Clara.

'Lex takes Teddy in to see Santa, which gives us time to get a few last-minute additions for his Christmas stocking,' explained Henry. 'Then we meet in the café.'

'But I'm sure Teddy doesn't really need *me* to go too. I—'

'Do relax, my dear. You've almost finished the second portrait and deserve a day out,' urged Clara. 'We're so glad you aren't going to rush off after the Solstice.'

Teddy appeared to want to include me in everything, even though I was sure Lex didn't . . . But then again, the old factory really *did* sound fun.

We all squeezed into the Range Rover and set off for the Pike with Two Heads, with Den driving. Clara would take the wheel when we left the pub for the school afterwards, so Den could have a pint or two of Gillyflower's Old Brown Ale.

Tottie's family name lived on, even though the brewery had been sold years ago.

It was a very old pub with modern extensions: a glass-roofed dining area had been added at one side, and a wing of motel rooms at the other. The old part was quite dark, but we detoured through it so I could see the famous mutant pike, proudly exhibited by the landlord, Fred Golightly.

It was in a glass case in the snug, with a light over it to illuminate the creature, which wore a severely pissed-off expression on both its faces.

'Fed up to the gills,' I commented.

'He does look a bit cheesed,' Lex's deep voice agreed from right behind me, and I jumped.

'There you are, Lex,' said Clara. 'Come along, let's go and have lunch. I'm starving!'

Den was going to eat his (probably non-vegetarian) lunch with the landlord and would join us for coffee later, but the rest of us followed Clara as she led the way into the large and light dining area, which was furnished with rattan chairs and glass-topped tables, and had been tastefully decorated with fake fan palms in large plastic urns and murals of camels plodding across deserts. I shouldn't think you'd see a lot of those round here.

I looked critically at the nearest camel as I sat down. 'I think they could rename the pub the Camel with Two Heads.'

'Reminds me of the horse in that School of Stubbs painting at Underhill,' Lex said, taking the chair next to me.

'You've seen it?'

'Mark insisted I go up and look at it weeks ago, though I told him my artistic expertise lay in pots, not paintings. But even I could see it probably wasn't even School of, let alone the real thing.'

'I think he's accepted that now,' I said, thinking Lex seemed a lot more chilled today and, if not friendly, at least not openly inimical.

'Mainly because you found him something probably a whole lot more valuable that it won't hurt Sybil to part with.'

We consulted the menus and then all chose the same thing: fish pie, followed by *crème brûlée.* I noticed Lex addressed the pretty blonde waitress as Susie and she had trouble keeping her eyes off him.

'It's like an annual outing of Pescetarians,' Tottie said, tucking in. 'I suppose we do all grab the opportunity of a bit of fish when we're out, even though we have it at home occasionally, too.'

'Lex fell into our ways when he used to stay with us over the years,' Henry said.

'Zelda's a little carnivore, though,' Lex said, and I wondered what this unknown younger sister, Teddy's mother, would be like.

'I don't really feel I *should* be eating fish,' said Henry, 'but I just can't seem to entirely break the habit.'

'I can manage anything fishy, so long as it isn't still wearing its head,' Clara said.

'Or two heads, if it was the mutant pike,' said Lex.

'Let's not go there,' I said, 'or it'll put us all off our lunch.'

'True,' said Clara. 'And I'm so glad you could join us today, Lex.'

'Perhaps you should have invited Mark, too,' Lex suggested. 'Meg seems to have sweetened his temper no end.'

I turned and looked suspiciously at him and he gazed blandly back.

'You mean, by finding that still life?'

'I expect that helped, because he seemed practically genial the other day. Something, or someone, has certainly softened him up,' Clara said.

'I think he's taken a liking to Meg – and who could blame him?' said Henry with a twinkle, and I blushed.

'It's no such thing. He's just delighted that I think his still life will fund the rest of his renovations.'

'What did you really think of his plans?' asked Lex.

'I'm no expert on it, but I think if he can persuade people that it's worth going all the way out to Underhill for a very upmarket wedding reception venue, he could be on to a winner.'

'He'll certainly have to charge a bomb if he's going to make enough money between spring and early autumn,' Lex said.

'What about this idea of turning Underhill into some kind of small country house hotel?' Tottie asked dubiously.

'I think it's more so he can accommodate some of the wedding party, rather than open it to the general public,' suggested Clara.

'I don't know if it would be worth it, really, and it would make a lot more work,' I said.

'I agree,' Henry said. 'He'd do better concentrating on the receptions and later, perhaps, hold weddings there, too.'

'It's all a big disruption anyway. Poor Sybil will be glad to get away to stay with us, though I noticed she was still fretting over that ghastly old reprobate Piers Marten,' said Clara. 'But if he's alone for Christmas, it'll be by his own choice.'

'Do you think there might be some kind of autumn/winter romance going on there?' asked Henry.

'I wouldn't have thought so, really,' replied Clara. 'I mean, she calls him "Uncle Piers" and he's the same age as George would have been . . . *and* he's not a very nice or attractive man.'

'I'm sure she just feels sorry for the old blighter,' Tottie said, spooning the last froth out of her cappuccino cup.

Den had arrived along with the coffee and, since we were all full, was eating the chocolate mints that had come with it.

'I think Sybil was hoping I'd suggest Piers come and join us at the Red House for Christmas, but I'd much rather not, so I didn't,' Clara said.

'Quite right too,' said Tottie. 'The man's a pain. Tried to get off with me after I inherited the Red House, till he found there wasn't any money to go with it. Then he cleared off.'

'Really?' exclaimed Clara. 'I had no idea!'

'Must 'ave known yer couldn't cook,' suggested Den.

'I can cook! Or *some* things, anyway.'

'A man can't live by jam and pickles alone, even if there's a bit of 'oney on the side.'

Tottie seemed about to take exception to this, but Henry hastily suggested it was time we made a move if we were to get to Gobelins in time for the Nativity play.

At the school we followed a stream of parents into what had once been a sizeable ballroom. The long curtains at the windows were drawn and rows of chairs had been placed in front of a raised stage, with steps up to it on either side.

Miss Aurora, an imposingly tall and deep-voiced woman, briefly welcomed us and then drew back the curtains to reveal Miss Dawn in the act of lowering a backdrop that had been painted by someone with little artistic skill, but a lot of enthusiasm.

It depicted a room with a window. A small and truculent Mary sat in a chair in front of it and proceeded to deal with the Angel of Annunciation, who was not seen, but merely a gruff voice heard offstage. First she told him to get lost, before finally being persuaded that what he proposed was a good idea.

After this she picked up her chair and trudged off, and in the next scene she was shown on her way to Bethlehem, well padded and saying she didn't much fancy riding a donkey in her condition.

I suspected she would grow up to be either a leading actor, or a leading feminist . . . or possibly both.

Another backdrop of a splashily painted open-fronted stable was lowered and Mary bossily ordered Joseph to sweep out the muck, but leave the donkey, the cow and the sheep, to keep it warm. The stage was quite crowded by this time.

Mary popped behind a group of donkeys and then came back and laid a baby in a manger that looked suspiciously like a wicker magazine basket.

'There we are, then,' she said. 'Come on, you lot, and have a look.'

The shepherds, several angels and the Three Wise Men all crowded on to the stage at once, so I was afraid the sheep would fall over the edge.

'I'm glad you didn't arrive early, because you don't want a load of strangers about when you're having a baby,' Mary told the Three Wise Men, raising her voice to compete with the cacophony of moos, baas and braying from the animals. By now, most of the children were hot inside their costumes, red-faced and very over-excited.

One angel had a drooping wing and another – Teddy – was throwing his halo like a discus across the room at a small papier mâché palm tree.

'Hush up,' Mary ordered everyone severely, then pushed her way to the front of the stage and announced brusquely, 'We're going to sing, and then that's it.'

They formed themselves into ragged rows and gave a stirring rendition of 'Jesus Christ, Superstar', before trooping off to loud applause.

'Oh, that was brilliant!' I enthused, as we rose gratefully from the bottom-numbing plastic chairs and headed for the refreshments at the back of the room.

Lex looked down at me with his arrowhead smile. 'Mary certainly stole the show, didn't she?'

'Well, naturally,' said Clara, overhearing.

The refreshments were exactly as Tottie had described them to me on the way there. There was non-alcoholic punch, sandwiches of all kinds and a large chocolate fudge cake, plus plates of small fondant fancies, meringues and vol-au-vents filled, according to Den, who was eating them with relish, with condensed mushroom or chicken soup.

'Do it meself fer the nibbles on Boxing Day, don't I?' he said. 'Just the mushroom, though.'

The children came back, now dressed in their own clothes, though one donkey still had his ears on and Mary had a halo rammed down firmly over the blue cloth that covered her head.

After we had admired Teddy's performance to his satisfaction, he told us about Santa's visit to the school earlier that day.

'I'll see him again tomorrow, at the cracker factory,' he added. 'Henry and Clara are taking me, but you and Uncle Lex are coming too, aren't you, Meg? The cracker factory is magic.'

'I'm sure you'll enjoy seeing it, Meg,' said Henry, and I said it did sound fun.

'Lex will meet us there in the car park,' Clara said, which reminder slightly took the icing off the gingerbread of anticipation.

'Wonderful,' I said, and turned to find him standing right behind me. He gave me one of his more adamantine stares from those dark, moss-agate eyes under drawn black brows, though I don't know what I'd done to deserve that.

He'd come to say he was leaving, and we did too soon afterwards, all cramming into the Range Rover.

Clara was driving – the long way round rather than the pass, I was happy to note – and when we finally scrunched up the gravel drive of the Red House, Henry said with a happy sigh, as if we'd been away for a year, 'How lovely to be home again!'

23

Present

Henry drove us to the mill next day in the Jaguar, by way of the Grimlike Pass, which was hairy since we met a delivery van coming up, hogging the middle of the road.

Beyond Great Mumming we took a narrow road that meandered off into the countryside between tall, dark, hawthorn hedges until we finally turned in through a pair of open wrought-iron gates between stone posts. A large sign next to them read:

WELCOME TO FRIENDSHIP MILL
THE HOME OF
MARWOOD'S MAGICAL CRACKERS

'Here we are,' said Henry gaily, heading up a thin tarmac road past a small terrace of cottages, to where the mill stood by a stream. The valley was narrow and woodland came crowding down behind the mill, but on the other side of the stream the ground opened up a bit and an old house sat there, on a green, grassy cushion surrounded by a moat, with ducks. It looked *very* improbable.

'Pretty, isn't it?' said Clara as we drew into a gravelled car park and stopped next to Lex's pick-up. 'It's in the Domesday Book and it still belongs to the Marwood family. We know Mercy Marwood, because her nephew, Randall, was at school with Lex, though he is a little older.'

'It's lovely, but certainly unexpected,' I said – unlike Lex, who had now got out and was shrugging a disreputable old waxed jacket over his slightly clay-smeared black jeans.

'There you are,' he greeted us, as if he'd been hanging around for hours, which he evidently hadn't, since the bonnet of his pick-up was still slightly steaming in the chilly air.

'Your jeans are covered in clay, darling,' Clara pointed out.

He looked down and grunted. 'They were clean this morning . . . but then I went into the workshop for a few minutes.'

'It doesn't matter anyway,' said Henry. 'Half the craftspeople from the workshops in the mill wander about covered in paint, or clay or whatever.'

Teddy, released from his car seat, bounced up and down impatiently, while the wind whipped his mop of black curls, so like Lex's, into a frenzy.

'Come on, Uncle Lex – come on, Meg!' he urged, grabbing our hands, so that we headed for the mill entrance with Teddy between us, the picture of a happy family outing, Clara and Henry following behind.

A large Christmas tree twinkled in the foyer and fragranced the air, but I barely had time to snatch a leaflet about the attractions within from a pile on a table before Teddy had dragged me through the double doors at the further end, highly excited.

'Slow down, Teddy,' called Henry. 'We want to show Meg the cracker making and the museum first. Then you can see Santa.'

'The cracker makers don't work weekends, but there are demonstrations instead,' Clara informed me.

I saw that the large interior of the mill had been divided by a partition with viewing windows, through which you could watch the crackers being made, while to the right were the windows of the Christmas shop and the side of a hut that said, 'Santa's Grotto', though it looked more like Santa's garden shed.

Above us, on a terrace reached by a flight of metal steps, was the café.

It was still quite early, but the place was already busy. In the background was some kind of electronic music . . . or sound, at any rate, for it conjured up wind whistling among snowy trees, icicles tinkling, sleigh bells jingling . . . It was very well done and a big improvement on the raucous Christmas pop songs usually blasting out in shops at this time of year.

We joined a group by one of the viewing windows and watched as a slender, elegant black woman with silvery hair and a tall, elderly man with improbably dark hair, parted in the middle and pasted flatly over his head, constructed large and intricately decorated crackers. I didn't think it could possibly be as easy as they made it look.

It was quite mesmerizing, watching their fingers nimbly assembling the various components: card centre, snap, joke, hat and some small gift, then enclosing the whole expertly in paper and patterned foil, before tying off the ends with ribbon.

There was an information board by the viewing window, but Teddy was too impatient to let me linger. Instead, he headed off to the back of the room where a sign indicated the museum.

That all looked riveting too, with the history of the mill, the cracker making and the Marwood family itself, which appeared to be Quaker and, like many of the early factory-owning Friends, benevolent and caring to its workforce.

'Look at all these old boxes of crackers in the display cases!' I exclaimed, fascinated. 'I love this Zoo box. Do you think that dates from the sixties?' I asked Henry.

'Probably, going by the clothes the children are wearing on the box front,' he agreed.

'We'll have to bring you back another day, dear, so you can have a better look around,' promised Clara. 'After Christmas, when they reopen.'

'That will be New Year – if you're still here by then, of course,' said Lex.

'We hope she will be,' Henry said. 'Come on. Teddy's just vanished into the Christmas shop.'

'The entrance to Santa's Grotto is just off it,' Lex explained to me as we threaded our way through racks of sparkling baubles, a rainbow of tinsel, festoons of fairy lights and great stacks of the various kinds of Marwood crackers. 'I always take him in and keep him occupied while Clara and Henry look for stocking fillers.'

Teddy reappeared from behind an illuminated wire polar bear and, taking both our hands again, urged us towards the arched door hung with the 'Santa's Grotto Entrance' sign.

'Looks like you're both going,' said Clara, amused. 'See you later.'

There was a queue of excited children that stretched from the entrance, along a snowy scene of lit fir trees and fairy lights and over a small wooden bridge to the door of Santa's cottage. When we'd shuffled nearer, we could see the man himself when the door curtain was drawn back to let in the next child, sitting in a big chair by a flickering fake log fire.

The children and parents were admitted through the door by a tall, green-clad teenage elf with a dark-skinned, serious face, horn-rimmed glasses and a very sweet smile.

The children must have made their exit from the other side, for no one came out again. It probably led straight back into the shop, I thought, as we inched over the bridge and stopped by a tableau of large reindeer.

The nearest one suddenly made a whirring noise and, moving its head up and down, said cheerily, 'Hi, I'm Rudolf!'

'Hello, Rudolf,' said Teddy, regarding him doubtfully, but that seemed to be the extent of his repertoire, for he fell silent until we heard him repeat himself ten minutes later as we finally arrived at the doorway.

'Are you ready for the next one, Nick?' asked the door elf, turning to look behind her through a gap in the curtain.

'That's Santa's real name – Saint Nicholas,' Teddy whispered to me. 'Uncle Henry told me.'

'Send 'em in,' said a high-pitched, fluting voice.

It was dark in the grotto, but we could make out Father Christmas by the light of the fire and a few dim lanterns. He was a tiny and ancient-looking man with what was clearly his own silvery-white hair and long beard. He had been having a refreshing cup of tea, but handed the empty mug to another elf and said, 'Ho, ho, ho, and who do we have here?'

Teddy approached him. 'I'm Teddy Mariner and I'm eight.' He frowned and then added suspiciously, 'You're very small and old, and you don't look the same as you did when you came to my school yesterday.'

'Good grief, have I changed size *again*?' exclaimed Santa, with commendable quick-wittedness. 'When I'm away from

Lapland, I never know what I'm going to look like from one day to the next. I could even be tall and black tomorrow.'

'You can change colour, too?' Teddy asked, impressed and round-eyed.

'Yes, it's one of my magic powers.'

'I think you look nice now, even if you are smaller than your elves,' Teddy told him.

'Thank you. Perhaps I'll stay like this today, then.'

'Can I ask you something, Santa?'

'Fire right ahead,' said Santa warily.

'Do you think Mummy will bring me a pony when she comes for Christmas? I put it at the top of the list I sent you.'

Father Christmas pursed his lips and ruminated. 'How is she travelling? Car or train?'

'Train, because she doesn't drive.'

'Pity,' said Santa, shaking his head. 'They won't let ponies on the train. I think she'll have to bring you something else off your list instead. Remind me of one or two other things you put on it?'

'A castle, and some dragons to live in it. A real geologist's hammer and goggles . . . and all the Narnia books in a box. I've seen them in the shop in Great Mumming *and* they've got a pirate game with a real wooden treasure chest and gold coins.' He paused. 'If I did get the pony, I'd need a new riding hat, because my old one is too small . . . Oh, and I'd like some proper paints like artists have, because I'm too big for poster paints and anyway, they run. I might be an artist when I grow up, like Meg.' He gestured to me, standing in the shadows with Lex. 'I was going to be a jockey, but Lex says I'm going to be too big, like him.'

'I suspect he's quite right, if you're eight now, because you're nearly as tall as I am.'

'But you're not very tall for a grown-up, are you?'

'No, that's true: I think living above the Arctic Circle must have stunted my growth.'

'But all your elves are very big – don't they live there, too?'

Teddy looked at the nearest helper, who was a tall, pale girl who reminded me of forced rhubarb and had pointed ears attached to her green hat. Then he leaned over and whispered, 'I know *that* lady's just pretending to be an elf, because she usually works in the Christmas Shop, but the other one at the door is a *real* one.'

'I have to get stand-ins sometimes to help me,' Santa whispered back gravely. 'Most of the real elves are still busy making the last toys to go in the sleigh.'

'But you only bring the presents that go in the Christmas stockings, don't you?'

I was starting to feel that whatever they were paying Santa, it wasn't enough. I wondered if he got this kind of inquisition from a lot of the children. No wonder the queue had moved so slowly!

'You're right, I bring enough presents to fill the stockings, and perhaps one or two more for children whose families are too poor to buy any,' he said.

Teddy sighed. 'I think the pony was too big an ask. They cost a lot of money.'

The tall, pale elvish helper was showing signs of restiveness, so we had clearly had our time – and a bit.

'Say goodbye to Santa, Teddy,' Lex said. 'There are lots of other children waiting to see him, too.'

Teddy, who had been leaning confidingly against Santa's red velvet-clad shoulder while they talked, straightened reluctantly.

'I bet *they're* surprised too when they see he's so small. Goodbye, Father Christmas, see you next year.'

Santa reached down into a hessian sack and handed Teddy a brightly wrapped parcel. 'Here's a little gift to be going on with.'

Even the subtle Christmas Shop lights seemed dazzling when we exited through another curtain, and I blinked.

'Come on, time for lunch,' said Lex.

Henry and Clara were waiting for us at a table upstairs in the café, bags of shopping next to their chairs.

Teddy told them all about Father Christmas and his amazing size- and colour-changing powers. Then he unwrapped his present, which was a large silvery egg, containing a purple and gold plastic dragon, whose wings were hinged and could be lifted up and down.

'He *does* know what I want, so he must read all the lists,' Teddy said, impressed. 'Do you think it means I'll get the castle, too?'

'I don't know,' said Lex. 'You'll have to wait and see.'

Teddy had a special children's packed lunch, which came in a reindeer-patterned card box. The rest of us settled for cheese and tomato toasties in thick wholemeal bread. They must have super toasters, and after I'd eaten I felt as if I'd had my roughage quotient for a week.

Afterwards, Henry and Clara took Teddy to select another glass bauble for the tree and a box of crackers, while Lex and I had a second cup of coffee in peace, before taking a look at the craft gallery and workshops.

The waitress who brought the coffee over greeted Lex familiarly and gave me daggers.

'Another ex-girlfriend?' I suggested sweetly, getting my own back for the digs about Mark. 'Like the waitress at the pub?'

He shrugged and said simply, 'I get lonely sometimes.'

'Yes, I've heard about Teddy's nanny too – Flora, wasn't it?'

He looked startled and then embarrassed. 'Oh, that was just a misunderstanding. Flora was about seventeen when she came to Starstone Edge to live with Deirdre and I was . . . off doing things by then. She was the same age as my kid sister, so later, when she was Teddy's nanny, I just carried on thinking of her that way.'

He brooded for a moment. 'She was always pestering me to do things, like run her into Great Mumming or take her out for some driving practice before her test . . . and I did once or twice. That was it: anything else was a figment of her imagination.'

Well, he should know all about *that*, I thought.

'I've given up asking anyone out now, because they all want more commitment than I can give. It doesn't seem fair to them.'

I suppose that when you've lost the love of your life in tragic circumstances, it *would* make it hard to settle for second best, even after all this time . . . especially if you're still carrying a load of guilt about your late wife around with you.

'What about you?' he asked suddenly. 'Are you seeing anyone? I mean, other than Mark.'

'Look,' I said through gritted teeth, 'stop winding me up about Mark! I've only just met him and I'm not remotely interested in him romantically. OK?'

'OK,' he agreed. 'I'm not sure he feels the same way about you, though.'

'He'd better learn to, then,' I said. 'And no, I'm not seeing anyone.'

Then I thought my answer might have given him the impression it was because no one was interested, rather than the choice it really was, so I said, 'I got engaged to Rollo Purvis six years ago. We might have done it earlier, except his mother really didn't like me and she was the one who paid for his flat and car and everything.'

'Didn't it work out?'

'No, but not because of his mother. He asked me just before he went off to do his annual summer stint at a creative writing retreat in the States, then something happened just after he got back and . . . I broke it off.'

He didn't ask me what had happened. Perhaps he could see from my face that it wasn't something I wanted to talk about.

'But he's still around, isn't he? Clara mentioned he'd rung you at the house.'

'We kept in contact, but only as friends – that was his idea – but not any more since he tried to use me to get access to Henry!'

'So, if you haven't been seeing anyone since you broke off your engagement, what do you want out of life?'

He seemed genuinely to want to know, so I said, 'I'd like a little cottage in the country. All my friends are married and having families and some have moved out of London already. Fliss was the last – remember Fliss? Tall, sandy hair and freckles, doing graphic design?'

He nodded.

'We've been sharing a flat for ages, but she's just got married and I realized there's nothing holding me to London, now.'

'But isn't it easier to get commissions if you're based in London?'

'Not any more, and I do have connections there now: there's a gallery that will show my work. Anyway, I'm on the Royal Society of Portrait Painters website and get most of my commissions through that. It's where Clara found me after seeing the portrait I'd painted of one of her friends.'

'One of life's strange coincidences,' he said, a trifle sardonically. 'Of all the painters that must be on their site, she chose you.'

He regarded me for a moment, frowning as if he was trying to puzzle me out again, then he rose to his feet. 'Come on, let's have a quick look round the rest of it.'

The gallery and craft shop could be reached from a door on this level, but I wasn't allowed to linger for long in either, though some of the paintings looked excellent and there were several amazing papercut pictures, one or two of which were literally leaping out of their frames.

'Those are made by Tabby, the wife of Randall Hesketh, who runs the mill. She's got a workshop downstairs,' Lex explained. 'We haven't got time to browse today, though, because the others will be ready to go shortly.'

'I'd love to come back and have a better look around, but I don't suppose I'll be here long enough,' I said, reluctantly following him out and down the stairs. There was a mix of workshops on the ground floor: jewellers, potters, leather workers, painters . . . The last one we came to was that of Tabby, Randall's wife. The workshops had stable doors, presumably so that the people working inside could open the top for viewers, or not, as they liked. Tabby's was open and at the far end of the studio, with her back to us, sat a tall slender woman with long, dark brown hair, intent over something on the table before her.

Papercut pictures hung along the walls, materials were stacked and rolled everywhere and scraps of paper littered the floor around her feet. She was so absorbed, I didn't think she even registered when anyone looked in.

'We won't disturb her,' Lex said softly, moving away. 'I occasionally meet up at the pub in Little Mumming with

Tabby and Randall, and Jude Martland and his wife, Holly, other friends who live nearby. But not recently, because Tabby and Randall had a baby boy a few months ago, and Holly's on her third, so my friends are procreating like mad, just like yours.'

'It's an age thing,' I said absently. 'We hit the mid-to-late thirties and realize if we want children we need to get a shift on.'

He gave me an unreadable look, but didn't say anything. As we went through swing doors and back into the mill, we spotted Clara and Henry waiting for us. Teddy was watching another cracker demonstration and we collected him on the way out.

'I saw Mercy in the shop,' Clara said to Lex. 'She had Tabby's baby with her – a sweet little thing.'

'We saw Tabby in her workshop, but we didn't disturb her,' he said.

We all piled back into the car and Lex into his pick-up and we followed him back down to the road, though by the time we'd waited for a cyclist to pass and pulled out, he'd vanished.

'I've told you the Martlands lived up at Little Mumming, haven't I?' Henry said, driving past the turn to the village. 'They hold a special ceremony on the green on Twelfth Night every year, but they don't encourage outsiders to go, so I never have. We wouldn't want to be swamped with outsiders for *our* Solstice rites, after all.'

'Fat chance of that, when the weather's so bad that sometimes even Fred from the pub can't get over to take part in it, and there's only a handful of people,' said Clara.

'Before the reservoir, anyone in the village capable of climbing the hill went,' said Henry. 'There was a torch-lit procession.

Someone went up earlier to light the fire and the torches round the stone first, of course.'

'Nowadays, someone usually pops up on the Underhill quad bike,' Clara said. 'And Old Winter goes with them to get in the cave before the rest of us arrive.'

Teddy was worn out with excitement and half asleep in the back next to me, holding his plastic dragon.

We went the long way round to get home, but Lex must have braved the pass, because he'd got there first. I hadn't realized he was coming back, but had assumed he'd go straight to Terrapotter.

'Lex has been quick! He was stopping to pick up our holly on the way,' said Clara, surprised. 'I hope he didn't forget.'

But we found him in the hall next to a heap of holly – red with bright berries – and another of tangled ivy, for Tottie had collected some from the Underhill estate with Sybil that morning after their hack.

Den had walked Lass already, so Henry disappeared straight into his study. Clara said she'd delegate putting the greenery up to me, Lex and Tottie.

'Well, that's why I came back here, after all,' Lex said, and went to fetch the stepladder.

Teddy went to watch a DVD in the morning room and I suspected he'd fall asleep to the sound of Disney-style singing.

Using green florist's wire, Lex twined ivy and holly round the big wooden wheel of a chandelier in the hall, while Tottie and I decorated the mantelpieces and stuck sprigs of greenery all over the place, until the house looked even more festive than before.

Teddy, flushed with sleep, reappeared just as we'd finished and then Den came out of the kitchen with the tea trolley. At the sound of the rattling crockery, or possibly the smell of hot, buttered crumpets, Clara and Henry's doors opened too, and for a few moments the hall was exactly like one of those wooden weather houses, only with multiple occupants popping out of doors.

Lex said he'd meant to go home way before tea, but he couldn't resist the crumpets. Afterwards he asked to see Henry's portrait.

He stood in front of it in total silence for ages, then gave me another of his long, puzzled looks.

'I'd forgotten how good an artist you were until I saw Clara's portrait, and this is going to be just as brilliant. You always took your work seriously, even when we were students.'

'So did you,' I reminded him. It had been something we'd had in common and we'd often been part of the small band of students who carried on working late until the caretaker threw us out into the night. It had made a bond, that unstoppable creative urge.

I could see he was remembering that and finding it hard to square with the person he'd thought me all these years.

He stared at me, frowning for a few moments, then turned and left without another word.

I felt too tired to settle to anything after that, so I sent Fliss a long email, telling her about the mill, and Lex's needling me about Mark, and finally what he'd said when he'd seen Henry's portrait . . .

It was all a bit tangled, but I sent it anyway.

At dinner, Clara said that while we were festooning the house with greenery, she'd written a little more of her memoirs and the part she'd reached now was causing her to come to a few interesting conclusions. This was mysterious, especially when she added enigmatically that presents came in all shapes and sizes, but were always welcome. I think her mind must have wandered off on to another track.

When Teddy had been put to bed, all his presents were brought down to the drawing room and we had a mad wrapping session, before they were locked away in the large cupboard under the stairs, ready to put around the tree on Christmas Eve.

My hoard of presents was still hidden away in my turret. but I gave Clara the bean-filled little dragon I'd picked up in Preciousss for Teddy's Christmas stocking, and she said it could guard the gold coins at the bottom of it until Christmas Eve finally arrived.

Clara

Lady Leamington's plan proved a good one, for though many people commented on how much weight Nessa was gaining, no one seemed to guess the truth.

There seemed no point in telling Nessa that our suspicions were correct and George's wife, Barbara, was expecting a baby not long after hers would be born.

We had plans for that summer vacation. Henry intended wandering around the remoter parts of Greece, while I had wangled my way on to an archaeological dig in Turkey, after which we'd go travelling together until the start of the Michaelmas term.

By now Nessa was turning quite militantly feminist, which made a pleasant change from her earlier romantic imbecility, and was looking forward to completing her degree in America. But first, Lady Leamington duly whisked her away at the end of term, and in the nick of time. The baby was born very early and by caesarean section soon afterwards.

I visited Nessa in her swish private maternity hospital before I left for Turkey.

I was glad to hear from the nurse who took me to her room that, despite being so early, the baby girl was a healthy five pounds and doing well. Nessa, who was looking pale and drawn, told me she hadn't seen her and didn't intend to.

'I'm going to recuperate at Godmama's house and we're going to tell everyone that I've had my appendix out.'

'A healthy, five-pound appendix,' I said drily, but she'd never had much of a sense of humour and this passed her by.

'I don't think I'll ever come back to England – and I'm going to focus on my career from now on,' she told me, before rambling on about how men conned women into the idea of romance in order to dominate and control them, and a lot more like that. When I got up to leave, she tearfully begged me to keep in touch.

On the way out I asked to see the baby, who was asleep in a clinical white room with a lot of other newborns, all looking much the same.

A private adoption had been arranged by Lady Leamington with her chauffeur and his wife, who were childless, and I hoped that would work out well . . .

Nessa wrote me several gushing letters, enthusing about her new life, but then slowly these missives dwindled, until at last they stopped. It took a lot longer, however, before Henry and I ceased to wonder how the baby was faring and where she was . . .

The knowledge of George's infamous behaviour (not to mention several other unsavoury episodes we heard about later) was to colour our relations with him for the rest of our lives. He, of course, had no idea we knew about Nessa, and he, in turn, had no idea about her pregnancy. There was no open breach: we were fond of his wife, Barbara, and their daughter, dear Sybil, but we had as little to do with him as possible.

24

Piked

Den drove Tottie to church in Thorstane on Sunday morning and Teddy went with them – not to church, but to the pub with Den, for a playdate with Fred Golightly's grandson.

Clara was working and Henry and I retired to the studio for what I thought might be the final sitting. There were still a couple of days to go until River arrived, so I would have completed both portraits in plenty of time, had I still intended leaving with him.

The house settled into quietness around us, apart from Lass's reverberating snores when she fell asleep on Henry's feet, and the ticking of the revived clock on the bookcase. Someone had reset the time and must be winding it up, but it wasn't me.

Clara was having a session on her memoirs and, since she was still writing about her Oxford days, she came in occasionally to ask Henry something.

I'd just completed the last touches to Lass and was contemplating a few small background tweaks, when she returned for a third time and said that if we were finished with the sitting, she'd like us both to come to her study so she could show us something.

I thought she must have switched to her work computer and had managed to piece another inscription together – a 'join' as she called it – or something like that, but when I'd cleaned up and followed Henry in there, only the laptop screen was glowing.

'I've found a photograph of one of the girls from my first year at Oxford University that I'd like to show you, Meg,' Clara said. 'She's called Nessa Cassidy.'

She exchanged a glance with Henry that I couldn't decipher and then brought up a picture of a plump woman in perhaps her late twenties, or early thirties, with very fair hair, a slightly tip-tilted nose, a babyishly short upper lip and a militant expression that sat oddly with all that cuteness.

'Nessa Cassidy? I think I've heard of her,' I said. 'Wasn't she a leading American gay feminist writer way back? There was a book . . .'

'Quite right,' said Clara, 'long before your time, of course. She went back to the States to complete her studies after her first year at Oxford and had a big hit with her book, *The Butterfly Kiss.* But she died tragically young in a car accident.'

I peered closer and frowned. 'She looks . . . sort of familiar. But then, I expect I've seen her photograph before somewhere.'

'It's an old photo, but Henry and I remember her very well. In fact, the memories have all come flooding back since I started writing that part of my autobiography.'

'Do you remember when you first arrived here and we said you reminded us of someone?' asked Henry. 'You hoped it might have been your mother.'

I nodded, puzzled.

'We hadn't met your mother, but we came to realize later that it was Nessa Cassidy you resembled. It's not so clear in the photo, but she had your unusual light greenish-blue eyes, silver-blond hair and creamy pale skin.'

'Really?' I looked again, with more interest. 'It's hard to tell from this, but other than her colouring, she doesn't look like me at all, does she?' I paused, then added slowly, 'She *does* look a bit like Mum, though!'

I turned to look at them both and Henry gave me an encouraging smile, as if I was a child trying to piece together a puzzle.

'The thing is, darling,' said Clara, 'that we think there may be a link between your mother and Nessa.'

'What kind of link?' I asked, though already my mind had begun to shove the pieces together, much as Clara did with her computer joins.

'Nessa had an illegitimate baby before she went back to the States, though it was all hushed up. We think that baby might have been your mother.'

'But just because my colouring reminds you of her, it doesn't necessarily mean there *is* a link,' I protested.

'There's a bit more to it than that, and you've just said yourself that your mother looked like Nessa,' Henry said. 'But let's go into the drawing room and discuss it more comfortably. The others won't be back for ages yet, and there's a lot to tell you.'

Once we were established around the fire, Henry said, 'I'm afraid this will all come as a shock to you, though we hope it's a nice one. We've had time to get used to the idea, because we've suspected you were Nessa's granddaughter for a few days, especially once you'd told us your mother was adopted and had the same unusual hair and eye colouring as yourself.'

'But that can't be unique to us, and Mum having been adopted could well be just a coincidence, too,' I pointed out.

'We've never met *anyone* who looked like Nessa until we set eyes on you,' Henry said.

'Let me tell you about Nessa, Meg,' said Clara, and described her first term at Oxford and meeting the half-American girl whose room was next to hers.

'Nessa was small – what they called then a Pocket Venus – and most people thought her very pretty. She took her studies seriously and had ambitions to work in journalism, but in other ways she could be very silly and talked a lot of romantic nonsense about men and love. But she had pashes on girls, including yours truly, so I suspected she was a lesbian long before she did.'

'I expect deep down she knew and she just pushed the thought away because she wanted to conform to the norm. This was 1959, after all,' said Henry.

'Very true, dear,' said Clara. 'Nessa talked a lot of romantic twaddle about looking for her perfect Sir Galahad and then, unfortunately, she convinced herself she'd found him . . . and he took advantage of her.'

'But he married someone else before she realized she was pregnant,' finished Henry.

'That's all very sad,' I said, still entirely unconvinced that there was a connection, 'but I really *don't* think—'

Clara did her human steamroller impersonation and just carried on as if I hadn't spoken. 'We hadn't even got to the swinging sixties by then, don't forget, and the pregnancy was quite advanced before she realized what was happening. I just thought she'd put on a lot of weight. But anyway, she confided in me and then decided to tell her godmother, who lived in London, and she helped Nessa to hush it up.'

'But surely she would have had to leave university when her bump showed?' I said, interested now, though still disbelieving.

'She *did* manage to conceal it till the end of term. Then the baby was born early by caesarean section and immediately adopted,' said Henry.

'How awful for her,' I said, sympathetically. 'To go through all that and then have to give up her baby.'

They exchanged glances again, like twins sharing a thought.

'She wanted to go back to America and put it all behind her,' Clara said. 'Which she did, and eventually we lost touch.'

'I still don't feel it has any connection to me,' I said. 'Anyone might have similar colouring to mine and Mum's, and just because this Nessa had a baby and my mother was adopted . . .'

'There's a bit more to it than that, my dear,' said Henry. 'And it doesn't reflect well on my family.'

I wondered what on earth was coming next!

'When Henry and I saw you and Mark sitting on the sofa together the other day, the similarity of your profiles was too striking to be dismissed. It confirmed what we already suspected.'

I stared at them in astonishment. 'But . . . I don't look anything *like* Mark! And what has he to do with anything?'

'In colouring, you're totally unlike, but the high cheekbones, straight nose and pointed chin are just the same,' explained Clara. 'You look a little like Henry, too. It's a Doome family resemblance.'

'Which is hardly surprising, because we *are* all related,' said Henry. 'I'm afraid the man who seduced Nessa was my elder brother, George – Mark's grandfather. He visited me soon after I went up to Oxford and unfortunately met Nessa then.'

'She was really very pretty, if you liked the type,' said Clara dispassionately.

'She was certainly George's type,' Henry said drily, 'and he always had to have what he wanted, no matter what the cost.'

'We were settling in and enjoying university life and being together again,' Clara said. 'I was just happy Nessa wasn't dogging our footsteps all the time, like she had at first.'

She pondered the past, then shrugged. 'We were very young and engrossed in ourselves, I suppose. Anyway, to continue this sorry tale, late in the autumn term, Nessa went off to London for the weekend, ostensibly to visit her godmother – but I'd glimpsed her getting into a car with George.'

'Yes, that gave us a bit of a jolt,' said Henry. 'We'd suspected they'd stayed in touch, but hoped it would fizzle out, because he was engaged to an heiress. He always loved money, so long as he didn't have to earn it.'

'Nessa was an orphan and would come into money one day, too,' Clara said, 'but at that time her guardians gave her an allowance, a very generous one.'

My brain was now reeling as it tried to come to terms with all this. 'So . . . you seriously think George Doome was my grandfather?'

Clara nodded. 'Nessa told me she'd arranged to spend the day with him in London before going to her godmother's house, but they went to a flat he'd borrowed from a friend first and that's where he seduced her . . . though, from what she said, that was too mild a term for it. It certainly shattered any illusions she'd had about romance and I think finally made her acknowledge her real sexuality.'

'Poor girl! I'm so ashamed of George,' said Henry.

'He knew Nessa was an heiress and told her afterwards that he didn't know why she was so upset, because he was going to marry her,' said Clara. 'Of course, he assumed she'd come into her capital once she was married, not that she'd have to wait till she was thirty, so when that came out in the big scene afterwards he turned very nasty.'

'He behaved very badly. We found it hard to forgive him, though of course he didn't realize that we knew what had happened – and he never knew about the baby, either,' Henry said.

'Nessa was absolutely adamant he shouldn't be told,' agreed Clara. 'And he'd got his fiancée pregnant soon after Nessa, so there didn't seem a lot of point.'

She sighed. 'The most awful things did just get hushed up then. Nessa wanted only to leave and put it all behind her. She wasn't interested in the baby at all and once the adoption was through and she'd gone off to America, that seemed to be the end of it.'

'I'm glad George's wife, Barbara, never knew about what happened,' said Henry. 'She was a sweet woman who put up with a lot from George over the years, but that would have really hurt her.'

By now, I was feeling so stunned and confused by all this that I was unable to speak. Henry fetched me a glass of Tottie's mead and a whisky and soda each for him and Clara.

When I finally got my voice back, I said, 'I still find it hard to believe that Mum could be Nessa's baby. There's no real proof, is there? Isn't it just conjecture?'

But even as I spoke I was examining Henry's features in a new light and noting similarities with my own, though his face had a bonier and more intellectual aspect.

'We're quite certain, though a DNA test would give concrete proof, if anyone wanted it,' Clara replied.

'To us, you felt like part of the family the moment you stepped into the house,' Henry said. 'Didn't you feel that, too?'

'I suppose I did,' I agreed, though I'd also been stunned by meeting Lex on the doorstep, so it hadn't hit me with great force at the time.

'We always wondered what had happened to the baby and hoped she was having a happy life,' Henry said. Then he and Clara filled me in a bit about Nessa's subsequent life and career, with the early success of her feminist book and the scandal of her having a female live-in lover when things like that were not openly talked about.

'Although what happened to Nessa was a terrible experience, it did seem to insert a backbone of steel into all that blancmange,' Clara said. 'You could see from the picture I showed you that she looked like an overweight Sugar Plum Fairy with attitude.'

'Mum looks like an overweight Sugar Plum Fairy *without* attitude,' I said. 'She drifts about like thistledown, though, wherever the current breeze takes her.'

Though this time, it seemed to have blown her totally off course.

'We must break it to Sybil that she has a half-sister and a niece,' Clara suggested.

'*Must* we tell anyone?' I protested. 'I mean, it's lovely for me if it's true, but I can't see the point in stirring things up after all this time.'

'Of *course* we must. We're quite sure about it, and you must be made part of the family, however belatedly,' declared Clara.

'Yes, we're very happy to have found you and we don't want to let you go again!' agreed Henry. 'But why don't we order the DNA testing kits online, to put your mind at rest? It could show up other interesting relationships, too, so it would be quite fun.'

'That's true,' said Clara. 'It might inspire you to write a little family history, Henry!'

I'd been working possible relationships out in my head and it was complicated. 'So . . . if it *is* true, then you, Henry, are my great-uncle? Sybil is my aunt and Mark . . . my cousin?'

'That's right, so you've acquired lots of relations in one fell swoop!' Henry said.

'But telling Sybil would surely upset her, and for no good reason?'

'She must already know what her father was like. He and that old reprobate Piers Marten were like two peas in a pod, where women and gambling were concerned,' said Henry. 'There were lots of unsavoury stories circulating about them when they were younger.'

'Sybil always managed to shut her eyes to anything she didn't like,' observed Clara. 'And of course after she married – Edmund Whitcliffe, a very nice Methodist minister, much older than herself, Meg – she didn't see a lot of her father because her husband disliked him.'

I wasn't surprised: I don't think I'd have liked him either. I much preferred having River as my grandfather.

'I think we should break the news to Sybil and Mark tomorrow,' suggested Henry, to my horror.

'And perhaps we should tell Lex at the same time,' said Clara. 'I know he's not related to you except through my marriage, Meg, but he'll have to know and it will save having to explain the whole thing over again.'

Lex! Amid all these revelations, I hadn't thought about how he was going to take the news! I hardly imagined he'd welcome me warmly into the family circle, especially since now there was a good chance he'd never ever quite get rid of me.

'I think you're being a bit hasty,' I said. 'We should at least wait till we know for certain.'

'We *do* know, and DNA testing will take some time, especially since it's so close to Christmas,' Clara said. 'But I've been thinking, and it occurs to me that your mother might have had some papers about her adoption, or even her birth certificate, since it was an unofficial adoption? Did she ever mention having anything like that?'

'She did tell me once that she'd brought her birth certificate with her when she ran away, because she thought she might need it for a passport one day. It's probably in the tin trunk she stored things in at the Farm.'

'Well then, if so, we might find some information on it to confirm who her mother was,' Clara suggested.

I got up, fired by a sudden need to know for sure. 'I'll ring River and see if he'll go and look.'

Luckily, I got hold of him right away and he said he'd send Oshan up to the attic for the trunk and call me back shortly . . . which he did.

And the mother's name on the birth certificate *was* Vanessa Cassidy; father unknown.

Suddenly it all seemed very real. Still holding the phone in a slightly shaking hand I relayed this information and then, prompted by Henry, suggested to River that he bring the birth certificate and any other documents with him when he came to stay.

Typically, River hadn't asked me why I was interested, but I told him anyway. 'Thank you for finding the certificate, River. It means I know now who Mum's biological parents were, and also that I'm related to the Doomes,' I finished.

'Karma,' he said, placidly. 'The Goddess works in mysterious ways.'

Then he added that he'd be setting off early next morning for Sticklepond and to stay overnight with his friend Gregory Warlock, as planned, and would then come on to Starstone Edge on Tuesday afternoon.

'How very satisfactory,' said Clara when I'd rung off, handing me another glass of mead. 'Here's to the newest member of the family!'

I found myself clinking glasses with them, while feeling as if I was trapped in the weirdest dream ever.

We hadn't heard the others come back, but now the door opened and Tottie said, 'Carousing already?'

'A little celebration – we'll tell you and Den all about it later,' said Henry as Teddy burst in, brandishing a long, foil-wrapped parcel like a slightly battered sword.

'Look, Uncle Henry! Fred's given us a pike he had in his freezer and Den says he's going to cook it for New Year!'

'I hope it's only got one head, then,' said Henry gravely.

'I checked,' Teddy said seriously, and then Den followed him in and took away the fish before it prematurely defrosted.

'Pike are carnivorous,' said Clara. 'Do we want to eat a fish that eats other fish?'

'A good point, my dear,' said Henry. 'But if we eat fish at all, then I suppose it makes little difference.'

'I've never heard of anyone eating pike,' I said.

Den returned in time to catch that and said he had an old recipe for the fish he'd like to try out.

Teddy asked if he could watch TV in the morning room till lunch was ready, and went off with Lass for company. As soon as he was out of earshot, Clara said to Den and Tottie, 'I've got something to tell you!' before explaining their discovery about me.

'Don't surprise me, does it?' said Den.

'How lovely,' Tottie said warmly. 'I mean, it was sad that your mother was adopted, but all's well that ends well, because we've found you now!'

'We're keeping it quiet until we've told Sybil tomorrow, and Mark and Lex at the same time, we thought,' explained Clara. 'We'll give Teddy a simple version a little later today.'

'He's going to be delighted,' Henry said, but *I* thought the rest of my new-found family might not be quite as keen on the idea . . .

'It did occur to me the other day that Meg and Mark looked as alike as two peas in a pod,' said Tottie. 'Only one was penny plain and the other tuppence coloured, as it were. Couldn't miss it, though,' she said, then searched out her pinafore from the collection stuffed under a sofa cushion and left with Den to help prepare lunch.

I felt quite dazed for the rest of the day as everything I'd learned sank in. Since I found I couldn't settle to do any work, I went out with Henry when he walked Lass.

On my return, I felt like making a statement, even if I wasn't quite sure what of, so I went straight upstairs and dyed my hair with the old-rose hair colouring I'd bought in Great Mumming.

'Gor blimey!' said Den, sounding like an escapee from Mary Poppins, when he saw me coming downstairs. Then he threw open the drawing-room door and announced, ''Ere's the bleeding Rose of Sharon, ain't it?'

After the initial surprise, everyone seemed to like the change, and Teddy said he was going to do a new portrait of me.

Clara explained to him that we'd just discovered I was related to the Doome family and then swore him to secrecy until everyone else had been told tomorrow.

'There isn't anyone I could tell,' Teddy pointed out.

'Well, just in case we have a visitor, or a phone call, don't mention it,' said Tottie.

'Does Mummy know?'

'Not yet,' said Clara. 'We'll give her a ring and tell her tomorrow, too.'

An idea suddenly struck Teddy. 'If Meg is Uncle Henry's niece . . .'

'Great-niece,' amended Clara.

'Then . . . does that make her my auntie?'

'More of a cousin,' Henry said. 'By marriage.'

'Good!' said Teddy.

I rang Fliss before supper and told her the momentous news. She was very excited, much more than I was, in fact, because I was still in a state of slightly disbelieving shock.

'It's like a romantic comedy film, isn't it, with you as the heroine? The lost heiress!'

'Except I wasn't a lost heiress, just a lost illegitimate relative . . . and the only candidate for the romantic hero part other than Mark, who turns out to be my first cousin, is Lex, who hates me.'

'It would all work out fine in a film, though, Meg.'

'Yes, but I'm not *in* a film and tomorrow is probably going to be more like a horror movie, because Clara has arranged for Lex to be here in the morning when she breaks the news to Sybil and Mark. I'm dreading it, because I don't think any of them are going to be as delighted as she thinks they will – why should they be?'

'Why *shouldn't* they?' Fliss countered. 'I mean, Henry and Clara are, aren't they?'

'Well, yes, but it wasn't a shock to them and it *will* be to the others. And I don't think Lex will like it in the least because I'm sure he's just counting down the days till he can see the back of me for ever.'

'But now you know you're part of the family, you're finally going to have to tell him the truth about what happened, aren't you?' she pointed out.

'I don't see why I should,' I replied stubbornly. 'Let him and Al think whatever stupid things about me they like! He probably wouldn't believe me anyway.'

'You know I'm right and he'd *have* to believe you,' she insisted. 'Ring me tomorrow, and tell me the next thrilling instalment. I'll be at a loose end, because Cal's not back from his business trip till early on Christmas Eve.'

'I don't suppose everything will have sunk in, even by then. Maybe I'll wake up tomorrow and find I dreamed it all.'

'No, I'm your reality check,' she said.

I googled Nessa Cassidy and spent a lot of time looking at old photographs online. There was no denying that, apart from the militant expression, she looked exactly like Mum.

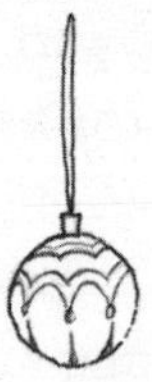

25

Relatively Speaking

Needless to say, I didn't sleep well that night, what with everything going over and over in my head, and the thought of the scene next morning when Clara and Henry told Mark, Sybil and Lex what they'd discovered.

We were all down to breakfast very early and Clara outlined her plans: she and Henry would break the news to Sybil, Mark and Lex. I still didn't see why Lex should be included at this stage, but my objections were overruled.

'We might as well tell them all at once,' she said. 'Then you, Meg, can come in with Tottie and Den afterwards and we'll have a little celebration together,' she added comfortably. I suspected the scene would not be as cosy as she pictured it.

'Not me,' said Den. 'I don't want to barge into this family reunion till the dust settles, do I?'

'There won't be any dust, and you're part of the family, Den,' said Clara, 'just as Tottie is.'

'I'll bring the coffee when yer give me the nod and see 'ow it's going,' he conceded.

'What about me?' asked Teddy.

'You could come into the drawing room with Tottie and Meg,' suggested Henry.

'There, that's all settled,' said Clara. 'Time for a little work before everyone gets here.'

She and Henry headed for their respective studies and Teddy and I went into the studio. Of course, I still couldn't settle to anything, so I didn't quite know what to do with myself. How would Sybil – my aunt (or half-aunt? And is half an aunt better than none?) take the news? She must be only a few months younger than Mum . . . And Mark, now revealed as my cousin – would his attitude change towards me?

Mind you, that might be a good thing.

Then there was Lex . . . A thought occurred to me: would he think I'd already known about the connection? Then I realized that was silly, for how on earth could I have? Without Clara and Henry's knowledge of the whole story, there was no way I could have found out.

Teddy began another picture of me, this time with pink hair, while I checked my iPad and phone for emails, messages and missed calls.

I certainly hoped I'd missed any that Rollo might have sent me, but to my surprise, the stream of communication from him had stopped dead. I hoped he'd finally got the message through his thick skull and wasn't just too busy at his event in York to harass me.

Then an even better scenario occurred to me: he might have finished his event by now and, having accepted there was no way I was going to play along with his plans, already be heading south, like a glossy, pouting homing pigeon.

Lex, Mark and Sybil had been invited for ten and I went up to my turret room just before that and watched for them from the narrow window: first Mark and his mother in his big, black, four-wheel-drive monster, and then Lex's familiar battered white pick-up.

I gave them a quarter of an hour to settle in and then crept down to my studio again. I could hear voices from the drawing room, even though the door was shut.

There were voices from the direction of the kitchen, too, including Teddy's, so in my studio I felt I was alone in a kind of limbo. Just me, and the old clock ticking like a time bomb.

Teddy's latest painting of me was still there, pinned to his little easel, and was really surprisingly good considering his age. He was going to love the artist's box I'd bought him.

I put my portraits of Henry and Clara on adjacent easels and contemplated them. Of course, I wouldn't touch Clara's again, but I decided Henry's still needed just a couple of tiny tweaks. Perhaps tomorrow . . .

The door suddenly opened, making me jump, and Tottie appeared to summon me. 'Come on! We're to go in now, Meg.'

When we entered the room it felt as if every eye was fixed on me and in that brief instant I recognized some far from joyful accompanying expressions.

Sybil's face looked both shocked and horrified, as if she'd reached the climax of a scary film (though perhaps a little of the horror was due to my pink hair). Mark's stare was hard and angry, and as for Lex, he was regarding me in the darkly brooding way that was so hard to read. If there had been the beginnings of a tiny thaw in our relationship, then it had frozen over hard again.

None of them was about to burst into rapturous welcome, that was for sure.

'Come and sit here, Meg, between Clara and myself,' said Henry, patting the seat next to him. Tottie took one opposite, next to Sybil, who was still gazing at me as if I had two heads, like the mutant pike.

'So, here's your new niece, Sybil!' said Henry.

'I . . . suppose she must be, if what you say *is* true, Henry,' she said reluctantly, finally dragging her eyes away from me. 'But the whole story seems so incredible that I'm afraid I can't quite believe it. I mean, I know you're sure who Meg's grandmother is, but there's no proof that Daddy . . .' She trailed off into silence.

'I think we've heard enough to know it must be true, Mum,' Mark said. 'I mean, now I *know*, even I can see Meg's got the family features.'

His hard expression turned into a twisted half-smile. 'We're first cousins, then, Meg.'

'But with different grandmothers,' said Sybil. 'And Meg's mother was illegitimate, of course.'

'I'm so sorry if it's all been a shock to you,' I apologized to her. 'I was stunned too, because I'd no idea at all.'

'Apart from the unedifying light it casts on my brother, I'm sure we're all *delighted* to welcome Meg into the family,' said Henry, and he and Clara smiled warmly at me.

Then Clara gave me a pat as if I was a nervous dog. 'Henry and I have always known about Nessa and George's affair and the baby, so once Meg arrived here it all quickly fell into place for us.'

Sybil said, 'Then I suppose it must be true . . . and I expect Daddy *was* a bit wild and thoughtless when he was young, but of course he was a wonderful husband to Mummy.'

There was a short and respectful, if incredulous, silence after this remark.

It was broken by Tottie saying, 'He treated her well enough when he was at home, but then, he didn't spend a lot of time at Underhill until the last few years, did he? And even *I* heard the rumours about what he and that Piers Marten got up to abroad!'

'*Piers!*' suddenly exclaimed Sybil, sitting bolt upright with her eyes widening. 'What on earth will he think when he knows about this?'

'Why should it matter what he thinks?' Clara asked. 'He may even know already. After all, he was George's oldest friend and they were practically inseparable for most of their lives.'

'Oh, no, if Daddy didn't know about the baby, then Piers certainly wouldn't have.'

'That's true,' said Tottie. 'I suppose Piers might have known about the affair, though.'

Mark's scowl had returned in force. 'Meg, I hope your mother won't think she has some kind of claim on the estate when she finds out she's related to us.'

I stared at him, astounded. 'I haven't seen her for a few years, but unless she's had a character transplant in that time, it would never even cross her mind! She's never been interested in who her natural parents were and she's the least materialistic person I know.'

I met his angry and suspicious eyes straight on. 'I can guarantee that she won't make any claim on the estate, even if she's entitled to – and nor will I.'

'Of course you wouldn't, dear,' said Clara, and Lass, apparently feeling some tension in the room directed at me, came and shoved her wet nose into my hand.

'I'm pleased to find I've got so many relatives, but I don't *need* anything from you, because I already have a family at the Farm *and* a profession.'

The black cloud slowly lifted from Mark's brow and he got up from his chair, came over and kissed me on both cheeks.

'Sorry, silly of me,' he said. 'I should have known you well enough by now to realize that.'

Sybil, rallying, gave me a slightly watery smile. 'I suppose we must welcome you into the family,' she said, though I noted she was still looking a bit rabbit-in-the-headlights. She must have closed her eyes and ears to what dear Daddy was really like for her entire life.

'That's the spirit!' encouraged Tottie.

I'd forgotten Lex was in the room, since he was sitting slightly back in the shadows behind me, until Clara said, 'What do *you* think of it all, Lex? You're very quiet.'

'It was a surprise, of course,' he said in his deep voice, 'but really, it's nothing to do with me, is it? Meg's no relation of mine.'

'She is by marriage, and she's now definitely part of the family,' Henry said.

'She's my sort-of cousin,' Teddy put in, from his perch on the camel saddle stool. 'I'm glad! Uncle Henry, can Meg live with us here for ever?'

'Of course, if she wanted to, but she has her own life to live, you know. But I hope she'll always treat the Red House as her second home and come here whenever she wishes.'

'Thank you,' I said, deeply touched.

'I'd better welcome you to the tribe, then, since clearly there'll be no getting rid of you now,' Lex said drily, though I'm sure everyone thought he was joking.

Den rattled in with the trolley, loaded with coffee and hot cheese scones. He was whistling 'Happy Days Are Here Again' between his teeth.

'All settled? The bleeding ewe lamb welcomed back ter the fold?'

'Very biblical, Den,' said Clara.

'I was saved once, wasn't I? But it didn't take.'

The conversation began to ease slowly into more everyday subjects and I let it ebb and flow around me as I sipped my coffee.

I didn't feel any sense that I was related to Mark or Sybil . . . and Mark had reacted to the news with anger, but once he'd accepted that his inheritance wasn't in any danger from me or Mum, he'd been quite sweet.

As for Clara and Henry, I'd felt a warm regard for them from the moment of my arrival; *they* felt like my family, and the Red House my home, rather than Underhill and its inhabitants.

Sybil, clearly now thinking some gracious gesture was required, broke into my reverie. 'You must come over to Underhill one day, Meg, and I'll tell you something of the family history and about your grandfather.'

I'd heard quite enough about George and I'd already had the guided tour of the house and the ancestors from Mark, but I smiled at her and said, 'That would be lovely, though what I'm really longing to see is the ancient inscribed stone Clara told me about. It was moved to the grounds of Underhill when the valley was flooded, wasn't it?'

'Yes, and you must see it,' Clara agreed. 'It's what first sparked my interest in ancient written languages. There are two different versions of the runic alphabet on it, one of them the earliest, with only sixteen letters.'

'We'll have all the time in the world to get to know Meg and show her the important landmarks and history of the valley,' Henry said. 'And what a big, jolly family party we'll be for Christmas dinner this year!'

I thought that was slightly optimistic under the circumstances. Unfortunately it also reminded Mark of something.

Turning to his mother, he said, 'I hope you've finally managed to get through to Piers and make sure he doesn't turn up for Christmas, Mum?'

She looked nervous. 'He isn't answering his phone, but I left several messages explaining, in case he hadn't got my letter, and I sent him another one. I do hope he's not ill, or anything.'

'He's probably just sulking,' said Mark.

Lex, who had lapsed into silence again, said he had to go back and do some work now, though I'm sure that was just an excuse. I knew the pottery was winding down ready for the Christmas break.

Clara pressed Sybil and Mark to stay for lunch, but Sybil said she thought she needed to ride out on the moors and think about things.

'Of course, I'm very pleased to find out about you, Meg, it's just that it's all been very *unsettling*, that's all.'

'Of course,' I said. 'I understand, because I felt exactly the same way when I found out, too.'

Tottie said she'd go with Sybil, since if the forecast was to be believed, they might not be able to ride for a couple of days. Sybil didn't object, so I expect she'd talk it all over with her friend, like I had with Fliss, and feel much better.

Den cleared the things away, with Teddy's help . . . or hindrance, since he insisted on pushing the trolley and it had the kind of wheels that tried to go in two different directions at once.

'That didn't go too badly,' said Henry when the others had gone. 'I knew it would be a bit of a stunner for poor old Sybil, but Mark took it quite well, really.'

'Yes, once he was sure Meg and her mother wouldn't try and claim anything from the estate!' Clara gave her wide, toothy grin. 'When we first told them who you were, Meg, Lex said he'd always felt there was something familiar about you and now he could see that it was a touch of the Doomes.'

That sounded about right.

After lunch I went up to my room to be alone for a while, and also to wrap the last of the little sketches I'd been surreptitiously drawing as gifts, then mounting in the card frames I'd bought in Great Mumming.

I looked out of my turret window from time to time and the sky appeared to be taking on an increasingly leaden, snowy aspect.

I rang Fliss up when I'd finished wrapping and gave her the latest instalment of what seemed to be turning into more of a saga than a romantic comedy.

'It just needs Mum to turn up on the doorstep now and drift about being ditsy and off the wall,' I finished, then sighed. 'I wish she *would* reappear.'

'I'm sure she's all right. I mean, River thinks so, doesn't he?'

Fliss liked River, whom she seemed to regard as somewhere between a fortune-teller and an oracle.

'Yes,' I agreed, with more positivity. 'He *is* certain she's alive, so she's bound to resurface one of these days.'

'I've found a lovely house online,' Fliss said then. 'It would be quite a long commute for Cal when he has to go into work, but then, he does travel so much, or work from home.'

'What about your job?' I asked.

'I'd have to give it up and perhaps do supply teaching for a while, but the whole point of moving out is to find somewhere cheaper in the country, where we can bring up a family. I'm getting on, so there's no time to lose.'

'No, I suppose not,' I said, with that familiar ache of loss. Motherhood was not going to be for me, though I'd probably have lots of fun being the mad auntie who turned up from time to time with presents.

'River's arriving tomorrow afternoon,' I said, changing the subject. 'He knows only that I'm related to the Doomes, so I can give him the whole story. I've decided that I'm going to tell him all about that night with Lex, too, and the fallout afterwards. Not to mention the way Lex and Al have behaved since I got here.'

'That's a great idea! He'll put it all into perspective for you and tell you what to do – but I think he'll say exactly the same as me: you must insist Lex hears what really happened!'

'I have a feeling you're right,' I agreed. 'I did *try* to tell Lex once, but he just walked off. I might have to tie him down and gag him before he'll hear me out.'

'I think you've been reading the wrong kind of novels, Meg.'

'No, only murder mysteries, and luckily, so far at least, I haven't felt homicidal.'

Tottie came back from her ride with Sybil, her face glowing.

'Weather's getting colder and it's starting to freeze. There's ice on the puddles.'

'Is Sybil all right about Meg now?' Clara asked. 'I didn't realize that she and Mark would be afraid that Meg and her mother would try and claim some money from the estate. Sybil has always been ready to fight tooth and claw to keep Underhill going for Mark.'

'She was a bit quiet, but it's a lot to take in at once,' said Tottie. 'When we got back, she tried to ring Piers Marten again, but there was no reply.'

'Perhaps he got her first letter and has already gone to stay with relatives?' I suggested.

'Yes, he might have gone to stay with one of the children, I suppose,' Clara said. 'He treated his wife very badly and there was a messy divorce when they were still small, but they seem prepared to invite him out of a sense of duty.'

'If he wasn't such a horrible man I'd have invited him here for Christmas,' Clara said. 'But I really don't want him under my roof and he'd be a total blight.'

I have to say, Piers Marten sounded *fascinatingly* ghastly . . . but not so fascinating that I ever wanted to meet him.

26

Left Luggage

I awoke next morning to a muffled white world and when I looked out of my window, I could still see large flakes of snow helicoptering slowly down from above, like the winged seedcases of sycamores.

It looked very pretty, though I thought the damp roads would have frozen yesterday evening, so that the covering of snow on top would make them treacherous.

River was supposed to drive over from Sticklepond today. I hoped he'd make it OK.

Tottie was in the kitchen, polishing off a poached egg, and she told me the local farmers had already been out to clear and grit the lane.

'They're on a contract from the council to do it, but actually, they need to give priority to keeping the road along the valley and up to the moors clear if they can, because of getting to the livestock.'

She pushed the coffee pot towards me and added, 'Clara and Henry are working and Teddy's going to help me this morning in the conservatory. I'd better go and winkle him out of the morning room.'

I didn't ask where Den was: he seemed to come and go as he pleased, with no set hours other than those involved in supplying an endless stream of good food.

I wandered off into the studio and propped the iPad, showing the photo I'd taken, next to the portrait of Henry on the easel so that I could compare the two.

The head and hands . . . nothing to do there. Or to Lass, a furry rug across his feet . . .

But the way the faded old jewel colours of the Persian carpet on the dais merged into the darkness behind Henry . . . yes, that needed just a *little* more.

When I resurfaced, it was late morning and the day had brightened. I heard the swoosh of snow sliding off the roof, so a thaw must have set in.

I cleaned up my palette knife, then went through into the drawing room, where I found Clara and Teddy doing a jigsaw puzzle on a board laid over the coffee table.

Teddy looked up. 'I don't think I want to be a gardener when I grow up,' he told me seriously. 'Tottie made me wipe *hundreds* of leaves, but they were shiny already.'

'I think you might become an artist,' I said, going over to the bay window and peering out past the Christmas tree. I could see stretches of the road along the valley and they looked dark and wet, with ragged white edges.

The road to Thorstane at its highest point over the moors probably wouldn't have thawed yet, but whatever state it was in, it evidently hadn't hindered River's arrival, for right at that moment his familiar ancient and battered Land Rover came chugging up the drive.

'Here's River now. He's early!' I exclaimed.

'Oh, good,' said Clara, who was slapping bits of jigsaw into place twice as fast as Teddy. I suppose it was finding all those joins in inscribed pottery and stone fragments.

A small figure, wrapped in a dark woollen cloak and wearing baggy black boots and a rainbow-striped knitted hat with a long point that ended in a tassel over one shoulder, climbed out.

I headed for the porch to find my wellies, but Den, with his sixth sense for visitors, got to the door first.

'You Meg's granddad?' he asked.

'Yes, I'm River.' He gave Den one of his singularly sweet smiles.

'Then go on in and I'll bring yer stuff, won't I?'

'How very kind of you, and I *am* a little chilled. Everything on the back seat is to come in,' he added, then caught sight of me.

'Meg, my dear!' He came up the steps and embraced me warmly and I hugged him back, realizing how pleased I was to have his familiar, reassuring presence there.

'How much better you look now! The air of the Lancashire moors must suit you. *And* the rose-pink hair, too – a bright and *hopeful* colour.'

Well, hope *is* supposed to spring eternal, and until the pneumonia wore me down, I'd always been more of a glass-half-full person.

'Oh, it's good to see you!' I said. 'But come into the drawing room and meet everyone.'

Alerted by the noise of arrival, Henry had come out of his study. Lass pattered past him into the hall to inspect River's legs while he removed his cloak and hat.

Without them, he was revealed to the assembled family in all his glory: a padded tabard of some greenish brocade, worn over a long black tunic. His white hair was loose down his back, but his beard neatly plaited. In one ear lobe shone a small silver star.

Teddy regarded him with awe.

'Are you an elf?' he asked, after a moment. 'Or maybe . . . a wizard?'

'Neither,' River said. 'Though it's an easy mistake to make. I'm Meg's grandfather-in-spirit.'

That made him sound as if I'd bottled him in vodka.

'I was worried the road over the moors would be too bad for you to get through,' I told him.

'I set out early and I had the snow chains, though I didn't need them. My friend in Sticklepond advised me to take the road from Thorstane, rather than use the pass and it was only tricky at the highest point.'

I remembered my manners and introduced him to everyone and he shook hands, just like an ordinary person, which he certainly isn't, but then, you could say that about any of the inhabitants of the Red House, too.

'I suppose you're quite used to bad driving conditions, living up in the Black Mountains,' said Henry.

'It can be a *little* extreme in winter,' agreed River, 'though the Farm itself is not quite as high above sea level as you are.'

Clara insisted he take the chair nearest the fire, though the room was so warm anyway that he'd probably thawed out instantly.

Den bore a succession of items from the Land Rover past the open doorway. It was like an economy version of one of those game shows, where things pass you on a conveyer belt and you get to keep everything you can remember afterwards.

A battered suitcase, tied with string, was followed by a large holdall covered in Air India stickers and several odd-shaped parcels, some of which River retrieved and pressed randomly on Clara and Henry.

'A little something from the Farm,' he said.

They contained the cake, goat's milk cheeses and various other edible goodies that Maj had packed up for him to bring. The Cellophane bag of crisp gingerbread stars were already pierced and threaded with thin ribbon loops and were a big hit with Teddy, who wanted to hang them on the tree in the hall right then and there.

'After lunch,' said Clara. 'The hall is full of luggage right now.'

We heard the inner door to the porch close and Den appeared with a small, brown painted tin trunk.

'That's the lot, ain't it?' he said, stopping in the doorway.

'Thank you so much,' said River. 'Do you want that trunk in here, Meg?'

'It's Mum's, the one from the attic!'

'Yes, I thought I might as well bring the whole thing. Luckily the birth certificate was on top, but you might discover other relevant documents further down.'

'Good idea,' approved Clara. 'But there's no rush to look through it, Meg. We already know Nessa's name was on the birth certificate.'

So the trunk was taken up to my bedroom, along with a large hessian bag full of brown-paper-wrapped packages, which were apparently gifts for me from my Farm family.

River's luggage was deposited in his room, apart from all the eatables, which Den carried off to the kitchen.

'Tottie's missing all this,' Teddy said, as if the circus had come to town.

'She's probably still in the garden or the conservatory and has forgotten the time,' Henry suggested.

'I'll go and get her,' said Teddy, heading for the door.

'Put your coat on if you go outside,' Clara called as he vanished, with Lass plodding after him, as one duty bound to keep an eye on the smallest member of the family.

Now River had warmed up, he discarded the quilted tabard. The hem of the tunic underneath was decorated with hieroglyphs rather than runes. His trousers were still tucked into the long black boots, which had pointy toes, but now he removed these too, revealing hand-knitted Welsh wool socks.

'Is there anything in my bag from the Farm that needs to go into the fridge?' I asked him, because it could contain almost anything.

'No, nothing perishable,' he assured me. 'It's just that once it became clear that you weren't coming back for the Feast, the Family decided to send you a few little Yule presents. And *your* gifts to us from the Green & Friendly Company arrived. Oshan has unpacked everything, ready to hand out after the Solstice.'

'I ordered them in a rush, but I got everyone a little eco-friendly *something*, so I hope they like them,' I said. Most people were getting sets of pencils made from twigs and bamboo toothbrushes, which were probably not that exciting. 'I had about five minutes to get everything done before I left London.'

'That was my doing, but look how well everything is turning out!' said Clara. 'Come on, let's have lunch and then afterwards, River, Meg can show you your room so you can unpack and settle in.'

Tottie came in from the garden as we reached the hall. She was introduced and offered River a rather earthy hand, which he grasped without hesitation. Her trug was full of long, pointed orange carrots that reminded me of River's hat.

'Pleased to meet you,' she said briskly, then added to the rest of us, 'Teddy will be along in a minute. He just wanted to check if the pineapple in the conservatory has grown enough to eat yet.'

'A pineapple? I'd like to see that,' River said interestedly.

'Tottie's got all kinds of exotic fruits and plants in her hothouse,' I told him resignedly. I clearly wasn't going to be able to keep its existence secret. 'Her fingers are so green, they're practically chartreuse.'

'Meg told me what you grow on the Farm. We must both be gardening at about the same elevation, so we can compare notes,' Tottie said. 'I believe we both keep bees, too?'

The way River was instantly fitting into the household, you'd think weirdly dressed elfin men with long silver hair and plaited beards arrived to stay at the Red House every day . . . though, of course, Clara had already met him. He had the happy knack of always being at home wherever he found himself, and in any company.

He had two bowls of mushroom soup and great hunks of wholemeal bread – I didn't know where he put it all. Then afterwards, they broke open one of the truckles of cheese he'd brought with him, which luckily for me was not goat. They must have done a trade with a neighbouring smallholder.

As we ate, we told him the full story of Nessa and George's brief and misguided romance, if you could call it that, which resulted in the baby who became my mother.

'So now you have two homes and two families,' he said. 'How fortuitous that you should choose Meg to paint your portrait, Clara. It must have been pre-ordained by the Goddess.'

Then he talked a lot about the mysteries of karma and predestination and so on, but I didn't take much notice. I already felt a sense of wonderment at the filament-fine thread that was woven through our lives, joining us together.

I came back to earth when they switched to talking about the Solstice.

'I'm so looking forward to the ceremony tomorrow evening,' River told them. 'I brought my own robes with me, because I thought I could wear them to add to the ambience of the occasion, if no one objects.'

River's robes are made of a kind of silver lamé with appliquéd symbols on the back and around the hem. They would certainly add to the ambience of *any* occasion.

'If you do, you must wear lots of clothes under them to keep you warm, like you do at home,' I told him firmly.

'Don't worry, we all pad up before the ceremony,' Henry assured me. 'I've had a thought, too: would you like to take part in the ceremony itself, River? Only, we lost our Old Winter and my nephew, Lex, had to take the part last year. He's too tall for the costume really and I know he'd rather watch than be in it.'

Clara suggested that if River took the part, he should wear his own robes, but with Old Winter's mistletoe crown.

River was, of course, delighted by the idea and Henry promised to explain the proceedings and the part he'd play in them later.

I showed River to his room and on the way up he admired the tree and all the baubles. 'The smell of pine is very invigorating,' he said, inhaling deeply through his small, patrician nose.

River's room looked out on to the back garden and I thought that once Lex and Sybil arrived, the house would be quite full up. No other visitors were expected so we could draw up a virtual drawbridge and let the revels commence.

While I unpacked and stowed away River's various strange garments and footwear, packets of twiggy stuff, sachets of herbal powders, crystals and other vital travelling accessories, he sat on the bed, cross-legged, and listened as I told him the whole sorry tale about the night Lex came back to my flat and what happened – or *didn't* happen – after that. And then the scene later, when his friend Al had cornered me in college and flung vile accusations at me, without giving me a chance to defend myself.

It was easier to tell him while I was moving around the room with my back to him, engaged in putting things away, but finally I turned and looked into his calm, deep celestial-blue and strangely innocent eyes.

'I see,' he said. 'They assumed the worst, even though you acted for the best, and then gave you no chance to explain.'

'I think I probably looked a bit guilty when Al cornered me, because there *had* been a moment that night when I'd been tempted . . .' I confessed, going for broke. 'I thought Lex was totally out of it, but he surfaced long enough to kiss me. It was only a split second before I realized what I was doing and pulled away, and by then he was out for the count again.'

'I think you can wipe that off your conscience entirely, Meg,' he said, as if it was a dirty mark on a plate. 'As to the rest, if he didn't fully recollect what happened that night, then he should have talked to *you* about it, rather than his friend.'

'Yes, that's what I thought. Instead, he's let all this unnecessary guilt fester away over the years.'

'So of course, he wouldn't be pleased when you suddenly turned up at the Red House.'

That was the understatement of the year.

'He looked angry and horrified! Over the years he must have built up a picture of me in his mind that really isn't like me at all. Now he's faced with the reality, I can see he's finding it increasingly difficult to square the two.'

'I should think he would!' River said. 'Since you say you knew him before the events of that night, he should have realized you wouldn't have acted in the manner he accused you of.'

'I think I just added another layer to his whole guilt trip over Lisa,' I said. 'I mean, that night in the wine bar he told me he and Lisa had married so he'd have the right to insist she didn't have chemotherapy, which she didn't want, but her parents were insisting on. There wouldn't have been much chance of it working in her case anyway, but when she deteriorated so quickly and had to go into the hospice, he was convinced that she'd probably have survived if she'd had it. Another guilt trip.'

'That was a heavy load to bear,' River said sympathetically. 'But he did the right thing in letting her choose.'

'Her parents didn't see it like that, and they were with her at the hospice that night when Lex came back to my flat. Then they couldn't contact him when Lisa took a sudden turn for the worse . . . It took Al to track him down, sober him up and take him there.'

River thought it all over. 'So Lex would feel guilt at not being there when he was needed, as well as guilt over what he thinks you did together?'

'But I didn't realize any of that, the day he came into college after it was all over. When he turned and walked away the moment he saw me, I thought perhaps it was because he'd poured his heart out to me in the wine bar and felt embarrassed about it. People do often avoid you, after doing that.'

'That's very true,' he agreed.

'It was only what Al said later that made me realize Lex had got totally the wrong idea about what we'd done in my flat. It was horrible.'

'I wish I'd known all this at the time, because I could have gone to London, sought out these young men, and put them right.'

I was very sure he would have done, too, but would they have believed him?

'The only person who's known about it all along is Fliss. She was the one who insisted I told you now.'

'Very sensible,' he approved. 'She's been a good friend to you.'

'She said you'd know what to do . . . Oh, and there's something else I didn't tell you,' I added, remembering. 'Al is now Lex's business partner in a pottery near here, and he's married to Lisa's younger sister! Henry took me to the pottery a few days ago and it was obvious Al had told her – Tara – all about it.'

River shook his head. 'Al sounds a rash and thoughtless person, lacking in empathy for others.'

'Yes, though I suppose in his way he's just being a good friend to Lex, and Lex *did* apologize later for the way Al and Tara spoke to me.'

'What is Lex's attitude to the news that you are now a member of the family?'

'He went very quiet, so I'm not sure. But soon after I arrived here he told me he'd forgiven me for the past, which was kind of him, considering I didn't do anything.'

'That was at least well-meaning,' River said.

'I did try to tell him the truth, but he said he didn't want to go over the past and walked off. That made me angry and determined to stay at the Red House over Christmas and not let him drive me away.'

'Very natural, Meg, but now the time has come for this misunderstanding to be cleared up so that old wounds can finally heal and you can both embrace a happier future.'

'You mean I have to tell him everything, whether he wants to hear it or not?'

'Yes, and I feel that if you do that before midnight on the evening of the Winter Solstice, it would be particularly fortuitous.'

'But that's tomorrow! It doesn't give me a lot of time to get him on his own for long enough.'

'A way will appear,' he said with certainty.

'He'll actually be staying here from tomorrow till New Year.' I gave a sigh. 'I knew you'd tell me to have the whole thing out with him, really, so the sooner the better, I suppose.'

River nodded. 'I don't feel your aura will recover until you have.'

'But what if he won't listen, or doesn't believe me?'

'He must believe the truth. And if necessary, *I* will also speak to the young man.'

I'd like to be a fly on the wall for that one.

I left him arranging his various crystals and stuff on the top of a chest of drawers and went to my room, where I opened Mum's tin trunk.

Immediately, I was enveloped in a wave of patchouli and sandalwood, and memories flooded in of my plump, pretty, feckless little butterfly mother, flitting in and out of my life . . .

Where was she now?

Clara

The ensuing years at Oxford were happy ones and though Henry went off on his globetrotting travels after he had completed his degree, while I continued with my studies, we would come together again whenever we could.

His poetry increasingly found its way into print, while I had already begun to make a name for myself as a 'joiner' of fragmentary pieces of epigraphy. You either have an eye for these things, or you don't, and I had it, along with a near-photographic memory of where I had seen other pieces of what might be the same inscription.

My doctoral dissertation eventually turned into my first non-fiction book . . . but I am running ahead again and must backtrack a little.

Even when pursuing our careers in different parts of the world, communications flew between us so that when we met, there was never any catching-up to do.

Henry would quite often just turn up while I was attached to a dig, so it was no surprise when I looked up one day from the trench in which I was sitting – Turkey again, as it happened – and saw him standing on the edge.

He was dressed in crumpled white linen and wore a broad-brimmed straw hat, somewhat frayed around the edges, to shade his familiar and very dear face from the hot sun.

'Hello, Henry,' I said, getting up as if only four minutes instead of four months had passed since we had last met.

I was holding a piece of clay tablet incised with cuneiform writing . . . though with some interesting variations. I suspected it was an early form.

'This fragment is fascinating. I was hoping to find a few more pieces, but no luck.'

He gave me his hand to climb out and then kissed me warmly, under the interested gaze of the workmen and my colleagues.

'I wasn't expecting you, was I?' I said.

'No, I just suddenly felt I'd had enough of travelling to last me a lifetime and wanted to go home – somewhere damp, and cool and probably grey. I thought I'd call in and propose on the way.'

'Propose what?' I asked absently, placing the piece of clay tablet in a tray and then brushing dust from my cotton trousers.

'Marriage. If I'm not going to be constantly travelling any more, I can be your base camp in London.'

His diffident, very sweet smile appeared and I exclaimed, 'I don't know why we didn't think of that before, Henry! I mean, not only do we love each other but it would certainly make life easier.'

'I'm so glad,' he said, then kissed me again, which I returned with enthusiasm, audience or no audience.

When we finally parted he dug a tissue-wrapped ring out of his pocket and offered it to me. 'Do you care for this carnelian seal I picked out, or would you rather choose something else?'

But the antique and very beautiful carved carnelian ring did indeed seal our union because we were married at the very first opportunity.

I ran our surnames together and became Clara Mayhem Doome, a conjunction that seems to have provided amusement for many.

27

Everyman

The birth certificate, in an old brown envelope, had been replaced right at the top. Apart from the mother's name, it gave little information.

Underneath it was an old, cancelled passport, in which Mum looked unbelievably young . . . and a lot thinner than the last time I'd seen her, when she'd been on the plump side of curvy.

Other than those, the trunk contained only a rainbow of discarded clothes in flimsy Indian silks and cottons . . . and all the gifts I'd made for her as a child, when she was paying one of her fleeting visits to the Farm.

She'd always expressed great delight in these offerings – and at least she'd kept them – but at some point in our relationship I'd begun to feel that *I* was the mother and *she* the feckless and irresponsible offspring.

While I was upstairs, the cleaners from Mary's Pop-ins had arrived to give the house a quick spruce up. Clara told me they were fortnightly, so this must be in lieu of the day they'd miss over Christmas.

They passed me on the stairs as I came down, kitted up like the Ghostbusters and ready, as Clara put it, to go through the whole house like a dose of salts.

'But not the studio,' I said anxiously. 'Could they leave that out this time? There's so much wet or tacky paint about!'

'Of course, dear, I'll let them know when they come down. We'll all have to shift then, so they can clean the rest of the house, but since Den always does the kitchen himself, we can hide out in there if necessary.'

Henry and River seemed to be getting on brilliantly, and took Lass out for a walk, even though she did her best to tell them that she was quite happy to skip it today and stay in the warm.

I'd taken the birth certificate down with me and Clara scanned it for the family records, so that I could replace the original in the trunk. River would return it to the Farm, ready for when Mum turned up again.

The sound of vacuum cleaners and voices upstairs continued, so I went to the studio and looked through my gallery of photographs, thinking how much I'd love to paint Tottie in her Carmen Miranda mode, and Den with his sleeves rolled up to show a bright assortment of tattoos as he chopped vegetables at the kitchen table. If Tottie would give me some sittings, I could make a start before Christmas.

I'd told Henry that I still wasn't quite happy about the way the shadows merged around him in the portrait and it would help if he sat in the pose for a little while when they got back. When they did, River came in with him in order, it seemed, to carry on a discussion about some aspect of poetic construction that would have been far above my head even if I hadn't been concentrating on what I was doing.

Their voices rose and fell, as did Lass's snoring.

'That's it, it's right now,' I said eventually, and they both came to look at the portrait.

'Truly, you have captured Henry's essence – it's a kind of magic,' said River.

'She did the same with Clara.' Henry indicated her portrait, which I'd propped up on the mantelpiece high above dog hair range. The surface was fairly hard to the touch now, though, so I brought it over and put it on the other easel.

I was amused when they both then fell back a few paces, hands clasped behind their backs and heads tilted consideringly on one side, like a parody of two art critics.

'Eventually we mean them to hang in the drawing room, one on either side of the fireplace,' said Henry.

'I hope you and Clara will let me show them in my small one-woman exhibition in London in February, first,' I said.

'We'd be delighted, and although I rarely go to London these days, I'll make an exception in your case.'

'Thank you, it would be so lovely if you could come, and River will be there, too, won't you?'

'I wouldn't miss it for the world. I might hire a minibus and bring a few of the Family with me.'

'That should liven things up a bit,' I said. 'Just don't stop at a pub on the way down for lunch.'

We opened the door to check the progress of Mary's Poppins and found they'd finished Henry and Clara's studies and Tottie's hide-out in the library, and were now in the drawing room, so Henry took River off to show him his Christmas ornament collection.

They roped in Teddy to assist and I went to look for Tottie, who was in the kitchen. When I explained that I wanted to paint her portrait – and in the conservatory, where I'd drawn her – she stared at me for a long moment.

'I suppose I *could*,' she said at length, with seeming reluctance, though I could tell she was secretly dying to be painted!

'I've promised to show River the hens, hives and garden after breakfast tomorrow – not that there's a lot to see at this time of year – and then the conservatory. Perhaps you could start it after that, before lunch?'

'Perfect! I'll set everything up in there ready,' I agreed. 'I'd like you to be holding some kind of basket of fruit and vegetables too, if you have anything that would do? In my head, I see it as a cornucopia, though you're not likely to have one of those!'

'I've got a big wicker cone-shaped container that might do. It's left over from when I made dried flower arrangements.'

'That sounds perfect!'

'I'll dig it out for you. It's in the library somewhere.'

The cleaners departed, leaving the scent of furniture spray to fight it out with the fir tree. The house settled down to await Christmas, now only a few days away.

During the course of that afternoon and evening, River seemed to engage with every member of the household, from Clara, who took him off to her study after tea to show him some interesting bit of inscription, to Den, with whom he discussed cars and cooking in the kitchen. I even found him laughing uproariously at something on children's TV with Teddy later.

Seamlessly transitioning from visitor to family member is his secret power . . .

After dinner, the drawing-room curtains were all drawn and a crackling log fire made it look cosy. The fairy lights on the tree in the bay window twinkled on and off, like little glow-worms catching the strange shapes of the antique baubles and making them sparkle.

Henry drew back one of the curtains and looked out.

'I noticed the barometer in the hall was dropping rapidly as we came through, so the roads will freeze again overnight. I hope we don't have more snow on top of it, or driving conditions will be bad tomorrow.'

'Perhaps it will thaw out again during the day,' suggested Clara. 'But I'll be happier when Lex arrives safely tomorrow.'

Then she explained to River, 'My nephew, Lex, always stays here for Christmas. He's a very talented potter.'

'Yes, Meg has told me a lot about him,' he said. 'I look forward to meeting him.'

'Let's hope the conditions aren't too bad tomorrow for the Solstice ceremony,' Henry said. 'We've held them despite the snow before now, but I'm not so young as I was for ploughing about in drifts.'

'None of us is,' said Tottie. 'But if it's like today the farmers will be able to grit the road all the way from here to Underhill.'

'It's not so bad once we've climbed the hill,' said Clara. 'The bonfire keeps the audience warm and the ceremony itself is brief, so the performers soon come down again.'

'I'm afraid Old Winter goes up with whoever is lighting the fire and torches, so he can get into the cave before the audience arrive,' Henry told River. 'Though if the track up the hill is clear enough, they can drive almost to the top on the quad bike.'

'That will be an interesting experience,' River said. 'And Tottie tells me that all the performers foregather at Underhill, where the costumes are stored, to get ready.'

'Yes, they've always been kept in a big cupboard in the tack room; then they're moved into the house in time to be handy for the ceremony.'

'I'm glad Mark has come round to the idea of taking his part in the ceremony and hosting the Gathering as usual,' said Clara. 'Sybil's so pleased.'

'The Gathering?' enquired River.

'Everyone goes back to Underhill for hot toddy and treacle cake afterwards – that's the Gathering,' Clara explained. 'In the past, before Starstone was drowned, so many people went that the courtyard as well as the great hall was full.'

'I'm surprised that Mark agreed to host the Gathering this year, what with his economy drive,' said Henry.

'He caved in.' Tottie grinned. 'Mrs Gidney just carried on and made the huge cake as usual – it's like a giant sticky ginger parkin, River – and Gidney ordered the ingredients for the hot toddy.'

'And since Mark's playing his role in the ceremony this year, *you* can be a spectator,' said Clara to her husband. 'And if Fred can get over from the pub, Lex can, too.'

'It's a pity Zelda won't be here in time for it. I can't remember the last time she was,' said Tottie.

'Not for many years,' agreed Clara. 'She either arrives too late, or not at all because she's in a pantomime.'

Teddy, who had been absorbed in completing another picture in his magic painting book, looked up worriedly at this.

'What if it snows a lot and Mummy can't get here for Christmas?'

'A thaw might have set in by Thursday,' I suggested.

'I'm sure she'll make it, even if she has to ski over from Thorstane,' Henry assured him and then, as if we'd summoned her, Zelda rang to speak with Teddy.

'Of course,' said Clara, who had picked up the receiver. 'I'll put him on. We've had some snow, so he's a bit anxious about whether you'll be able to get here on Thursday.'

Zelda must have reassured him, because Teddy relaxed after a few moments of listening to her and turned to the topic most absorbing him at the moment: what he was getting for Christmas.

'Father Christmas explained you'd probably come on the train and they wouldn't let you bring me a pony, so perhaps you've got me something else, like a dragon?'

The phone squawked faintly and then Teddy said, 'All right. Night-night, Mummy,' and put it down.

'Mummy says I'll have to wait and see what she brings me,' he said, then added, darkly, 'There's too much *waiting* at Christmas.'

We all laughed and Tottie said, 'Well, it wouldn't be a surprise otherwise, would it?'

'You like dragons?' asked River.

'Yes, and I know lots of stories about them,' Teddy said enthusiastically. 'Bilbo told me a good one and there's another in my book about a dragon who ate four knights for breakfast. But I don't like the story about St George because he kills the poor dragon.'

'I see where you're coming from,' said River. 'Meg told me about Bilbo and I know his wife, Moonflower. I haven't seen her for several years, though, so I look forward to meeting up with her again.'

'If you go down to their shop – Preciousss – Flower will sell you something. She's keen as mustard,' I warned him.

'Preciousss – and Bilbo? Do I detect a slight interest in Tolkien?'

'You could say that,' Henry said drily. 'They called the baby Grace-Galadriel too.'

'Pretty,' approved River.

Teddy yawned hugely.

'Time for bed now – it's very late, Teddy,' said Tottie, getting up. 'Come on, let's get you ready.'

'Will you come up and read me a story, Uncle Henry?' he asked.

'I'll be there when Tottie calls me,' he promised.

When they'd gone up, Clara explained to River about Zelda.

'Teddy's mother is Lex's sister and so my niece. They're my sister Bridget's children, but she and her husband live in New Zealand now. She's much younger than me, which is why Lex, Zelda and Henry's great-nephew, Mark, are all about the same age.'

'And Meg, too,' said Henry, smiling at me. 'Another great-niece.'

'Zelda is an actor, so she finds it more convenient for Teddy to live here, and it's better for him to be settled in one place,' continued Clara. 'She loves him dearly, but I'm not sure she's cut out for day-to-day mothering.'

'She sounds a bit like my mum,' I said. 'The love is there and they want to know you're safe, but out of sight, out of mind!'

Tottie called downstairs and Henry went to read Teddy his story, though he'd been so sleepy he'd probably have nodded off in moments.

But none of us stayed up late that night: we were all tired.

'Truly, you are a Renaissance man and know something about everything, River,' I told him as I wished him goodnight. He'd come upstairs carrying a glass beaker of some strange herbal tea that he liked to drink last thing. It smelled like old hay sprinkled with earthy spices, and possibly was.

When I looked out of my bedroom window next morning, the sky was still a heavy, half-mourning lavender grey and a fresh layer of snow gleamed below. But then the first pale tinge of rose-gold appeared behind the furthest hills and I thought perhaps it would be another day like the last, with the sun eventually thawing the snow and ice from the roads.

That would be good for the Solstice ceremony . . . and I'd promised River I'd have that talk with Lex today, if I could get him alone long enough. I hoped so because, now I'd made up my mind, I wanted to get it over with.

Wondering exactly what I'd say and how he would take it made me late down for breakfast, but I found everyone still seated around the kitchen table, the air redolent with the mingled scents of freshly baked bread and coffee.

'We thought you were going to stay in bed for ever, like Sleeping Beauty,' Teddy said, waving his cereal spoon at me, like a slightly dripping and utilitarian magic wand.

'*You* did,' said Tottie. 'The rest of us didn't get up that early this morning, either.'

'I thought if Meg was still asleep when Lex came, he could be Prince Charming and kiss her to wake her up,' Teddy said, and I felt myself go pink.

'I was just looking out of the window and daydreaming, I'm afraid.'

Den cut me a couple of slices from the still warm loaf, which had sunflower seeds on top, and Tottie passed the honey.

They'd all been discussing the weather when I came in and, like me, thought it would thaw later.

'Once the sun goes down again, it'll be very cold for the ceremony, but we start as soon as it's dark, which, of course, this being the shortest day of the year, is mid-afternoon. We'll be back at Underhill carousing before the roads start to freeze.'

'I've rung Lex to tell him you'll take the part of Old Winter, River,' Henry said. 'Unless Fred can't get over, he can just watch this year.'

'Fred's the Straw Man, with bundles of straw tied round him,' explained Tottie. 'It was probably corn originally, but the heads have dropped off over the years.'

'Interesting,' said River. 'What are the other characters?'

'Mark will be the Green Man, with a leafy mask affair, Bilbo has antlers attached to a leather hood, Tottie wears a bird mask and Len, who is the gardener and groom at Underhill, has a hood with ram horns. I'm sure it's all to do with ensuring fertility, abundant food and that kind of thing, after the birth of the New Year.'

River nodded. 'I'm sure you're right, and we do something similar at the Farm, though when I began it I took elements from several ancient rituals to add to my own.'

'Having enough food was the important thing when our ancestors first began holding the rite – animals, crops and game,' agreed Clara. 'And the symbolic banishing of Old Winter to make way for spring.'

'I like Tottie's bird mask best,' said Teddy. 'I'd like to wear that one, when I'm grown up.'

'You can, because I'll probably be past it by then,' said Tottie. 'I'll be able to watch you instead of the other way round.'

'Clara and I remember the ceremony from when we were children in Starstone,' said Henry. 'The whole village used to walk up there in procession with torches, it was wonderfully exciting: the dark night, the sky and the bright star over the stone, the fire crackling and the strange figures moving around the Starstone.'

'It still *is* exciting,' said Clara, 'especially when Old Winter suddenly appears from the cave. Even though I know what will happen, it's a thrill when he emerges and walks around declaiming his lines.'

'I hope I do the part justice,' River said. 'Henry is going to run me through my lines later.'

'I was a baby when the reservoir flooded the valley,' said Tottie regretfully. 'I only remember the ceremony from later, when there weren't so many people left to attend it. But still, it's really magical. Even when I knew who the performers were, they took on the persona of their characters during the ceremony. And now I'm part of it!'

After breakfast, Clara and Henry went off to work and I borrowed Lass and took her into the study to draw. I'd taken a couple of biscuits with me, so I had her complete attention.

When I'd finished – it was another little sketch intended as a gift – I moved my easel and painting gear into the conservatory at the spot where I'd drawn Tottie.

A large wicker cone-shaped basket lay on the table, already filled with fruit, glossy citrus leaves and the feathery ends of carrots: the perfect cornucopia!

When I was ready for action I could still see Tottie and River meandering round the garden as if it was midsummer and not a freezing cold and snowy day, so I went into the kitchen to fetch a cup of coffee.

Teddy and Den were in there and very mysterious about a surprise they were cooking up . . .

Tottie was in the conservatory when I went back, and she took up her pose. Through a gap in the foliage we could see River, wrapped in his flowing cloak, standing in the middle of one of the knot gardens by a spiral box tree, with his arms raised up to the sky. His back was turned to us and, apart from the rainbow-striped pixie hat, he looked rather impressive.

'What's he doing?' asked Tottie.

'Invoking something, I expect.' A good outcome for this talk I hoped – and dreaded – to have with Lex, perhaps?

*

River was in the kitchen again, writing down a recipe for Den, by the time we ended the sitting and went to find something to eat.

Teddy proudly displayed the surprise he'd cooked up with Den – cupcakes topped with edible Santa and snowman decorations – and we were allowed one each.

Henry came in and suggested to River that they take Lass and walk over to Underhill to check on the costumes, and he could teach him his lines on the way.

'Perhaps on the way back, I might call in at Preciousss, to catch up with Moonflower,' said River. 'What about you, Meg? Would you like some fresh air?'

'No, thank you, I'm going to the conservatory again for a bit,' I said, which I did, working on the rainforest of foliage in the background of Tottie's portrait.

I'd already sketched in her head: she had the sort of plump, round face that seemed to have sunk in the middle around the nose, like a slightly deflated sponge cake.

Then I went up to my turret and read another of Clara's books, to which I was becoming addicted. In fact, I was so engrossed that I entirely missed Lex's arrival. When Teddy came to call me down, I was surprised to see him there, seated next to River on one of the sofas, deeply engaged in some discussion.

Tea was early, but fairly substantial today, since the ceremony would make dinner extremely late.

There was an extra layer of anticipation in the room added to that already sparked by the countdown to Christmas Day.

Soon it started to go dark and it was time for the advance party of players, Tottie and River, to leave for Underhill. Lex was going to drive them over, and then go up on the quad bike to light the fire and torches, taking River, in his Old Winter guise, with him.

I made sure River had several layers of warm clothing on beneath his silver lamé before I let him go out into the cold: he could be careless about these things and he wasn't as young as he was.

28

Headlong

Once the advance party had left, the rest of us began to get kitted out for the cold weather, before piling into Clara's Range Rover, which was a bit of a squeeze, though of course, coming home, we'd have Lex's pick-up too.

There were already a few vehicles parked along the road below the hill and a group of people had gathered, ready for the ascent. In fact, the number of Starstone Edge inhabitants there that I hadn't yet met was a surprise, but I supposed some of them were from the farms and outlying cottages.

As we got out to join them, a bonfire suddenly burst into life high on the hill, just below the Stone, and there was a ragged cheer. A few moments later, the Stone itself was ringed in fire.

'See up there, Meg? The performers are almost at the ledge,' said Clara, pointing, and I noticed for the first time the bobbing line of torchlight ascending the hill.

Sybil, in a dark blue Puffa jacket and ski trousers, materialized from the darkness of the Underhill drive.

'Come on, we'd better get going,' she urged us, and we followed the stream of people heading slowly up the path, which was mercifully clear of snow, though there were great patches of it on the hillside.

The route was wide and zigzagged to and fro, so that the gradient was never very steep. I found myself next to Flower and Bilbo, who had the baby inside his padded coat. You couldn't see anything of her, except a knitted hat and a bit of cheek and nose. Apart from Teddy, who was walking ahead with Clara and Henry, I didn't see any other children.

The path opened out just below the plateau and Lex was waiting there by the quad bike to give Sybil the keys.

'Sybil will want to go down ahead of the rest of us, to make sure everything's ready for the Gathering,' Henry explained.

'Teddy, I'm relying on you to pull me up this last stretch of hill,' Clara told him, as he tugged impatiently at her hand.

'Come along, everyone. They'll start in a minute!' urged Henry.

We gathered around the fire on the ledge below the Stone, sheltered from the wind by a half-circle of rocky outcrops, one of which held the deep fissure in which River was concealed. Henry warned me not to go beyond the white-painted boulders that ringed the other side, since there was a steep drop down.

'Quiet!' someone shouted, and then a faint drumming and chanting drew our attention upwards, to where the strange shapes of the performers had begun to circle the Starstone.

The flames from the torches seemed to leap, twirl and gesture with the figures, and snatches of words, borne by the breeze, floated down to us. They sounded like doggerel, and I remembered Tottie saying that's what they were.

The tempo picked up and the figures gyrated, gestured and stamped faster and faster and faster, until it all came to a climax with a sudden great shout!

In the following silence, the audience turned as one and spread around the fire, their attention now all on the rock face at the back of the ledge, where Old Winter had appeared, ghost-like and startling in sparkling silver, as if covered with frost. He wore a gilded mistletoe crown on his long white hair and carried a tall staff twined with ivy. As he reached the firelight, his eyes gleamed an almost unearthly blue.

For someone the size of an elf, he made a *very* impressive entrance, even to me, who had seen him garbed in those robes many times before, though not, of course, with the mistletoe crown. He'd probably incorporate that in his own rites next year.

'I am Old Winter, here to stay. None of your magic will drive *me* away,' he chanted, circling the fire and occasionally pausing to shake his staff in one of the spectators' faces, so that they fell back in mock fear.

Then the audience drew aside, making way for the other performers to come forward, one by one, until they were all gathered together, facing the now isolated figure of Old Winter.

What with the cloaks, masks, leather tabards and bizarre horned headgear, it was like the heavy metal version of *West Side Story*.

Then the Green Man, easily recognizable by the oak leaves that spouted from the mouth of his mask (and I had forgotten he was Mark until that moment), stepped forward and loudly proclaimed that Old Winter's day was done and he should be gone forthwith.

Something must have been thrown on the fire at this point, because it suddenly and effectively flared up in a rainbow of colours, before dying down again, and by the time our eyes had readjusted, Old Winter had vanished.

It was very effective and there was a spatter of applause, but this was not quite the end. The Green Man and the others took up stations around the fire and recited in turn a line or two more, though what I could catch made little sense. I expect it's like Chinese Whispers and changes a little every time it gets passed down a generation.

The fire was starting to die down now, but there was enough light to make out the antlered or horned headdresses, a kind of Straw Man figure and the scary hawk-like bird mask that must conceal Tottie.

It would make *such* an amazing surreal picture! I moved backwards into the darkness behind the others to take it all in, especially the way those masks seemed to contort and come alive in the flickering light of the fire . . .

Then I suddenly remembered Henry's warning to keep inside the border of white-painted rocks and turned to see if I was close.

I was, and beyond them the dark, opaque density of the sky seemed to merge into nothingness.

'The *star*!' someone shouted behind me and I looked up in time to see a bright diamond pinprick briefly appear between heavy clouds over the Stone.

The wind had been changing directions and picking up for the last few minutes, tugging and gusting around me. Then it suddenly buffeted my back, sending me off-balance . . . then again, but this time a hard blow that made me stagger forward between the white boulders. One foot came down into heart-stopping emptiness . . . and then

I was desperately twisting sideways, grabbing at a nearby bush, to save myself. The sharp thorns of gorse pierced my hands, but I hung on for dear life.

'Help!' I shouted. 'Help!' But the wind snatched my voice away.

Then, miraculously, a dark shape bent over me and I was seized in a strong grip and dragged back to safety.

'Oh God, Meg, I thought you were going to fall before I got to you,' said Lex's voice. He sounded shaken, and I clung to him.

'What on earth were you doing?' he demanded, gripping my arms to hold me upright when my knees threatened to buckle. 'Didn't you realize those white boulders were there for a purpose?'

'I . . . yes,' I stammered, beginning to tremble.

'A gust of wind hit me, and then I was pushed over the edge,' I gabbled, hardly knowing what I was saying. 'I just managed to grab that bush in time and—'

'Do you mean the *wind* almost blew you over?' he said sharply.

'No, someone did. I felt hands . . . a shove in the small of my back.'

Even as I said it, it sounded unlikely and though I couldn't see Lex's face, I could hear the scepticism in his voice.

'When I spotted you, there was no one near, and most people had started to leave. It was lucky I'd noticed you walking away from the fire and looked to see where you'd got to.'

There was certainly no one near us now and the last stragglers were heading for the way down – the long one, not the steep and deadly route I had inadvertently nearly taken. There was only Lex here . . . and *he'd* rescued me.

I trembled again from head to foot and he said, a little more gently, 'You're safe now, however it happened.'

I pulled myself together a bit and said uncertainly, 'I must have imagined it and it was only another strong gust of wind after all. I mean, who would want to push me over the edge anyway?'

'No one that I can think of. I suspect all that ritual and old magic has made your imagination go into overdrive.'

I realized I was gripping the front of his coat and unloosed my hands. 'I expect you're right,' I agreed. He *must* be, even if I could still feel those hands in the small of my back, shoving hard . . .

'Come on,' he said, taking my arm and urging me towards the path. 'Almost everyone's gone.'

He was right. Someone had extinguished the torches around the Stone and raked the fire into dull embers. The temperature seemed to have dropped rapidly too as the wind got up, and now a spattering of hard, crystalline snow stung my cheeks and made my eyes water.

As we started down there was a loud roaring noise and Lex said, 'That must be Tottie and Sybil on the quad bike. They were going on ahead to make sure everything's ready for the Gathering.'

That must have been quite a sight, the bird-headed Tottie and Sybil, hurtling off into the darkness.

'Did she still have her head on?' I asked.

Lex gave me a strange look. 'Have you taken something?'

'Oh, don't be so stupid,' I snapped, anger dissipating some of the lingering shock. 'I don't even drink that much, let alone anything else! I just had this vision of Tottie driving off on the bike with her mask still on, that's all.'

'I suppose that would be fairly weird,' he admitted. 'But I expect she's taken it off, though Sybil's probably driving.'

We mingled with the last of the audience walking down the track and River, still a spectral symphony in silver, fell into step next to us. He had Tottie's bird head mask under his arm, which answered that question.

River seemed to sense some tension between us, or perhaps it was the way Lex was still gripping my arm, like a gaoler.

'Are you all right, Meg?'

I shook Lex off and linked my arm through River's instead.

'Fine. I just had a bit of a stumble near the edge of the ledge and almost went over. It was quite a shock.'

'She thinks someone tried to push her over,' said Lex sardonically.

'No, I don't really, it just *felt* like that, but it must have been a gust of wind, catching me off balance,' I said shortly. 'Now I'm just cold. Come on, River, let's walk down together.'

Lex strode off ahead, but when we got to the bottom he was waiting by the pick-up and insisted on driving us up to the house. It was hardly worth the drive, really, for although Underhill was hidden round a bend of the tree-lined drive, it was barely a couple of hundred yards away.

There were a few other cars parked in the courtyard, including Clara's. The big front door to the house, illuminated by twin lamps of giant dimensions, was open on to the inner passage that led to the hall. Warm yellow bands of light fell across the steps and the snow-sprinkled cobbles.

When Lex turned the engine off we could hear the whispering of crisp snowflakes hitting the windscreen.

'Now for the Gathering,' said River, adjusting his mistletoe crown and gathering his long robes together preparatory to getting out. 'Come along, Meg.'

At that moment I'd rather have simply gone home because not only had I turned shaky again, but I felt as if I'd been dragged backwards through a thorn bush, which, actually, I had. Bits of me were starting to hurt where I'd landed hard on the edge of the drop and my hands felt like prickly pears.

However, since River was already out of the pick-up and waiting, there was nothing for it. He gave my arm an encouraging squeeze. 'Let's see if anyone looks guilty,' he suggested, as if this was some kind of murder game. Lex gave him one of his sardonic looks and walked off ahead of us.

The hall, which I'd previously thought a dark, chilly, echoing space, now presented a totally different aspect. It was ablaze with light and a huge log fire burned brightly in the vast hearth. It was so warm, that I suspected that someone – probably Sybil – had turned up the heating as far as it would go.

She'd probably been the one who'd decorated the room with swags of ivy, holly and mistletoe, too.

Clusters of people were gathered about, several of them around a long trestle table that bore a glass punch bowl at either end and, in the middle, a giant dark cake, from which a large portion was already missing.

The players had taken off their costumes and parked the heads, cloaks and tabards under the table, but most people were peeling off layers now.

I removed my own anorak and tried to smooth my hair down, but it hurt my hands. I noticed one or two of the nearest people were staring at me, so I must have looked dishevelled . . . or maybe it was just the pink hair?

Most of them, though, were so busy eating, drinking and talking that they hadn't even been aware of our arrival, and those who had, didn't look particularly guilty. It was just a group of ordinary people having a good time, most of them total strangers to me, and I began to feel a bit silly and wished I hadn't told Lex I thought I'd been pushed.

I was just wondering whether to try to find a cloakroom to clean myself up a bit when a small black and brown shape wriggled through the forest of legs and threw itself at me, barking ecstatically.

'Pansy!' I scooped her up and held her tightly, while she licked my chin enthusiastically.

Lex appeared with three steaming glasses, the kind in metal holders with handles, and gave one to River and another to me. I tucked Pansy under one arm and took a cautious sip.

'Hot toddy – you look as if you need it,' he said.

It was an unexpectedly kind thought and I took another sip. It tasted spicy and of oranges and . . . something else. 'Is it alcoholic?'

'Yes, but not very, so I got Gidney to put a tot of brandy in yours.'

'I don't like brandy!'

'It's for the shock, and you won't taste anything much except spices and lemon.'

River, holding his drink, smiled at us and then wandered off to talk to someone. He'd removed his robes and a layer or two of padding, but not the gilded mistletoe crown. It did sort of go with the black tunic bordered with gold runes that was now revealed in all its glory.

As I drank the toddy, warmth began stealing down inside me, thawing out the frozen knot of cold and shock. Pansy wriggled and I put her down, but she stayed next to me, looking up with dark, trusting eyes.

Everyone was happily chattering, eating cake and drinking – a small community, who all knew each other – and

I felt strangely outside it all, as if I was looking in from a window.

Up on the hill it had been another world entirely, which probably accounted for my imagination running riot. Lex must have been right.

Mark, looking almost genial, now that hospitality had been forced upon him, finally spotted me and made his way over.

'Meg, there you are!' he said eagerly. 'I was looking out for you and—'

His voice stopped as he took in my state, before asking in concern, 'Have you had an accident, Meg? You look as if there's a bruise on your cheek and—'

'I think it's probably mud, rather than a bruise,' I said, fingering my face cautiously. 'I did have a bit of a fall up on the hill, but I'm fine.'

'Meg nearly fell off the ledge after the ceremony and thought someone pushed her,' Lex said, and I glared at him.

'I don't *really*. It was just that the wind caught me and nearly sent me off.'

Mark gazed blankly at me. 'Why would anyone want to push you off?'

I flushed, feeling foolish. 'They wouldn't – don't take any notice of Lex! I shouldn't have gone so near the edge anyway, and I was lucky Lex spotted me and pulled me up.'

'Weren't you wearing gloves?' asked Mark, noticing my poor, punctured hands.

'I took them off to find a tissue. The wind was making my eyes water.'

'It's a steep drop from there, so you were lucky,' he said, looking so concerned that I was touched.

I drained the glass beaker and suddenly felt a lot better.

'Here, you might as well have my toddy, too,' Lex said, exchanging my empty beaker for his untouched full one. 'I'll get another.'

Mark put an arm around my shoulders – in a cousinly, rather than an amorous way, I hoped – and said anxiously, 'Meg, you must come and let me put some antiseptic on your hands. That scratch on your face needs cleaning, too.'

'Oh, I'm all right,' I said, smiling up at him and feeling warmed by his concern. 'I expect we'll be going back to the Red House soon and I can do it then.'

'I'd run you back now, except that as the host—'

'I can run Meg back any time she wants,' Lex interrupted shortly.

I was just about to disclaim any wish to leave the Gathering before the others, when a sweet little voice at my elbow said, 'Lex, there you are! *And* Mark, darling – I was looking for you.'

A small woman of about thirty, with big brown eyes and feathery chestnut curls, stood fluttering her long eyelashes at both men, as if semaphoring a message.

Whatever it was, it didn't get through, because Lex just nodded at her casually and Mark's greeting was far from enthusiastic.

'Hi, Flora.'

So this was Teddy's former nanny!

Ignoring me, she was turning her full focus on Mark, who now removed his arm from my shoulders and said, slightly sheepishly, 'I didn't realize you were home, Flora.'

'Didn't Clara tell you? The last job simply didn't work out because the husband couldn't keep away from me, no matter what I said, and his wife was getting jealous. I handed in my notice and came home.'

'She did mention it the other day but I'd forgotten,' he said tactlessly. 'Sorry about the job.'

'Oh, well, at least it means we can see each other over the holidays, while I look for another post. I've *so* missed you, Mark.'

She cast him a special, intimate smile and there was an unmistakable intensity in her voice.

Mark began to look slightly hounded, though I remembered hearing he'd gone out with Flora on a previous visit. It looked like she wanted to take up where they'd left off.

'I'll be really busy working on the renovations, right over Christmas,' he said quickly.

'So I've heard, and I'm just *dying* to see what you've been up to,' she said, undeterred. 'I could help you while I'm here, if you like?'

Mark was now looking increasingly uncomfortable and kept glancing at me, though Flora was still pretending I didn't exist.

Lex was impervious to her tactics, though, and introduced me. 'Meg, this is Teddy's former nanny, Flora Johnson. Flora, Meg Harkness.'

She turned reluctantly. 'Oh, yes, the portrait painter. I know all about you, because I've brought someone with me that you know *very* well.'

A horrible suspicion was already forming in my mind when, with a certain Parting of the Red Sea effect, she pointed and a path to the fire opened up, revealing, huddled in a chair, a familiar but unwelcome figure.

'It's someone *I* recognize too,' Lex said. 'Rollo Purvis.'

'Oh?' she sounded surprised. 'He's Meg's boyfriend.'

'No, he's not!' I snapped. 'He's not even a friend any more, just someone trying to use the fact that he knows me to meet Henry.'

'He said you'd been cold-shouldering him since you came up here to paint Clara, so he thought you might have found someone else.'

Her limpid gaze looked me over, battered and dishevelled, then her eyebrows rose and she looked from Lex to Mark, as if inviting them both to find this idea as ludicrous as she did.

'Rollo only wanted to see you,' she said. 'So he thought he'd take you by surprise.'

'I'm certainly surprised he was stupid enough to drive over the Pennines in the middle of winter in his soft-top sports car,' I said tartly.

'He stayed at the Pike with Two Heads last night, but his car wouldn't start this morning and the garage have taken it away,' she said. 'That's why I offered him a lift over.'

'I hope you'll give him a lift back, too, and soon,' I told her. Then I marched up the room to Rollo and paraphrased my favourite film quote.

'Of all the ancient manorial halls in all the world, you had to choose this one?'

'*Casablanca*,' said Clara, who was standing by the fire with one booted foot resting on the fender. 'Flora picked him up at the pub, Meg, and brought him back with her. She's offered to put him up for the night.'

'I just heard about your car, Rollo. You were an imbecile to drive over the Pennines in it. Didn't you listen to the weather reports?'

The others had followed me and Flora said, 'It was lucky I'd stopped in Thorstane on my way home, to buy some supplies, and then decided to have lunch at the pub. Poor Rollo's car was just being towed away by the garage when I got there.'

'It was late by the time I got to this Thorstane place yesterday, so when I saw the pub had a motel sign, I checked in,' said Rollo.

'We got talking,' said Flora, 'and of course, as soon as I knew where he was heading, I offered him a lift.'

'Of course you did, dear,' said Clara, ironically.

'The journey from York took me *hours* longer than I expected,' said Rollo, looking at me as if expecting sympathy. Getting no response, he added peevishly, 'If you ever checked your phone, Meg, you'd have known I'd had the journey from hell and you'd have driven over to the motel to fetch me yourself.'

'In your dreams!' I said, but he was lost in the remembered horrors of his journey.

'I was stuck on the motorway in the snow for hours and got totally chilled. You know I've got a weak chest and Mother was beside herself when I rang her last night and told her about it.'

He shivered pathetically in his vaguely Byronic jacket, worn over a thin cashmere jumper, and then sneezed.

River materialized out of nowhere, as usual, his bright, deep blue eyes glinting from under the mistletoe crown, and quoted, '"I had a grievous ague."'

'I haven't got an ague,' snapped Rollo. 'And I didn't expect to see *you* here.'

'*Brief Lives* by John Aubrey,' Clara said, delightedly. 'My favourite line of his is the one that goes, "Sciatica; he cured it, by boiling his buttocks."'

They smiled at each other, which seemed to annoy Rollo even more. He'd never really taken to River on the few occasions that they'd met.

'Clara kindly invited me to stay for the Solstice,' River told him. 'I was Old Winter – were you not at the ceremony?'

'No, it was late afternoon before we arrived at Flora's aunt's guesthouse and since I appear to have caught a chill, only the hope of meeting the great Henry Doome induced me to come out tonight.'

He employed the languishing look from under his long eyelashes that he considered irresistible to women. It was the male version of Flora's technique, which I found amusing.

'I doubt the feeling is mutual,' Clara said, dampeningly. 'And if you're breeding a cold I'd much rather you didn't meet Henry because he might catch it.'

'It's not a cold, but a chill,' Rollo said. 'My room at the pub wasn't very warm either, though the food was good and—' He broke off and stared across the room. 'Isn't that the pub landlord over there, near the table?'

'Yes, Fred plays a part in the Solstice ceremony. If you have a word with him, he'll probably take you back with him tonight, and then you can get straight off home again tomorrow, once the garage have finished with your car,' Clara suggested sensibly. 'I expect he'll be leaving soon, in case the road up over the moors freezes.'

'Oh, I couldn't face that chilly room again tonight,' Rollo protested faintly, with a shiver. 'I feel so ill.'

'You don't have to face it,' Flora assured him. 'You can stay at the guesthouse tonight and I expect you'll feel much better in the morning.'

Rollo gave her a look of gratitude. 'You're so kind.'

Flora cast me a triumphant glance, as if she'd put one over on me. Clearly Rollo had convinced her that we were in some kind of relationship.

'You don't mind, do you, Mark?' she said, turning to him and taking him by surprise.

'What?' He gave a start. 'No, why should I mind?'

Then his eyes caught sight of his mother and he beckoned her over.

'Mum,' he said, putting his arm around me again and drawing me forward, 'Meg had a fall up on the hill. She almost went over the steep drop near the bonfire. Her hands and face are a bit scratched and could do with some antiseptic.'

'Oh, you poor thing!' said Sybil sympathetically. 'Didn't anyone warn you to keep away from the edge?'

She didn't wait for an answer, but added firmly, her maternal instincts clearly roused by my state, 'You come with me and I'll do a bit of first aid.'

I was glad to go. Not only were my hands stinging terribly, but by then I was desperate to get away from Rollo.

29

Prickly

Sybil cleaned up my face and then competently removed several thorns from my hands. I bet she wielded a mean hoof pick.

'You're so kind; thank you,' I said gratefully when she'd finished. 'My hands feel so much better already!'

'Good, and the scratch on your face is barely visible, though I'm afraid there might be a bruise tomorrow.'

'Never mind, I think I got off lightly.'

'How did you come to fall?' she asked curiously. 'No one had moved the white stones marking the edge, had they?'

'No, but I was standing very close to them and a sudden gust of wind caught me. I just managed to grab that gorse bush as I was going over!' I shivered in recollection. 'Lex spotted me and pulled me back.'

'Thank goodness he did,' she said. 'I know you've only been here for a short time, but I'm sure everyone at the Red House is fond of you already – and Mark certainly is, too!'

She paused, though continued packing away the scissors and plasters in the first-aid box. 'I . . . may not have given you the warmest of welcomes into the family, Meg, but your existence came as quite a surprise to me and . . . well, it's taken me time to come to terms with it.'

'That's all right. It's taken me time to get my head around it, too,' I assured her.

'Of course at first, like Mark, I was worried that you might have a claim on the estate, which would make things very difficult for him.'

'I can understand that, but even if that were possible, I don't want anything more than to know I'm part of the family. Mum will feel exactly the same.'

'Thank you,' she said, then added, with a smile, 'You and Mark hit it off immediately, didn't you? And I'm sure you'll soon grow attached to Underhill.' She gave me a look that I couldn't quite fathom. 'Mark said you were very interested in his plans.'

'It's a charming old house,' I said, though actually the Gothic excesses of the Red House were more to my taste.

'Mark likes you *very* much – I could see that tonight – and it doesn't really matter if you're cousins, after all,' she said more to herself than me, evidently pursuing some inner train of thought. 'It would be perfect!'

There was no mistaking the direction of her remarks *now*, so I said firmly, 'I'm sure being cousins will make us even better friends.'

Even if Mark had been my type, which he wasn't, he had a few drawbacks, like being several years my junior and appearing to have previous relationship issues to resolve. I'd already had one love rat in my life and I wasn't looking for a replacement.

'I look forward to getting to know you better during Christmas,' Sybil said. 'It'll be good to get away.'

'That reminds me,' I said, 'Mark might have an assistant over the holidays, because Flora just offered to help him with the decorating while she's home.'

Sybil's expression, which had been pensive, darkened. 'I hope he turned her down. She's a man-eater under that sweet and fluffy "poor little me" act! She hounded poor Lex when she was Teddy's nanny and then, last time she was home between jobs and Mark happened to be here too, sorting out the estate after probate had been granted, she wouldn't leave him alone. Just because he felt *sorry* for her and took her out for dinner a couple of times, she seems to think they're in a relationship.'

I thought there'd been a bit more between them than that, even if not serious on Mark's side. Perhaps he should have made that clearer from the start.

'Well, we'd better get back,' she said, and when we reached the hall it was clear we'd been away longer than I'd thought, for lots of people had already left and the rest were getting back into anoraks and overcoats and wrapping scarves around their necks.

Lex was leaning against the bottom of the staircase and seemed to be waiting for me, but I couldn't see any sign of the others.

'There you are, at last,' he said, straightening up. 'Den's taken everyone else home, except Tottie, who's walking up by way of the fields with Len Snowball, to help him catch the horses.'

'That's so kind of dear Tottie,' said Sybil. 'There's heavy snow forecast for tonight, so I asked him to bring them down to the stables.'

Then she excused herself and went to speed her departing guests homeward.

Lex looked down at me. 'Mark offered to run you home himself later, but I said I'd wait for you.'

I suddenly realized that here would be the perfect opportunity to have that private talk with Lex I'd promised River, even if it *was* the last thing I felt like doing right then. My head was a bit fuzzy, too, which I think must have been the generous shot of brandy in the toddy earlier. I'm not used to spirits.

'It was kind of you to wait,' I said formally.

'Not really. I thought it was time we had a little talk.'

I stared at him in surprise. 'You're right, and *I* was going to suggest we stop somewhere on the way home to have things out, too.'

'River told me earlier that I had a closed mind and needed to open the door and listen to you,' he said.

'That makes it sound like I've been shouting at you through the keyhole,' I said shortly, and the ghost of a grin touched his lips.

'Well, this is your chance to shout at me face to face.'

When I'd fished my coat out from the depleted pile under the table and put it on, I joined Lex and Mark by the door.

Mark smiled at me warmly. 'I see Mum fixed you up. You look a lot better now.'

'It's amazing what a difference washing the mud off my face and combing my hair made,' I agreed. 'I'm really fine, just a few scratches and bruises.'

'We'd better get off,' said Lex. 'Is it still snowing?'

'Yes, though that sudden wind has dropped as quickly as it got up.' Mark's eyes went beyond me and I turned to see Flora with Rollo, though I hardly recognized him, since he was enveloped in a battered caped raincoat that covered him from collar to heels. He was in the act of pulling the wide hood over his head to complete the mad monk impersonation and avoided looking at me, but instead thanked Mark for the loan of the coat.

'That's all right. It's an old one of my grandfather's that hangs in the back hall for anyone to borrow, so there's no hurry to return it.'

'I'll bring it when I come over tomorrow afternoon, once I've run Rollo back to Thorstane, Mark,' Flora said brightly. 'We have *so* much to catch up on and I want to hear all about these renovations.' She smiled winsomely up at him, her face framed in snowy white fake fur.

'I'm afraid I'll be too busy for visitors,' he said with more haste than tact. 'Mum's going to the Red House tomorrow to stay over Christmas, so I can press on with the work here.'

'Really? But you don't want to be alone at Christmas, surely?' she said, widening her big eyes at him. 'And anyway, *I'm* not a visitor, am I? I can help you, too.'

Mark might have behaved badly, but she was now starting to remind me of a small, pretty, but predatory fairy, red of fang and sharp of nails. The dark sort you found in some old stories: a bit Grimm.

Rollo had sidled up to me unnoticed and now said in a low voice, 'Meg, since I've come all this way and caught a chill, surely you'll let me come and see you in the morning, before I go?'

'Now, how can I put this tactfully, Rollo?' I mused aloud. '*No!*'

'You're terribly *hard*, aren't you?' said Flora, gazing at me sadly, with her head on one side, like a bird. A small vulture, possibly. Or maybe a buzzard, circling over a new kill. 'Poor Rollo!'

'Poor Rollo nothing,' I snapped. 'And if it was me he came to see, then he's standing right in front of me now, isn't he?'

Rollo glowered in his best Byronic fashion, though under the hood and with a pink-tipped nose and watery eyes, it didn't come off too well.

'Apparently, the forecast is for heavy snow tonight, so you'd be better going straight back to the motel while you can,' I suggested.

'Oh, it won't be *that* bad – and don't worry, because *I'll* look after him,' Flora told me.

I bet she would.

Then she turned her full wattage on Lex, smile and fluttering eyelashes working overtime: she obviously couldn't be near any personable man without giving it her best shot.

'Oh, Lex, will you tell Clara that I'll pop in and see Teddy some time soon?' she cooed and then added to me, 'He adores me. I was his nanny, you know. I saw him earlier, but he can't have spotted me or he'd have come over to say hello.'

'He did, but Fred was teaching him the vanishing handkerchief trick with Clara's bandanna,' Lex said. 'That was much more exciting.'

'Oh, thanks,' she said, pouting.

'I'll just say goodnight to Sybil and then I'm ready to go,' I said quickly to Lex, suiting the action to the words.

I'd have liked to have said goodbye to Pansy too, but Mark had shut the dogs up in the morning room.

We were the last to leave, and the Gidneys had already half-cleared the trestle table. The platter that had held the huge treacle cake was now bare, apart from a scattering of crumbs.

Rollo and Flora had gone, and I thought if she had any sense at all, she'd drive him straight back to the pub tonight and leave him there.

Mark had taken me by surprise by kissing me in an uncousinly way under a bunch of mistletoe before I left, and as I climbed into the front of the pick-up next to Lex, he said, 'Perhaps you'd rather have let Mark drive you home? He seems to have recovered from that slight hiccup when he heard you were related and suspected you were after his money, doesn't he?'

'No, I wouldn't, and what I said at the mill was true: I'm not interested in him that way and I'm sure he isn't *seriously* interested in me, either.'

I did like him, though, and he'd been kind tonight. When we'd first met I'd thought he was mean to Sybil, but I'd come to realize that he was driven by his love for Underhill to do whatever it took to keep it.

'I'm sure he'd like your help with the decorating,' Lex suggested.

'He'll have to make do with Flora's. I'm a portrait painter, not a decorator's mate.'

The front seat of the pick-up was a long bench-style one and I kept a good space between us, hoping the heater would soon kick in, as Lex headed down the drive.

In the headlights the snow was swirling down in quite large, flat wafers that settled on the ground.

'It's starting to look as if the weather forecast got it right: heavy fall of snow overnight on the moors,' Lex said. 'So if Flora doesn't want to be stuck with Rollo for longer than one night, it's to be hoped she's halfway to the pub by now.'

'That's what I thought. I'm still furious with him for turning up, because I'd already told him I never wanted to see or hear from him again after he rang Clara that time.'

'I don't think he got the message, *and* it sounds as if he's been spinning Flora a tale about being in a relationship with you.'

He had, of course, but I wondered now if his survival instinct had kicked in when he'd met Flora at the pub, warning him that he'd better tell her he was involved with someone else?

As we drove through the village, the only sign of life was a few lit windows, including those at Preciousss.

'We can park by the Sailing Club under the pine trees for a bit, where it's sheltered,' Lex said, turning down a track that ran through the woods until he pulled up facing the glimmering reservoir, next to the dark outline of a building, and cut the lights.

It was a bit like the start of a murder mystery . . . but perhaps we'd already had act one? As we'd driven here I'd let my mind go back to that awful moment when I'd almost fallen and, no matter how irrational it might be, I was sure I hadn't imagined the hard shove of two hands in the small of my back.

Lex switched on the interior light, which shed a dim glow, and turned to face me. He seemed to sense what I was thinking, which was disconcerting.

'Do you still think someone tried to push you off the hill tonight?'

I answered indirectly. 'I don't see why on earth anyone would, unless you have a local practical joker.'

'No, and it would have been way beyond a joke if you'd fallen down there.'

I shivered. 'Then it must have been an accident. And anyway,' I said, getting my resolve together, 'that's not what I wanted to talk to you about. River said it was time I told you exactly what happened between us that night you came back to my flat. Not that I haven't *tried* already,' I added tartly.

'But I already do know what happened – or enough. What good will it do to rake over the ashes now?'

'But you *don't* know, that's the whole point,' I said forcefully. 'You only *think* you know. You and Al built up a whole picture from a few pieces without asking me for my side of it.'

He sighed, running one hand through his already tangled hair, his handsome, dark, hawk face brooding in the dim light.

'Look, we'd both had a lot to drink that night, Meg, and I've already said I don't blame you for what happened, but myself for getting so drunk that I didn't really know what I was doing.'

'You don't actually have anything to blame me for, magnanimous though it is of you,' I said sarcastically, but he was back in the past and swallowed up in a sea of old guilt.

'If Al hadn't managed to track me down, I might have got there too late to see Lisa. I can't bear to think of that!'

'Yes, I know,' I said, softening slightly. 'But you'd been under a lot of strain for weeks and you'd no way of knowing she'd need you that night. Now, perhaps you'd like to stop wallowing in guilt for a few minutes and just listen.'

That was harsh, but it got through, because he said tightly, 'You're obviously determined to go through it all again, so let's get it over with.'

'I don't know how much you recall about the start of that evening we met in the wine bar,' I said. 'When I went in with a group of my friends, you and Al were already there and you insisted we join you. You'd already had quite a bit to drink by then.'

'I was trying to blank out what was happening for a few hours.' He rubbed his forehead as if his memory hurt him. 'Lisa had finally had to go into the hospice and her parents had come down that day to be with her . . . so rather than let me go home on my own, Al took me out for a drink.'

'Which turned into several drinks,' I said. 'I'd had a couple myself, but then switched to coffee when the others left and we stayed behind, talking.'

'Al had a job as a hotel night porter, so he had to go, too. I remember that part . . . and when they'd all left you told me your boyfriend had just dumped you by email – was that Rollo?'

I nodded. 'Yes, the first, but not the last, time. I was mad to give him a second chance.' And a third and final one.

'It starts to get hazy after that,' Lex admitted. 'I think . . . I talked to you about Lisa.'

'You totally unburdened yourself on the subject,' I said frankly. 'All about how you'd supported her decision not to have chemo in the face of her parents' wishes, because the chance of it working had been so slim and she'd wanted to enjoy what life she had left. And how guilty you felt about it, after she'd worsened so quickly.'

'I really did bare my soul, didn't I?' he said wryly. 'I knew we'd talked a bit, but I didn't realize how much I'd told you.'

'I thought that was why you turned and walked away the next time I saw you – because you felt embarrassed about having told me so much personal stuff.'

'No, it wasn't that. I hadn't remembered what I'd said.'

'I know that now, but it was only when Al raged at me like a madman later that day that I realized the truth – and what you both thought of me!'

'He shouldn't have taken it on himself to say anything at all, and I told him so. But he's been a good friend throughout everything.' He paused. 'So, I remember being in the wine bar with you . . . but not how I ended up in your digs.'

'You'd carried on drinking, but since you were talking perfectly well, I didn't realize how drunk you were until we left. When we got outside it was bucketing down with rain and the cold air just hit you for six: I had trouble keeping you upright. We were the last out of the wine bar and they locked the door behind us, or I'd have rung for a taxi to take you home.'

He was looking intently at me now, though I couldn't see his expression clearly enough to read.

'I lived only round the corner, so I thought the best thing to do was take you there, pour black coffee down you and call a cab.'

'Very practical,' he said drily. 'What went wrong?'

'I managed to get you there, though it was a bit of a struggle, and we both got very wet. I hung your coat up to drip and you headed for the bathroom, while I went to put the kettle on.'

'I don't remember any of that,' he said blankly. 'The first thing I remember about your flat is . . . being in bed with you.'

'You were *not* in bed with me,' I said forcefully. 'I'd got *into* bed because I was freezing – that was the coldest, dampest flat ever – but you were lying on top of it, under a duvet.'

'But I remember—'

'You're supposed to be letting *me* tell you what happened,' I interrupted. 'When we'd got back to the flat and I'd put the kettle on, there was no sign of you – and I found you crashed out on my bed. It was next to the bathroom, so I expect you just stumbled in there and passed out.'

This time he said nothing, so I carried on. 'I did try to wake you up, but I couldn't, so after a while I thought I'd better let you sleep it off. I took your boots off and covered you with a spare duvet. Then, since I was damp and freezing, I got ready for bed and got in. I left the bedside light on in case you woke up and didn't know where you were.'

'Yes . . .' he said slowly. 'There was a light, because I remember seeing you in bed next to me – and kissing you.'

'You did briefly surface and kiss me, just after I got in bed, but I don't think you really knew what you were doing and you passed out again almost straight away.'

He was frowning heavily now, brows knitted. 'You're trying to tell me we *weren't* actually in bed together? That we didn't—'

'I'm not trying to tell you – this is the truth! Apart from one brief kiss, we didn't do anything other than sleep, so whatever else you remember, it only happened in your head.'

'But how do I know that's really what happened and you're not just saying it to make me feel better?'

'Because I've never had a one-night stand in my life. I'm not that kind of person,' I snarled. 'Look, that evening I was heart-broken because I'd just split with Rollo, so what makes you think I'd have jumped straight into bed with you?'

'But . . . I knew you had a crush on me, because Al used to joke about how pink you went whenever we spoke.'

'I'm glad I provided you both with some amusement,' I said coldly. 'And yes, I did have a crush on you – in my first term! Once I'd met Lisa, it just wore off, because she was so sweet and lovely, and you were perfect together.'

'She was one in a million and I didn't deserve her,' he said, still frowning as if trying to put the pieces of the past together again. 'When I told Al what I remembered, he said you'd always had a thing about me and had seized the opportunity when I was drunk to—'

'Drag you to my lair and have my wicked way with you?' I finished for him sarcastically. 'Al is mad!' I added with conviction.

I decided to tell him my clincher: 'What you don't know, Lex, is that I have a witness to back my story up. There was someone else in the flat that night.'

There was a silence. Then he said, 'But I don't remember anyone else.'

'No, but then, you only seem to have a selection of small and distorted memories of what happened, don't you? But Fliss *was* there.'

'Fliss? You mean, Fliss from college?'

'That's the one. She was in the flat that night, because she had flu.'

'You're trying to tell me she was there the whole time?' He sounded disbelieving. 'But I suppose even if that's true, she must have been in her room, if she was ill.'

'She was over the worst by then, just wobbly. She came out to see what was happening when we arrived and then after I found you out cold on my bed, we discussed what to do. In the end, we thought you'd be OK and just sleep it off, so she fetched a spare duvet and we covered you up. Fliss and I had some cocoa, then I got into my bed and she went back to hers. But it was only a short time later that she came back in with your phone in her hand. It had been ringing on and off in your coat pocket for ages and she'd heard it because she slept next to the living room.'

He was still silent, so I carried on. 'When she came into the bedroom, I was asleep in bed, and you were still out for the count under the duvet, just as she'd left you. She gave the phone to me and when I answered it, it was Al, looking for you.'

Lex stirred at last. 'Lisa's parents rang his mobile when they couldn't get hold of me . . . and I do remember him turning up to fetch me. I was still wet—'

'No, you were wet because we splashed your face with icy water to try to get you to wake up,' I said. 'The sound of your phone seemed to bring you round a bit, too, so after the icy water and a couple of mugs of black coffee, you were almost coherent by the time he arrived.'

'But Al didn't see anyone else in the flat, either, or he'd have mentioned it. He only saw you, in your dressing gown.'

'Fliss had gone back into her room by then; she didn't feel in a fit state to see anyone.'

There was another long silence and I had no idea what he was thinking, until eventually he said slowly, 'I don't know what's true and what isn't any more, but once you'd turned up at the Red House, it was hard to square what I'd been thinking of you with the reality. Now . . . I don't know what to believe.'

I got out my phone and rang Fliss's number, praying she'd answer. It was early still, despite the darkness.

'Fliss! I'm sorry to bother you, but I need your help.'

'Meg? Your voice sounds shaky – what's up?'

'I had a fall earlier, but I'm OK, and now I'm in a car with Lex and I've just told him the truth about what happened in the flat that night. Only I'm not sure he believes *you* were there, too.'

'You give him the phone and I'll put him straight!' she declared belligerently, and I passed it across.

The ensuing conversation was mostly one-sided – Fliss's.

His expression didn't change as he listened, but when he did finally speak, he said, 'Yes, OK, I believe you, and I agree I was a fool for not talking to Meg afterwards.'

Then he thanked her and handed back the phone.

'The truth will out,' Fliss said cheerfully. 'It's just taken a hell of a long time.'

'Better out than in,' I agreed. 'Thanks, Fliss.'

'That's OK, and if Al and his wife don't apologize, you can put them on to me and I'll sort them out as well.'

She'd wanted to have it out with Al years ago, when I'd told her what he'd said to me. Maybe I should have let her?

'I hope that won't be necessary. In fact, I'm hoping I never have to see them again.'

'Well, if you're OK we can catch up again tomorrow?' she suggested. 'I'll go back to my virtuously alcohol-free celebration.'

'Why alcohol free?' I asked, but I think I knew the answer before she announced it.

'Because I'm pregnant!'

I made the right noises but suddenly I felt like the last barren woman in the world. She must have guessed that for she said, 'I'm sorry, I forgot and I—'

'No, don't be sorry, I'm so happy for you,' I assured her. 'Just because *I* lost my baby, it doesn't mean I don't want to hear my friend's good news. I'll be Auntie Meg, instead.'

When I rang off, Lex said in a changed voice, 'Meg, I seem to have been entirely wrong about you all along the line, and I couldn't help hearing what you just said. You've lost a baby, haven't you? I'm so sorry.'

'I miscarried after an accident. I made the mistake of telling Rollo I was pregnant when he was driving and he went off the road. Since we were supposed to be defying his mother and getting married at last, I didn't think he'd be as horrified as he was.'

I remembered the expression on his face just before he lost control of the car, and shivered . . .

'Why didn't his mother want him to marry you?'

'She didn't think I was good enough for her precious son, especially when she found out Mum was adopted: all those random unknown genes in the grandchildren.'

'Well, they're not unknown any more,' he pointed out.

'No, but it's too late now.'

'With Rollo, perhaps, but not with someone else.'

'No,' I said with finality. 'I'll have fun being an auntie to my friends' children. That'll be enough.'

There was a long silence, broken eventually by Lex.

'I don't know how to start apologizing for all the things I thought about you *and* said to you, since you came here. I still feel guilty about the past and Lisa, but at least none of it was anything to do with you.'

I decided to clear my conscience once and for all. It took quite an effort. 'I *do* have a touch of guilt about that night in the flat,' I confessed. 'Because when you kissed me, I went with it at first. But then I realized what I was doing and pulled away and you passed out again. I was surprised you remembered it.'

His lips twisted. 'Oh, I remembered it all right, and that I knew it was you I was kissing. *And* I wanted to. That was part of the guilt.'

'You did say my name before you passed out again,' I admitted. 'I never told Fliss that.'

'If we're being totally honest with each other, I kept something back that night in the wine bar that's been gnawing at me ever since: I wasn't in love with Lisa any more and I was trying to find a way of telling her, before she fell ill.'

I stared at him, stunned. 'But you always seemed the perfect couple!'

'We fell in love at sixth-form college and we'd been together ever since. But first love doesn't always last, does it?'

'No, that's true,' I said, remembering the few weeks I'd had my mad crush on him.

'I might not have been still *in* love with Lisa, but I did love her: she was sweet and kind and beautiful.'

'She was the most genuinely good person I've ever met. *Everyone* loved her,' I agreed.

'I finally felt I'd have to try to end the relationship just before she was diagnosed. I think seeing you with Rollo one day was the decider – I felt jealous.'

'What, of *me*?' I exclaimed incredulously. Even in the throes of my brief crush on him, I'd thought he was way out of my league.

I was still feeling stunned when he said, 'Yes, of you.' He gave that twisted smile again. 'There was some connection between us from the moment I first saw you in that dark corridor.'

I'd thought that feeling was all on my side! But he had seemed to like my company . . . until that fateful night.

'Of course, once Lisa was diagnosed I had to stay with her. I still adored her and I did my best.'

'You certainly did,' I assured him.

'Near the end, she said she hoped I'd be able to move on and have a good life with someone else. She wanted me to remember only the happy times, if I thought of her.'

Tears filled my eyes: that was so typical of her.

'But you haven't done that, Lex, have you?'

'No, because I've been too busy wallowing in self-pity and guilt ever since. And making *you* part of that, too.'

'Don't be too hard on yourself, Lex,' I said, reaching out and placing my hand over his. 'You can put it all in the past now, can't you? River was right: getting everything out into the open has cleared the air. We might be shaped by the past, but we don't have to constantly relive it.'

'That sounds very like River! And it has freed me: I feel a weight has dropped off, though I think we both need a bit of time to get readjusted to the new status quo.'

His hand turned under mine and closed around it, strong and warm.

'Can we be friends?' he asked.

'Yes, as well as relatives,' I agreed. 'Though as you keep pointing out, only by marriage and that doesn't count. *And* the wrong side of the blanket.'

'What an old-fashioned expression!' he said, his seriousness suddenly softening into amusement. He pulled me towards him and kissed me on the lips so lightly and quickly that he'd started the engine before I'd taken in what he'd done.

'I'd forgotten how off the wall and funny you are,' he said, and while I was still pondering that one – and the kiss – he pulled out and headed up the dark track. The star had moved and was now hanging over the turn on to the road, as if waiting for us.

It was probably a sign, though I'd no idea of what. And now I came to think of it, I hadn't thought about my near-Icarus over the precipice for at least half an hour.

Clara

Married life heralded a new phase in our relationship.

Henry's mother had left him what money was secured to her, since George would inherit the Underhill estate, an arrangement that must have seemed eminently fair at the time.

Henry had entrusted his legacy to an old school friend to invest. His trust had not been misplaced and we were able to buy a tiny flat near the British Museum, where I now worked. We even had household help, in the form of our good friend Den, who had attached himself to Henry during one of his trips to Greece.

Having absorbed from the wider world all that he needed, Henry began to focus more on the past: he was continually drawn back to Starstone Edge – indeed, it always exerted a pull on both of us.

I consolidated my professional standing and wrote papers, articles and books, while frequently being called in for my opinion by museums, galleries, private collectors and archaeological digs.

I had another string to my bow, too. In the first year of our marriage I had written, purely for fun, a crime novel, my heroine being an epigrapher not entirely unlike myself. It had found a publisher and my subsequent yearly offerings built up a surprising following.

Henry, for the most part, divided his time between the flat and Underhill, while his father still lived, though he avoided Underhill when George was visiting, so far as possible.

Henry's first poetry collection had been met with wonderful reviews and great acclaim and he was embarking on the second. His reputation as a poet grew, despite his refusing to do any kind of public event, other than radio broadcasts, reading his own works.

We had many friends in London and our years spent living there were extremely happy.

As our careers took off, we were aware from the media that so too did Nessa Cassidy's, in the States. She espoused a militant form of feminism, lived openly with a female lover, Suzanne Dell (also a writer), and her book, The Butterfly Kiss: A History of the Suppression of Female Love, *became a runaway bestseller.*

It did bring back the past and made us think of that little girl out there in the world, whom we would never know. But we were pleased that Nessa appeared to have found love and forged a career for herself. The book was well written, though I felt she often relied on conjecture, rather than fact, when dealing with the past. However, the dead could not sue her, of course.

Henry's father died suddenly and George inherited the Underhill estate, which made visiting difficult. It was not that we weren't welcome to stay, but we were not keen on the company of George and his cronies, especially one, Piers Marten, who seemed to encourage George to drink and gamble to excess. Not that he needed much encouraging. There were also some unsavoury tales about what the pair of them got up to abroad . . .

Now a widower, George spent a lot of time on the Riviera or at Monte Carlo, where the money ran through his fingers like sand.

He fancied himself an expert on investments, and though Henry advised him to let his own broker handle them, it was to no avail.

30

Advent

With everything that had happened – more than enough not only to make my head spin, but entirely rotate like something from *The Exorcist* – I hadn't expected to sleep well that night. But I must have been exhausted by all the emotional turmoil, because I went out as soon as my head touched the pillow and the next thing I knew, it was early morning.

I lay there, mentally shuffling through the events of the previous day like a deck of cards and picking out a random selection.

Did I fall, or was I pushed?

The ceremony had been a strangely surreal experience, as if we'd all passed through a portal into a darker and more mysterious past, where anything might happen. But unless the villagers harboured a homicidal maniac among their number (probably something they would have noticed by now), my imagination must have gone into overdrive.

The unwelcome appearance of Rollo while I was still in a state of shock had only added to the element of unreality. Then there were Flora's relationship issues with Mark and what seemed like his renewal of an uncousinly interest in me . . .

Sybil, too, had definitely been hinting that she hoped Mark and I had a future together . . . Perhaps she felt if we married it would neatly legitimize my place in the family?

But real life tends not to tie itself into pretty ribbon bows with swallow-tail ends and, unfortunately for her plans, I didn't fancy Mark in the least.

I know who you do fancy – you always did, whispered a tiny demon in my head, and I told it to shut up and go away, because life was complicated enough already.

I hoped – but doubted – that Flora had had sense enough to return Rollo to the pub last night, because there was a certain still, heavy silence about the morning that told me, even before I hopped out of bed and looked, that the world was blanketed in thick, white snow.

I got back in bed again, snuggled under the duvet and this time let myself think about Lex and last night.

River had been right: forcing Lex to look back at the most painful time of his life and re-evaluate my part in it had been cathartic. But then, as River often said, wounds never healed until they'd been cleansed.

But what my mind had really been skittering round the edge of was Lex's bombshell revelation that he'd once had feelings for me; had even been jealous of my relationship with Rollo! *And* that that night at the flat he'd *wanted* to kiss me, his inhibitions washed away by alcohol.

And I'd certainly wanted to kiss him back, until I came to my senses.

It seemed there was a whole world of what-might-have-beens out there, like one of those films with several alternative parallel realities.

But it was all a long time ago and now we were both older, wiser and, it seemed, destined to be friends.

I hoped Lex would now be able to cast off the shackles of guilt. The ghost of Lisa, beautiful and sad, would always be there, but she wouldn't have wanted her death to blight his life.

Lex's brief kiss before he drove me back last night had been meant to mark the end of hostilities and the start of a new relationship . . . of some kind.

Kissing cousins . . . Mark certainly thought *he* was! I'd have to disillusion him about that pronto, before Sybil called the banns and Flora decided I was her love rival.

I wriggled down a little further under the warm duvet and remembered the scene when Lex and I had arrived back at the Red House last night. It had struck me as odd that nobody asked what had kept us so long.

'Oh, there you are,' Clara had said casually, with a beaming smile. 'Just in time for a late dinner, or early supper. Den and Tottie are just putting the finishing touches to it, whatever it is.'

'Cheese and onion pie, with winter slaw and red cabbage,' River said. 'Blackberry crumble and custard.'

'Very hearty and warming,' approved Clara.

'It's starting to snow hard out there,' Lex told them. 'Just as well it wasn't like this earlier, or we'd have had a struggle to get up to the Stone for the ceremony.'

'We've never postponed one yet, even if it's only been the performers who made it to the top,' Henry said, then added to River, 'I'm afraid you might not be able to leave in the morning, but you're very welcome to stay as long as you like.'

River thanked him and said it was in the hands of the Goddess and he would wait and see how she directed things. I had a mental image of her as a kind of celestial Traffic Officer.

Teddy said anxiously, 'Will Mummy make it tomorrow?'

'Yes,' Lex assured him, 'even if I have to borrow Uncle Henry's skis and carry her here on my back.'

Teddy had thought that very funny and he was quite talkative and lively during dinner, until the excitement of the day caught up with him and he'd have gone face down in his dessert, fast asleep, only Tottie caught him in the nick of time.

I'd felt a bit self-conscious with Lex – OK, a *lot* self-conscious – and tried to avoid looking in his direction, but on the one or two occasions when I did glance his way I found him smiling at me with a kindness that I found more difficult to bear than the animosity that had gone before.

It hadn't stopped me eating as if I'd been famished for a month, though. That must be what a near-death experience, followed by a lot of soul-baring, does for you.

Everyone seemed to know I'd had a fall, but no one mentioned it as anything other than an accident.

I couldn't lie there for ever and it was starting to get light, so I showered, finding a few more bumps and bruises down one side, though you could barely see the thin thread of the scratch on my face, or the surrounding bruise, and my hands were only a little pink and puffy from the gorse, thanks to Sybil's ministrations.

As I reached the bottom of the stairs, giving the now-familiar wooden eagle a friendly pat on the head, Henry and Lex came in through the front door, stamping off the snow in the porch.

'Is it still snowing?' I asked Henry, avoiding Lex's eyes, because I felt even more shy this morning than I had last night, having had time to think about it all.

'It's snowed a lot during the night, but it's stopped now and the sun's trying to break through.'

'Some of the farmers have been out gritting the road through the village, so it's passable from here to Underhill,' Lex said. 'It gets steadily deeper as you climb up towards the moors, though, so they're going to see if it thaws out a bit this morning and then try the snowplough later.'

'Yes,' Henry said, 'even if they can't get all the way through to Thorstane, they'll still need to take feed to the sheep, one way or another.'

They'd already had breakfast, but I found most of the others still in the kitchen and I apologized for my lateness.

'I wasn't even asleep, just lying there, too snug to get up.'

'That's all right, all our usual routines are slowly dissolving into the Christmas spirit,' said Clara. 'Tottie's only just gone to let the hens out.'

'If we had a pond, we could have a duck,' Teddy suggested.

'What do you call a duck at this time of year?' asked Clara.

'A Christmas quacker,' Den answered, spooning loose leaf tea into the pot with a generous hand. 'That one fell out of crackers in the Dark Ages, didn't it?'

I put two slices of wholemeal bread into the toaster while Clara poured me a mug of coffee and pushed it towards me.

'Flora rang first thing to see if we knew how the roads were,' she said. 'I told her the Thorstane road was blocked, but perhaps they might clear it later.'

'So she *didn't* take Rollo back to the pub last night?' I asked.

'No, he's still at the guesthouse and she says his chill is much worse, so he's staying in bed at the moment.'

'He's such a hypochondriac that if he's really got something wrong with him it'll send him into a panic without Mummy to hold his hand. He'll be the patient from hell and have Flora running round after him.'

'Oh, Flora's adept at doing only what Flora wants,' Tottie said, entering the kitchen in time to hear this. 'The hens didn't really want to come out,' she added.

'Not bleedin' surprised. Even an 'en's got more sense than to be out in this weather,' said Den, opening a tin of digestive biscuits and dunking one in his mug of tea, which was a dark, rich mahogany colour. Half of the biscuit fell into the cup and vanished.

'Bugger,' he said.

Teddy, who was picking the last bits of his cereal out of the bowl with his fingers, looked up and said thoughtfully, 'Bugger's one of the special Den words I'm not allowed to use till I'm grown up, isn't it?'

Tottie agreed that it was.

'But Sybil said it too, when that Shetland pony she borrowed for me in the summer holidays bit her on the bum.'

'I'm not surprised,' said Clara. 'We're going to fetch Sybil and the dogs right after an early lunch and bring them here for Christmas. That'll be fun, won't it? Lex will run me and Henry there in my car with the snow chains on, if we need them.'

'I should be on my way home by now,' said River. His tunic today was the clear deep blue of his eyes and I now easily recognized the lettering around the bottom as cuneiform. 'Perhaps the road *will* reopen later.'

'I doubt it, and I don't think you should try it today. Do stay until at least tomorrow,' urged Clara. 'We like having you.'

'You're very kind,' he said, with one of his warm, serene smiles. 'I'm enjoying being here immensely.'

Lex came to report that Henry had gone back to his study, because being so near the completion of his epic work was too tantalizing to resist, even at Christmas. Then he asked what the rest of us meant to do for what was left of the morning.

'I'm carrying on with my memoirs,' said Clara. 'I feel much the same as Henry: I can't leave them alone for long. But now I know what happened to Nessa's baby, I'll have to resist the urge to jump ahead of the timeline.'

Tottie said, 'Olive was coming over to make up the bed in Sybil's room and then give all the bathrooms a once-over, but in this weather—'

'That's Olive now – or the Abominable bleedin' Snowman,' said Den.

Lex suggested he and I and Teddy clear the steps at the front of the house, but first, Teddy insisted we make a snowman and Den provided a carrot and lumps of charred wood from the embers of last night's drawing-room fire for nose and eyes.

Lex and I began shovelling the snow from the steps after that, while Teddy went round the house to help Den clear the path to the garage.

We didn't talk, but the silence was thick with unspoken words, possibly in one of Clara's ancient languages, because I had no idea what they were.

'That's it, then,' Lex said finally, as he sprinkled grit on the cleared steps. He smiled at me in a tentative way that I found somehow heart-wrenching, so I returned it warmly.

The cold air had whipped some colour into his cheeks and tangled his mop of dark curls. I suspect in my case it had just given me a cherry nose.

'Shall we go and help the others now?' I suggested.

'OK,' he agreed, shouldering his shovel and heading for the corner of the house . . . but suddenly the sight of that broad back was just *way* too tempting. I scooped up a handful of snow and threw it, hard. It splattered right on target.

He turned slowly, regarded me with a serious expression that made me feel nervous, then dropped the shovel, grabbed a handful of snow and threw it right back.

A battle ensued until I admitted defeat by running off round the side of the house, though wading through snow required a lot of effort and Lex got me with one last snowball.

River, bundled up in layers and with the rainbow pixie hat pulled firmly over his pointy little ears, was gritting the part of the path already cleared in front of the kitchen door, while Henry had now joined the party and was helping Teddy and Den shovel snow from the rest of it.

'It's good to hear the sound of laughter,' River said, beaming at us. 'Meg, I rang Oshan before I came out, to warn him not to expect me yet, and then I went down the garden to talk to the bees and the hens.'

'The bees are all fast asleep. Tottie told me,' said Teddy, leaning on a child-sized red shovel.

'Bees can absorb words even when they're asleep,' River assured him.

'Did the hens say anything interesting?' I asked, and he gave a puckish grin.

'They said they were glad they lived in a vegetarian household.'

'Except fer the fish,' pointed out Den. 'Come on, let's finish this, before I die of the perishin' cold.'

The snowball fight seemed somehow to have broken the ice between me and Lex. Though we still didn't speak much to each other, at least now the silence was comfortable.

We thawed ourselves out with hot soup and then, when Lex was getting ready to take Henry and Clara to fetch Sybil, we heard the sound of a tractor and saw it slowly ploughing its way past the Red House and up towards the moors.

There was a Land Rover parked at the bottom of the drive, with bales of hay and two lively Border collies in the back, and Den went to find out what was happening. He reported that Billy was waiting to see how far up the tractor got.

'That's Billy Banks from Berry Edge Farm,' Henry told me, then smiled. 'What a lot of alliteration!'

'Pete's the one on the tractor and 'e'll plough as far up as 'e can, won't 'e?' said Den. 'Billy'll follow 'im up and drop some 'ay off fer the sheep.'

'Do they think Pete will be able to get all the way over the top?' asked Clara. 'Zelda will be getting a taxi from the station this afternoon and I hope it can make it through.'

'Told 'em about Zelda,' Den said. 'They'll do their best.'

'Being Zelda, she'll probably bat her eyelashes and someone will carry her over the drifts,' Lex said cynically. 'I think we'd better go and fetch Sybil now, while the road through the village is well gritted, don't you?'

When they'd gone, Tottie agreed to sit for her portrait for an hour or so in the conservatory.

Den had vanished, probably to his flat, and River said he and Teddy were going to construct a Christmas collage to brighten up the hall.

In the conservatory, Tottie took up her pose and then became lost in thought, her expression rapt.

I stopped after a while – I was already laying paint on the face – and enquired what she was thinking about.

'Spring bulbs,' she said simply.

I asked her to hold the pose for another few minutes while I quickly blocked in the fruit and vegetables spilling out of the end of the cornucopia, so they could be returned to the kitchen. I'd put in the final details later, from the photos I'd taken.

Teddy came round a bend in the path and stopped under the large fan of a date palm.

'You've been ages. We've finished our picture and put it up. Don't you want to see it?'

'Of course we do,' I assured him. 'Just let me clear up here and we'll be there in a moment.'

We duly admired a panorama that featured a lot of dragons circling the Starstone, while tinfoil stars peppered the heavens.

'Where's River now?' I asked.

'In the kitchen with Den, baking,' he said, and when we went to make coffee we found a caraway seed cake cooling on a rack. It was a favourite of River's and he'd got Oshan to email the recipe over.

Tottie and I took our coffee into the drawing room and she put a match to the laid fire, which soon blazed up. Teddy had followed us and spread out his magic painting book on the coffee table, but he'd barely dipped his brush in the water pot when there was the sound of wheels crunching up the drive and then a horn beeped.

'They must be back with Sybil,' I said, going to the window to see. But instead of Clara's car, I saw that the farmer's Land Rover was pulling up, with two familiar Border collies jumping about in the open back. No hay this time, though.

Tottie looked over my shoulder as the driver got out and waved to us, then pointed at the cab.

'That's Billy Banks again, and I think he may have brought Zelda!'

'Mummy?' exclaimed Teddy eagerly, and beat us to the front door by a head.

Billy had hurried round to the passenger side by then and was tenderly helping down a small woman in a long, pink quilted coat and with a ridiculously huge Russian-style fake fur hat pulled low over a lively, pretty face with dark eyes and a tilted nose.

I didn't need Teddy's cry of 'Mummy!' to know who that was.

Tottie put a hand on his shoulder in time to stop him dashing out in his slippers.

'*Darling!*' cried Zelda, her red lips curving in a warm smile, and she practically swam towards us, arms outstretched. You could tell she was an actor.

Behind her, another figure was emerging more slowly: a tall, elderly man with white hair, dressed in an old-fashioned thick woollen overcoat and Burberry scarf. He turned and surveyed us with the palest of ice-blue eyes.

'We thought you'd make it, one way or another, Zelda,' said Den, edging past the mother and son reunion. He'd discarded his brown linen overall in favour of a battered donkey jacket and slipped his feet into wellies.

Then he spotted the extra passenger and said, disgustedly, 'Gawd! Yer running a taxi service now, Billy?'

'Aye, seems like it,' he said laconically. 'Makes a change from carting sick sheep about.'

He grinned, gap-toothed, at Zelda.

'You've been *so* kind – you and Pete are angels!' she told him.

'It's nothing,' he said, then explained to us, 'The taxi got as far as the pub. Then when the snowplough went up from that side, Fred followed it with his Land Rover – and the post van followed him. The top's too deep to plough, though, so they hailed Pete on this side and we managed to get them across.' He grinned again, good-naturedly. 'We had a bit of a job, what with the drifts and the old gent, and them having luggage.'

The 'old gent' didn't look too pleased to be described this way.

'Is the luggage in the back? I'll help yer get it out, won't I?' said Den.

Teddy and his mother had vanished inside, but Tottie and I were still blocking the entrance and the elderly man gave us a frigid glare from under bristling white eyebrows and snapped, 'Well, Charlotte, are you going to let me in before I die of hypothermia?'

From Tottie's expression, she thought that would be a good outcome, but she reluctantly made way and he pushed past us into the hall.

We followed and Tottie demanded, 'What are you doing here, Piers? Nobody's expecting you.'

So this must be the Piers Marten that Sybil had been angsting over, though from what everyone else had said about him, he hadn't sounded the most pleasant of characters.

'Then they *should* have been,' he was saying. 'I knew Sybil would want me to come for Christmas, whatever plans that young cub of hers had. He never liked me, so I thought he was just getting her to put me off, until Zelda told me that Sybil is spending Christmas *here*.'

'She is, because Mark's going to be doing a lot of work on the house over Christmas. I know she's been trying to ring you and leaving messages to tell you so,' said Tottie. 'The others have gone to fetch her. They'll be back soon.'

'I only saw the first letter and then I moved to my club, because my central heating boiler broke down. No one seemed to want to fix it this side of Christmas.'

He turned and gave me what he obviously imagined was a charming smile, though it didn't warm his eyes.

'Zelda told me about her new-found cousin, too. You must be Meg. I'm Piers Marten.'

'Yes, I'd gathered that, because I've heard about *you*, too,' I said, shaking the hand he held out, which was encased in unpleasantly clammy thin leather.

'I can't imagine why you're here, if you got Sybil's letter putting you off *and* after Zelda told you why,' said Tottie. 'You should have turned round and gone back to your club. But perhaps Billy wouldn't mind dropping you off at Underhill on his way home – he goes right past.'

'I'm too frozen to go any further and if Sybil is staying here, then there's no point in it. Mark's unlikely to give me a warm welcome.'

I suddenly remembered Clara saying that she wouldn't have him staying under her roof, so I didn't think that she would welcome him with open arms on her return, either.

'You can't be frozen, Piers, because it was toasty warm in Billy's cab,' Zelda said. She shed her quilted coat and the huge hat and then, having hugged Teddy and patted Lass, looked up and added, 'I did tell you you should go back to London on the next train, but you *would* insist on coming.'

'I *always* go to Underhill for Christmas,' he snapped. 'Done it for years.'

'No, you don't. Sometimes you've spent it at your club, or with your children,' Tottie pointed out.

Den and Billy had now brought in the luggage and Zelda told Teddy he wasn't to look at the big bag with parcels sticking out of the top. 'And no touching them to see if you can feel what they are.'

'Are they all for me?' he asked, eyes shining.

'You'll just have to wait and see, darling, won't you?'

A small figure emerged from the kitchen passage, seemingly borne along on a zephyr of deliciously aniseed-scented air.

River was wearing one of Den's huge striped blue and white aprons over his tunic and trousers, which enveloped him from head to toes. A fetching smudge of flour lay across one cheek and he'd tied a red and white checked tea towel pirate-fashion over his head to hold back his long silver hair.

'Greetings of the Goddess be upon you,' he said to Zelda, who smiled enchantingly at him. He turned his limpid azure gaze on Piers and added, generously in the face of an affronted glare, 'And upon you, too.'

'This was always a madhouse,' Piers muttered, tossing his coat and scarf over a chair.

Billy was holding a very large canvas sack, the last thing to be brought in. 'This is the mail for Starstone. I told the postie I'd drop it off here and take anything for the farms on with me.'

'Okey-doke,' said Den. 'I'll sort it and someone can walk down and deliver it tomorrer.' Then he added, 'Yer going to stay fer an 'ot drink, or maybe a cup of soup to thaw you out, Billy?'

'No, thanks. I'd better get off.' Billy jerked a thumb at Piers. 'What about him?'

'I don't know . . .' sighed Tottie. 'I expect you'd better leave him here and we'll see what Clara and Henry say when they get back. We'll have to do *something* with him.'

'*I'd* certainly like some of that soup, and perhaps a snifter of brandy,' Piers said autocratically.

'The only brandy yer likely to get in this 'ouse is the drop I put in the Christmas pud,' Den said. 'I'll put yer stuff in yer room, Zelda.'

She protested and said she could carry it up herself, but he insisted, so the rest of us went into the kitchen and had coffee and mince pies, while Zelda and Piers drank their soup. Lass, having expressed her pleasure at seeing Zelda again, now seemed compelled to keep a wary eye on Piers, though I'm not sure what she thought he might get up to.

'That mutt keeps staring at me,' he said.

'She's not a mutt, she's a cocker spaniel,' Teddy told him in surprise. 'Didn't you *know* that?'

'Lass probably suspects you're going to steal the family silver,' Tottie suggested.

'Do we have any?' asked Teddy. 'Is it in a box, like treasure?'

'No, only a set of fish knives somewhere in the attic,' she said. 'Oh, and that silver wine coaster in the dining room.'

Piers brightened. 'I wouldn't mind a drop of something now, but whisky for preference.'

No one took him up on this and, after a moment, he took a hip flask out of his pocket, shook it, then upended it over his coffee cup till a few slow drops trickled out.

'Those cakes smell wonderful,' Zelda said.

'Yer can have some fer tea,' Den said. 'They're seed cakes. River gave me the recipe.'

'And you would be . . . ?' said Piers, looking at River with disfavour.

'He's sort of Meg's grandfather, Teddy told me,' Zelda said, smiling at River. 'Since Meg is my new cousin, then I suppose he's my sort-of great-uncle!'

'I think I'm only a remote connection by marriage,' I said. 'It's all a bit complicated to work out.'

'Meg's sort-of grandfather? Curiouser and curiouser!' said Piers, staring at River.

'I came for the Solstice, but the snow is delaying my departure.'

'Well, no rush fer yer to go, is there?' said Den, with a pointed look at Piers. I'd initially felt rather sorry for Piers after his chilly reception, but really, his attitude did him no favours!

'Will anyone still want any tea this afternoon, after the soup and all these mince pies?' Tottie asked.

'Clara will, fer a start,' Den said. 'And they'll be back any minute – the light's going.'

Looking at the kitchen clock, I was surprised to see that it was almost mid-afternoon by then and the sky outside the windows looked as if it was thinking of dumping the next lot of snow.

'Let's go back into the drawing room and wait,' suggested Tottie, but River said he'd help Den clear up the kitchen first and then they were going to make a kissing bough.

We always had one at the Farm, so he obviously thought it was a vital part of the proceedings.

Piers' belongings were still stacked in a heap near the front door: Den evidently hoped for his imminent departure.

Piers seemed *very* unpopular, and I can't say I'd really taken to him either. Now he bagged one end of the sofa nearest the fire and, leaning back, closed his eyes. 'Such a long, cold, wearisome day . . .' he murmured histrionically.

Tottie switched on the Christmas tree lights and went to draw the curtains behind them.

'There's the car now: the others are back,' she said, peering out into the gloom.

'They're going to be so surprised to see Mummy got here through the snow!' said Teddy.

'They'll be even more surprised to find Piers did, too,' Zelda said drily.

31

Baggage

'Hello, everyone!' said Henry cheerily as he came into the drawing room. 'Zelda, my dear! I'm so glad you made it.'

'Hello, Henry,' she said, getting up and kissing him fondly, and then embracing Clara, who'd followed him in.

'Lex's just taking Sybil's bags up to her room and they'll both be down in a minute,' Clara said. 'And look, here's Mark! He's come back with us for tea, isn't that lovely?'

'Well, actually,' he said, 'I came to ask Meg if—'

But I was destined never to know what he was going to ask me, for at that moment his eyes fell on Zelda, who'd returned to sitting on the end of one of the window seats by the Christmas tree, and their gazes locked. Neither seemed able to look away. There might have been no one else in the room – or even in the world – but the two of them.

It was like all the classic moments in rom-com movies rolled into one and I felt myself grinning. I mean, they must know each other already, but now they stared into each other's eyes as if they'd instantly been hit by a thunderbolt.

The sharp yapping of the little dogs as they rushed in ahead of Sybil finally broke the spell and Zelda and Mark blinked, dazed, then looked away.

Pansy hurtled over and threw herself on to my lap, while Wisty and Lass greeted each other in a more matronly manner.

The yapping had also awoken Piers, who had been snoring in his corner of the sofa, hidden by Tottie's angular figure at the other end.

'*What?*' he barked, sitting bolt upright and glaring wildly around him. 'I wasn't asleep.'

'You were,' said Teddy, who was sitting on the floor, absorbed in sending tiny toy cars hurtling down some kind of vehicular helter-skelter. 'You were snoring and your mouth was wide open.'

'Oh God, what are *you* doing here?' Mark exclaimed, with a heavy scowl. Turning to Sybil he added accusingly, 'Mum, Piers is here. I thought you'd told him we couldn't have him for Christmas?'

'That could have been put so much better,' said Henry critically. 'You sound like a pair of cannibals.'

Sybil turned pale. 'But . . . I did tell him it was impossible for him to visit Underhill this year! I wrote twice and left several messages on his phone.'

'Ah, dear Sybil!' Piers said, hauling himself to his feet and coming over to kiss her on both cheeks. 'A little misunderstanding and some crossed wires, but I'm here now and I'm sure things can be arranged. How delightful to see you again.'

She looked totally distracted. 'Of course, I'm pleased to see you, Uncle Piers, it's just we weren't expecting you. Didn't you get my messages?'

'He only got your first letter and thought you were putting him off because Mark didn't want him to come,' said Zelda.

'He got that right,' said Mark.

'Boiler broke – had to move to my club till it was time to come up here,' Piers explained succinctly.

'I'm going to be too busy working on the house for guests, even welcome ones,' Mark said.

'Clara told me about your wedding reception venue plans and it sounds a really fun idea,' Zelda said enthusiastically to Mark.

But before he could answer her, Piers said indignantly, 'But I'm an old friend of the family!'

'You were Grandfather's friend,' Mark said pointedly.

'You'll have to take this boy of yours to task, Sybil,' Piers said, turning to her. 'His manners leave a lot to be desired. But I know *you're* always pleased to see me.'

'I . . . of course,' Sybil stammered. 'It's just . . . well, I've no idea what we're going to do—'

'Zelda kindly updated me on *all* the recent events – especially the news about Meg. You must be delighted to have a long-lost cousin, Mark? And what a wonderful surprise for you, too, Sybil, to find a new niece – and possibly a half-sister, I understand, if Meg's mother can be found?'

He made it sound as if Mum was playing hide-and-seek somewhere, like a mature Mistletoe Bride.

'Yes, we are, though it was a bit of a shock at first, to find that Daddy—' she began, then stopped dead, before gathering herself together with an obvious effort and saying with dignity, 'Naturally, we're all delighted to welcome Meg into the family. She's a dear girl.'

'I'm sure you are. And I expect Meg will be moving to Underhill soon?'

'No, why should I?' I asked, surprised. 'It's lovely to find I have some relatives, but Underhill isn't my home.'

'Underhill will soon be a business, rather than a family home anyway,' Mark said, sparing me a glance that I was amused to see no longer held any spark of his previous interest. 'But Meg's welcome to stay with us whenever she wants to.'

'Well said,' applauded Henry.

'That's very kind of you, Mark,' I said gratefully.

'But Underhill is a lovely old house and needs to be a home as well as a business,' Zelda protested. 'It could be both, couldn't it, Mark? I mean, you're not going to turn it into a hotel as well, are you?'

'I think Mark's plans for the house can be discussed at a later date, darling,' Clara told her. 'And we hope Meg will look on the Red House as her second home, somewhere she'll always be welcome, like you and Lex.' She looked over her shoulder as the door opened. 'And speaking of Lex, here he is. Have you heard Zelda's here, Lex?'

She pointed at Piers. '*And* an unexpected item in the baggage department.'

He closed the door behind him and surveyed the scene with a slightly sardonic expression in his dark eyes.

'Den filled me in. He and River will be along with tea shortly.'

'Good, it seems for ever since lunch,' Clara said.

'We finally get to eat the seed cake they made earlier, too,' Tottie said. 'The smell's been tantalizing me since they took it out of the oven.'

'I dislike seed cake, so I hope there's something else on offer,' said Piers.

Nobody replied to that one. Mark had gravitated to Zelda's side, as if drawn by a magnet, and now they were sitting together on the window seat, talking in low voices, the auburn head and the dark curls, so like Lex's, close together.

Sybil looked at them in a puzzled kind of way and then at me and I smiled at her. She'd have to readjust her romantic notions a bit if I'd read the signs aright and Mark had finally met his match in both senses of the word.

'Sybil,' Piers said, claiming her attention, 'we must have a little private conversation shortly. We have so much to talk about!'

This got through to Mark, who looked up. 'You won't have time; you'd better return to Thorstane before it snows again. I expect Lex or Den will run you up as near to the top as possible – I'd do it myself, if I had the Jeep with me – and we can ring Fred Golightly and ask him to collect you on the other side and put you up for the night.'

Piers looked aghast. 'But we had to plough through snowdrifts on foot – and I'm too old for repeating that kind of caper.'

'Clara and I are only a couple of years younger than you are, so you're hardly heading for the Last Post,' Henry said.

'You're an old ham, Piers, because Pete and Billy actually *carried* you in a fireman's lift through the worst of it. *I* was the one who fell into that snowdrift and had to be pulled out!' Zelda broke into an infectious peal of laughter. 'I must have looked like a snowman!'

Mark, who'd begun scowling at Piers again, grinned at her.

'It's too dark now to attempt the return journey today, anyway,' Lex said. 'And the temperature is dropping, so it wouldn't be a good idea.'

'Well, Piers, if you can't get back tonight, what *are* we going to do with you?' asked Clara. 'Perhaps you ought to ask Mark very nicely if he'll put you up till the road is open.'

'I'd much rather not,' Mark said shortly. 'And he wouldn't find it comfortable with the place upside down. But I've had an idea: Flora might take another lodger at the guesthouse.'

'A guesthouse? But surely it can't be open at this time of year?' Piers said.

'No, and Deirdre's over-wintering in Australia, as usual,' said Henry. 'But her niece, Flora, who I expect you met when she was Teddy's nanny, is there and she's already taken in one stranded visitor.'

'*He* turned up uninvited too, and he's stuck there till tomorrow, at least,' said Clara. 'Flora might take you in as a paying guest.'

Piers appealed to Henry. 'Henry, you and I have been friends for years – you can't really mean to turn me out of the house!'

'You were George's friend, never mine,' Henry said. 'And of course I'm not proposing to throw you out into the snow, like in some Victorian melodrama, just find you alternative accommodation.'

'I don't see why I can't stay here,' Piers said, reseating himself comfortably on the sofa. 'I'm sure you must have a room for me in a place of this size.'

'No, actually, every single room is occupied by my *invited* guests,' Clara said.

'Then I expect a couple of the younger ones won't mind sharing, to make room for me,' he suggested.

'*They* might not, but *I* would,' said Clara. 'I've allocated the rooms and that's that.'

She sounded totally inflexible, and River, who had quietly come in just at that moment, said apologetically, 'I fear you may also be stuck with me for a day or two more, though I'm sure Moonflower and Bilbo would put me up if—'

'Oh, we don't want *you* to leave us at all,' said Henry.

'No, you're welcome to stay as long as you want to,' said Clara, and Piers glared at River.

Sybil timidly faltered out, 'I . . . expect a bed could be made up for me elsewhere, Uncle Piers. Perhaps Tottie wouldn't mind if—'

'Now, I thought we'd dropped the "uncle" long ago, because we're on such *different* terms these days, aren't we?' Piers said to her in a far from avuncular way, and she blinked at him, nervously.

'Sybil is *not* giving you her room and that's that, Piers. I'm not changing *any* of my arrangements to suit your convenience . . . though I suppose if we can't find an alternative, it will have to be a camp bed in the library.'

'A camp bed? You can't be serious!' Piers turned to appeal to Mark. 'Dear boy . . .'

'Mark is economizing on his central heating at the moment, but I expect you'd soon get warm, helping him to strip wallpaper and that kind of thing,' said Henry with a gentle smile.

'I'm afraid my health would not allow that,' Piers said, horrified.

'Perhaps it would be best if I rang Flora, then, to see if she can take you – at a special Christmas rate, of course,' Clara said.

'Best idea,' agreed Tottie. 'You'd be warm and well fed till you can get away and, with luck, the road will be open enough tomorrow to let you go home.'

'But you wouldn't want an old man to spend Christmas alone?' he said pathetically.

'You have two adult children and several grandchildren,' Henry pointed out.

'They don't *really* want me. Their mother poisoned their minds against me years ago, after the divorce.'

'Then you could spend Christmas very cosily at the club with your old army cronies, couldn't you?'

Den brought in the trolley, laden with china, teapot and cut slices of seed cake.

Teddy stopped making vrooming noises and crashing his toy cars about and crawled out from behind one of the sofas.

'Yer still 'ere, then?' Den said to Piers as he set the teapot before Clara.

'As you see,' Piers said loftily. 'And I'd like something else to eat other than that cake.'

'Tough titties, I don't do individual bleedin' menus,' said Den.

I heard Zelda giggle and had to choke down a laugh myself.

Lex got up and silently passed the biscuit barrel to Piers, who took it without thanks.

'Can *I* say tough ti—' began Teddy.

'No, you can't,' Tottie told him quickly.

'Oh.' He sounded disappointed, but began to eat a slice of cake. 'If there are seeds in this cake, will plants grow in my stomach?'

'No, it's not a suitable habitat for germination,' said River, who had seated himself on a small, low, padded chair that might have been made for him.

'It's an interesting idea,' said Henry.

Sybil was sitting in the corner of a sofa as far from Piers as she could have got, but was looking slightly revived by her tea. It was odd, I thought, that despite being so anxious about him before his arrival, now he was here she seemed more nervous of him than fond.

Mark and Zelda took their plates and cups back to the window seat and carried on their intimately low-voiced conversation, and Sybil gave them another puzzled glance.

I found Lex was looking at me in a frowning sort of way and when I took my cup and plate to an armchair just outside the fireside circle, he followed and sat down next to me.

'Mark seems surprisingly happy to see my sister again, doesn't he?' he said drily. 'They had a bit of a boy and girl romance years ago, before Zelda went off to drama school, but they haven't seen much of each other since.'

'When you haven't seen someone for ages, it can feel as if you're seeing them for the first time,' I said.

He looked at me seriously and said, 'That was certainly true when I saw you again.' Then he gave me a searching look. 'I thought Mark was keen on you. From what Sybil said to me at Underhill earlier, she seems to expect an engagement announcement at any moment!'

I felt myself blushing. 'Sybil got the wrong end of the stick.'

'Well, you keep telling me you aren't interested in Mark, but when he suddenly announced he was coming back with us, I did wonder. He *said* he wanted to ask your advice about paint colours.'

'I expect he's asking Zelda's instead now,' I said. 'Look, I know he was a bit keen on me, but I'm more than happy he's switched his attention to Zelda. I'm sure Sybil just thought that if Mark and I married, it would . . . sort of make everything tidy.'

'I expect you're right and I'm glad you're not nursing a broken heart.'

'No, though there is someone here I do have a soft spot for,' I admitted.

I'd put Pansy down while I had my tea and she'd gone to join the other two dogs, who had strategically placed themselves near the coffee table.

'I'm going to ask Sybil if she'll sell me Pansy, so long as I can pay her in the New Year.'

'I'm afraid she told me earlier that she'd accepted an offer for her,' Lex said, dashing my hopes.

'Oh, now I wish I hadn't waited!' I said sadly. 'I didn't realize how quickly I'd get attached to her.'

'And vice versa. She makes a beeline for you whenever she sees you.'

'I hope the people who are buying her are nice.' I sighed. 'Oh, well, it wasn't meant to be. I'll just have to enjoy playing with her over Christmas.'

Mark had torn himself away from Zelda to fetch another slice of cake. He looked a bit more mellow: food did seem to sweeten his temper . . . unless it was love.

I *hoped* it was love this time, for Zelda's sake, because I'd taken an instant liking to her.

'I'd better head back to Underhill shortly,' he announced, but refused Lex's offer to drive him back.

'No, that's all right, the walk will do me good.'

'If the road through Starstone Edge is clear tomorrow, then perhaps I could come over and see what you're doing with the place?' suggested Zelda. 'I'd love to and I'll help, if you like?'

'That would be great,' he assured her warmly. 'Why don't you come for the day?'

'I'll do that,' she promised.

'I suppose Meg and I could help out for a couple of hours in the morning too,' volunteered Lex, without consulting me.

'Every extra pair of hands welcome,' Mark said.

'Let's see what it's like tomorrow,' suggested Clara, 'then we can all make our plans accordingly.'

'Wasn't Flora going to go to Underhill this afternoon? I'm sure she said so at the Gathering,' Lex said.

Mark looked a bit uncomfortable. 'Yes, she did mean to, but then she rang me this morning to say her visitor was stuck there. She's got a Mini and it's not built for these road conditions.'

'Flora took pity on a rather persistent young man who wants to interview Henry,' Clara explained to Zelda. 'He was a boyfriend of Meg's years ago.'

'We all make mistakes,' Lex said to me gravely and I gave him a look.

'If Flora's stuck with him till the road is clear, she really might as well have Piers too,' reiterated Tottie.

'I don't think anyone will make it over to Thorstane tomorrow if it snows again tonight and then freezes hard,' said Lex.

'If not, you may just have to put up with me over Christmas, after all,' Piers said. 'I'm sure with a little goodwill and rearrangement—'

'I'll ring Flora,' interrupted Clara decidedly, getting up. Just at that moment, the doorknocker thumped heavily. 'Now, what fresh hell is this?' she muttered.

'It's not,' Lex said, going to pull back the curtain and look out. 'I think it's the woman of the hour: Flora.'

32

Star-Crossed Others

The knock was clearly a token gesture, for the inner door to the hall opened and a light voice trilled, 'Coo-ee!'

'In the drawing room, Flora,' called Clara, and a moment later, having divested herself of boots and coat, she came in as one sure of her welcome.

Her chestnut curls were feathery with damp, her brown eyes shone and her cheeks were rosy from the cold. She looked very pretty, in a slightly marmoset kind of way.

'Hi, everyone!' she said, looking round. 'Zelda, you made it, then? Oh, and Mark, I didn't expect to find *you* here.'

She gave him a very special smile and he shifted uneasily on the window seat, but didn't get up.

'I came over with Mum, but I'm going back in a minute.'

'I'm so glad you did come, Mark, because it's wonderful to see you again,' Zelda said, turning to smile dazzlingly at him and he gave her a besotted look.

Flora's eyes narrowed and she looked uncertainly from the pair on the window seat to where I was sitting, evidently puzzled and unsure who her main rival now was. And I couldn't blame her, because Mark seemed to change direction like a weathercock. First it was Flora, then me and now he only had eyes for Zelda.

I became aware that Lex was now standing so close behind my chair that we could have been posed for one of those Victorian photographic patriarch-and-wife combos, which couldn't have helped poor Flora figure it all out, either.

Baffled, she smiled largely on the assembly and, with a sudden change of tack, said reproachfully, 'Teddy, darling! Don't you have a kiss for your old nanny?'

Teddy got up rather reluctantly and allowed her to embrace him, then released himself politely and went back to sitting on the floor next to River's chair, where they'd been poring over a large book about dragons.

'We didn't think anyone would come to call on a day like this, Flora, but cometh the hour, cometh the woman,' Lex said.

'I simply had to get out for some fresh air, because I've been cooped up all day looking after poor Rollo, who has a *really* bad chill. I thought Meg might like an update on how her *boyfriend* was.'

This with a sharp sideways glance at me, but if her innuendo was meant for Mark's benefit, then it had missed its target, because he hadn't been listening to a word she said.

'I think we've established that Rollo's not Meg's boyfriend, or partner, or whatever they call them these days, Flora,' said Clara. 'So if he told you he was, then he's trying to take you in.'

'Oh, sorry! I should have said *former* boyfriend,' she amended hastily. 'And there seems to have been a little misunderstanding, because he only wanted to pop in and see Meg while he was in the area, though of course, being a poet, he'd love to pay his homage to Henry, too.'

'Let him pay it by email, then,' said Henry.

'Yes, we certainly don't want his cold germs invading the Red House,' agreed Clara.

'Like Typhoid Mary,' suggested Tottie and, seeing Flora's blank expression, elaborated: 'She was a typhoid carrier, infected dozens!'

'Rollo hasn't got typhoid!' exclaimed Flora. 'It's just a chill, nothing infectious, though I was afraid it might turn into pneumonia. However, he's started to take a turn for the better.'

'I've just got over pneumonia. It's a viral thing,' I said. 'I'm glad he's feeling better, though, and I hope his mother isn't ringing you twenty times an hour.'

'She's naturally very worried about him, poor woman,' Flora said.

'Well, Flora, whatever your reason for coming, your arrival is very opportune,' Clara told her.

'In fact, we were just talking about you,' put in Tottie.

'In a good way, I hope?' Flora said, though as if there couldn't possibly be any other.

'I hope it will be good for all of us,' said Clara. 'We have a proposition to put to you. But do come and sit here, near the fire, between me and Sybil and get warm. You met River and Meg at the Gathering, didn't you? And here's Piers Marten, whom you've certainly met before.'

I don't think Flora had taken in his presence till this point because he was somewhat obscured by Tottie until she sat back.

'Of course, though not for some years,' Flora said, shaking hands. 'How are you?'

'Exhausted and, it appears, unwelcome,' he murmured with patently false pathos, before adding bravely, 'but I'm an old soldier, you know: I'll carry on.'

'But you won't be able to carry on back to Thorstane till the road thaws enough, which is the root of the problem,' Tottie said, and Flora looked puzzled.

Henry explained. 'Sybil put Piers off coming for Christmas this year because of Mark's renovations, which is also why she's spending it with us. But he ignored her letter and turned up this afternoon with Zelda.'

'It was all just a misunderstanding,' said Piers. 'But I'm here now and—'

Clara ignored him and carried on in her best human bulldozer manner: 'The thing is, Flora, we have a full house and Mark can't have Piers. He's told the Gidneys to take a few days off over Christmas, since he can look after himself while he's working on the house, and they're looking forward to it.'

'And Piers'd probably freeze, because I'm not turning the heating up till Mum's back,' said Mark, joining in the discussion. From where I was sitting, I could see he and Zelda were holding hands, which was pretty quick work.

'Really, Mark, you've turned very hard!' said Piers sadly. 'When you were a little boy, wasn't I like an uncle to you?'

'No,' said Mark. 'I used to dread it if you were staying at Underhill when we were. You made fun of me because I hated hunting and killing things. Then later you told Grandfather I'd had to take my degree in hospitality management because I hadn't got the brains for anything else!'

Piers looked taken aback, but before he could speak, Sybil's maternal instincts made her say, 'That's quite true, Piers! I heard you say so myself, on several occasions.'

'Sybil, you can't possibly believe that I'm not fond of the boy. I was merely joking,' he said. 'You know I'd do anything in my power to protect his interests.'

She met his eyes briefly, paled and looked away uneasily. 'Of course . . . I mean, it's only that you weren't very kind to him and . . .'

'Never mind the past,' Clara cut in. 'Let's get back to the problem in hand: the road is blocked and may stay that way for at least a couple of days. You already have one stranded visitor, Flora, so we wondered if you could also take Piers?'

'But the guesthouse isn't open,' she said, taken by surprise by this suggestion. 'I mean, I contacted Auntie and told her I was home and had a friend staying with me, of course – and Rollo and I have become *such* good friends already,' she added, with another pointed glance in my direction to gauge how I felt about *that*.

'How nice,' I said pleasantly. 'He can be very good company, when he wants to be.'

'Of course, Auntie was quite happy to know I had a friend staying, but to have Piers as well . . .'

'He'd be a paying guest, of course,' said Tottie. 'And I expect Deirdre would want you to charge double, or triple rates over Christmas, with full board.'

'She certainly would,' agreed Flora. 'But although I've often helped out with the guesthouse, I've never run it myself.'

'I imagine Deirdre won't object if you take Piers in, as long as he's paying. And really, you might as well be looking after two visitors, as one,' Clara said reasonably.

'I'm sure you wouldn't want to charge me more than the usual rate, my dear, when I'm so unfortunately stuck here,' Piers began, giving Flora his best brave old soldier smile.

'You don't know Deirdre,' put in Tottie. 'She's a business-woman to the core.'

'And you can't be poverty-stricken if you can afford to be a member of the In & Out Club,' Clara told him.

'We'd be very grateful if you could accommodate Piers, my dear,' said Henry, with his charming smile.

Flora wavered. 'Well, I'd have to try and get in touch with Auntie again and get her permission, though in the circumstances I expect she'll agree. But Tottie's right and she *would* expect me to charge you at a higher rate, Piers. And she *always* insists on taking her guests' card details on their arrival,' she added firmly.

She seemed to be a chip off the old block and there was more than a hint of the steel hand that lay within the velvet glove.

'But surely not in my case?' Piers protested. 'This is an unexpected expense, so I'm not sure if . . . But then,' he added, brightening, 'I'm sure Sybil would settle my bill and then I can reimburse her later.'

'Since Mum seems constantly broke these days, I wouldn't advise that, Flora,' Mark told her.

'No, it would have to be *your* card details up front, or Auntie would be really cross,' Flora told Piers.

'So, if Deirdre agrees, will you take him, Flora?' asked Henry.

'I suppose so. I'll go back and see if I can get hold of her now, then get a room ready for him.'

'Wonderful! And do let us know if you get through to her. We can give Piers dinner and then bring him down to the guesthouse after that,' suggested Clara. 'Will that help?'

'Yes, though I'm not quite sure how I'll manage with the catering if both he and Rollo end up staying over Christmas. I got only enough groceries in to keep me going, and though of course there's a freezer full of food, we're likely to run out of fresh things quite quickly. And then there's Christmas Day itself . . .'

Clara sighed. 'I can see your point, dear, but we can probably let you have anything you're short of. And I suppose if your guests *are* still here by then, you can all come to the Red House for Christmas dinner.'

'How lovely! That's so kind of you,' Flora said.

'And you might as well bring them both to the Boxing Day drinks and nibbles party, too,' Clara added generously.

'But warn this Rollo that there'll be no interviews with me, no taking notes, and no writing about us when he gets home, or he'll be sorry,' Henry said. 'I'm not without some influence in the world of poetry.'

'I'm sure he wouldn't dream of it! He'll be delighted just to meet you,' she assured him.

'But if his chill turns into a cold, he can stay in bed and we'll send his dinner down,' qualified Clara.

'I don't think it will. He's really improving this afternoon.'

'Good, because *I* don't want a cold either,' said Piers. 'Especially if I'm paying through the nose for the privilege of staying in your establishment.'

At some point, River must have quietly slipped out, for now he returned, bringing fresh tea and a clean cup for Flora, for which she thanked him prettily. She seemed able to turn on a lighthouse beam of charm at the drop of a hat, but it did sometimes switch off again very quickly.

The pressing problem of Piers seemingly solved, the atmosphere in the room lightened, though Sybil was still quiet and looked anxious, while Piers appeared to be trying to catch her eye. Perhaps he wanted sympathy and thought she was the only person in the room sure to provide it.

Mark brought his and Zelda's cups over and Flora patted the empty seat next to her.

'Do come and talk to me, Mark! I hardly had the chance to exchange a word with you at the Gathering.'

'Sorry, I'm afraid I'll have to be going in a minute,' he said shortly.

She pouted charmingly and appealed to Sybil. 'He's such a grouch, isn't he? You'd think he wasn't pleased to see me again – and after all the fun we had together last time I was home, too!'

Sybil gave her a chilly smile that barely twitched her lips, but Mark flushed.

Zelda, though, was regarding Flora thoughtfully. Then she said, 'How long are you staying in Starstone Edge, Flora?'

'Until I find a new post, I suppose . . . unless something better offers.'

There was no mistaking the innuendo of this remark or who it was aimed at, though Mark avoided her eyes.

'I expect *you'll* have to return to London straight after Christmas, Zelda?' Flora asked with a glittering smile.

'Oh, no, I don't have to rush off again this time. In fact, I've been thinking about my future, now I've hit thirty.'

'You don't look thirty, you poor old thing,' said Lex, and she made a face at him.

'I don't think you look old, Mummy,' said Teddy, distracted from his dragon book.

'Thank you, darling, that's so sweet of you.'

'Thirty's nothing. You're a mere slip of a thing,' said Henry.

'It's a bit of a milestone when you're an actor, though, and, let's face it, my career has never really taken off. I didn't even get into a panto this year.'

'But you hated spending Christmas in digs,' Clara reminded her.

'It is a bit miserable, but this time I never even got *asked.* And that advert I've just done was for toilet tissue – hardly the pinnacle of my career.'

'Was it soft and strong and very long?' asked Lex, and she threw a cushion at him, which he fielded neatly.

'So, what would you do instead of acting, darling?' asked Clara.

'I don't know. I'll have to think about it.' She smiled. 'Though I did have the *glimmer* of an idea a few minutes ago!'

'You're always welcome to move in here while you decide,' said Henry, and Clara agreed.

'That will be fun, Mummy,' said Teddy, though since he'd previously told us that Zelda had described Starstone Edge as 'the arse end of nowhere', I couldn't really see that happening.

Zelda appeared to feel the need to explain it, too. 'I like fun, meeting new people and travelling, but of course I love being here as well. So I need to find a way of combining the two.'

'If you discover how to have your cake and eat it, we'll all be interested to know,' Tottie said drily.

'The idea I had came while I was talking to Mark about his plans for Underhill. I wondered if he might give me a job when his wedding reception business is up and running.'

He smiled at her and said, 'I just might, at that! We can discuss it tomorrow, when you come over.'

'Oh, are you going to Underhill tomorrow?' Flora broke in jealously. 'Perhaps you could pick me up on the way? You promised to show me what you'd been doing and all your plans, Mark.'

'Did I?' he said, breaking eye contact with Zelda with an effort and looking harassed.

'Actually, Meg and I are going to Underhill with Zelda in the morning too,' Lex said. 'But to help out with the work for a couple of hours, not just look around.'

'I could help, too,' Flora said eagerly. 'I may not be able to stay long, because of my visitors, but I can always walk back. My old Mini really isn't good in the snow.'

There was no putting her off. When Mark said he really would have to go home now, she said she might as well walk back with him, because she needed time to get things ready for her unexpected visitor.

'Poor Mark!' said Clara obscurely as they left together.

'He brought it on himself,' Tottie pointed out fairly.

'I'd forgotten what a man-eater she is, under that cute fluffy-little-me exterior,' Zelda said.

'Just a little over-keen,' Clara said charitably. 'She does tend to think that going out for a drink with a man means you're practically engaged, though I'm afraid Mark *did* give her a little encouragement last time he was home.'

'I've always thought she seemed a very sweet girl,' Piers said. 'I don't know what you've got against her.'

'We haven't got anything against her,' Clara said. 'She was a very competent nanny, too, and I found her a good post in London when Teddy didn't need her any more.'

Sybil was looking alarmed. 'I really don't want her as my daughter-in-law,' she said. 'And anyway, I thought—' She broke off, her gaze resting on me in a baffled way.

'It will all work out fine in the end, don't worry, Sybil,' Clara said. '*I* never do.'

'It's like one of Shakespeare's plays, where everyone is mistaken in everyone else's character, and it takes a lot of untangling before it all comes right in the end,' agreed Henry. 'Christmas should be *very* interesting this year.'

'I have no idea what you're all talking about,' Piers said testily. 'Now, if I'm to stay here for dinner before being carted off to this godforsaken bed-and-breakfast place, I'd like to freshen up a bit and then have a lie-down. It's been a very exhausting day.'

'You can use my room,' River offered generously. 'There's a bathroom opposite. I'll show you.'

Piers didn't thank him, but followed him out. In the hall, we heard him say to River, as if he were some kind of minion, 'I'll need that small Gladstone bag there.'

'Fine, you bring it with you,' said River's voice gently.

'River's a kind and generous soul, but he's nobody's fool,' I said.

'I'd better go up and unpack and freshen up too,' said Zelda.

'Usual room, darling,' said Clara. 'I'm starting to think we'd all be better for a lie-down in a darkened room.'

Tottie heaped the tea things on to the trolley and Lex took them out to the kitchen. Lass slipped out behind him, probably hoping for leftovers, but Wisty was fast asleep in front of the fire and Pansy had climbed back on to my lap again, without my noticing.

River returned and, taking the seat nearest the fire that Piers had vacated, beamed round at us and said without apparent sarcasm, 'Well, this *is* jolly!'

Clara

Starstone Edge was exerting an ever greater pull on us and we discussed whether we might be able to afford a cottage in the valley, where we could spend time, either separately or together, without having to stay with George.

Then my beloved aunt Beryl died and left her considerable fortune to be divided between myself and my sister, Bridget.

What with this and Henry's flourishing investments, we suddenly found ourselves surprisingly affluent, and travelled up to Starstone Edge to see the few houses that were for sale.

After inspecting a couple of claustrophobically tiny cottages and a thirties villa with some serious damp issues, we were beginning to despair, when we went to tea with Tottie Gillyflower.

She had been only a tiny baby when I'd left Starstone, but of course Henry knew her well and we had often met her on our visits. She lived at the Red House, a substantial Victorian house at the further end of the village from Underhill and, over tea, we learned that her attempts to turn it into a bed-and-breakfast establishment since her mother's death had not been the success she had hoped. The upkeep of such a large house was expensive and she feared she would have to sell it and move away. It was the idea of losing her garden that seemed to upset her most.

Henry had always adored this bizarrely over-the-top Victorian Gothic relic and I also had a sneaking likeness for it – and also for Tottie, a no-nonsense, angular youngish woman with a passion for gardening and beekeeping. So we came to an arrangement and bought the Red House from her with the proviso that she was to continue to make it her home and take over the housekeeping, devoting the rest of her time to her garden and bees. Den, our loyal friend who had cooked and looked after us so well in London, would continue to do so there, but could have his own flat over the garage, once we'd completed a scheme of much-needed renovations.

Though the arrangement with Tottie might seem strange and fraught with possible difficulties to many, we soon all settled down into one happy family – and still are, over thirty years later.

Eventually, although officially still attached to the British Museum, I could divide my time between my work on epigraphy, lectures, and the writing of books, both erudite and fictional.

Of course, I am now retired, but I can't say that it has made any great difference to my life, except that through the innovations of technology, I can do quite a bit of epigraphic reconstruction right here on my computer screen, via a wonderful program.

Our lives have been full and happy ones and though we had no children of our own, my sister Bridget's have spent so much time here at the Red House that they have more than made up for it . . .

33

The Kissing Bough

Sybil had been huddling quietly in a corner of one of the sofas, but now looked up and said, in a distressed voice, 'I'm so sorry about Piers trying to impose on you like this and, really, I know I should have made Mark take him back to Underhill . . . and gone with them.'

'Oh, nonsense, Sybil!' declared Clara roundly. 'You're too kind-hearted for your own good. Just because he was your father's best friend, it doesn't mean that he's entitled to hang around your neck like an albatross for the rest of his life.'

'But . . . I mean, I've known him since I was a little girl,' she protested. 'And I do feel sorry for him, because he says his family don't really want him for Christmas.'

'He probably makes himself such an odious nuisance that it's not surprising,' Henry said.

'But Piers isn't all bad,' she insisted.

'Sybil, we know he and George used to drink themselves senseless every night after dinner when he was staying at Underhill, not to mention the gambling . . . and the other things that they got up to when they went off on one of their jaunts to the South of France,' said Clara. 'We heard the rumours.'

Sybil didn't try to deny this.

'Don't worry about him, Sybil,' Lex told her kindly. 'He'll be more comfortable at the guesthouse than he would have been at Underhill with all the work going on, and Flora will look after him.'

'As long as she doesn't find him too much trouble, because he *is* a little set in his ways,' said Sybil. 'But then, perhaps the road will thaw tomorrow and he can get away,' she added optimistically.

'I doubt it, Syb,' said Tottie. 'Den told me the Met Office forecast said there wouldn't be a thaw for a few days. So it looks like he could well be here on Christmas Day, with his feet in the trough.'

'In which case, I'd better keep the key of the drinks cabinet on me, when he's in the house,' Henry said thoughtfully. 'And tell Den to keep the larder door locked, too, though we don't stock a large supply of alcohol, other than Tottie's mead and fruit wines.'

'There's whisky and sherry, but I think that's it,' agreed Clara.

'*And* several bottles of elderflower champagne for the Boxing Day morning party,' Tottie reminded them.

'Oh, I adore elderflower champagne!' I said. 'Maj at the Farm makes it, too.'

'Indeed she does,' said River. 'They'll all be drinking it now at the feasting . . .'

He looked slightly pensive, probably remembering that this time he had abdicated his role in the proceedings to Oshan.

I was right, for he added, 'Oshan poured a libation of mead over the stone cairn on the hill behind the Farm at the Solstice, as usual.'

'I expect Den has a crate or two of Guinness in the flat,' Henry said. 'But he's not going to share with Piers. They've never taken to each other.'

'That's because Piers is a snob and tries to treat Den like some kind of servant,' Clara said.

Sybil made a token protest, but her heart wasn't in it.

'I expect Den puts him right,' Henry said.

The phone rang. It was Flora to say Deirdre had agreed that Flora could take in Piers as a paying guest on full board terms, but at double the usual rate.

'Pretty much what I thought she'd say,' said Clara. 'So that's that sorted.'

'I'll take him down there in the pick-up after dinner,' Lex offered. 'It's probably started to freeze, but I can put the chains on.'

'I think I might lie down till dinner, once I've fed the dogs,' Sybil said. 'I have a bit of a headache.'

I felt no urge to lie down, but I did want to get away to my own little Rapunzel turret for a bit and once I was there, dashed off a quick email to Fliss.

> Lex being very kind to me, to make up for thinking I was an evil seductress. I've just watched Mark, the only romantic hero material, fall head over heels for Lex's sister on sight. Ex-nanny furious, had designs on him herself. Ghastly old gent arrived earlier, but he's going to stay somewhere else. Rollo still in Starstone Edge too – he has caught a chill, the roads are blocked and we're snowed in. The thick plottens.
> Meg x x

I hadn't mentioned that I thought someone had tried to push me off a precipice because in retrospect I could see how silly the idea was.

Lex *was* still being almost unbearably kind to me: before I came upstairs, he'd caught me up and asked me if I was sure I wasn't hurt by Mark's sudden defection and I'd told him not to be daft.

Henry was right, it was all just like one of Shakespeare's more confusing romances. I only hoped it would be all's well that ends well.

I'd just sent the email to Fliss when I heard a scratching noise and yapping. I went down the turret stairs to find Pansy outside my bedroom door, bright eyed and wagging her tail.

'How on earth did you know where I was?' I exclaimed, scooping her up.

And I felt a horrible pang, knowing that after Christmas she would belong to strangers. I only hoped they'd love her as much as I'd grown to.

She lay on the rug and watched me as I brushed my hair and then rendered my eyelashes and brows a slightly more dramatic shade than their natural fawn.

A pale face framed in rose-pink hair, with eyes of a strangely light duck-egg blue, stared back at me from the mirror. With my high cheekbones and straight nose, I wondered how I could possibly have missed the Doome family features that I'd painted in Henry, and must have noted in Mark.

On impulse, I opened Mum's tin trunk and Pansy sneezed as a wave of sandalwood and patchouli hit her.

I rummaged among the clothes. I had an urge to bring her close tonight by wearing something of hers, and chose a heavy silk top with bell sleeves, an embroidered yoke and tassel-tie front.

I wore it over a long, go-anywhere, dark green skirt with a hitched-up side that revealed a silk chiffon layer beneath. I'd found it in a charity shop years ago and it looked sort of Victorian.

Malachite drop earrings completed the look . . . whatever the look was.

I felt cheered by the spirit of my freewheeling mother and it suddenly struck me that Zelda's style of mothering was very similar to hers.

I knew Mum loved me, but it had never stopped her going off on her own adventures. *I* seemed to have assumed the maternal, worrying role . . . especially since she'd vanished.

Down in the hall I found a scene of activity. Henry and Teddy had upended the big canvas postbag on to the side table and were sorting the contents into heaps, while Den and River had got out the long stepladders and were hanging up the kissing bough.

'I knew there was something missing in here,' River explained.

'Yeah, and 'ere's one we prepared earlier, ain't it?' said the voice from above.

'It's lovely,' I said admiringly, though this one wasn't so much a bough as a large twig, wound with ivy and decorated with a few sprigs of berried holly. From it hung a large bunch of fake mistletoe, which they'd probably purloined from one of the swags.

'Holly and ivy to represent the male/female yin/yang element of the season, of course,' said River. 'And mistletoe for obvious reasons.'

'Kissing,' said Den, starting to descend.

'No, I meant the deeper magical significance, but kissing is good too,' said River, and kissed my cheek.

I returned the salute and gave him a hug.

'How lovely you look tonight, dear child,' he said.

'This is one of Mum's tops, out of the trunk. I thought I'd wear it because she feels very close tonight, for some reason.'

'Yes, I feel that too, and I'm sure she will come back to us soon.'

I hoped he was right and my worst fears weren't true . . .

Tonight River wore the tunic with the runes. Around his neck hung a silver wire mandala and a chakra necklace of variously coloured stones.

'You look very fine, too,' I told him. 'Did you manage to get into your room to change?'

'Yes, though Piers was still flat out on my bed asleep. In fact, we might have to wake him for dinner.'

'And we'd better get back and bleedin' finish cooking it,' Den suggested, and they went off, carrying the ladder between them, like a comedy act.

'Do go in the drawing room and have a drink, my dear,' suggested Henry. 'Clara, Tottie and Sybil are already down – and we assumed Pansy must be with you when she vanished. Lex has gone to fetch in more wood and Zelda's been holed up in Clara's study for the last half-hour, having a long phone conversation with someone. We suspect it's Mark.' His eyes twinkled. 'I've never seen such a *coup de foudre*.'

I laughed. 'Nor me! They were both struck all of a heap, weren't they?'

Teddy, who was clutching a large parcel, said, 'Look, Meg! Uncle Henry forgot he'd left a bid in an auction for some more Christmas decorations ages ago and they've just arrived.'

'Haven't checked my emails for a couple of days, or I might have known they were on the way,' he admitted. 'I can't even remember what was in this lot.'

'Can we open it now?' demanded Teddy.

'No, let's tantalize ourselves and save it for tomorrow,' he said. 'Carry it carefully into my study and put it on the desk with the typewriter. That's another antique: they can keep each other company overnight.'

'You're very silly, Uncle Henry,' Teddy said severely.

'I know, but I'm afraid I've left it too late to change now.'

Teddy carried off the box and Henry quickly whipped out another package from the post sack and stowed it in the hall-stand cupboard. 'Another parcel with American stamps, but this one is for Clara and has Radnor Vane's address on the back, so I expect it's something for Teddy.'

I hoped, for Teddy's sake, that it wasn't more Mickey Mouse slippers.

'We've sorted out the post now. That was the last,' Henry said, as Teddy returned. 'I've given Clara ours, which was mostly cards, and Sybil is looking through the mail for Underhill. I thought you and Lex could take that up with you tomorrow morning, Meg.'

'There's still a lot more to deliver, though,' I said, eyeing the heaps on the table.

'I'll probably take it round tomorrow, when I'm out with Lass, but it shouldn't take long because most of it is for the Adcocks and Bilbo.'

In the drawing room, the tree lights and chandelier sparkled, and with the curtains drawn and the fire glowing warmly, everything looked very cosy.

Clara was drinking her usual whisky and soda, and Sybil and Tottie held glasses of golden mead.

'. . . strong fetlocks and a sweet nature,' Sybil was saying, so I deduced they were discussing something equine.

'Everything I always looked for in a man,' I said, and Tottie gave her bark of laughter.

'What is?' asked Lex, coming in with a laden log basket. There were starry drops of melting snow in his dark curls.

'Strong fetlocks and a sweet nature,' said Sybil, smiling.

'That's me to a T, then, but unfortunately, I can't marry all of you.' He put the log basket next to the fire and carefully added one or two more to the blaze.

The door opened again and Zelda wandered in, a slightly dreamy expression on her face. She was dressed in something short, holly-berry red, and with interesting cut-out bits that revealed selected portions of her curvy, but petite, anatomy.

'Mark all right?' asked Clara.

'Yes, he's—' She broke off and blushed. 'How did you know I'd been talking to him?'

'Intuition, darling,' said Clara.

Sybil stared at Zelda, a frown between her eyes. She looked as if she was about to say something, had Henry, Teddy and River not joined us at that moment.

'No sign of Piers yet,' observed Henry.

'No. Perhaps you should rattle the whisky bottle and a glass together at the bottom of the stairs?' suggested Clara.

'Actually, when I went up to change and found him still flat out on the bed, there was a distinct smell of brandy,' said River. 'I think he may have had further supplies in his Gladstone bag.'

'I suppose if he doesn't appear by the time Den beats the gong, we'll have to wake him up,' Tottie said. 'And we still have to get him down to Flora's once he's been fed.'

'Some solid food and a cup of coffee should do the trick,' Clara said.

'I hope Flora won't find him too much of a pain,' said Henry. 'Perhaps I should warn her to lock up the mini-bar in the guest lounge?'

Sybil looked unhappy again. 'Piers does drink rather a lot. Daddy was always much worse when Piers was staying with us.'

'I'd back Flora to cope with Piers any day,' said Clara. 'There's no need for you to look so guilty and worried, Sybil: it's not your fault he's here.'

'What are we all doing tomorrow?' asked Henry, changing the subject. 'I know you young ones are going to Underhill in the morning, to help Mark.'

'Yes, if the road is clear enough I'll run us all up there. Zelda's staying on but I'll bring Meg back for lunch,' said Lex.

'I'm hoping you might give me another sitting in the afternoon, Tottie?' I suggested.

'I don't see why not,' she agreed.

'I'm steaming full ahead with my memoirs,' said Clara. 'I'm going to finish the current volume, before starting my next crime novel.'

'There *is* to be another volume, then?' enquired Tottie.

'Oh, yes, because I feel that finding Meg heralds the start of a new chapter in our lives, don't you?'

'I do,' agreed Henry. 'And now my own work is finished, bar the final polishing, perhaps I might also start a second volume: about the village coming back like a ghost during the last dry spell.'

'It really did look odd when walls and ruined houses started to reappear,' Tottie said.

'I wish I'd seen that,' said River.

'I've got some photographs in the library. I'll show them to you later,' she promised.

'I'll be the village postman as well tomorrow,' said Henry, and River offered to go with him to help.

'What about me?' asked Teddy. 'Shall I come to Underhill, Uncle Lex, or be a postman with Henry and River?'

'Den said earlier that he'd really like some help in the kitchen tomorrow morning,' River said. 'It was something about a chocolate log, and that he was counting on you.'

'Oh, yes, the log!' Teddy exclaimed. 'I'd forgotten we were going to make that.'

Den threw open the door and ushered Piers through it with a mock bow and the words, ''Ere's 'is nibs down fer 'is dinner.'

Piers must have applied cold water to his hair, for it lay in flat, dull white locks across his head. His glacial eyes watered and he was preceded by a strong smell of brandy.

'Light blue touchpaper and retire,' suggested Den.

Lass, fixing her eyes on Piers, growled low in her throat. It was quite impressive for a dog who spent most of her time either eating or fast asleep. Wisty and Pansy, curled up in a heap before the fire, took no notice at all.

'Den, I'll help you with the chocolate log tomorrow,' Teddy offered.

'I was counting on it, Teddy, wasn't I? And I've made you a treat for dinner – a rabbit.'

This seemed unlikely, but Piers brightened up.

'I'm partial to a bit of jugged hare, or rabbit with mustard sauce.'

'Don't be silly,' said Clara. 'It's a pink blancmange rabbit for afters, isn't it, Den?'

'That's right. There's rice pud fer anyone who don't fancy that.'

'Hare today and gone tomorrow,' joked Tottie, and we all groaned.

'Is no one going to offer me a drink?' said Piers.

'Dinner's ready, ain't it?' Den said, brandishing the gong. 'And yer already smell like a distillery.'

'Let's all go in,' Henry said, hastily getting up, and we all followed suit.

I'd never seen Sybil wearing anything but riding clothes before, but tonight she'd put on a wrap dress in an old gold colour that suited her very well.

Unfortunately, this had the effect of turning Piers gruesomely gallant.

'How lovely all the ladies look tonight,' he said, leering at Zelda, 'but especially *you*, Sybil. You must let me take you in to dinner.'

He drew her arm through his and led her into the hall, as if they were in some period drama set in a stately home. I noticed Sybil's perfume as she went past, something very strong and unusual, yet somehow familiar.

In the hall Piers came to a sudden stop under the kissing bough.

'Well, well, here's an opportune bunch of mistletoe!' he said, then kissed Sybil, though she turned her head at the last minute and it landed on her cheek rather than her lips.

Undaunted, he said gaily, his eyes moving from me to Zelda in her red mini dress, 'Now, who's next?'

'Nobody wants to kiss you, Piers,' said Clara firmly. 'But we *do* want our dinner, so let's go into the dining room before it goes cold.'

'I feel I've just had a narrow escape from a ghastly experience,' I whispered to Lex.

'I can't remember anyone ever kissing *me* under the mistletoe,' he replied. 'But I like to think I'm a more attractive proposition than Piers.'

'Maybe you haven't tried his scattergun method of asking?' I said, grinning.

'No, but there's no one left to fire *at* now, except you and Pansy . . . and call me picky, but I'd prefer not to kiss a dog.'

I looked up and found his dark green eyes looking down into mine were not agate-hard at that moment, but soft and a little sad.

On a sudden impulse, I stood on tiptoe and kissed him quickly . . . or at least, it was *meant* to be quickly, but his arms went round me, holding me close and the moment went on for ever.

Then Pansy suddenly emitted a sharp and jealous volley of yapping and we fell apart, staring at each other, before bursting into speech at once.

'Meg! I—' Lex sounded oddly shaken.

'Sorry, I didn't mean—' I began.

A voice interrupted us. 'You two want yer dinner out 'ere?' asked Den, who was heading for the dining room with a covered dish, followed by River, carrying a basket of bread rolls.

'I see the Goddess put the idea of the kissing bough into my head for a purpose,' River said, and smiled benignly on us.

34

Well Spiced

Lex and I took our seats at the dining table, carefully not looking at each other, which wasn't easy, since we were directly opposite. Another leaf had been added to the table to make room for us all. As well as Sybil and Piers, Den was dining with us and had laid a place for himself between Tottie and Clara.

We passed round the basket of rolls and the butter and Den uncovered the serving dish to reveal two smaller ones inside, which Piers regarded with disfavour.

'What on earth are those?'

'This one's vegetable pâté, and the other mushroom,' said Tottie.

'Mushrooms *are* vegetables,' Teddy said.

'Fungi, smarty-pants,' said Tottie amiably.

'Oh God, I'd forgotten you were all vegetarians. I should have remembered those weird snacks you serve up at your Boxing Day party,' said Piers. 'It's a wonder anyone goes to it, what with that and the lack of a decent drink.'

'If you haven't managed to get away by then, Piers, do feel free to give it a miss and stay at the guesthouse,' Clara told him.

'Ditto Christmas Day,' agreed Henry.

Piers' brandy-clouded mind seemed to find the concept of a vegetarian Christmas dinner impossible to grasp.

'But you *must* be having turkey on Christmas Day, surely, if only for your guests?'

'No, of course we're not. It'll be a delicious savoury nut roast instead,' Clara told him. 'We usually have mini salmon en croûte parcels for starters, though.'

Piers' mouth had dropped open, which wasn't a pretty sight. 'But . . . not even a Christmas ham?'

'At the Farm, we keep two pigs just to dig up the soil where we wish to plant,' said River gently. 'They're better than any Rotovator.'

Piers ignored him and appealed to Sybil, who he seemed to feel was his only ally in the present company.

'Surely the Westphalian ham you always have at Underhill could be brought over here and—'

'Not into my house, it can't,' said Henry firmly.

'There is a ham, Piers, but that's going to keep Mark going over Christmas, while he's working. But he'll join us here for Christmas dinner, of course.' Sybil gave Piers a timid smile. 'I really don't mind being vegetarian while I'm staying here, because Den cooks such delicious food!'

Den looked flattered, though we were always praising the wonderful things he produced for us to eat.

'We do have Christmas pudding and a cake and trifle,' Tottie said, offering a sop.

'I need *meat*,' he said. 'I can't live on lentils and lettuce leaves.'

'I expect Flora will cater to your inner carnivore at the guesthouse,' Lex said. 'You'll probably get a full English breakfast.'

Piers grunted. 'It's to be hoped so.' He looked around the table and said, 'You've forgotten the wine.'

'We don't really go in for wine with dinner much,' said Clara. 'In fact, we're not great drinkers at all, any of us. Shall I pass you the water jug?'

'*Water?*'

You'd think she'd suggested passing him a poisoned chalice.

'My apple wine is very good, so we could open a bottle of that, if you fancy it?' offered Tottie as a concession, but Piers just stared at her blankly.

'Well, please yourself.' She shrugged.

'What are we having for our main course tonight, Den?' asked Henry.

'Kedgeree, but without any 'addock, though I cooked the rice in fish stock, didn't I? Lentils, spices, eggs and cream.'

'Sounds delicious,' I said, wondering if he would give me the recipe for Oshan. If he replaced the fish stock with vegetable, used vegan cream and omitted the eggs . . . No, on second thoughts, perhaps not.

'We're going Angular Indian tonight,' said Den. 'Afters is rice pud with cardy-moms.'

'*Anglo*-Indian,' corrected Clara.

Den seemed to be about to dispute this point, but Piers said, 'That's rather a lot of rice and I'm not fond of it, or anything spicy.'

'*We* all love anything spicy,' said Tottie. 'Syb does too, don't you, Syb? We usually have a good hot curry on Boxing Day evening, so it's just as well you won't be here for that.'

The kedgeree was golden and delicious, though Piers made a show of picking at a mere spoonful. Afterwards, River carried in the big tureen of rice pudding and Den a pink blancmange rabbit, quivering on its dish.

'I like rice pudding, but not when it's got big green seeds in it that taste like perfume,' said Teddy, as Tottie scooped blancmange into his bowl.

'I don't see how you can tell what perfume tastes like, Teddy,' said Zelda. 'It's hardly part of your normal diet.'

'I know what he means, though,' said Clara. 'It does taste odd when you inadvertently bite into a cardamom pod.'

'I think Sybil's wearing pod perfume,' said Teddy, looking fixedly at her.

'Is it a bit strong?' she asked, anxiously. 'I don't usually bother, except for a splash of Penhaligon's Violetta, but they sent me a trial size of this new one. I'm not quite sure if it's *me* or not. I did dab a bit on when it arrived on the day of the Solstice, but I was mostly outside, so I didn't notice it.'

'I *thought* it was familiar!' I said. 'I must have noticed it at the Gathering, when you were cleaning up my hands and face.'

'I like it, but I think it's wearing you, rather than the other way round, Syb,' said Tottie.

'It's a delightful scent,' River assured her kindly. 'Perfect for special occasions, like this happy gathering.'

He beamed around the table, though not everyone was looking entirely happy and at that moment I saw Zelda's face freeze and her eyes suddenly widen. Then Piers, who was sitting next to her, gave a yelp and snatched his hand from under the tablecloth.

'I think my bloody finger's dislocated!' he exclaimed.

'Oh dear, have you hurt yourself?' Zelda said sweetly. 'You really should be more careful!'

'I caught it on the table edge,' he said, seeing all our eyes on him and swallowing down the angry remark he was clearly about to make.

'I'd try not to do that again,' suggested Clara drily.

Sybil had missed this byplay, for she was deeply engrossed in a comfortable chat with River about gardening. They appeared to be getting on *very* well, something Piers didn't seem pleased about, because he kept scowling in their direction until we rose from the table.

Zelda and Tottie took a very sleepy Teddy straight up to bed. Lex and I helped Den clear the table while the others went into the drawing room.

'Nearly time to get rid of ghastly Piers,' Lex said, closing the door on the dishwasher. Then he grinned. 'I don't think he'll try anything on with Zelda again, do you?'

'No, it served him right! Though I do feel a *tiny* bit sorry for him,' I confessed. 'I mean, he doesn't *know* he's ghastly, does he? He thinks he's God's gift to women. And then, he *is* very old.'

'Late seventies isn't that old these days and, anyway, being old doesn't entitle you to be obnoxious, does it?'

''E's always been bleedin' obnoxious,' observed Den, who was now making the coffee. 'A nastier pair than 'e and that George were, yer'd never find. 'Ard to believe 'e was 'Enry's brother.'

And *my* grandfather, I thought, though I didn't feel madly keen to acknowledge the relationship with him.

Den went off to his flat and we took the coffee through. Predictably, Piers spurned it and demanded something stronger.

'If you're not having coffee, Piers, then I might as well take you down to Flora's now,' suggested Lex. 'She's expecting you, and we don't want to leave it too late because the roads will be freezing again.'

'I don't think I want to go out into the cold again this evening,' he said pathetically. 'It's too much to ask of a man my age and—'

'I'm driving you down; it's not as if you're going to walk,' pointed out Lex. 'I'll bring the pick-up round and you can get in when it's warmed up, so you'll only be out in the cold for two seconds.' He got up and left the room.

Piers turned to Sybil. 'I wanted to have a little private chat with you after dinner, dear girl,' he began. 'Perhaps before I leave we can—'

'You'd better start putting your outdoor things on now, Piers,' Henry interrupted. 'Lex has gone for the pick-up and he'll be ready for you in a few minutes.'

'Yes, you mustn't keep him waiting,' Sybil said.

I thought she looked relieved, until he gave her a hard stare and snapped, 'Come and see me at this guesthouse tomorrow morning, Sybil. I'll be expecting you.'

'Oh . . . but I'm not sure I . . .' Sybil stammered.

Piers' voice became oily. 'I came all this way to see you, my dear. You don't want to *disappoint* me, do you?'

She stared at him, swallowed hard and then, summoning up a weak smile, said, 'No, of course not. I'll walk down if there hasn't been heavy snowfall overnight.'

Lex sounded his horn and everyone enthusiastically bundled Piers into his coat and scarf, then urged him out. It was snowing, but in a half-hearted way. Lex helped Piers to get in and then went back round to the driver's side.

Before I could stop myself I'd called anxiously, 'Be careful, Lex!'

'Don't worry about me. I'm used to the weather up here,' he said, smiling at me, and got in.

'He'll be fine,' Clara assured me, giving my arm a pat. 'Come along in before we let all the warm air out.'

Back in the drawing room, there was a palpable lightening of the atmosphere.

Zelda and Tottie returned from putting Teddy to bed and reported that he'd fallen asleep instantly.

Sybil said, 'Teddy's such a lovely little boy. I remember Mark at that age . . .' But then her face clouded over and she looked anxious again. During the course of the evening I'd become sure she had something on her mind, but I'd no idea what.

River went to sit next to her, with Tottie on her other side, and soon the three of them were deep in horticultural conversation. At least, I hoped it was, because I caught the words 'cross-pollination' and 'hot beds'.

Zelda suggested she, Lex and I go into the morning room to watch a rom com, called *While You Were Sleeping*, which I loved. All those crossed wires reminded me a bit of our own complicated Lex/me/Zelda/Mark/Rollo/Flora situation.

On my way to bed later I popped my head into the drawing room to say goodnight and found River, Sybil, Clara and Henry playing mah-jong. Tottie was sitting nearby, knitting a rainbow-striped scarf.

It was a cosy scene, with Lass and Wisty curled up together under the table.

'Pansy's just been out,' I told Sybil, pushing the little dog into the room, even though she obviously wanted to stay with me. I had to harden my heart.

'Fine, dear,' said Sybil absently, then she smiled triumphantly at River and said something that sounded like, 'Pung!'

When I woke up next morning, I thought about Pansy and wondered if I could beg Sybil *not* to sell her to someone else after all . . . even offer her more, if she could wait for the money?

The light filtering in was the soft white kind bounced by snow and it still felt quite early. Was Lex awake yet? Was he thinking about that kiss last night? *I* might have been the one to initiate it, but he'd turned it into something deeper and . . . well, resistance was useless.

Of course, he'd been very kind to me since we'd had that talk in the car, but that kiss had travelled beyond mere kindness. I just wasn't quite sure where to.

I told myself not to read too much into it: he might once have had feelings for me, but all that lay in the past, on the other side of the emotional chasm of his loss, grief and guilt.

My own feelings were confused. When we were students and I'd got over my crush, we'd been friendly, and because of Lisa I'd never let myself think of him in any other way.

But now, I was, and that *so* wasn't a good idea because, given the past, how could things ever work out between us? I needed to get a grip on myself before I lost my heart, though that wouldn't be easy when we were living in the same house.

I turned my thoughts to Zelda, instead, whom I liked very much and who was so very different from her brother.

Her casual mothering reminded me so much of Mum: loving but always ready to leave the responsibility of raising a child to someone else. A cuckoo mother. It was just the way some women were.

Watching the film together last night had been fun: eating snacks from a kitchen raid and drinking home-made ginger beer, as if we'd escaped from an Enid Blyton novel.

Zelda had dragged Mark's name into the conversation a couple of times and I wondered where that would go. *Could* she settle down in one place? And Mark – how constant was he likely to be?

But no, love at first sight is unmistakable . . . or, in this case, love after a long gap in sightings.

I turned on the pillow, releasing the faint fragrance of lavender, which I found very soothing, unlike Sybil's unsettling perfume the previous night.

And then, quite suddenly, something connected in my head and I sat bolt upright, eyes wide.

I *hadn't* first noticed Sybil's pervasive, unusual and strangely familiar scent at the Gathering at all. Instead it was ineradicably associated with the moment I'd nearly gone headlong over that precipice! No wonder I'd found the perfume unsettling.

But did that mean I *had* been pushed, and by *Sybil*? I surely must be going mad if I thought Mark's mother was a homicidal maniac! I mean, after we'd got to Underhill she'd been so kind, patching me up and then saying nice things about my joining the family, and then insinuating how much Mark liked me.

But of course, when she'd first known about our relationship she'd been horrified and looked afraid. Mark had been wary and angry, too, until I'd reassured them both that neither Mum nor I would be remotely interested in pursuing a claim on the estate.

Perhaps Sybil hadn't really believed me and I'd still seemed to pose a threat? But then later, after seeing Mark and me together at the Gathering, she'd decided our marriage would solve the problem much more easily?

Unless she was completely mad, though, my theory seemed entirely unbelievable. Yet somehow, now, I *did* believe it. I just didn't know what to do about it.

I put my dressing gown on and padded across the landing to the bathroom, pausing for a moment to listen to the faint clack of typewriter keys. It was not that early, for Henry was already at work . . . and was that murmuring noise Clara dictating into her microphone?

When I went down, almost everyone else was eating breakfast or, in the case of Henry and Clara, a second breakfast.

'There you are, dear,' said Tottie. 'We've saved you some fried eggs and potato cakes: we're having a blowout.'

'Mummy says she can eat what she likes now, if she's not being an actor any more,' Teddy told me.

'To a degree: I don't want to turn into a barrel of lard,' said Zelda, who was looking workmanlike in a retro film-starry way, in jeans and a jumper, a scarf tied pirate-fashion over her hair and big gold hoop earrings.

Sybil didn't look as if she'd slept very well and wished me a wan good morning. I couldn't imagine anyone looking less like a homicidal maniac. She was feeding bits of toast to Wisty and Lass under the table, while Pansy was polishing three dog bowls with her tongue, in case any last morsel had been overlooked.

In this warm domestic scene, what I'd been thinking about Sybil seemed impossible. Perhaps all those crime novels of Clara's I'd been reading had pervaded my imagination?

'Henry and I were working, but we couldn't resist the smell,' said Clara.

I sat down next to her and Den whipped the cover off a dish with a flourish and set it in front of me.

'Thanks, Den,' I said. *I* might be the one turning into a tub of lard, but I couldn't resist it.

'Coffee?' asked Tottie, pushing the pot in my direction. 'Just made it. Lex has gone out to look at the road, but he'll be back in a minute.'

'I am back,' said Lex's deep voice behind me. 'Pete was out on the tractor gritting and he said he'd spoken to Fred at the pub on the phone and there's no snow at all in Thorstane.'

'Typical,' said Henry. 'You only have to get to the pub and they have a whole different weather system from ours.'

'Pete thinks we'll be snowed in for Christmas,' Lex said. 'They're going to try to keep the road open up towards the tops, if they can, because of the animals, so someone could always get across if there's an emergency.'

'I sincerely hope there won't be, though after a few days of Piers, Flora may possibly consider getting him out of her house an emergency,' suggested Clara.

Lex sat down and I passed the coffee pot across. I'd avoided looking at him till now, but when I did he smiled warmly at me and I returned it before looking quickly away again, feeling my face going pink. The trouble with having such pale skin is that every change of colour shows, however slight.

Clara finished the last of her egg and sighed with satisfaction. 'I'm going back to the memoirs shortly, because I want to bring this volume to completion by Christmas, if I can. And I think you all have plans for the morning?'

'Me and Den and Tottie are going to make a chocolate log,' said Teddy importantly.

'And then we'll ice the second Christmas cake, the one for the Boxing Day bash,' said Tottie.

'Do a lot of people come to that, even in this kind of weather?' I asked.

'Oh, yes, if they can get through, then they wouldn't miss it for the world,' said Henry. 'Like the Gathering.'

A door opened somewhere and I could hear the tinny sound of radio music and running water from the scullery.

'That's Olive. She's giving the house a final tidy up before Christmas,' said Tottie.

'Her only drawback is that she carries her radio around with her and is addicted to the inanities of Radio 2,' said Clara.

Olive's head appeared round the side of the scullery door. 'I heard that – and I find it soporific.'

'I think you mean calming, otherwise you'd be sleeping while you cleaned,' suggested Henry.

'Soothing,' amended Olive.

'Would you like a cup of tea or coffee and some toast, Olive?' asked Clara.

'No, I'll do the upstairs bathrooms and then have me elevenses after that.'

'Fair enough,' said Clara, and the head vanished.

'We're heading up to Underhill shortly,' said Lex. 'Meg and I'll be back for lunch, but I expect Mark will run Zelda home later.'

'And you will give me a portrait sitting later, won't you, Tottie?' I asked her.

'I expect so,' she said, assuming the off-hand air that didn't disguise her pleasure in having her portrait painted.

'I suppose I'd better ring Flora and see if she still wants a lift to Underhill,' said Lex, but when he came back, he reported that Flora would be going there under her own steam.

'She remembered Deirdre's four-wheel-drive was in the garage and found the keys, so she rang Gil – that's Olive's son, Meg – and he's clearing and gritting the drive for her. But she won't be able to stay long, because of her guests.'

'Piers will certainly expect to get his feet in the trough for every meal,' Henry said.

'Flora says Rollo's much improved and up and about,' Lex said, then gave that arrowhead grin and added, 'She said that last night she'd warned Piers that if he wanted a cooked breakfast, then he had to be down before eight thirty, so she seems to have him organized.'

'I knew she would. She was a very efficient nanny and I expect she's using the same technique,' said Clara drily.

'Piers had just asked her to ring us and remind Sybil that he wanted to see her this morning. I'd let him stew, though, Sybil.'

Lex smiled at her. 'There's no reason you should have to traipse down there at his command, if you don't feel like it.'

'You could just ring up,' suggested Clara.

'No . . . I'd better walk down and see Uncle Piers,' she said.

Clara was now looking at her narrowly, possibly puzzling about why Piers seemed to have such a hold over her. It was very odd. Perhaps he and her father had always barked their commands at her and she was used to obeying? But though she called him 'Uncle Piers', his attempt to kiss her last night hadn't seemed very avuncular at all.

'River and I are going to take the post round the village shortly, Sybil, so you could walk down with us as far as the guesthouse?' suggested Henry.

'That would be lovely. I could take the dogs with me for some exercise, if you don't think Flora will mind them in the guesthouse.'

'They'll probably be a welcome relief after Piers,' said Clara.

35

Stripped

Flora's car was creeping down the drive of Bella Vista as we passed and she followed us up to Underhill. The journey was a little hairy, despite a fresh layer of grit on the road, and I suppose she was unused to her aunt's car, because she fell back and arrived a few minutes after we did.

Mark came out, but had eyes only for Zelda, so I don't think he even registered it when Flora parked next to the pick-up and got out with a palpable expression of relief on her face. We'd waited for her and followed the other two in, and then Mark gave us very much the same tour he'd given me, though in reverse order, starting with the almost-finished new reception room in the coach house and then through into the bare catering kitchen-to-be.

Lex and I hung back; I think *he'd* heard enough about the plans already too. But Flora stuck with Mark and Zelda, asking questions and enthusing about everything until slowly it became clear even to her that she was an unwelcome third in the conversation. I felt a little sorry for her.

Zelda was coming up with some practical ideas of her own and by the time we'd toured the upstairs, she and Mark had begun an impassioned discussion.

'Starting off in spring with the wedding receptions is very achievable, because the new catering kitchen will easily be ready in time,' she said. 'And, of course, you'll need an en-suite room for the bride to use on the day, but it doesn't have to be in the family wing, does it?'

'But it's one of the bedrooms I'm already renovating for guests,' he pointed out.

'Forget those for the moment, Mark. Why not turn the rooms over the old kitchen, which you've earmarked for your friends' accommodation, into the bridal suite, instead?'

'But why?' demanded Mark.

'Because when you go upstairs from the hall, those rooms are to the right, but the family ones are to the left. So if the bridal suite was there, it would leave the whole of the family part of the house separate.'

'But only until the other guest bedrooms were finished.'

'You'll have to scrap that idea,' she said decidedly. 'I don't think letting a few bedrooms would be worth the effort, and anyway, Underhill should remain a family home as well as a business.'

'I don't know about that,' he said. 'And where would I put Art and Gerry?'

'If Sybil still has her old bedroom, then that little housekeeper's parlour, with its own staircase up to a bedroom, could be made into a perfect little apartment for them.'

I thought she had something there, and Mark was beginning to look more thoughtful.

He turned it all over in his head for a few minutes and then said slowly, 'It *could* work.'

Zelda took his arm and gave him a starry smile. 'I'm certain it could, and it would still be a lovely home as well as a business. We'd easily make enough money just from the receptions, providing it's all *really* high end.'

'I'd thought of holding weddings later, too,' he said. 'The actual ceremony on the top landing and the guests in the hall below.'

They moved off in that direction and we followed. I was amused to notice that at some point Zelda had stopped saying 'you could' and replaced it with 'we could'.

Flora, who had found herself sidelined for the last half-hour, now said, '*I* think Mark's original idea about the guest bedrooms would work much better, and half the en-suites are put in already.'

'No, on that scale it wouldn't be financially worth it,' Zelda said dismissively. 'A lot of trouble and disruption for not much return.'

'But Flora's right about my having already put in the en-suites,' Mark said.

'The rooms wanted updating anyway, didn't they?' said Zelda.

'Sybil will be very happy if she doesn't have to live in the housekeeper's room,' Lex put in.

'I do think that was a bit of a mean suggestion, darling,' said Zelda, giving Mark's arm a squeeze. 'Never mind, we'll redecorate her old room and I'm sure she'll love having an en-suite.'

'I suppose we could do it the way you suggest and then, if it doesn't work out, we still have the country house hotel option,' Mark conceded. 'But my plan is not only to make enough money to keep Underhill going, but also be able to spend my winters in my house in Italy . . . and go skiing, too.'

'It sounds so perfect, working all summer and then playing all winter,' she said, smiling up at him. 'And I'm dying to see your little house in Italy!'

'And I can't wait to show it to you,' he said warmly.

'That's what you said to *me*,' piped up Flora tartly. He'd said it to me, too, but though fickle might have been his middle name, I was sure he really meant it this time.

Flora evidently thought so too, for she was admitting defeat. 'I'm afraid I'll have to go, Mark,' she announced. 'I need to see how Rollo's doing. He's really not very strong. His poor mother's so worried, though she knows I'm taking the best care of him.'

'And Piers?' said Lex.

'There's nothing wrong with his health, though he is a bit crotchety and demanding,' she said. 'I gave him Deirdre's rules of the house after breakfast and pointed out that he has tea- and coffee-making facilities in his room, as well as the use of the visitor lounge with a TV. I don't suppose Rollo and I will see much of him, except when I serve his meals in the dining room.'

Rollo was clearly living in the family part of the guest-house, which all sounded very cosy. I wondered if this morning's visit to Underhill had simply been a last testing of the waters with Mark and now, seeing she was getting nowhere, she would turn her full attention to the hapless and helpless Rollo?

Perhaps she'd eat him afterwards, like a spider.

'I hope you hid the keys of the roll-down shutters over the bar in the dining room somewhere Piers won't find them?' asked Lex.

She gave a thin smile. 'I wasn't born yesterday: they're in my bag. Not that we keep a huge stock of spirits. And we always sell it by the glass, never the bottle, as I explained to Piers last night.'

'At a mark-up, too, I expect?'

'Of course. I'm afraid his bill is going to be rather large.'

Lex saw her out and came back to find us standing in the hall, discussing what to do next.

Lex said, 'I suppose we'd better get on with doing something, before it's time for us to go, too.'

'We've decided to paper and paint what was going to be the bridal suite first and turn it into Mark's bedroom,' said Zelda. 'And then the same with your mum's old room, so she can move back into it after Christmas.'

'I think that's a really nice idea, Zelda,' I agreed.

'I suppose it shouldn't take too long with a bit of help,' Mark said. 'Then we can move on to the new bridal suite.'

'Sounds like a plan,' said Lex. 'Why don't Meg and I strip wallpaper in Sybil's room and you two take on the other?'

We collected buckets of water to soak the walls, and scrapers, and set to.

'Flora's nose is well out of joint,' Lex said. 'She could hardly wait to get away.'

'I suspect that's because she's realized that though she might have lost Mark, she still has a bird in the hand with Rollo.'

'You think she's going to set her sights on him, now?'

'He's dependent on her at the moment. He can't escape, even if he wants to,' I pointed out. 'But good luck to her. I'm starting to think she could even cope with his ghastly mother, too. Clash of the Titans.'

After a few minutes of wall scraping I said, 'I did feel worried about Zelda falling for Mark, when he seems so quick to switch from one girl to another.'

'So did I,' Lex admitted. 'But she seems to know what she's doing – and that's rearranging Mark's plans for Underhill to suit their future life together, just the way she wants it!'

I laughed. 'Including the winters in Italy and skiing! You know, I think they're made for each other.'

We set to again with the scrapers and there's something very satisfying about peeling off long damp tendrils of old wallpaper, several layers deep, to reveal the plaster beneath . . . even if it was the bedroom of the person I suspected had tried to kill me.

That was a bizarre thought.

On the way back to the Red House, Lex suddenly surprised me by saying, 'There's been something on your mind all morning, hasn't there? You were looking very oddly at Sybil at breakfast, too.'

'Was I? I was trying *not* to look at her.' I paused, then made up my mind to tell him, even if he thought I was mad.

'Remember at dinner last night, when we were talking about Sybil's perfume? It's overpoweringly distinctive, isn't it? I knew I'd noticed that scent before.'

'Yes, you said – at the Gathering.'

'I assumed that was it, but when I woke this morning I realized that I'd found it unsettling because I connected it with that moment when I nearly went off the ledge.'

He pulled into a passing place and turned to stare incredulously at me. 'You mean . . . ?'

'Yes, I really am sure now that I was pushed and, however ridiculous it seems, I think Sybil did it.'

'But why on earth would old Syb try to kill you?' he said blankly.

'I don't really know, unless it was just a sudden impulse when she saw me standing there alone in the dark.'

'That's not exactly a reason,' he pointed out. 'When I spotted you, there was no one remotely near.'

'She could have slipped away quickly, and she was wearing a dark blue ski jacket and trousers.'

He looked frowningly at me, as if I might indeed be mad, so I said, 'I've been giving it a lot of thought and I think she still saw me as a threat to Mark's inheritance, even if she was putting a good face on it. But afterwards, at the Gathering, she noticed Mark was . . .'

'All over you like a rash?' he finished.

'Something like that. So *then* she got the misguided idea that he was seriously interested in me, and of course, if we were to get married, that would make his position safe.'

'But it's all so far-fetched! I mean, even if you or your mum made a claim, there's no guarantee you'd get anything,' he said.

'Neither Mum nor I would dream of doing that anyway. I'm happy to have found out about my heritage, but it doesn't mean they *feel* like family – or not Sybil and Mark. Henry and Clara do, and I'm very attached to Teddy.'

'And do I feel like family?'

'No, not in the least,' I said frankly.

'Good,' he replied enigmatically, and pulled out into the lane again.

He was frowning. 'I don't know if I believe it or not, but I think I should tell Clara and Henry what you suspect,' he said, to my dismay.

'Oh, please don't tell them, Lex! Let's just forget it.'

'You can't simply forget attempted murder. And what about Zelda?'

'But Zelda isn't a threat, is she?' I said, astonished. 'In fact, Sybil seems fond of her and I don't see why she should mind if she and Mark get together. It might have been different if it was Flora.'

'I suppose that's true. I'd still like to run the whole idea past Clara and Henry, though, and see what they think.'

'I don't want anything to spoil Christmas. It's bad enough Piers having to be invited for dinner, isn't it? I can't imagine he'll be able to leave before then.'

'No, we're stuck with the old soak. Or rather, Flora is.'

He gave me a sideways grin that made him look suddenly and heart-wrenchingly like the old, carefree student Lex from long ago.

'But Nanny Flora will sort him out and probably keep him in line during Christmas dinner, too!'

When we got back the house was quiet.

'Where is everyone?' asked Lex, when we found Tottie sitting in the kitchen over a cup of coffee, while the three dogs snored in their baskets by the range and Teddy industriously blobbed glitter glue on a sheet of card at the other end of the table.

'Clara had emails to answer and then she was going to do some work, and Henry is printing out the final version of his book.'

'I thought I heard the sound of a printer as we were coming in, but I assumed it was Clara's,' I said.

'Sybil came back from Bella Vista with a headache that turned into a very bad migraine, so she's taken some pills and gone to her room, and River and Henry delivered the mail and then called in on the Bagginses.'

'River's just gone to do some wrapping,' Teddy said, looking up. 'Do you think he bought me a present at Preciousss?'

'I don't know. We don't usually do Christmas presents, but he might.'

'I like River and I'm making him this picture for Christmas. It's a dragon, sitting on the Starstone.'

'So I see – he'll love it.'

'Me and Den and Tottie made the chocolate log this morning and iced the Boxing Day Christmas cake,' Teddy said, and when he'd finished his picture he insisted we go into the larder to admire them.

The large chocolate log was covered in dark butter cream, artfully scraped into bark-like patterns and adorned with holly and a plastic robin. The cake had been royal-iced, whipped into little peaks like rough plastering and studded with random plastic decorations – a red postbox, a bristly fir tree, a little snow-covered house and a signpost pointing to 'Merry Christmas'.

'Lovely,' I said. 'And what's this in the big glass bowl?'

'The base for the special trifle we'll have on Christmas Day,' said Tottie. 'Madeira sponge spread with raspberry jam and soaked in a little sherry, then covered in a layer of raspberry jelly – vegetarian, of course.'

'I've got to help Den cook lots of things tomorrow,' said Teddy.

'Yes, he'll be baking cheese straws and other nibbles ready for the Boxing Day bash,' Tottie said, then added that she would be in the conservatory when I was ready to paint her.

I popped upstairs to change first, because I was sure I smelled of old, damp wallpaper. On my way down I noticed that River's door was ajar and I peeped in. He was sitting cross-legged on the bed with his eyes shut and the room smelled faintly of burnt herbs and joss sticks. He opened his eyes and smiled.

'Ah, there you are, Meg. Just the person I want. I have purchased a few small things from dear Moonflower. When in Rome, do as the Romans – and the Doomes exchange gifts on Christmas morning.'

'That was a kind thought,' I said, and fetched him the left-over wrapping paper and my Sellotape. The gifts were all contained in one of Flower's smaller brown carrier bags, so goodness knows what he'd bought.

I debated telling him my suspicions about Sybil, but since he liked her so much I hesitated, and then in the end I didn't.

Tottie was waiting for me in the conservatory and through a gap in the foliage I spotted Lex and Teddy going down the garden to clean out the hens.

I hoped Lex had thought better of telling my wild suspicions to Henry and Clara.

Tottie took up her pose, holding the now empty wicker cornucopia – the fruit, vegetables and leaves were almost completed, but the wicker itself needed a few touches. The pineapple, seemingly poised above her head, looked just about ripe enough to eat.

Tottie's face had come together amazingly quickly yesterday and I'd already worked on some of the background. This, I thought, might be my fastest portrait yet!

Her expression had turned dreamy and absent again and at one point she murmured, 'Snake's head fritillary . . .'

It was some time before I surfaced again and the garden was empty, the daylight fading into darkness.

'I think it's finished, Tottie,' I said.

She came over to look, stretching as she did so. 'I look quite exotic, don't I?' she said, in a pleased voice.

'You were the perfect sitter,' I told her. Then she pottered off in the direction of the garden hall while I moved the easel and my painting gear back into the studio, and propped the portrait up to have a good look.

Three portraits, all – even if it sounded immodest of me to say so – very good. I'd produced my best work here and I knew who I *really, really* wanted to paint next.

Lex.

I tracked him down to the kitchen, where he was with River and Teddy, making what River always calls God's

Eyes: odds and ends of coloured wool woven on to a frame of sticks.

Pansy woke up and hurtled towards me as if she hadn't seen me for a week, yipping round my ankles till I picked her up.

'We'll have to clear up soon,' said River. 'It's not long till tea. Cheese scones, they just want warming.'

'Lex,' I said abruptly to him, 'can I paint *you* next?'

He looked up at me for a moment, seeming slightly surprised and then said, 'Of course. When do you want to start?'

'Tomorrow . . . though perhaps we could set the pose now? I seem to be on a roll after not being able to paint for so long and I just want to keep on going.'

'All right, just let me wash this glue off my hands and I'll come to the studio.'

When he joined me, I'd arranged the dais and chair the way I wanted them.

He stopped dead in front of the old easel on which I'd placed Tottie's portrait and said admiringly, 'Wow! You're right, you really are on a roll. All three portraits are *brilliant*.'

'I think I'm doing my best work here and though I usually do paint quickly, here it's been fantastically fast.'

'Let's hope mine doesn't break your run of success, then,' he said with a grin. 'Where do you want me?'

I suppressed the unsettling image that popped into my head and said, 'On the dais – if you could just go and sit down, I can fiddle with the lighting a bit.'

I'd already put a fresh canvas on my easel – I'd soon run out of large ones at this rate – and thought I'd draw straight on to it. I'd already done a small sketch of him anyway, without him knowing, as a gift for Clara . . .

He sat in the tall, carved chair looking as if it had been made for him. He'd taken off his green fleece in the kitchen and one arm, in a loose white shirtsleeve, lay along the padded armrest, his hand, with its long, mobile fingers, relaxed.

I studied the pose, angling the lights. 'I like the white of that shirt you're wearing and the way your throat rises from the open neck . . .'

'I'm flattered.'

'To *paint*,' I said pointedly. I rearranged the drapes behind him, but it needed something more.

'I wonder if Clara would let me borrow the totem pole from her study. If it was turned so that the hawk head was just behind yours, I think that would give me what I need.'

'The beak echoing the curve of my big hooter, you mean?'

'It's *not* a big hooter, it's a very fine aquiline nose, like Clara's. But yes, one shape echoed by the other.'

'I'll go and ask her, if she's in the study,' he offered, and came back a few minutes later, carrying the heavy wooden post as if it weighed nothing. He arranged it as I directed until I was satisfied and had taken a few pictures of him sitting in front of it.

'There,' I said, 'that will do for today.'

'Then if you're done, Clara and Henry want us to go into the drawing room before tea.'

I looked at him with sudden suspicion. 'You've snitched about Sybil, haven't you?'

'I have told them, yes. It seemed the best thing to do. Come on.'

36

Tryst Issues

'There you are, darlings,' said Clara, when we went into the drawing room. 'Sybil hadn't stirred when I looked in on her, and Tottie and River are in the morning room with Teddy, watching an old film, so with luck we won't be disturbed for a little while.'

I must have looked worried because Henry smiled at me encouragingly. 'Lex told us after the Solstice that you'd thought at first you'd been pushed off the ledge, then decided you'd imagined it.'

'Yes, because who would do that? It just seemed so improbable.'

'But I shouldn't think you could really mistake the feeling of being pushed for even the strongest gust of wind,' Clara said. 'So Henry and I are inclined to believe you.'

'*I* thought she'd imagined it, but when she said about Sybil's perfume earlier, I started to wonder,' Lex said.

'You explained everything very clearly, darling,' Clara told him. 'And I'm afraid Meg might be right. Sybil's horrified reaction when we told her who Meg was quite took us by surprise. It had never crossed our minds till that moment that she and Mark would be worried Meg and her mother would make a claim on the estate!'

'At the Gathering, Mark certainly made me think *he* wasn't worried about it any more – *or* about Meg being his first cousin,' Lex said drily.

'He *was* rather smitten with her at the time, wasn't he?' Henry agreed.

'The trouble is, Sybil noticed it and suddenly got it into her head that Mark and I were serious about each other and that our marriage would make everything right,' I said.

'Her assumptions seem to have been a little premature, to say the least,' Clara said. 'It certainly isn't you he's got his eye on now, is it?'

'Most definitely not, and Sybil's noticed, too.'

'You'd have to be blind to miss it,' Lex pointed out. 'He and Zelda have hardly taken their eyes off each other since she got here.'

'It still seems very bizarre that Sybil should attempt to get rid of Meg in such a dramatic fashion,' Henry said.

I thought that that was the understatement of the year.

'Only to realize shortly afterwards – though mistakenly, as it turned out – that there was a better way to neutralize her,' he continued.

'Nicely put, Henry,' applauded Clara. 'I believe Meg's story and I think we must accept that Sybil was the culprit, however unlikely it seems.'

'Though we have noticed that she's looked very stressed, lately,' said Henry.

'Yes, so perhaps that night the darkness and the strange rites might have combined with her fears into some kind of nightmare scenario, and when the opportunity presented itself to get rid of Meg, she acted,' suggested Clara.

'A moment of temporary insanity, which she probably instantly regretted,' Henry finished.

'Meg would have regretted it even more, had she fallen right over,' Lex said drily.

I shivered. 'It was a horrible experience. Thank goodness you spotted me, Lex.'

'But what are we going to do? That's the question,' said Henry.

'Oh, nothing!' I said. 'I mean, there's no actual *proof*, is there? She could just deny it and then everything would be very uncomfortable.'

'Hmm . . .' said Clara. 'I'm a great believer in having things out in the open, as you know, so that goes against the grain. Though I do think something's been going on with Sybil for a while.'

'A kind of midlife crisis, perhaps?' suggested Henry. 'Piers seems to exert quite a hold over her, too, though he's no Svengali.'

'Yes, that's very odd,' agreed Clara. 'Tottie's her best friend, but even she doesn't know what's worrying Sybil.'

'*Could* they be having some kind of autumn/winter romance?' asked Henry.

'Not on Sybil's side at least, Henry, though Piers may have some ideas in that direction. But I expect Sybil's just wondering how to repulse him, without hurting his non-existent feelings.'

'She definitely looked repulsed when he kissed her last night,' Lex said.

'Let's not do anything hasty, but take a couple of days to think over the situation,' Henry suggested. 'Put it out of our minds till after Christmas.'

'I'd be happy just to forget about what happened altogether,' I said. 'I'm sure you're right: it was just an unbalanced moment and she'll never do anything like that again.'

'I think we'll still need to get to the bottom of it eventually,' Clara said. 'But Henry's right, we should just carry on as normal over Christmas and not let it spoil the festivities. After all, it's Christmas Eve tomorrow, so it's almost upon us.'

'And here come some of the others . . . and Den with tea, because I can hear the trolley rattling,' said Henry.

Since there was no sign of Sybil, Tottie took a cup of tea and a scone up to her room and reported that she was feeling slightly better and hoped to come down for dinner.

Teddy and Henry went into his study afterwards, to unpack the box of baubles that had arrived yesterday, and I felt strangely tired, so went up to my room with Pansy in attendance.

I gave Fliss a quick ring and she said she was looking forward to Cal coming home next morning and she was going to tell him about the baby then.

'He's going to be so excited, but we'll really have to get going with the house search, because it's sooner than we planned.'

I updated her on the Sybil Saga and how I was sure now it hadn't been an accident and it all sounded more like the plot of a bad thriller than reality.

Then when she'd finished exclaiming over that, I said that I'd finished Tottie's portrait and was going to paint Lex next.

'So . . . you're friends now?'

'I suppose we are. He's being . . . very kind.'

'Hmm,' she said noncommittally. 'If your other possible romantic lead has gone off with Lex's sister, then that leaves only him for the part, doesn't it? And there you both are, snowed in at a remote house for Christmas – so romantic!'

'It might have been, if we didn't have a shared painful past to come to terms with and a whole house party looking on! I think you'll have to abandon this whole rom-com idea of yours, Fliss.'

When I'd rung off, I lay back on the bed with Pansy curled up close and just closed my eyes for a moment . . . The next thing I knew was when I was woken by the sound of the dinner gong.

It was just as well I was not high maintenance, because I'd changed, brushed my hair, applied lip gloss and was downstairs so quickly that I'm sure the air was still reverberating in the hall from the gong.

It was a strange evening. Sybil came down, but was very quiet at dinner, while Zelda was dreamy and preoccupied. Mark had dropped her off while I was sleeping, but not stayed, because the roads were freezing over again already.

Back in the drawing room we all gathered round the fire while Henry read us the opening chapters of *A Christmas Carol*, apparently another family tradition. He read so beautifully and Teddy, who had been allowed to stay up for it for the first time, was enthralled.

'I only hope it doesn't give him nightmares,' Henry said, when Teddy had gone up to bed with Zelda and Tottie. Tonight River had been commanded by Teddy to go up later and read the bedtime story.

'I don't think so,' said Lex. 'He's got the Muppets version of it on DVD, hasn't he? So he's used to the idea of the ghosts and the chains and all that.'

'They're exposed to a lot worse than that these days,' said Clara. 'We can only protect him to a certain extent.'

'He'll find his own way through life, as we did,' Henry said. 'He's a clever, sensible child.'

Since Sybil had gone to bed early, Lex and I let the dogs out last thing.

It was bitterly cold and all was silent, except for the sound of the snow crisply scrunching under the dogs' feet.

The sky was a clear, translucent ultramarine, scattered with sequin stars, one of them very bright.

'That's a wishing star,' Lex said, when I pointed it out. 'What will you wish for, Meg?'

I wish I could stay here for ever, with you, a traitorous voice in my head whispered.

'If I told you, it wouldn't happen,' I said quickly. 'What about *your* wish?'

'Ditto,' he said, and smiled.

I thought it would be difficult to put the whole Sybil thing right out of my head over Christmas, but actually, at breakfast she was again so very ordinary that I found myself questioning my own sanity. Surely we were *all* mad to suspect quiet, plaintive Sybil, with her faded prettiness, of doing something like that? But then, of course, she was a horsy person too, out in all weathers and hefting bales of hay about, not some fragile hothouse flower.

Tottie said that, Christmas Eve or not, Clara had been up and working long before I came down, while Henry and River had just gone into his study together, where River was going to read through the manuscript of Henry's book as a final check.

There hadn't been any further snowfall overnight and the farmers would have already been out gritting the road, so Zelda said she intended spending the day at Underhill again, which was no surprise. Sybil and Tottie decided to go down with her and hack around the estate, to give the horses a bit of exercise.

'Would you like to go to Underhill with me today, Teddy?' asked Zelda, but he looked dubious.

'Aunt Clara said she'd teach me to read more hieroglyphs this morning,' he said. 'And Den's got lots of cooking to do, so I need to help him. I think I'll stay here, Mummy.'

'Then I'll see you at dinner, darling, and you can tell me all about it,' she said, smiling at him.

'Where's Lex?' I asked.

'He and Den went out to start your van's engine – you'd left the keys in the studio. They thought it might be an idea to run it for ten minutes, because it's been standing there in the cold for a few days.'

'I hadn't given it a thought!' I said, and thanked them when they came back in, before taking Lex off to the studio to give me the first portrait sitting.

He removed his warm fleece without my asking him and resumed the pose in his shirtsleeves and black jeans.

I checked the iPad photo, then took up my soft black pencil and began to sketch directly on to the canvas.

My concentration was intense and soon that hawk profile, half-turned away (the hardest of portrait poses to paint), took shape, the faint scaffolding of bones and tendons, the strong line of the neck rising up from the open V of his shirt . . .

Finally, I stepped back and stared intently from outline to sitter: this way of drawing straight on to the canvas without preliminary sketches was new but it seemed to be working well.

I'd been looking at him impersonally as a series of lines and shapes, but now, suddenly, I was aware of him as a man – the one he was now, damaged and haunted by his past, perhaps, but still sweet-natured, kind and with courage. There was humour in that arrowhead smile, too.

All that I knew of him, past and present, must somehow be distilled into paint. The mysterious alchemy between eyes, mind and hand had never failed me yet and I prayed (to the

Goddess? Gaia? Whatever divine being happened to be listening?) that it would not fail me now.

Den broke the spell by coming in just then with coffee and a few of the cheese straws he'd been making for Boxing Day. Pansy was hard on his heels, though I didn't know if that was from greed or whether she was in search of me.

'That's definitely 'is 'ead,' Den said, pausing behind the easel.

Lex stood up and stretched slowly. 'I don't think I want to look yet, because you've been staring at me so intently that I'm afraid of what I'd see.'

'It's just the pencil sketch, anyway,' I said. 'I'd like to start putting paint on, but you might have had enough of sitting for one day?'

'I don't mind, so long as I can have a little break now and walk about first,' he said obligingly. 'I'll probably need to go and do something physical afterwards, like chop logs, though.'

'I'll take this 'ound with me, shall I?' Den said.

'No, don't bother, just leave the door slightly ajar, so she can get out if she wants to.'

I set out my palette while Lex was having his break and then he took up his pose again.

My hand, holding the small trowel-shaped palette knife, with which I could produce a line, a scraping, a smooth sweep, or a thick curl of paint, trembled slightly with excitement . . . and then that inner force took me over and the shadows, planes and angles of his face began to emerge.

Apart from the curve of his nose, it was mostly angles. His skin tone was a warm, pale olive, a family colouring he shared with Clara, Zelda and Teddy, along with the black curls. His dark eyes should have been brown, not that agate-dark green . . .

Lex's voice, slightly plaintive, finally woke me to the present.

'Meg?'

I blinked at him and then looked at the canvas before me, on which his face seemed to have materialized. How long had I been painting?

'I think all of me has gone numb and Pansy's been staring at you for the past half-hour,' he said. 'I think she wants her lunch – and so do I. *And* someone to make soothing noises at me, because I feel like a scoured-out shell of my former self.'

'I expect you're just exhausted,' I said contritely. 'And I know having someone staring at you for hours on end can feel weird.'

'I think I'd like to get my own back and make a clay portrait bust of you, one of these days.'

'Really? But there might not be time after Christmas, because now I've finished the commissioned portraits, there won't be any real reason for me to stay on.'

'But you're working so well that maybe you *should* stay on and paint some of the others, too?'

Clara pushed the door wide and wandered in. 'Yes, why not make it a full set? Den, Teddy and Zelda, for a start.'

'I could paint Zelda and Mark as their wedding present,' I suggested, half-joking.

'Now, there's an idea,' she said. 'I don't expect to see Zelda again till tonight, but Tottie and Sybil came back over an hour ago and they're helping Den in the kitchen.'

'So Sybil hasn't been summoned again by Piers today,' Lex asked.

'Actually, he *did* ring first thing, but I answered it in my study and told him she couldn't go down to see him today. He wasn't pleased, but then he does seem to want to have his own way in everything, doesn't he?'

'Did you tell Sybil he rang?'

'No, I'm afraid it entirely slipped my mind. It'll do her good to have a nice, quiet day doing things she enjoys instead. And I've had a lovely morning, too,' she continued. 'An old friend sent me photographs of a broken stone marker and we're agreed it's written in an early form of Ogham. It was broken into pieces and a digger turned it up, but we seem to have most of it.'

'Ogham?' I echoed.

'Don't ask, the explanation would take us to teatime,' Lex said.

'Just another early written form of language, darling, that developed in Ireland, separately from others in use at the same date,' said Clara. 'One written language does not follow the other in a neat fashion, but instead they often overlap in time. Rather like the evolution of the human race as we currently know it,' she added.

'See what I mean?' said Lex. 'Come on, let's go and have something to eat. I'm famished.'

'Cheese and tomato quiche,' said Clara. 'Den's been baking up a storm in there and Wisty's covered in so much flour, she looks like a ghost dog.'

The ghost dog had been dusted off, but Den was still at work, mixing up a savoury nut loaf for Christmas dinner. Bizarrely, this was to be baked in a large early Victorian pottery mould, shaped like a capon.

'That should confuse Piers even more than the rabbit,' I said.

'Got a few more things to do,' Den said, 'then that's it. Fill the volley-vaunts on Boxing Day morning, won't I?'

'With condensed mushroom soup?' I asked, remembering.

'That and Eggwinas.'

'Eggwinas?'

'Curried eggs. It's an old family joke,' said Lex.

'It was that Edwina Curry, wasn't it?' Den said, bafflingly, though as long as she wasn't in the vol-au-vents, I was fine with that.

When I'd eaten I went back to the studio for a brood over the portrait, then I checked my iPad and phone.

There was a brief email from Fliss, telling me Cal was home and ecstatic at the news, to which I replied suitably.

And there were several missed calls from Rollo, who I'd thought would have given up by now. Then, disconcertingly, he rang, as if he knew I'd turned on the phone.

'What on earth do you want now, Rollo?' I said wearily. 'If you're still angling for an interview with Henry, it's not going to happen. I think you're jolly lucky to be invited to dinner tomorrow and you'd better be on your best behaviour!'

'It's nothing of the kind,' he said indignantly. 'I just thought you might feel some slight concern about my health, seeing you were the cause of my getting such a bad chill.'

'*I* was?'

'Yes. So I was sure you'd want to know that I feel much better.'

'I already knew, because Flora's kept us up to date. It was just a chill, anyway, wasn't it?'

'*Just a chill?* When you *know* how weak my lungs are? It could have carried me off.'

There had never seemed anything wrong with his chest or lungs that I'd ever noticed. I thought the only thing likely to carry him off in the near future was Flora herself.

'You could come and visit me,' he suggested.

'I'm too busy working and, anyway, I'll see you tomorrow, won't I?'

'But I'm feeling cooped up and bored, because that dreadful old man is always in the guest sitting room, drinking and complaining.'

'He's another uninvited visitor, but never mind, at least Flora seems to like *you*.'

His voice stopped being die-away and warmed to enthusiasm. 'She's been quite wonderful! Mother is very grateful to her for looking after me so well. They talk on the phone every day.'

'How nice,' I said, thinking that perhaps a nanny was really what he'd needed all along.

'Well, see you tomorrow,' I said briskly, preparing to ring off, but I wasn't to get away quite that easily.

'That's another thing,' he said. 'You told me a whole lot of lies about Henry. All that guff about only wearing green and his being a recluse.'

'Just joking. And he loves being surrounded with people – he just likes to choose them himself.'

I hoped Rollo would behave himself tomorrow at dinner. But Flora would have her eye on him, and also I didn't think he was so stupid as to forget that Henry still had many influential contacts in the world of literature.

After this I felt like some fresh air and thought I'd walk down to Preciousss and visit Flower.

The house was quite quiet, though I thought I could hear Clara's voice through her study door.

I got my coat and boots on and, while I was scrunching down the drive and on to the ice-rutted road, I did a mental tally of my Christmas presents. I had made lots of little sketches of everyone, including the dogs, and I already had one or two gifts I'd got at Preciousss, but I could do with a few extras . . . like something for Den.

Flower, carrying Grace-Galadriel on her hip, opened the shop door to me and was delighted I'd come to visit – and even more so to hear that I wanted a few small gifts in case I had forgotten anyone.

'I don't know what, though.'

'Sweets?' suggested Flower. 'Everyone likes sweets.'

'I didn't know you sold them, Flower!'

'I have my own range,' she said proudly, leading the way over to a dim and distant shelf that had previously escaped my notice. Flower's range had been created by filling old jam jars of various sizes and shapes with bought sweets and then covering the lids with miniature bath caps in shiny purple. Handwritten paper labels gave a new slant to the contents.

'Wizard's Wands' were just liquorice sticks, the soft, twisted sort with one end dipped in little coloured granules. 'Tasty Spells' were old-fashioned humbugs and 'Magical Mints' were the soft kind covered in chocolate and individually wrapped in foil.

Den liked liquorice; I remembered Teddy saying he was going to save him some liquorice allsorts the first time we collected him from school.

I bought several jars and Flower's eyes shone so much she looked quite beautiful for a moment, in a slightly Drowned Ophelia kind of way.

'As long as my card doesn't spontaneously combust when you put it in the machine,' I said glumly. The rent for the flat would have gone out of my account, and now I was paying it all on my own it was quite a burden. I really must start cottage hunting as soon as I got back after Christmas.

Flower made me coffee in the kitchen and left me minding Grace-Galadriel while she was packing my purchases. I just had time to whip out my sketchpad and do a quick drawing of the baby before she came back. I still had a few mounts left and even if I couldn't give the drawing to Flower for Christmas, I'd see her on Boxing Day.

When we'd drunk our coffee and eaten some home-made biscuits that looked like perforated cardboard and tasted much the same, I said I'd better get back.

'I've just remembered there's a letter for the Red House here,' she said, getting up and fetching a battered envelope from the dresser. 'Here we are! It must have been damp in the post bag, because this was stuck to the bottom of a parcel. We had to peel it off.'

'The snow probably got in, while they were dragging it through the drifts,' I said. 'But at least you can still read the address label.'

It was a long brown envelope, with American stamps and interesting stains, addressed to Professor Clara Mayhem Doome.

'I'll give it to Clara when I get back,' I said, pushing it down inside my large tapestry shoulder bag.

I'd only just set off up the road when a dog-walking party consisting of River, Henry and Lex caught me up.

Lass was proceeding under her own steam, but River was carrying Pansy and Lex the more substantial Wisty.

'They've such little legs,' said River when I commented on this. 'They were tired and their tummies were cold.'

'I don't suppose they are the most suitable of country dogs,' I said.

'They can walk a surprisingly long way, when they don't have to wade through snow,' Henry said. 'Sybil is a good dog breeder. Her puppies are always healthy and win lots of prizes.'

'I don't think Pansy will,' Lex said. 'She looks like a collection of all the things dachshunds shouldn't be.'

'She's healthy, though, that's the main thing. And she is beautiful in her own way,' Henry said.

As soon as we got in, the door to Clara's study opened and her head of grey and silver curls appeared.

'Psst!' she hissed thrillingly. 'Come in here, all of you!'

'Me too?' asked River.

'Why not?' said Clara. 'I feel you're quite one of the family.'

'Just let me put the dogs in the kitchen so they can dry off by the stove,' Henry said, suiting the action to the words.

Tottie was already in the study, pacing about restlessly.

'Shut the door, Henry,' Clara said when he came in.

'Who are we shutting out?'

'Sybil,' Tottie said. 'While you were all out, Piers made Flora bring him up here and I was in the drawing room with Sybil when they rang the doorbell. We had the lights on, so of course they could see us through the window and we couldn't pretend there was nobody home. Piers said he'd just wanted a quick word with Sybil on a private matter.'

'What private matter?' asked Henry.

'It wouldn't have been private if he'd announced it, would it?' Clara pointed out. 'Shush and let Tottie tell the story.'

'Well, I suggested she take him into the library and I'd make us all some coffee. You know the library door never catches properly . . . Anyway, on the way back I could hear them talking, and I wouldn't have stopped and listened if I hadn't heard Piers say something that caught my attention.'

'Well, you've got us all agog now, Tottie: what did he say?' Lex demanded.

'That something – I don't know what – was the only solution, because otherwise, if the truth came out, things could be very difficult for her. Then he said he looked forward to spending more time at Underhill and that it was still her home, after all, so Mark couldn't stop him.'

'That sounds a bit like blackmail to me,' Henry said thoughtfully. 'Did you hear any more?'

'No, because I thought I'd better take the coffee through before they came out. When they did, Sybil was white as a ghost and looked totally trampled, but Piers seemed pleased with himself. Flora insisted they leave as soon as they'd had the coffee and Sybil said she'd started another migraine and went upstairs to take a pill.'

Tottie looked at us all, as if trying to read an easy answer on our faces. 'What does it all mean?'

'I smell a rat,' said Clara. 'A Piers-shaped one.'

'Can he possibly have some hold over Sybil?' I asked.

'I can't imagine what,' said Clara. 'I do suspect he's been sponging on her since George died and that's why she's always short of money, but she might just feel she owes it to him in some way.'

'What are we going to do?' asked Tottie.

'I think we need to have a serious talk with Sybil and get her to open up – and there's another matter we want to talk to her about, too,' she added. 'But let us have a peaceful Christmas first! Then I'm sure we can sort this all out afterwards.'

'Yes, though I think we should try to keep Piers away from Sybil as much as we can until then,' suggested Henry. 'Certainly no more tête-à-têtes.'

Clara checked her watch. 'It's almost time for the carol service.'

'Which carol service?' I asked, puzzled.

'It's on the radio: Nine Lessons and Carols with the choir of King's College, Cambridge,' explained Henry.

'Yes, so do go into the drawing room while I quickly put Tottie in the picture about the night of the Solstice,' urged Clara.

Since there was no way of stopping her telling Tottie, I thought perhaps I'd better put River in the picture too, at the first opportunity. I hoped it wouldn't be too great a shock to him.

Henry switched on the radio just as Tottie and Clara came in, with Teddy following, still lightly dusted with flour or icing sugar from helping Den in the kitchen.

Tottie was carrying a large box and while we were listening to the service, she and Teddy unpacked a set of beautifully carved wooden Nativity figures and a crib and set them up on a wide window ledge.

'It's lovely,' I said, admiring it after the radio was switched off. 'But where's the baby Jesus?'

'He hasn't been born yet,' Teddy told me. 'It's his birthday tomorrow.'

'Of course, silly of me,' I apologized.

Clara told me later that Tottie thought the idea of Sybil attempting to push me over a precipice was ludicrous, and just the product of an overactive imagination.

But River, when I got him alone for a few minutes and told him everything, just said sadly, 'Poor lady! I suspected as much at the Gathering.'

'You *did*? And it would have been poor Meg if she'd succeeded!'

'The Goddess protected you. I saw straight away that you believed you'd been pushed and knew it must be Sybil, for her aura was not right . . . and her expression when she saw you enter the hall for the Gathering was one of pure relief.'

'Well, that's something! Why didn't you tell me?'

'I thought it better to let the pattern work itself out,' he said obscurely, then smiled like a wise but infuriating elf. If he'd been wearing his pointy knitted hat, I'd have been tempted to ram it down over his eyes, like those little Scandinavian nisee or tomte gnomes.

'Violence is never the answer,' he added, though whether he was continuing his original train of thought or had read my mind, I had no way of knowing.

Clara

This next part of my memoir deals with more current events although, as you will see, connected with the past.

Recently our lives took another new and surprising turn when I was struck by an idea that was to have far-reaching consequences.

An old Oxford friend, Professor Priscilla Longridge, had recently had her portrait painted and had crowed about how she intended to leave it to posterity, i.e. the National Portrait Gallery. (This was amusing, since the portrait was such a speaking likeness that I could tell she secretly hated it, even though it was so brilliant that she couldn't reject it!)

But having seen it I felt it would be great fun for Henry and me to have our portraits painted too. I very much liked the way the artist had caught the more crocodilian aspects of Pookie Longridge's face. She was the artist for me and since I had to be in London to give a talk, I thought I would arrange the matter at the same time, though this proved slightly more difficult than I had anticipated.

However, in the end all was arranged and within a couple of days Meg Harkness, a delightful young woman, was established at the Red House and beginning the first of our portraits.

She soon became one of the family. Indeed, both Henry and I felt from the start that there was something oddly familiar about her unusually pale colouring and light, almost turquoise eyes.

But it was only when I reached that part of my memoirs dealing with my first year at Oxford that the penny dropped and I slowly came to realize that she must be the granddaughter of Nessa Cassidy and Henry's brother, George.

How strange are the twists of fate that brought us all together!

37

Gifted

Sybil came down looking as if this might be her last meal before doing a Nurse Cavell next morning, rather than an enjoyable family Christmas Eve dinner.

She had applied a brave red lipstick, but entirely forgotten to change out of her breeches, so that a faint but not unpleasant fragrance of horse hung about her.

I preferred that to the unsettling perfume.

Everyone was very kind to her, as if she was ill . . . which I suppose she was, or at least had been at the point where she attempted to kill me. But I, too, found myself talking gently to her about innocuous subjects, like favourite honeys and the way bees danced to communicate with one another.

'As a written language, that could present some interesting translation problems,' said Clara.

'Bees don't have hands,' Teddy pointed out. 'I don't see how they could write.'

'It would certainly make things difficult for them,' agreed Henry.

Den joined us for dinner, but then said he was off to his flat afterwards, since he'd marked a full evening's TV viewing in his *Radio Times*. 'And I've got a tub of Cheese Footballs and some Twiglets, 'aven't I?'

'The old ones are the best,' commented Henry, though I thought it was odd that a man who could whip up delicious party savouries would prefer bought snacks himself.

Teddy grew steadily more excited as the evening progressed and I didn't see how he'd ever calm down enough to go to sleep that night.

We listened to Henry read the second half of *A Christmas Carol*, then Lex, Zelda and I played Monopoly with Teddy until he began to flag a little.

'Time to get the snack ready for Santa and the reindeer?' suggested Tottie eventually.

A mince pie, two carrots and a small glass of whisky were laid out on a pedestal table by the fireplace, and Lex promised he'd be sure to extinguish every last ember of the fire, long before Santa was due to descend the chimney.

Teddy was finally persuaded to go to bed and Tottie took him up, but not before he'd issued his commands: 'Mummy has to come too and sing "Little Donkey", then Uncle Henry can read the special book.'

'Special book?' I asked.

'*The Night Before Christmas* by Clement Clarke Moore,' explained Henry. 'Do you know it?'

'No,' I said.

'I'll bring it down with me afterwards and then you can read it. It's a lovely little story.'

When he was called upstairs to perform this annual rite, Clara said cheerfully, 'There we are, then: we're on the last lap before the big day! Just the presents to arrange and Teddy's stocking to fill.'

'I did love filling Mark's stocking when he was a little boy,' Sybil said. 'It seems odd not being with him on Christmas Eve . . . or when he opens his gifts in the morning.'

'But he'll be here for Christmas dinner,' said Clara. 'River, do drink Santa's whisky and eat the mince pie if you fancy them. We can return the carrots to the kitchen. Teddy won't notice.'

'I've never had a Christmas stocking,' I said. 'Do you hang it on the end of his bed?'

'No, Teddy hangs his on the outside door handle to his room and Santa then fills it and hangs it on the inside.'

'That way, you don't have to wait hours for him to fall asleep before you fill his stocking,' said Lex, then added, 'It's odd that though Zelda and I never hang our stockings up any more, Santa still keeps leaving them.'

He grinned at Clara, who remained deadpan.

Zelda and Tottie came down and Henry soon followed, carrying a large, knitted stocking with a red velvet ribbon loop at the top.

'Fast asleep,' he reported. 'I barely finished reading the book and he was off.'

He handed me *The Night Before Christmas*, an illustrated version, and I read it with interest: I could see why it had annual appeal.

The presents were brought out and Teddy's ranged around the tree in the drawing room, while ours went under the one in the hall.

We all added our own contributions and there was something for everyone . . . including, to my surprise, Piers.

'We had a couple of spare bottles of whisky in the larder, so we thought we'd let him have one,' said Henry. 'Deirdre runs the alcohol stocks down for autumn at the guesthouse, so he's probably down to a choice of crème de menthe or Curaçao by now.'

'It'll keep him quiet when they get back to the guesthouse on Christmas Day, and give Flora a little peace,' agreed Clara.

In a generous moment, I'd wrapped a jar of humbugs up for Rollo. He was full of humbug, but I didn't think he'd get the joke. I didn't feel the need to give anything to Flora . . . though perhaps I already had, in the form of Rollo, if she'd got a grip on him and could negotiate a deal with the Mother Dragon.

The gaudily wrapped presents added the final festive touch to the scene: the fairy lights twinkling on the trees, the spice and cinnamon smell of baking and the fragrance of pine underlying all.

I could feel the magic seeping into my bones and the house itself seemed mysteriously to be expectantly waiting for something.

I didn't understand any of it, but on some level I *got* it – and I was hooked!

Hello, my name is Meg and I'm addicted to Christmas . . .

To my surprise, River had thrown himself into the whole thing, too, and I thought a few new elements might creep into the Farm's Solstice ceremony and the Feast next year.

In the drawing room, Clara, Tottie and Zelda began stuffing Teddy's stocking. The traditional tangerine went in the toe, where it made a satisfying full stop of a bump; then a net bag of chocolate coins and one huge penny in a round tin, which Zelda had bought in Fortnum and Mason.

She also contributed a pencil case shaped like an Egyptian sarcophagus and a small model of the cat god, Bast. Tottie's additions were a pink sugar mouse, a retro ray gun that made a noise and flashed lights and a small paper accordion. I thought we might all come to regret that last one.

To finish, Clara pushed in one of the *Horrible History* paperbacks and then my beanie dragon, with his purple corduroy head poking out of the top.

We all agreed that it looked *very* exciting and, more to the point, would keep Teddy occupied for a while, after he woke up at some unearthly hour of the morning.

Henry was dispatched to hang this on the inside of Teddy's door, first donning an ancient and tattered red Santa jacket and a pair of spectacles with white beard and moustache attached.

'We really must replace this,' Henry said, cinching red folds in round his narrow waist with a black belt.

'It'll look fine, if Teddy wakes up, which he won't,' said Clara.

'And he didn't stir,' reported Henry, coming back down with an air of relief.

In fact, there was now a general feeling of unwinding and we broke out the mead and mince pies.

Henry, Clara, Sybil and River settled down to mah-jong while the rest of us played Scrabble, though Zelda wasn't concentrating. I guessed where her mind was from her dreamy expression.

I *really* wanted to beat Lex, though I don't know why, but my letters kept forming themselves into words so rude, I simply couldn't bring myself to use them, even when they'd have got me the triple word score.

We wished each other happy Christmas at midnight with a toast of elderflower champagne, and then Tottie popped the baby Jesus into his crib in the Nativity scene before she and Sybil went up to bed.

Lex had volunteered to let the dogs out for a last run in the garden again and I went with him for a breath of air before I went to bed. It was very still out there, just glimmering snow and darkest indigo skies, studded with a million stars.

The dogs raced around as if the cold had sent them crazy, and a window over the garage, from which the light of a TV flickered and glowed, was flung open. Then a voice called, ''Appy Christmas and Gord bless Tiny Tim!'

'Happy Christmas, Den!' I called back, laughing, and the window closed again.

Lex was throwing snowballs for the dogs to chase, though they broke into pieces the moment they caught them.

I looked back up at the stars. I thought I could feel the world turning and planets moving in their ordained paths . . .

Something light and cold touched my face.

'Snowflakes are fallen feathers from angels' wings,' Lex said whimsically, then spoiled the effect somewhat by adding, 'I heard Flora telling that to Teddy once. But if it was true, then there'd be a lot of bald angels circling over Starstone Edge.'

'Chilly bald angels,' I agreed.

'How are you enjoying your first Christmas so far?' he asked, sending the dogs racing after another snowball.

'It's certainly different from anything I've *ever* experienced before,' I said truthfully.

I woke very early on Christmas morning with a strange sense of anticipation. I could understand Teddy's feelings entirely now! It was still dark, so I switched on the bedside light . . . and immediately spotted that there was something hanging on the handle of my door!

It was a long, knitted sock, to which had been roughly sewn a ribbon loop. It bulged enticingly.

I stared at it . . . and then I remembered Clara's insistence last night that she was still so wide awake that she intended working for an hour or two before she went to bed . . . and Lex saying earlier that he and Zelda still got Christmas stockings. Now *I* had one, too!

I fetched it, got back into bed, then began to delve into it. The contents were loosely wrapped in light green tissue paper and out came Clara's latest paperback, personally signed to me, a small bottle of Tottie's mead, a chocolate orange, a set of tiny Mexican worry dolls and a very pretty long silk scarf, marbled in shades of green, that I was sure I'd seen in Preciousss.

In the toe was a tangerine, which I ate, then went across to the bathroom to wash the citrus off my hands.

On the way back there was a thudding of bare feet as Teddy hurtled down the landing, hissing loudly, 'Meg! Meg!'

'Shhh!' I warned him. 'It's still very early and I think everyone's asleep.'

'I know. I've already tried Lex, Mummy and Tottie,' he said disgustedly. 'I'm glad you're not, though, because I want to show you what was in my stocking!'

'I had one too,' I told him, getting back into bed.

'Lex and Mummy always get one. Santa mustn't have realized you've all grown up.'

He made a nest of the eiderdown that had been folded across the end of my bed and emptied out his treasures.

Of course, I already knew what was in there, but I pretended I didn't. Like me, he'd eaten his tangerine, but also the bag of chocolate coins, which had been reduced to empty foil cases.

'We've both done pretty well, Teddy, haven't we?' I said finally, looking at my watch. 'I think I could decently have a shower and go downstairs, now.'

'Everyone has to get up soon, because I'm not allowed to open my presents till we've had breakfast – and I can't wait!'

'I know what you mean,' I admitted. 'The stocking was an unexpected surprise, but now I want to see what's in those other parcels under the tree with my name on them!'

'I bet Den's in the kitchen by now,' he said, sliding off the bed. 'I'll go and see. Then I can show him my stocking, too!'

'Good idea, but after that I'd come back up and get washed and dressed, Teddy—'

But he'd vanished before I'd finished.

I showered and came back to my room to find Pansy waiting inside. And unless she'd learned to open and close doors, somebody must have let her in. She was trying to chew something attached to her collar, but abandoned the attempt in order to greet me with near hysterical pleasure.

'What's that on your collar, Pansy?' I asked, picking her up to look – and found a slightly chewed, though still legible, cardboard tag, which read:

To Meg,

Wishing you a very happy Christmas.

If you accept Pansy as my gift, I'll know you really have forgiven me.

Lex xx

I stared at it, especially those two kisses at the end.

'Did Lex put you in my room?' I asked Pansy, and she wriggled till I put her down and then ran to the door, looking back at me as if inviting me to follow. When I opened it, I was somehow not surprised to find Lex standing on the other side, as if uncertain how his present had been received. I left him in no doubt.

'Oh, Lex, thank you!' I said with heartfelt gratitude. 'You couldn't have given me anything I wanted more than Pansy – but she was so expensive. You really shouldn't have!'

'Sybil gave me a family discount,' he said with that familiar, sharp smile. 'So . . . you'll accept her and my apologies for the past?'

'Of course I will. There's nothing left to forgive. It was all a misunderstanding and we're friends again now, aren't we?'

On impulse, I stood on tiptoe to kiss his cheek, but instead our lips met . . . and then I was lost again in his arms, which held me close.

'Uncle Lex! Uncle Lex! Are you coming downstairs?' called Teddy's voice and we fell apart, staring at each other. My heart seemed to be doing some kind of gymnastic routine and I was having trouble breathing.

'We'll have to stop meeting like this,' Lex said, his voice sounding strange.

Teddy came to a halt in front of us and demanded, 'Why were you kissing Meg? There isn't any mistletoe up here and anyway, I think that kind of thing's soppy.'

'*I* kissed Lex to say thank you for giving me Pansy for Christmas.'

'You mean, she's all yours *for ever*?'

I nodded. 'Yes, she's a special early present, but if you want to see what *you've* got for Christmas, you'd better go and get dressed, hadn't you? I think everyone's getting up now.'

He shot off and, seeing Lex looking at me with a serious expression, as if he was trying to work something puzzling out, I said quickly, 'I'd better get dressed too – and my hair's drying all over the place, so it's going to look like a pink haystack.'

And I whisked into my room and closed the door, fortunately with Pansy on the inside.

Whoops, I'd done it again! I mean, apart from that brief kiss Lex had given me in the car on the night of the Solstice, a friendly salute to mark the end of hostilities, *I* seemed to be the one making the first moves, though he wasn't exactly pushing me away when I did.

Did that mean he still had some feelings for me? I knew now that if I let myself, I could fall really hard for Lex. But even if he felt the same way, could we *allow* ourselves to fall in love when the ghost of the past would be forever haunting us?

38

Entirely Engaged

I had to damp my hair again before I could do anything with it, then took a while dressing in my new jewel-coloured patchwork corduroy dress in honour of the day, before going downstairs with my very own dog at my heels.

Everyone was now down and a space was made for me at the table. *I'm sitting here with my family*, I suddenly thought. *My* new *family.*

In the general confusion of thank yous for the stockings, and Sybil telling everyone how she'd been sworn to secrecy by Lex when he'd bought Pansy for me, there was no time for introspection.

The New Zealand branch of the family rang while we were still in the kitchen – Clara's sister, Bridget, and her husband, Lex and Zelda's parents, were spending Christmas at their elder son, Christopher's, house and the phone was passed around the table.

After that, Teddy didn't let us linger long in the kitchen and we carried our coffee through into the drawing room, where he was finally allowed to open his presents, while a CD of carols played quietly in the background.

There was a frenzy of paper-ripping, though Tottie sat nearby and listed who had given him the various gifts, so that Teddy could write thank-you notes later.

Lex and Den brought in our presents from the hall and soon we all had a little heap next to us, even River, the unexpected guest.

Teddy ran over with each new treasure to show us and, if the giver was there, to thank him or her.

The castle from Clara and Henry, with the dragon family provided by Den, was greeted with ecstasy. Then the art box from me, and a folding artist's easel and a pack of small canvases from Lex . . . jigsaws, books, puzzles and games . . . Soon the floor around the tree was piled high with his spoils and he was down to the last few. By then, he was wearing the geologist's goggles that were one of Zelda's presents to him, along with the pirate's hat from the game he'd so much wanted.

'Look,' he said, 'Daddy's sent me a light-up sword and a picture of his friends.'

It was a *Star Wars* light sabre and the picture was a signed one of some of the cast. One of Daddy's friends was *extremely* hairy.

'I expect Daddy will ring you later, Teddy,' said Clara. 'They're several hours behind us there, I think.'

'Radnor's got a wife and family over there. They were separated when I met him, then got together as soon as he went back,' Zelda confided to me in a low voice, though Teddy had gone back to his presents and probably wouldn't have heard her if she'd shouted through a megaphone.

We were sitting on the same sofa, our heaps of presents between us, and she'd just put on a pair of earrings with dangling silver llamas and was looking at herself in a jewelled pocket mirror, another gift.

'He didn't believe Teddy was his until the DNA test proved it, but he does keep in contact with him now; just birthdays and Christmas really, though.'

'I suppose that's better than no contact, and at least Teddy knows who his father is.'

'Yes, I've always been *entirely* open with him,' said Zelda, earnestly. Then, after a pensive moment when she was clearly following some inner thought, she added dreamily, 'Mark said he'd try and come over early.'

Teddy's last present, a small rectangular one, was a joint gift from Tottie and Sybil. Inside was a framed photograph of a sturdy brown pony with a long mane and tail.

'That's Conker,' explained Tottie. 'He's an Exmoor and he's coming here on long loan at half-term to be your pony.'

'You can graze him with my horses, like we did with the Shetland we borrowed,' said Sybil. 'In fact, he's coming from the same friends, whose youngest has just outgrown him.'

'I'll buy you a new riding hat and paddock boots when he arrives,' promised Tottie.

'And *we'll* cover any insurance and vet's bills,' said Clara. 'What a lovely idea!'

Teddy was so delighted by this that after a speechless moment he was moved to kiss both Sybil and Tottie, despite his earlier assertion that such goings-on were soppy.

Then Lex helped him gather up all the discarded wrapping, so that we didn't feel adrift in a sea of lurid Santas, reindeer, snowflakes and penguins.

Teddy settled down on the floor with a jigsaw puzzle of the Rosetta Stone and a chocolate selection box, while we all finished our own unwrapping in peace.

Clara had a lovely long string of chunky real amber beads from Henry, to whom she gave a cashmere jumper in the same colour as his eyes. My sketches seemed to be a hit with everyone and River was pleased with the book about ley lines that I'd bought him.

It became increasingly obvious that several shopping sorties had been made to Preciousss over the last few days, as a stream of pretty, useful or just interestingly bizarre items emerged from their wrappings.

River had chosen a theme and stuck to it for his offerings: everyone got a small smooth pebble painted in Gothic script with words like 'Blessings', 'Peace' and 'Tranquillity'. Mine said 'Love'. He'd also brought me a pair of long blue velvet gloves in an Elizabethan gauntlet style, the cuffs quilted and sewn with pearls, which had been made by one of the craftworkers at the Farm.

To Teddy, he gave a set of reed panpipes, and since he'd already demonstrated the paper accordion several times, I could see we were in for a noisy Christmas, though the breathy sound of the pipes was definitely the less irritating of the two.

Tottie had also given everyone the same thing, a knitted rainbow scarf, though she pointed out that she'd helpfully sewn on name labels so we didn't mix them up.

Den offered to swap his new leather driving gloves for the velvet gauntlets, but he was only joking. He had the hands-free torch that Lex had given him strapped around his head, the light like a kind of bright Cyclops eye in the middle of his forehead.

I'd kept the bag from the Farm till the last. It held a terracotta ocarina, a small, hand-turned bowl made of sycamore wood, a pair of moonstone and pearl earrings, and various hand-made face creams, bath lotions and hand balm. The craftworkers at the Farm were very diverse in the things they made.

But finally, the unwrapping was done, the paper collected and tidied away, the dogs calmed down – they'd had special

Christmas chews – and we could have more coffee and relax for a while.

When Den and River went off later to make a start on dinner, I helped Tottie to lay the dining table, now extended as far as it would go, to accommodate the extra guests.

There was a special crimson damask tablecloth and a long runner embroidered with snowflakes and gold tassels hanging down at each end.

When the shining cutlery, festive paper napkins and crackers were all laid out, I thought it looked quite perfect. Tottie added the centrepiece, a real log decorated with holly, snowy cotton wool and glitter, which Teddy had made at school.

Lex suggested he and I take the dogs out after that, before our guests arrived, and we took them down the fields at the back of the house, where the snow still lay in drifts. We didn't talk and I wished I knew what he was thinking about our earlier kiss . . . if he was thinking about it at all. But our silence was companionable and at one point, when I slipped and nearly fell, he took my hand and didn't release it till he had to open the gate on the way back.

We dried off the dogs in the garden hall before we let them into the rest of the house: legs and tummies, in Wisty and Pansy's case, but *all* of Lass, since she'd been rolling in the snow.

Mark must have arrived early, because he, Zelda and Henry emerged from his study just as we had shut the still slightly damp dogs into the kitchen. I thought perhaps he'd been showing them the latest additions to his bauble collection. One of them, shaped like a hot-air balloon with a basket beneath, had especially taken my fancy.

Just before half past one, Flora drove up in her aunt's car with Rollo and Piers.

Rollo looked pale and interesting after his illness – a look he'd spent his entire life striving to achieve – and had a tendency to gaze adoringly at Flora.

I was relieved to see he seemed subdued, and when introduced to Henry, shook hands in a quiet and respectful manner before seating himself next to Flora. I suspected she'd given him instructions.

Piers, who was a little glassy-eyed, glanced uneasily at Flora and then drifted hopefully towards the drinks cabinet at the other end of the room.

'Piers *would* insist on a drink before we came,' Flora told us in a low voice. 'And his hands shake a lot, so I think he's a near-alcoholic! He's finished the last of the Bombay gin now and at this rate his bar bill alone is going to be into three figures before he leaves.'

'He's an awful old man, but you manage him wonderfully well, darling,' Rollo said adoringly.

Darling? That was quick work!

Flora gave me a complacent – even smug – sideways smile, a marmoset Mona Lisa.

'You're so sweet, Rollo,' she cooed.

Lex leaned over the back of the sofa and murmured in my ear, 'Love is in the air, and not just Zelda and Mark! Flora already seems to have her claws firmly into Rollo.'

I turned my head and looked up at him. 'She doesn't hang about, does she?' I whispered.

'At least it doesn't look as if he'll make a nuisance of himself with Henry, so if we can keep Piers from getting near Sybil, everything should be fine.'

There had been no room for Piers on the sofa next to Sybil, when he returned from the drinks cabinet, having helped himself uninvited to a whisky, for she had Tottie on one side and

River on the other. I could hear snatches of their conversation: River seemed to be translating the strange symbols round the hem of his purple tunic to them, with occasional interpolations from Clara, sitting opposite.

Piers had had to settle for the less-favoured man-eating sofa, and when Den beat the gong for dinner it didn't want to disgorge him. It must have spat him out eventually, though, because he arrived in the dining room just as we were taking our seats around the table, at Clara's direction.

Sybil was placed at the opposite end to Piers and next to River, while Piers was safely corralled between Lex and Mark. The old convention of alternating male and female guests was not something Clara went in for anyway.

In honour of the occasion, we drank rich ruby elderberry wine with our dinner, with lemonade for Teddy. Piers took a sip of his wine and pulled a face, then drained the rest in one.

That was no way to treat something so delicious. I bet River asked Tottie for the recipe later.

We pulled the crackers, which were the ones Teddy had chosen at the Friendship Mill and contained small vintage wind-up cars, hats and jokes.

Everyone, even Piers, put on their paper crowns and read out the bad jokes while we were eating our hot mini salmon en croûte. Then Lex and River helped Den bring in the main course: the large, capon-shaped nut roast had turned out perfectly and sat on a lordly willow-patterned platter. It was flanked by dishes of glistening golden-brown roast potatoes, sprouts, bread sauce, glazed carrots, and a large blue and white striped jug of thick gravy. There were jars of relish too, including the Fiery Fiesta chilli one I'd brought with me. I hoped the picture of a red chilli wearing devil horns and holding a pitchfork on the label would warn everyone about the strength of the contents.

The elderberry wine was obviously strong too, for after Henry filled Piers' glass a second time, his nose and cheeks became even redder and his eyes more glazed.

The curtains were drawn to gain the full effect of the flaming Christmas pudding when it was carried in. I'd never actually eaten it before and it was very rich and solid, served with white sauce and brandy butter. I could have had trifle instead, but I thought the pudding would be worth experiencing, even if I had indigestion for a week after this crowning moment of gluttony.

At the end, when the plates had been cleared, champagne glasses were put out and a bottle of Tottie's elderflower champagne poured for a toast.

'Happy Christmas, everyone,' said Henry, and we all echoed him and clinked glasses. Then he tapped a spoon against the bottle for silence and said he had a second toast to propose: 'I'm delighted to say that Zelda and Mark are engaged.'

This was unexpectedly fast, though of course not really a surprise to most of us except Teddy, who stared at his mother, brow wrinkled, as if trying to work out the implications of this news.

We all offered our congratulations. Then Flora called down the table to Henry, in her sweet, carrying voice, 'You have another toast to propose too – Rollo asked me to marry him earlier today!'

Rollo took her hand. 'Yes, this wonderful woman has agreed to take me on!'

That sounded more like she'd accepted the position of his nanny, but then, I suppose in a way she had because she must have grasped what he was like by now: needy, self-obsessed and not quite as talented as he thought he was.

'We knew we were right for each other from the moment we met, didn't we, Rollo?' she said.

'We did and now I've told Mother our news, she's longing to meet you even more than before,' he agreed.

Good luck with that one, Flora, I thought, but maybe she'd be equal to the task.

'Good heavens, that was quick!' said Tottie, and I thought Zelda and Mark looked slightly put out at sharing their special moment.

Henry hastily proposed the toast. 'Rollo and Flora!'

'Rollo and Flora!' we all echoed, except Piers, who had remained slumped silently in his chair, drinking the elderflower champagne in small sips as if it was medicine.

By now the proceedings finally seemed to percolate through to what was left of his brain, for his eyes suddenly focused on Sybil at the far end of the table, whose hand River was squeezing as he murmured in her ear – probably assuring her that the Goddess had arranged the union of Zelda and Mark and would pour blessings down upon their heads – and he said loudly and commandingly, '*Sybil!*'

She started and turned her head to stare at him like a rabbit in the headlights.

'I believe *we* also have something to celebrate, my dear, do we not?'

Sybil turned ashen and her mouth opened and closed silently.

'Sybil and I decided yesterday to tie the knot, for why live apart when we can live together?' Piers said, only slightly slurring the words. 'We will be able to divide our time between Underhill and my flat in Chelsea, the best of both worlds.'

The reaction to this announcement was not quite in the same league as the previous two. In fact, there was a stunned silence, broken only when Mark stared at his mother aghast and demanded to know if this was true.

'You can't possibly want to marry Piers, Mum!'

'Why wouldn't she?' said Piers. 'I'm a damned good catch.'

'Piers did . . . *suggest* it yesterday, when we had a little chat, Mark,' she faltered. 'But I – I mean, I didn't say . . . nothing was *decided*. And . . .'

She wrung her hands, which I'd never actually seen anyone do before, until River reclaimed the nearest one and patted it soothingly.

'Since your announcement seems to have taken Sybil entirely by surprise, Piers, perhaps we should postpone *your* celebrations for another time,' said Clara drily. 'Let tonight just be for the young ones.'

Piers glared at Sybil and she shrank back towards River, which hardly poured oil on the waters.

'I thought we were in agreement yesterday that it was the best thing to do,' Piers said. 'But perhaps we can have a few moments together now, so I can make my proposal in form.'

'I doubt there's any form you can make it in that she's likely to accept, Piers,' said Clara. 'So, come on, everyone, let's all go into the drawing room.'

Henry turned to Piers and said cunningly, 'I believe there's a present for you under the tree in the hall and it looks remarkably like a bottle of whisky.'

Love – or whatever it was – went out of the window as Piers almost knocked his chair over in his eagerness to get his hands on this unexpected prize.

Lex and I helped Den clear the table and load the dishwasher, to the accompaniment of Mark declaring to Zelda that he'd never let his mother marry Piers and he'd certainly never live under his roof.

He sounded very feudal and lord of the manor. You could practically see the generations of squires lining up behind him, ready to horse-whip someone.

'Oh, I agree with you, darling,' Zelda said. 'But I'm sure she doesn't want to marry him at all.'

Clara arrived in search of the coffee and, shutting the door behind her, leaned against it and said dramatically, 'What an ending to the dinner!'

'What's happening out there?' Lex asked.

'Tottie and River have got Sybil between them on the sofa again, so ghastly Piers can't get near her, and Henry gave him a large drink to keep him quiet. Now Rollo's telling Henry about his poetry magazine, but as soon as we've had the coffee, I'll get rid of the guesthouse contingent, though, of course, we don't want to get rid of *you*, Mark.'

'I'd like to get rid of Piers permanently!' he said savagely. 'I can't imagine what on earth Mum is thinking of.'

'Well, as to that, I meant to have a little chat with her after Christmas, because he does seem to have an unhealthy influence over her. But don't worry, because Sybil doesn't *want* to marry him at all. I'll have to bring that little talk with her forward to tomorrow morning and get to the bottom of it all.'

I sincerely hoped the little talk wouldn't also cover the question of whether Sybil had tried to push me off the hill. Really, I thought, it would be best forgotten and I certainly didn't want poor Mark to know about it.

'I'm sure you and Zelda will be very happy, Mark,' Clara said. 'And Flora strikes me as just right for Rollo, don't you think, Meg?'

'Yes, I'm sure she'll turn into a clone of his mother and they'll manage him between them.'

Zelda got up. 'Come on, let's take the coffee through and act out this final scene and then we can all relax.'

The welcome sound of Flora's car receding into the distance was music to our ears. Our farewells had been enthusiastic.

'Thank God they've gone,' said Clara, settling back by the fire with a sigh of satisfaction.

Sybil had vanished up to her room in the flurry of the departure, but Tottie said she was all right and would be down later.

'But she can't possibly want to marry that man.'

'No, of course she doesn't. He must be holding some threat over her head but we'll find out what it is tomorrow, before the party. I don't want to upset Sybil any more tonight.'

'I'll come over early, then,' said Mark.

'Really, darling, it's hardly worth your going back to Underhill,' said Clara. 'You might as well have come to stay when Sybil did.'

'I know, but I hadn't factored in falling for Zelda when it was arranged,' he said, his scowl dispelled by an engaging grin.

'I've given you lots of help peeling wallpaper off, so I haven't held the renovations up,' pointed out Zelda.

'I don't like Piers,' announced Teddy, looking up from his castle. The towers had tiny lights inside and one of the dragon family was sitting on the tallest.

'You have very good taste,' said Lex.

The landline rang and it was Radnor Vane, calling to wish Teddy a happy Christmas. Teddy thanked him for his gifts and said, with the frankness of childhood, that he liked them much better than the Mickey Mouse slippers.

After this call, Teddy was quiet for quite a while and must have been thinking, for he suddenly asked if he would have to live at Underhill if his mummy married Mark.

His tone made it clear that he was not keen on the idea. Zelda, slightly taken aback, said that she and Mark would be so busy getting the business up and running that he'd probably stay at the Red House for the immediate future.

'I expect eventually you'll have a bedroom there as well as here and can divide your time between the two,' suggested Henry, and Teddy cheered up.

Mark left after we'd had a simple supper of Welsh rarebit followed by trifle or Christmas cake, Den having long since retired to his flat and his telly for a well-deserved rest.

Teddy was distinctly flagging by then and made no objection to going to bed early, so long as he could take a selection of his favourite presents upstairs with him.

I went into the studio to email Fliss and wish her happy Christmas, then told her about the two engagements, especially the amazingly speedy one of Rollo and Flora.

> She pinged one right back: There's still one romantic lead left in this rom com, and we all know who he is!

And I hadn't even told her about Pansy, or the kissing . . .

When I returned to the others, Henry's mind must have been moving along similar lines, because he suddenly announced, channelling Mr Bennet in *Pride and Prejudice*, 'I'm going to my study now, but if any man should come asking for Meg's hand in marriage, I'm entirely at leisure to receive him.'

'I think you'll be quite safe from interruption,' I said, and then caught Lex's eyes on me and went pink, though I hoped no one, including Lex, noticed.

*

On my way to bed I passed Clara on the landing, who had just looked in on Teddy, and thanked her for a wonderful Christmas and all the gifts and the stocking.

'I hope we have many more like it, because you're part of the family now, Meg,' she said, 'even if we do have to share you with your family at the Farm.'

'If you talk to Sybil in the morning, you won't mention about what happened at the Solstice, will you?' I asked anxiously.

'I might, if it helps me to get to the root of what's happening with her,' she said. 'This Shakespearian comedy of errors needs all the knots untangling, and the sooner, the better.'

Then she startled me by saying warmly, 'I'm so happy that you and Lex have become such good friends! I realized there must have been some misunderstanding in the past and that you'd finally cleared it up. I haven't seen him so much like his old self for years. Bless you for that, Meg.'

I felt myself blushing again, but fortunately the landing lights were quite dim. I had my tapestry bag slung over my shoulder and suddenly, something made me remember the letter that Flower had given me to deliver to Clara.

I rooted round in the bottom of the bag under the iPad, a sketchbook and a dozen other odds and ends, and apologetically proffered an even more crumpled envelope.

'I'm so sorry, I entirely forgot about this! It went to Preciousss by mistake with their post and Flower gave it to me to bring back.'

'Oh, not to worry. I see it's from America and probably one of those long round robins from an old acquaintance, because anything important seems to come by email these days.'

She kissed my cheek. 'Goodnight, dear Meg: we are so glad you are a Doome!'

39

A Family Affair

None of us was up early next day, except Clara, who emerged from her study to join us at breakfast and seemed to be in an unusually quiet and thoughtful frame of mind.

As soon as we'd finished, she said that she wanted us all to come into the drawing room for a big family pow-wow and that Mark would be arriving at any moment to join us.

This didn't sound at all like the quiet little talk she had proposed having with Sybil and I wondered what on earth was to come. Would she bring up my fall and our suspicions about Sybil being responsible?

'I want *all* of you there, though Den, perhaps you wouldn't mind staying here with Teddy and we'll fill you in later?'

'All right by me. Got to get the food ready fer this bleedin' party, 'aven't I? And I need Teddy to 'elp me.'

Teddy, who had been looking as if he would object, now subsided.

'We have a couple of hours until the first guests arrive,' said Henry. 'Plenty of time.'

'This is all very mysterious,' said Sybil, looking nervous.

'I'd better stay here, too,' River suggested.

'No, River, I think we might need you,' Clara said, and he obediently followed the rest of us into the drawing room. 'Family' seemed to be as infinitely flexible a term to the Doomes as it was at the Farm.

I looked at Lex as we went in and he smiled reassuringly at me, which made me feel a little better.

Mark had just arrived, and he and Zelda perched together on the window seat, while the rest of us spread out on the sofas and chairs before the fire, which was laid, but not yet lit. River discreetly removed himself to a more distant seat.

'There we are, and you're probably all wondering what this is about,' said Clara. 'Henry and I have had some unexpected news, which has put a fresh complexion on some of the things that have been happening lately.'

'Yes, indeed,' he agreed. 'We were going to have a little chat with you this morning anyway, Sybil, but this news has clarified everything no end.'

Sybil gave a great start and looked about her, slightly wildly. 'With *me*?'

'Yes, dear,' Clara said, 'because we'd realized even before Piers announced last night that you were engaged, that he had some hold over you. And given that, despite an ample annuity, you were always broke, we put two and two together and came up with blackmail.'

'But until last night, we didn't know what he'd got on you, as it were,' said Henry, then added gently, as she remained transfixed, 'We know the whole truth now, Sybil.'

'You mean Piers was *blackmailing* you, Mum?' demanded Mark, springing to his feet.

'Oh, no, not at all . . . I mean, he wasn't—' stammered Sybil, incoherently.

Tottie said soothingly, 'It's all right, Syb.'

'Mark, do sit down and just listen for the moment,' said Clara. 'All will be revealed, as they say.'

Mark subsided, glowering.

'Meg gave me a letter last night that had got mixed up with the post for Preciousss, and which she'd subsequently forgotten till that moment.'

Lex, who was seated in a chair just behind me, leaned forward and whispered in my ear, 'Do you know what this is all about?'

I shook my head. He didn't sit back, but continued leaning forward, one arm across the back of my chair, and I was very conscious of him.

'The envelope contained a letter written to me by Nessa Cassidy and found among her papers by her lover after her unfortunate early death in a car crash.'

'It was marked to be forwarded to Clara if anything happened to her,' continued Henry. 'But for various reasons, it wasn't, until now.'

'And just at the right moment, too,' said Clara.

'Well, we're all now agog to know what astounding revelation was contained in this letter,' Lex said. 'Spit it out!'

'Quite simply, it stated that she'd married Henry's brother, George, late in the Michaelmas term of 1959.'

'He . . . married this Nessa?' said Mark, stunned, and I felt my own mind turning over and over like a fruit machine, until it stopped with a resounding thud and more than a couple of lemons.

'Yes. He thought he could get his hands on Nessa's substantial inheritance once they were married, and *she* was a very romantic and silly girl. In the event, after the wedding he discovered she couldn't touch her capital until she was thirty and she found that she was mistaken in her man. Or indeed, in *any* man. They had a furious row and agreed to part and forget the marriage ever happened.'

'Though since it actually had, it made his subsequent marriage to Sybil's mother bigamous,' Henry finished.

That was a curve ball I hadn't been expecting, or anyone else, except Sybil, whose face told a different story.

Henry said, into the stunned silence, 'George had lied about Nessa being of age and other details on the marriage licence and he told her that made it illegal.'

'It only occurred to her later to wonder if it *had* been legal or not,' Clara said. 'Of course, it was, as I'm sure George realized, but I expect he thought no one would ever find out. And he never knew about Nessa's baby.'

'It's all true!' wailed Sybil suddenly. 'I found the certificate among Daddy's papers after he died, though something he'd said towards the end made me wonder . . .'

'But Piers knew?' Lex said.

She nodded. 'He was actually at the wedding and it was his sister's flat they went to afterwards. And then, when Daddy died, Piers told me he knew, but that he'd keep it a secret for my sake, and for Mark's.'

'And then proceeded to blackmail you,' said Tottie. 'What a rotter!'

This old-fashioned term seemed to sum Piers up perfectly: rotten to the core.

'Piers didn't put it like that. It was more that I'd be helping out Daddy's old friend, by having him to stay and—'

'Bleeding you for increasingly large sums of money?' suggested Lex grimly.

'How horrible for you, Sybil,' said Zelda sympathetically. I don't think she'd quite grasped the implications of this news yet, but I had begun to, and I could see from his face that Mark had, too.

'When Meg turned up and we worked out who she was – though of course *we* thought her mother was illegitimate – you realized it would give Piers an even bigger lever for his blackmail,' said Clara.

Tears were now running down Sybil's face and she was wringing her hands. 'Yes, because Meg became such a threat to Mark's inheritance! Since her mother had disappeared years ago I thought *she* was probably dead, so that just left Meg. And then, I thought—'

She came to an abrupt stop and did that hand-wringing thing again, staring at me from wide, anguished blue eyes. Doome eyes.

'Yes, we know what you thought, Sybil,' said Clara. 'That it would be better if you got rid of Meg. So you tried to push her over the steep drop on the bonfire ledge, on the night of the Solstice.'

'What on earth do you mean, Clara?' Mark demanded angrily. 'Mum couldn't possibly have—'

He came to a sudden stop as Sybil just looked up and said quietly to Clara, 'How did you know?'

'I was certain someone had shoved me,' I explained, 'though I'd no idea who. But then, you were wearing that very distinctive perfume again the other night and I realized later that it wasn't the Gathering it was associated with in my mind, but the moment you tried to kill me.'

'You mean, you really *did* try to push Meg off the hill, Mum?' demanded Mark incredulously, going white.

'Now, now, Mark, we're sure it was simply the instantly regretted impulse of the moment,' said Henry soothingly.

'I thought I was protecting you, darling. I was confused and didn't know where to turn,' pleaded Sybil.

'You should have told me the truth the moment you found that wedding certificate. Then none of this would have happened,' Mark told her.

'I . . . expect I should.' Her voice quivered and Tottie put an arm round her shoulders.

'Steady, Syb!' she said, as if Sybil was a nervous horse. It seemed to have the right effect, for she sat up straighter.

'I deeply regret it, Meg. I didn't really mean to do it, but something desperate came over me. It must have been a moment of madness, for I was totally appalled the second I'd done it.'

But not, I thought, appalled enough to stop and see if I actually had fallen over. But then, I suppose the instinct for self-preservation had kicked in and she'd darted off ahead of the others down the path.

'You *must* have been mad, because it would have been a much better idea to try and kill Piers off, instead,' Clara pointed out. 'Still, Lex luckily spotted Meg hanging on to that gorse bush for dear life, and came to her rescue.'

'My hero,' I said to him, trying to lighten the mood.

'I didn't believe anyone had pushed you at first, though, Meg,' he said. 'It seemed so incredible.'

Sybil shuddered and said, 'I went back to Underhill, not knowing what had happened, and it was such a relief when you walked into the Gathering, Meg. And then I thought Mark seemed to be seriously interested in you and that perhaps you'd get married, and then . . . well, that would make everything all right.'

Mark turned slightly pink and Zelda looked at him quizzically.

'Mark and I were only ever friends,' I said.

'I can see why you thought Meg and Mark marrying would be the best solution,' Henry said.

Sybil nodded. 'Even if Piers told everyone the truth about the marriage and Meg's mother being legitimate, it wouldn't matter, would it? Meg would be in her rightful place at Underhill and part of the family.'

'Then *I* turned up for Christmas and spoiled it all,' said Zelda.

'There was nothing to spoil,' I assured her.

'It's not that I don't *want* Mark to marry you, dear, but you can see how easy his marrying Meg instead would have made things,' Sybil told her earnestly.

'Well,' said Tottie thoughtfully, 'what happens now? Would Meg's mother, if she's still alive, be the rightful heir, or Meg, if not?'

'Since I'm the daughter of a bigamous marriage, I think she must be,' said Sybil.

'So Underhill might not be mine after all?' Mark said, looking stricken.

'Not necessarily,' Clara said. 'When Henry and I talked it over last night, after I'd read Nessa's letter, it seemed to us to depend on the terms of George's will.'

'But I don't *want* to claim Underhill, or any part of your inheritance, Mark!' I burst out. 'And nor will Mum.'

'Just as well,' said Henry, 'because George's will was very carefully written; I remember thinking so at the time: he named exactly who was to inherit. And Underhill wasn't entailed, so he could leave it to whoever he wanted. I think Meg or her mother probably *could* have a strong claim to some money from the estate if they went to court, but I'm sure it won't come to that.'

'No, absolutely not,' I declared. 'In fact, when Mum comes back and I explain all this to her, she'll hardly take in the facts.

She only lives in the moment and this story all belongs to the past.'

'But what are we going to do?' said Mark.

'Keep it in the family,' I said firmly, 'and carry on as if that misguided marriage between George and Nessa never took place.'

'I think that's the only sensible way forward,' River agreed, speaking for the first time. 'Nothing need change: Meg has already become a part of your family.'

'Clara and I thought that was the easiest solution, too,' said Henry. 'And Mark needn't think he isn't entitled to the estate, because his grandfather very obviously intended him to inherit it.'

'Piers might tell people, though, in a fit of pique,' suggested Tottie.

'I doubt it. There's the blackmail angle, for one thing,' said Henry. 'And who would he tell? I doubt he has any real friends left, and no passing acquaintance at his club is going to take any notice of his stories. Or not to the extent of searching the wedding registers, at any rate.'

'And since we can arrange it among the family, it's nothing to do with anyone else,' agreed Clara.

'I still don't feel that it's right that—' Mark began, looking pale and stubborn.

'Just think of all those complicated noble families over the years, leaving property to their illegitimate, as well as legitimate offspring,' Henry said.

'And perhaps Meg *will* marry into the family, anyway,' Zelda said brightly. 'What do *you* think, Lex?'

'Now, Zelda, don't tease your brother,' Clara said absently, as I went scarlet under the interested gaze of several pairs of eyes. 'We have to decide now how to handle things at the party – or handle Piers. At this point, we can't really ban him from coming.'

'And I can't hit him, because he's too old,' Mark said, with one of his familiar dark scowls.

'You'd better leave it to me,' Henry told him. 'I'll remove him for a quiet conversation, after which he'll no longer be welcome in this house, or to contact any member of my family.'

Sybil was wearing the sort of expression you see on the faces of people getting off a rollercoaster, though tinged with faint hope.

'There,' Clara said. 'That was just like the denouement at the end of a Poirot novel, wasn't it? Do we all feel better for our complete catharsis?'

'*I* feel like getting into a hole and never coming out,' said poor Sybil. 'I don't know how I can ever look any of you in the face again, especially Meg.'

I found myself assuring her that all was forgotten and forgiven and, in fact, that I really didn't mind her having tried to kill me in the least . . .

River moved to sit next to her on the sofa. 'Meg is quite right: you were momentarily unhinged, after all the stress of the burden you'd been carrying alone. You must be quite exhausted.' Then he suggested that when he returned to the Farm, she go with him for a short visit.

'A change of scene will do you good and you'll receive a very warm welcome,' he added.

'Good idea,' Tottie endorsed, from Sybil's other side.

'I hope you'll visit us too, in the spring, Tottie,' River said. 'Perhaps you and Sybil could come then together.'

'How nice it is to have no more mysteries and misunderstandings,' Clara said cheerfully with one of her widest and most Cheshire Cat smiles. 'Now we can just get back to enjoying Christmas!'

*

The hour of the Boxing Day drinks party approached, and Den and Teddy already had the preparations well in hand: the long table in the hall had been spread with a white cloth and laden with glasses, jugs of orange juice and bottles of elderflower champagne, chilling in a galvanized pail full of ice.

The gate-leg table in the drawing room would bear the paper napkins, plates and platters of cold nibbles, and Den assured us that the hot ones were ready to pop into the oven, once everyone had arrived.

'Teddy's the waiter; 'e'll 'elp carry them round.'

There was just time to tidy ourselves up, attempt to slip back into our right minds, and assume an appropriate expression, before the first of the guests arrived.

By eleven fifteen the rooms were quite full. There had to be even more people there than had made it to the Gathering. The drive and the snowy road verges were lined with vehicles, ranging from tractors to Land Rovers and the battered open-top truck that belonged to Olive Adcock's husband.

There were all the farmers from up the valley and their families, a handful of elderly residents from the village that I hadn't seen before, Bilbo, Flower and the baby, Len Snowball and the Gidneys . . .

I didn't see Flora and her entourage arrive and I was circulating Den's hot 'volley-vaunts' among the throng in the hall, when Lex told me that Rollo, with prompting from Flora, was in the drawing room sucking up to Henry and doing what he called 'a misunderstood young poetic genius' act.

'I know that one, but he's a little too old to carry the role now,' I said. 'Where's Piers?'

'He was trying to get near Sybil, but Henry took him into his study and when they came out, Piers looked pretty sick. I should think he's gone to find a dark corner to lurk in till it's time to go.'

After a while, Henry asked everyone to gather together. Those who couldn't fit in the drawing room crowded round the open door while he raised a toast to Christmas and to old friends, which seemed to mark the official end of the party, because people began to leave.

Clara had been taking her guests into the studio in relays to admire the portraits, and eventually that's where Lex found me, contemplating his picture.

'I thought you might be in here. Have you had enough of people?' he asked anxiously. 'It's been one hell of a day and we're not even halfway through it yet!'

'I'm all right, though I'm not sure I've really taken it all in. But I hope I've put Mark's mind at rest, so that everything carries on exactly like it did before.'

'I think Zelda took him into the library earlier and talked some sense into him.' He looked with critical appreciation at his portrait. 'You've certainly caught me . . . and I could give you a long sitting tomorrow, if you like?'

'Great,' I said, my spirits lightening. 'I hated leaving it even for one day, but there hasn't been a moment till now, and I feel totally wrung out and exhausted. I suppose I should be helping clear up.'

'No, Sybil's expiating her sins in a frenzy of helpfulness, with River and Tottie.'

Someone must have released Pansy from her incarceration in the kitchen, for now she nosed the door open and ran in. I picked her up, somehow soothed and comforted by her warm little body in my arms.

Lex took hold of my shoulders and looked down very seriously at me over her head. 'Are you *sure* you're all right? You're happy to just let go any claim on Underhill, or your real place in the family?'

'Yes, totally,' I assured him. 'I'd like us all to forget that marriage certificate ever existed. It was all a mistake anyway.'

'You're a very sweet and kind person, Meg Harkness,' he said, and after kissing me lightly, let me go and went out of the room.

I escaped upstairs without seeing anyone else and fell asleep on the bed with Pansy, the ultimate comfort blanket.

When I woke up I felt *much* better: it was as if the past I'd been told about had been just a play I'd seen, and nothing to do with me. The curtain had fallen and now we could carry on with our lives . . . wherever they took us.

Mine would presumably be in a little cottage somewhere and I'd only see Lex when I visited the Red House: Clara wasn't likely to let me escape the family orbit now that she'd found me.

I discovered I was hungry and we went down to find everyone except Zelda and Mark in the drawing room, drinking tea and consuming leftover canapés.

'There you are, dear,' said Clara. 'Lex, Henry and Teddy took Wisty and Lass out for a run earlier, before it got dark, but we thought Pansy must be with you.'

'We were both asleep,' I said, taking my cup and helping myself to a cheese and tomato tartlet and an Eggwina.

'It's starting to thaw in earnest,' said Henry. 'I'm sure the road to Thorstane will be open again tomorrow.'

'You're not leaving yet, though, are you?' Teddy asked me with flattering concern.

'No, I've got Lex's portrait to finish first.'

'And there's no rush anyway,' said Lex, moving over to sit beside me on the sofa.

'Zelda's gone back with Mark. She thought it would be a good idea not to leave him alone tonight, since everything's been a bit of a shock to him. She's a dear girl,' said Sybil. 'She says Mark has given up the hotel idea and they're redecorating my old bedroom for when I return.'

If, as seemed likely, Zelda was staying at Underhill overnight, I hoped she liked ham . . .

'Piers will go scuttling off back to London as fast as he can,' Henry said. 'He didn't know what to do with himself when I told him we knew what he'd been doing and threatened to inform the police if he ever bothered any of us again.'

'There,' said River to Sybil, with one of his tranquil smiles. 'It's all turned out very well.'

It wasn't quite ended yet, but there *was* a sense of a journey undertaken and successfully accomplished.

'I love a party, but how nice it is to be just *us* again!' Clara's happy gaze encompassed family, visiting pagan, would-be murderess and Den, who was eating three cheese straws at once, while assisting Teddy to construct a 3-D triceratops out of slotted wooden pieces.

'A little more work on my memoirs before dinner, I think,' she added.

'And I,' said Henry resolutely, 'will press the button marked "Send" and dispatch my book to my agent as a slightly late Christmas present.'

Life at the Red House had begun to return to its familiar pattern.

Later, Lex helped Teddy set up his easel in the studio, where he laid out his new paints and embarked on his first portrait on canvas. I was the sitter on the dais this time, which was a novelty.

Lex stayed, sitting in one of the battered armchairs and vatching proceedings, with Pansy curled on his knees.

Teddy seemed to have turned into an even quicker painter han I was and had just told me that he'd finished when I ıeard the phone ring, and Clara's voice from the study next loor, so she must have picked it up. Then, a few moments later, vhile I was admiring my likeness (*very* pink hair, slightly green ace), it rang again and this time she came to fetch me.

'Meg, it's a call for you. Do take it in my study.'

'For me?' I asked, following her. 'I suppose I've left my phone urned off again and Oshan or someone from the Farm is rying to get hold of me. I hope nothing's happened.'

'I'm sure it hasn't, darling, or they'd have asked for River,' he said. 'There's the phone, on the desk.'

'Oshan?' I said, picking it up.

'Is that you, Meg?' said a faint and faraway sweet voice that vas instantly familiar and most definitely *not* Oshan's.

'Mum?' I exclaimed incredulously and out of the corner of ny eye saw the door close behind Clara.

Clara

Late on Christmas Day, I was given a letter sent from America b Nessa's former lover, Suzanne Dell, which was to throw a new light on past events.

She had found among Nessa's papers an envelope to b forwarded to me in the event of her death. Of course, she hadn been able to resist opening it and then, fired by jealous induced by the first paragraph, suppressed it. But now, with onl weeks to live herself, she had finally sent it on. I will present i here in full.

Dear Clara,

If you get this I will be dead, though I hope you will still be hale and hearty and enjoying life as much as ever. You will probably be horrified to learn that you were the love of my life, something I only realized long after my ghastly mistake with George.

Making a clean break with the past was the best thing I could have done, and I have been happily settled with my lover, Suzanne Dell, since I met her at college after the move.

I'm writing this letter, because I have something I want to share and you are the only person I feel I can tell.

Cast your mind back to that weekend in London when George took advantage of me. I told you the truth about this incident, just not the whole of it.

I was a naïve, romantic idiot and had convinced myself we were in love. But in fact, I was in love with the idea of love and in denial about my true sexuality.

However, the moment we arrived in London he announced that he had arranged for us to be married at a registry office that morning! He gave me no time to think, but swept me off my feet and, before I knew it, I was coming out of some anonymous Victorian building as Mrs George Doome.

But it was all some horrible mistake, as we discovered back at the flat. There was nothing loving about what happened then . . . and it was a moment of blinding revelation for me. My revulsion, along with the discovery on his part that I would not gain control over my capital for another ten years, led to a terrible scene.

He said our marriage wasn't legal anyway, since he'd lied about several things to get the licence – I was under age for a start – so we could just forget it had ever happened. This entirely suited me and I got in a taxi and went to Godmama's house. Thank God she was out, so that by the time she returned I was in control of myself and could pretend nothing had happened . . . Inside, I was just numb with shock, which is why I was in denial about the pregnancy for so long.

It was not until a couple of years later that I began to wonder if our marriage had been legal after all and so his subsequent one not, but I was living with Suzanne by then and it was of no importance to me.

I now lay the matter in your – and Henry's – hands to decide what, if anything, to do about it. The best course is probably nothing.

I hope you sometimes think of me kindly, as I think of you. You were a great support to me when I needed it most, even if you could never return my affection in the way I wanted.

I will sign this with my love, in any case,

Nessa Cassidy

40

The Elephant in the Room

I hadn't known until I heard Mum's voice just how much I had feared she was dead. For a moment my throat closed up and I couldn't speak.

Then I said shakily, 'Where on earth *are* you, Mum?'

'Mumbai, of course,' she said. 'Didn't Oshan tell you? He gave me this number when I rang the Farm earlier.'

'No, he didn't tell me. Perhaps he wanted it to be a surprise . . . which it certainly is. Have you been in Mumbai all this time?'

'Oh, no, I was in a very remote ashram for ages. They took me in after I had some kind of accident, and when I got better I simply couldn't remember who I was.'

'Didn't they try to find out?'

'No, but I was quite happy there, so I didn't want them to.'

'We were worried. We had no idea what had happened to you. River even went out to India to look for you.'

'Dear River!' she said. 'I'm sure he enjoyed the visit even if he didn't find me.'

'But you're not at this ashram any more?'

'No, because some other Europeans visited and one of them had met me years ago at a party and recognized me . . . and then it all came back to me in a rush.' She sighed. 'I was sad to leave the ashram but I felt I'd had enough, so when my new friends left, I went with them.'

That sounded a lot more like Mum than staying in the ashram for a few years.

'I've got my luggage back, but my passport's expired, so I'll have to visit the Embassy. But there's no rush.'

'But you'll need one to come home, won't you?'

'Eventually,' she agreed. 'Luckily, my friends are *terribly* rich and have paid for me to stay in this lovely hotel . . . and actually, I met someone wonderful in the bar, and I think I'm going to marry him. He's a maharaja, or a prince or something,' she added.

I held the phone away and looked at it as if she might pop out, like a genie from a lamp, but could still hear her soft, dreamy voice droning on about Prince Charming, whoever he was. I was pretty sure his real name *wasn't* Darling Boo-boo.

Eventually I broke into this catalogue of his finer points and told her, as succinctly as I could, that actually, her biological parents had been married and her father, now deceased, was the brother of the man I'd come here to paint.

'How wonderful!' she said vaguely.

I tried again. 'It means you were legitimate, Mum. But then your father married someone else, bigamously, and you have a half-sister.'

'Is she nice?'

'Lovely,' I said, leaving out the whole trying-to-kill-me bit. 'And she has a son, my half-cousin, Mark. He inherited the family estate, but actually, if you took it to court, you might have some claim on part of it. But I've told them you won't do that, so we've decided to forget about the first marriage.'

'That's all very confusing, darling, but you do what you like about it. I'm a child of the Goddess; that's enough for me.'

She sounded like River.

'Don't you want to come over and meet your new family?'

'No, though it is nice to have a sister – do tell her I hope she'll come out and visit us one of these days. Boo-boo's got a palace. You must come out too, Meg,' she added kindly. 'I'm not sure I'll be back any time soon: too cold, too wet. I feel my home is here in India now.'

Yes, I thought, probably in a lavish palace with servants and hot and cold running elephants, if such places still existed.

'Are there elephants?'

'In India, there are *always* elephants, darling.'

When she'd rung off, I went out of the room rather blindly and literally ran into Lex in the hall.

And it must have been the relief and shock, for I threw my arms around his neck and burst into tears all over his broad chest.

'Mum's *alive*!' I sobbed as he gathered me into his arms.

'I know. Your brother rang Clara earlier and warned her she was going to call you, but Clara thought it should be a surprise. Is your mother all right?'

I stopped crying and mopped my face with a tissue I fished out of my pocket, then told him what my totally ditsy mother had said. And as I did, I began to see the funny side . . .

'It's exactly like her: the moment she remembers who she is, rich friends whisk her to a smart hotel, where she bumps into a maharaja, who instantly proposes to her.'

I realized Lex's arms were still around me and he was gazing down at me, suddenly sobered and intent. 'We could go and visit her – together?' he suggested, tentatively.

'What do you mean?' I said stupidly, feeling the world whirl dizzyingly round.

He turned my face up to his and kissed me, long and hard, and my knees went weak. It didn't help with the dizzy feeling, that was for sure.

'I think you know what I mean,' he said finally. 'I love you and I think you love me. So, are we going to let the past keep us apart, or bring us together?'

'*Could* it bring us together? Won't the memory of Lisa always be there?'

'Yes, but in the way she wanted to be remembered: fondly, as a happy memory, not a sad ghost.'

I looked up at him and saw that his face was not sardonic, or sombre, or even kind, but instead filled with tenderness and love.

I pulled his head down for another long kiss . . . eventually broken by River's voice exclaiming in pleased tones, 'How wonderful that your stars have now aligned! The blessings of the Goddess be upon you!'

At dinner, we opened yet more elderflower champagne to toast Mum's reappearance, but *not* another engagement because Lex and I had decided there had been too many of those lately. Instead, we'd have the honeymoon in India first and then a quiet wedding later, or possibly while we were still out there.

Clara and Henry seemed to think this was a perfectly reasonable suggestion.

'Just as well it was a good year for collecting elderflowers,' Tottie said, topping up the glasses. 'Otherwise, we'd be running out of fizz, by now.'

Later, when I wished Lex goodnight, he said, 'It's been one hell of a day!'

'You can say that again,' I agreed whole-heartedly. 'Half-nightmare, half—'

He kissed me before I could complete the sentence. 'I hope I'm in the good half now, whatever it is.'

'Always,' I assured him.

As one elderly farmer had predicted at the party, the temperature had risen radically overnight and we awoke on the morning after Boxing Day to the sound of dripping everywhere. The snow still covered everything, but as the morning went on it was rapidly sinking like a deflated soufflé.

By the time Lex and I had finished a long portrait sitting, followed by a kiss or two, slightly impeded by one jealous small dachshund, we emerged to the news that the tractor and snowplough had gone up the lane earlier . . . and then a little later returned, followed by the mail van.

The road to Thorstane was finally reopened!

After lunch, Flora rang to tell us that Piers had insisted on leaving the moment he heard the road was open and had paid Gil Adcock to drive him to the station.

'She said he kicked up a huge fuss when she gave him his bill and said she was charging twice as much as his London club. But, of course, he had to pay it,' Clara said.

'I should think Gil will charge him quite a bit, too, if he's taking him all the way to the station,' Henry said.

'He wanted Flora to take him, but she was too nervous to try it until the road thaws a little more tomorrow. When it does, she and Rollo plan to leave her car at the motel and then drive to London in his, so he can introduce her to his mother.'

'Really?' I said. 'She doesn't let the grass grow under her feet, does she?'

'No, I think she's got her man and she isn't going to let him out of her sight now,' agreed Clara.

'They could have taken Piers back to London with them,' suggested Tottie.

'Rollo's got a ridiculous little two-seater sports car,' I said. 'They couldn't have taken him, even if they'd wanted to.'

Zelda was still at Underhill, and River drove Sybil there that afternoon, so she could pack for her trip with him to the Farm.

'We've told Mark about your mother's call,' Sybil said when they returned. 'I'm sure it's put his mind totally at rest, so that now we can forget all that tangle in the past.'

Tangle was one way of putting it.

'What about you, dear?' Sybil asked me. 'So lovely that you and Lex are . . . well, *together*. Are you going to stay here a little longer, or are you coming to the Farm tomorrow, too?'

'Oh, I'll stay here until I've finished Lex's portrait at least, and then I suppose I'd better tell my landlord I'm not renewing my lease on the flat. Luckily it expires just after my exhibition in February.'

'And after that, we'll go India,' Lex said with the special smile that made my knees turn into jelly. 'I must get back to work in a few days, though. I'll "get potting", as you once suggested!'

'Potted,' I corrected, but I smiled.

I knew at some point I'd have to meet with Al and Tara, to lay the foundations for our future relationship. I wasn't looking forward to it, but I'd already had an abject apology by telephone from Al, so I was prepared to forgive and, if not forget, put it behind me.

'We'll have to make our plans, so that after your exhibition and our trip, you can move up here permanently,' Lex said.

'We'll all go to your exhibition,' declared Clara.

'And I'll hire a minibus for the Farm contingent,' said River. 'We can all meet up there!'

It sounded like it would be one of my more memorable one-woman shows.

'There'll be lots of coming and going between Starstone Edge and the Farm in the years to come – what fun!' said Clara happily. 'It's all working out surprisingly well!'

Then a frown crossed her face and she added, 'Oh, but there's just one thing! Henry, I'm afraid Rollo is coming for tea today with Flora, to say goodbye. He behaved himself quite well at the party, so it seemed mean not to let him.'

Henry sighed. 'I expect I'll end up letting him print one of my poems in his ghastly magazine. But I'm definitely not writing a foreword to his collected poems!'

'Meg, you've enlivened and enriched our lives!' declared Clara.

And Lex, sitting next to me, gave me his sideways arrowhead smile and said, with a hint of his old sardonic self, 'She's a gift that just keeps on giving.'

Epilogue

Twelfth Night

It was Twelfth Night and an icy wind prowled around the Red House, occasionally casting a handful of snowflakes at the window, or howling menacingly down the chimney.

The two dogs were shut up with Clara in her study, out of the way, and though the spaniel, Lass, snored gently under her desk, Meg's young and excitable dachshund, Pansy, barked madly at the unseen menace, whirling round in a circle like a little dervish.

Out in the hall, the huge Christmas tree was being denuded of its ornaments and tinsel by Lex and Meg, while in the drawing room Henry and Teddy were carefully removing the antique baubles from the artificial tree in the bay window.

Clara heard Lex's deep laugh and Meg's voice protesting about something and, as always, it did her heart good to hear her nephew happy again.

Zelda, always a creature of impulse, had already packed up her possessions from the shared flat in London and moved straight into Underhill.

Teddy, reassured that he could continue living at the Red House, yet still spend time with his mother, seemed remarkably sanguine about this change now, while Zelda's soon-to-be mother-in-law, Sybil, had just returned to Underhill from her visit to River's Farm and seemed to have dropped ten years and revived like a flower in water. Clara was not sure if that was from relief that the truth about the past had come out and the blackmail stopped, or from River's company. She was already talking about another, longer visit . . .

Clara was sitting at her U-shaped desk, supposedly waiting for inspiration for the next crime novel to strike, which she had decided to call *Scratched Out*. She had summoned the Muse and confidently expected her to arrive at any moment, or she would want to know the reason why.

There was still a good hour before she could decently eat lunch – though good smells were wafting beneath the door from the direction of the kitchen.

Cheese and onion pies, that comforting winter alternative to hearty soup, she rather thought, and perhaps some of Den's special savoury scones to have for tea later . . .

Food was such a pleasure.

The voices of Henry and her great-nephew Teddy sounded louder, so they must have removed the decorations and now be headed for Henry's study, to put away the valuable vintage and antique glass baubles in their places among his extensive collection.

Later, Lex and Den would take the pine tree outside, and then store the boxes of decorations back in the attics. Being so substantial, the Victorian Gothic house wasn't short of them and there had been some talk about perhaps turning some of them into an apartment for Lex and Meg. The Old Smithy cottage attached to Terrapotter could then be turned over to

Al and his family, who were bursting out of their tiny rented terraced house.

How amazing and wonderful it was that the tangled interactions between the Doomes, herself and Nessa Cassidy had finally woven themselves into a complete and very lovely design!

And now, the loom seemed to have been set up to begin a new one . . . *and* a new volume of her memoirs.

She found she still had a lot to say . . .

Perhaps it had been a mistake to mention to the publishers of her crime novels that she was at work on her memoirs? They had seemed surprisingly keen on the idea of publishing them!

They would certainly need some severe editing first, to protect the guilty. But the new volume could start in the present and travel backwards, as she recollected the wonderful times she and Henry had had abroad, roaming in remote areas and working on archaeological sites. She had lots more stories to tell.

She opened a new file and began to type:

Second Impressions
The Memoirs of
Clara Mayhem Doome
Volume 2
Foreword

Acknowledgements

I would like to thank Oliver Mahony, Lady Margaret Hall Archivist, for his invaluable assistance in researching and understanding what life was like for a female student in Oxford in the late fifties and early sixties. (Though of course, any errors or instances of artistic licence are entirely my own doing.)

Also with gratitude to my son, Robin Ashley, for general research, technological support and ordering the takeaway dinners when the deadlines approached.

And finally, a huge thank you to my wonderful agent of many years, Judith Murdoch, for her constant support and encouragement.

About the Author

Trisha Ashley's *Sunday Times* bestselling novels have twice been shortlisted for the Melissa Nathan Award for Comedy Romance, and *Every Woman for Herself* was nominated by readers as one of the top three romantic novels of the last fifty years.

Trisha lives in North Wales. For more information about her please visit www.trishaashley.com, her Facebook page www.facebook.com/TrishaAshleyBooks or follow her on Twitter @trishaashley.

Recipes

Old Fashioned Sticky Treacle Cake

I do not imagine that Clara does much cooking herself but, if it were to take her fancy, I like to think that this is exactly what she would make on a cold wintry night. Warming, nostalgic and comforting, this is the perfect dessert to make on those days in between Christmas and New Year's Eve for guests, children or even just for yourself. Enjoy with custard or on its own.

You will need . . .
225g (8 oz) butter
225g (8 oz) light muscovado sugar
1 tbsp (1 oz) treacle
2 large eggs
½ pint whole milk
450g (16 oz) self-raising flour
4 tbsp (4 oz) golden syrup

Before you do anything else, preheat your oven to 140°C fan/160°C/gas mark 3. Combine the butter, sugar and treacle in a large pan and place over a medium heat until the ingredients have melted together, stirring as needed.

Leave the stovetop mixture to cool and, in the meantime, mix both the eggs and milk together. Once there is no danger of the eggs being cooked, add the eggy-milk and the flour to the original mixture. Beat everything together with brute force inspired by Clara's iron will.

Once fully combined, pour the mixture into a greased and lined 23cm (9 inch) baking tin and bake for around 50 minutes. Test the cake by inserting a skewer and checking whether it comes out clean. Allow the cake a few minutes to cool and then poke the cake all over with a clean skewer and dollop the golden syrup all over the sponge. When the cake has fully cooled, turn it out of the tin and cut yourself the first, sticky piece.

Meg's Mother's Anglo-Indian Cardamom Kheer (Rice Pudding)

When Meg's mum does eventually come back from India there is one thing she would certainly be bringing back with her: this recipe. Kheer is the Indian version of Rice Pudding and it's delicious. This recipe takes its inspiration from the Indian dessert but uses pudding rice in place of a more traditional basmati, although you can use either.

You will need . . .
2 pints whole milk
1 tsp ground cardamom
120g (4 oz) pudding rice (or basmati should it take your fancy)
100g (3.5 oz) sugar
1 tsp vanilla essence

35g (1.2 oz) unsalted pistachios, roughly chopped
Nutmeg, to garnish

Bring the milk to boil over a medium heat in a large pan. Add the cardamom and rice to the boiling milk, stirring constantly. Lower the heat so the mixture is barely simmering and cook for 45–50 minutes, stirring every few minutes to stop the rice from sticking. The pudding is finished when the grains of rice are soft enough to squish between two fingertips. Add the sugar, vanilla, and two thirds of the pistachios. Stir and turn off the heat. Serve either warm or chilled, garnished with extra pistachios and a sprinkle of nutmeg.